"Ling writes with a distinc
genuine. His life story tea
and opens doors to perception of other cultures and of self. Words paint pictures with the insight of the best anthropological works. An amazing read, one feels like they have taken an incredible journey."

—Stephen Brown, an educator

"This book is an insightful look into how historical circumstances affect flesh and blood individuals. Rather than pontificate on academic abstractions, Ling brings geopolitics to the good Earth by focusing on life in a poor, rural, Chinese village located in Malaysia. Readers wishing to understand how others live, particularly how young children endure, should read this book. Most remarkably, this is the story of the American dream an ocean away from America. A young man born into poverty seeks a better life for himself by working hard and developing his innate talents to their fullest. He seeks to create and define his own life rather than have his family and community decide what is life should be. The ideals of freedom and opportunity that are often identified with America are not just American, and they smolder within the heart of one Eng-Huat Ling."

—Dylan Duke Gintz, a college scholarship student

"***For My Hands Only*** provides fresh insights into the rich experiences of growing up in Malaysia. The diverse culture in the land has emerged through the multiple voices that the author struggled with in this coming-of-age memoir. He orchestrates all these voices to depict the complex life of growing up in a truly multicultural world."

—Dr. Belinda Louie, professor, University of Washington

"Shades of Dick Whittington, Horatio Alger and Oliver Twist—one young man's quest for freedom, an education and a new life. ***For My Hands Only*** accounts such a struggle by one undaunted by life's hurdles and vicissitudes."

—Lorraine Hildebrand, author of *Straw Hats, Sandals and Steel*

"With a unique voice, the author offers a fascinating look into his early life as an adopted child in mid-20th century Malaysia. He shares with us the details of everyday life as a Chinese immigrant living in poverty in a small village. ***For My Hands Only*** is a thought that shapes his life as he labored tapping rubber trees or killing pests in the tobacco field. Using language that depicts vivid pictures of his pain and hardship, Ling also enables us to see the small joys he finds in his life. Through it all, the author maintains a sense of purpose and knowledge that he is destined for a life outside his village. This compelling memoir offers an intriguing look into a culture that often is shrouded in mystery."

—Mary Ann Miller, a librarian

"***For My Hands Only*** is both fascinating and multilayered. One layer is a personal memoir of growing up poor in Malaysia before, during, and after WWII. Another layer isw a detailed, well researched historical account of those same years. His use of personal anecdotes and his willingness to open up about both the good, the bad, and the terrible of his growing up years, places the reader right in the time and place along side the author. The final layer is a complex study of the Chinese culture from the inside out. Put all the layers together and you discover that the author has created an indispensable learning experience disguised as one good read!"

—Erica Lustig, an attorney at law

FOR MY HANDS ONLY

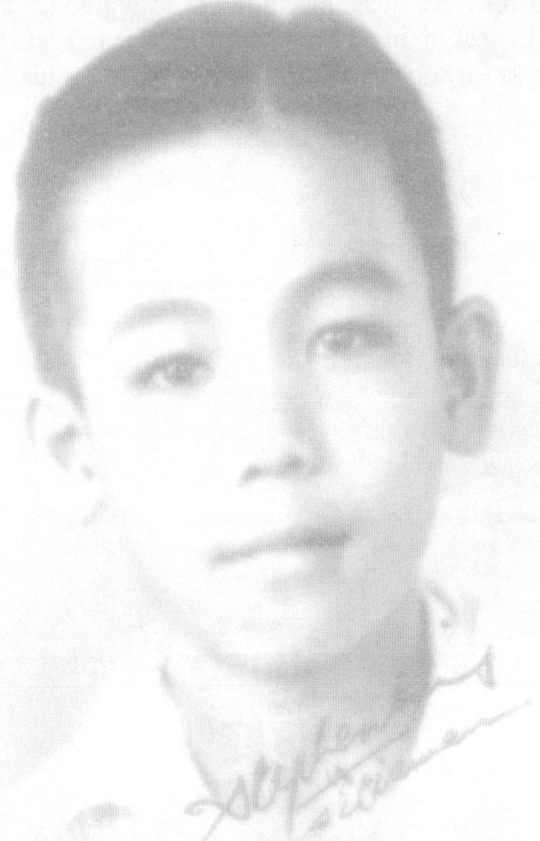

Stephen Eng-Huat Ling

ISBN: 0-9774906-4-5

Library of Congress Control Number: 2006926088

Counterbalance Books
Seattle

This is for my godson
Jim C. Hsu

He knows in his heart
there are people in this world
who care for him deeply
and support his every step
as he embarks unwaveringly
on life's exciting journey
of learning, discovery,
and personal achievement.

Foreword

S. Eng-Huat Ling's new book, For My Hands Only, is the equivalent of cultural anthropology with a wicked sense of humor. Ling lays out his own story, set in Malaya (now Malaysia), with sensuality, humor and brutal honesty. Along the way we learn more than a bit about the stories of a Chinese people who were trying to find a better life in their adopted Malayan home while being beset by hardship after hardship, from the Japanese Occupation to the communist insurgency, the declining British influence and the economic uncertainty caused by major international events. Under this backdrop, we are treated to the art of match-making, weddings, the secrets of outdoor wok cooking, the delicate relationship between the Chinese and the Malays (the sons of the soil), Chinese traditions, the culture and trade of opium, sex, family ties, and much more.

How many lively accountings do we have of Chinese life within Malaysia? I'm certain that this will add to the record with a huge dose of humor and flair. Ling's style is anything but dry. He's funny, as he meanders then returns to his own life strand. Each chapter is a cultural primer, focusing on wedding traditions, Chinese customs, wok cooking, rubber tree harvesting, tobacco cultivation—even the nefarious opium operation gets a heavy dose as Ling's Father refined small amounts of opium for meager sums.

Beneath narrative, however is a more intimate story of Ling's efforts to belong and his growing awareness of betrayal and servitude, which doesn't sit well with Ling and his restless liberation-seeking soul.

This is a lively book, with a funny, thoroughly enlightened author doing his best to tell his story and the story of one Chinese village in Malaya with tremendous insight, detail and compassion. The wok is waiting, with thorough mix of oils and flavorings. Dig in!

Lucas Smiraldo
Playwright and Rostered Teaching Poet
Washington State Arts Commission

Preface

In sooth this book started as a series of anecdotes of my pathetic upbringing to entertain my dinner guests at my American home, a measured, palatable dose at a time, my preferred dessert. Sister in England objected vehemently the first time she heard it and advised me against "telling your American friends about our family secrets!" Obviously we are an ocean apart in this and other matters! She chooses to carry the label of the mysterious and the inscrutable one!

Then, as an English teacher, I realized profoundly that I have my own unique, inimitable story to tell my students, less to entertain than to instruct, inspire, and instill in them the understanding that they too, with all the enviable privileges and material abundance showered on them on a silver platter from an early age, can accomplish what I have, despite the seemingly insurmountable hurdles that once stood formidably in my way, growing up adopted, neglected and deprived in a God-forsaken, poverty-stricken, secluded village somewhere in a remote corner in a country called Malaya (now a part of Malaysia). They are a crucial reason why I wrote my book, a living testament to one person's determination not only to survive but also to venture indefatigably into the unknown world of hope and possibilities beyond the village of despair.

It grieves me to watch many of my American students unwilling to make the sacrifices and stringent efforts required of them to succeed—academically and economically—in this growing competitive world but corrupted, retarded and detoured by instant gratification, easy money, sex, inferior jobs, cars, and apartments, leaving our government dumbfounded as to why fewer males each year are pursuing higher education in our land.

Helen Keller remains my hero. And if she could do it, I should accomplish more with all my faculties intact and my innate talents. And if I have achieved a modicum of success in America, despite growing up poor and deprived, many of my students, to whom poverty is just a word, have no reason to fall behind their contemporaries in China and India in many human endeavors, especially in the areas of math, science, medicine, and technology. It might be too late that the president of the United States is now pushing for more emphasis on and funding for science and math in our public schools! Matter-of-factly India is producing more engineers each year than the United States of America and India has become a land of opportunities for the educated and skilled Indians.

More importantly, I am also witnessing more and more Asian-American writers on the American literary scene. Yes, we are living in a shrinking global village and a "flat" world and a more diverse American society. Bill Gates travels the world, picks and chooses the best brains to staff his incomparable and renowned Redmond campus (my nephew works there). I am an immigrant. We are a nation of immigrants and our voices and experiences are woven inextricably into the emerging literary mosaic. We should all be eager to learn and know more about people—beyond the cursory enthralling, at times provocative *National Geographic* images—whose ethnic cultures, traditions, beliefs, practices and experiences continue to enrich the salad-bowl culture of this vital nation of ours. I am a proud American, an Asian-American, and I want my voice heard. That is the other reason why I wrote the book.

I wrote *For My Hands Only* not for fame or fortune. I penned it because I believe everyone has a story to tell. In the words of one insightful reviewer, "This is the story of the American dream an ocean away from America. A young man born into poverty seeks a better life for himself by working hard and developing his innate talents to their fullest.... The ideals of freedom and opportunity that are often identified with America are not just American, and they smolder within the heart of one Eng-Huat Ling."

And I hope my modest endeavor is worthy of your attention and perusal.

Stephen Eng-Huat Ling
Puyallup, Washington

Acknowledgments

Thank you, Jim, my godson, for graciously moving to the PLU dorm so I could have all the space and time, in addition to a busy schedule teaching English, to focus on reflective thinking and composition of this book.

To Hey Moi, my beloved niece and a psychiatric nurse in Australia, who early must have suspected but understood why I asked many questions about our family since she is the self-appointed "family historian." She is Mother's first grandchild and knew intimately, more than all her eleven siblings, her grandma's joys and sadness. I knew I had her unstinting support when she said unequivocally, "Uncle, you have a right to your story. It's your perspective that counts."

To Toong-Siong Shih, a high school classmate, for his book *The Foochows of Sitiawan: A Historical Perspective*, which includes the story of my grandfather, one of the early pioneers in the development of the Foochow community in Malaya at the beginning of the twentieth century.

To the "chosen six" of my friends in western Washington for reading the manuscript and goading me on to seek a wider audience for my voice.

To Luke Smiraldo, an accomplished playwright, for believing in me and my writing. Following his invaluable critique, I rewrote the ending of the book.

To Dena Hughes, a parent, a teacher, and a voracious reader, for her wisdom and humor, making me appreciate the beauty and validity of all human experiences.

To Jesus A. Carrero for allowing me to be a friend and a parent during the formative years of his life, teaching me patience, love, and humility.

To Keith Lim, the eldest son of my sole blood brother, a computer genius and a software engineer (with Microscoft), teaching his stubborn uncle how to use the computer effectively.

To Morten Nilsen, a generous editor, for promising to preserve, but enhance, the flavor of my cooking. "This is your book," he assured me, "but I will make it more palatable for public consumption."

To Assunta Ng, publisher of *Northwest Asian Weekly* and *Seattle Chinese Post* and founder of Rainbow Bookfest: Celebrating Authors of Color, for inviting me to showcase my debut coming-of-age memoir at the 2006 Seattle Rainbow Bookfest, allowing me also the opportunity to engage in creative dialogue with minority authors of national renown who live and write in the Pacific Northwest.

If I am not for myself,
Who will be for me?
If I am only for myself,
What am I?
If not now,
When?

—Rabbi Hillel

ONE

Bad woman...evil...sell her sarong...gamble...whore...you *sima-yan*."

In the Hockchiang dialect, *sima-yan* stands for *son of Siam*, not exactly a term of endearment or a nickname, but more of an epithet Mother would hurl at me, like stones against a harlot in biblical times, when she was annoyed with me. Or caught in a personal dilemma, unsure of what to do with her wayward adopted son. My birth mother, according to hearsay, hailed from Siam (today Thailand). But Mother never announced that it was my birth mother she was denouncing. Disparagingly. Even though deceased, my mother could hear the echo of Mother's mockery of her. (Chinese say some spirits of the departed are alive and restless, stealthily roaming the earth seeking solace or revenge.) Her language veiled, Mother's target was unquestionable. It was *me* she was after, unequivocally. I was here; my mother decomposed six feet underground, many moons ago. It was more like "This is who you are, you bastard," a product of someone despised and ostracized by her own people. Mother's voice was unflappable, direct, and clear as the tropical blue sky. But this castigation was worse than a malicious bee sting. The problem was it didn't come through one ear and out the other, like drops of water on a duck's back, but sank and anchored deep in my soul, exacerbating my feeling of uselessness and of being unwanted, like a pariah, a scrub, through no fault of my own. And forever branded a *sima-yan*. An invisible badge of shame she nailed to my chest. I was coerced into wearing a false identity.

Like the refrain of a dirge, I had heard this evil song before: "Bad woman...evil...sell her sarong...gamble...whore...you *sima-yan*." Many times. Somewhere. Usually in private. Was this a manifestation of her inner turmoil? Or prolonged sexual dysfunction?

Or was I the catalyst for her indecent tirade? Whatever the reason, I was *doomed* to hell, in her eyes.

Mother was using her scolding voice in Hockchiang, a Chinese dialect of our family. This was the only tongue she knew. She had been robbed of a decent education. I was about seven years old then. Like a dog gone berserk, ready to snarl at its foe, Mother's voice was vociferous. Unabashed. Its high pitch, loud and evil, carried by the warm evening breeze to my ears, spelled trouble for me.

"Your mother calling," one of the boys sensed the vibrations in the air. I was in the middle of playing marbles. Serious marbles! With three of the neighborhood kids, childhood buddies, an arm's throw away. Mother had found another excuse, I thought, to interrupt my joy and summon me home. Another way to belittle me in front of my peers. Or was she effortlessly following her maternal instinct, like feathers sailing in the wind?

"Who?" I said, taking the nudging seriously. Who else could be calling my name? *Ardi-yan* (small boy) and *Ngulan-dea* (milk boy) were my Hockchiang nicknames, encouraged and employed by members of the family. Small boy because I'd a grown-up brother and milk boy because I had been fed condensed milk, diluted with warm, boiled water, when I was a baby…so they told me. The preference among certain relatives was *Ngulan-dea* for no particular reason except they didn't know my public name. "*Ardi-yan…*" Mother called.

"She's coming…better get moving," another one joined in, like a line in a song. "My fingers or my ass you want me to move?" I mused. They knew Mother, a martinet, meant business. She was a veteran in bringing up the young and many years older than most mothers in the village. I could either tarry and finish the game now, increasing her anger, or haul my fingers and ass home without any delay, for my own good.

Quickly abandoning my playmates, I hurried home like a bullet train. Might as well. I was losing my marbles. One at a time. Big and small. To my friends.

I tried to keep my personal marbles intact, despite a sudden insight of the imminent crisis that was unraveling before my eyes. Ooooh shit! Three times I cursed. Damned! Once only, whimsically. The conundrum was of my doing!

Approaching the front of the house, her voice had shifted from scolding to punishing, suggesting the gravity of the situation. Sooner or later (I was hoping for later) I would appear involuntarily before Mother (the judge) to answer a few delicate questions concerning a certain gross misconduct. Or was it vandalism? There was only one niche in the house I could, seemingly, hide from Mother's wrath. Under Father's opium bed in the room downstairs that served as Father's opium den. A place where he smoked opium and conducted his business with his opium friends from the village. All men. Openly. I had been there before. I mean under the bed. There was room for ten kids my size.

In many Chinese homes in the tropics, a standard size bed has four sturdy poles for a mosquito net and stands about three feet high. With plenty of room for hiding or storage underneath. A mosquito net is a must, since most homes do not have screened windows or doors. Because of the perennial tropical heat, many prefer a cool reed or bamboo mat to a mattress on the hard solid wooden bed. "Mattresses are too hot," they complain. "They don't breathe easily," they add. And carved wooden pillows, blocks harder and taller than soft-cushioned pillows, are favored by grandpas and grandmas.

Mother was standing stiff and adamant, guarding the front entrance to the ground floor—like one of the fierce-looking concrete lions flanking the front steps to a Chinese mansion—with a slender but a lethal stick in her right hand. In the blink of an eye, I'd traveled to Egypt, witnessed the wounds inflicted on the Israelites by the Egyptian taskmasters (reliving my Sunday school stories), and returned to wait for the slashing by Mother's cat-o'-nine-tails. I felt like someone marooned on a deserted island alone with Mother. Brother and his wife were upstairs on a different planet listening to some Chinese music from the Phillips radio. Eighth Auntie and her children were in their kitchen at the back of the ancestral home. And Sister must have been watching gleefully from behind a wall somewhere, thinking, "Sorry, your butt is going to get it this time!" I was to face the music all alone.

"Bad woman…evil…sell her sarong...gamble…whore..." That was the ugly picture Mother had painted of my blood mother. The only one I would ever know of my dear departed mother. Morally degrading. Defenseless. But Mother had her reasons, right or wrong, true or false, for putting me in my place. Why was Mother so hateful of my mother? Was I a chip off the old block? Did I remind her of this whore? This evil, bad woman? Maybe one of Father's mistresses? Was I an accident of their passions, their illegitimate offspring? Her face I had never seen. Her warmth and bosom I had never felt. Till I ran away at fifteen, I accepted and respected the uncompromising silence the adoptive family had maintained about my origins. (Dutiful Chinese children don't question their elders.) And the family secrets entombed, forever. But Mother repeated it like a mantra as I flew by her, seeking immediate refuge under Father's opium bed.

Villagers gossiped that Mother was never happy with my adoption. A child of one of Father's mistresses? A bastard? An unwanted one dumped on her lap? Simply conjectures from an overactive child's imagination? *My* imagination? After all she had three grown children of her own: a daughter (Big Sister) married to a farmer a long time ago, a son (Brother) recently married, and a younger daughter (Small Sister) soon to be married to a nobody in some far off village. And out of pity, I reasoned, for one of her brother's many daughters, Mother had adopted one of her nieces, two years older than I. A practice, I understood, of one relative extending a helping hand to another relative in good and bad times, for motives known only to the parties involved. Everybody, including myself, called her Ah Lang (Sister, to me). Years later I heard rumors that Mother had adopted her niece for a reason: she was to be, in Mother's scheme of things, my chosen bride. Another practice, I was informed, in the culture of the Hockchiang people. Incestuous, grotesque and morally disgusting—in my view. Then I wouldn't be the first in our clan to do so. To follow the mandate of the Hockchiang people, as if sanctioned by the gods! My personal individual views didn't matter to the Hockchiang people, tempering my insolence somewhat. Eighth Auntie was adopted by Grandpa, so I heard, and later became Eighth Uncle's wife. I wondered if this had anything to do with his leaving her after fathering three children (they adopted a girl) and living with a mistress in Ipoh, a town thirty miles or so away from the village. The mistress was my biological mother's sister and had adopted my oldest blood brother. Sadly, my adoption was like an imposition on Mother, a sort of cruel and unwanted punishment for someone in her early forties. She endured years grieving invisibly over an unfaithful husband, Father. His dalliances with women were accepted, not glorified.

Only Father, and he alone, knew why he abandoned Mother and ended up with a mistress. Having a mistress or a concubine is as old as China itself, from the imperial families down to the commoners. Literary or musical entertainment by a courtesan in the imperial court or the soft touch of a geisha wasn't satisfactory for many Oriental men! There could be a number of reasons that concubinage—this overtly male prerogative and behavior—has withstood the test of time and is beneficial to both sexes: women's magnanimous social attitude or public endorsement encourages it; strong belief in male progeny views it as a viable solution if a wife is barren; and concubinage, not divorce, brings joy to the man, keeps the family intact, and saves a wife's face, allowing her to maintain some dignity and her established position, thus perpetuating her dependency. A smart Chinese wife, having failed to conceive or produce a son, follows ancient custom, suppressing her libido and pleading with her husband to take a concubine for the sake of producing a son. A legitimate heir, in some cases!

Mother's life wasn't made any easier with Father's infidelity and now a new baby on her lap.

The rumors of an impending Japanese attack sweeping steadily southward from Indochina, unbridled, were flying everywhere like discolored leaves breaking loose from dead branches. The British could not protect my country, Malaya, from the Japanese invasion. Emotions ran amuck. At that precarious time, an additional mouth to feed in the home was as welcome as a filthy, emaciated rat in Mother's kitchen. She did it, dutifully.

Years later I was told my biological mother died of complications from her pregnancy in a hospital in Ipoh, the capital of the state of Perak. The hospital was ill-equipped to handle her abnormal case. She hemorrhaged to death, relatives remembered. My oldest brother, five or six years old, cried and clung to her hospital bed as he watched her die.

My father couldn't handle a brood of four financially. He literally gave us away, two to the people related to my mother. I was the youngest of the four, less than a year old when I was adopted by a relative who brought me from the state's capital to a remote village called Kampong China.

I spent a great deal of my early months in Kampong China conspicuously in the opium den with Father. At least during the daylight hours when the rest of the family were out tilling the soil for tapioca or sweet potatoes or catering to the needs of the pigs, vital sources of the family income. Yes, the sweet smell of the opium den! There was a distinct smell, maybe not as sweet as I would like to think. Replicating the scent of showy white magnolia? It was not. I was raised here. Father could kill two birds with one stone single-handedly, tending to my needs—few—and the needs of the opium smokers—few—who frequented the den.

I was a lovable, cuddly baby, according to Father's paying guests. The dense opium smoke, saturating the air, probably had something to do with my being a quiet sweet-natured baby. That close to the operation—inches away—I might as well have been smoking the opium myself! The effect was immediate—the mind and the body in a blissful dreamlike state, sauntering in the Garden of Eden. The reality was I spent my time on a hard wooden bed with Father and his gentle cohorts in crime. That might conveniently explain why the back of my head was asymmetrical. Imperfect.

There was seldom any light in the opium den other than the oil lamp sitting in the middle of the bed, aiding in the final processing of the opium before someone, lying on his side, smoked and inhaled it through the bowl of a long pipe directly over the flame. As a baby my head would naturally turn to the source of light, the oil lamp sitting in the middle of the bed, like an indoor plant turning imperceptibly to an open window. Since nobody straightened my head, it faced the lamp sideways for a long period of time—days, weeks, and months—and the back of my head inevitably became asymmetrical. I suspected Father was preoccupied with smoking or preparing opium for his clients. I never asked and nobody cared to explain why my head wasn't perfect or normal like the boys in my neighborhood.

Female luxuriant hair could easily have camouflaged this imperfection. Or an Afro! As I grew older, it pained me each time when the barber, after a cut, handed me a round mirror, swiveled me around, and said perfunctorily "Is the back okay?" "Of course it's not okay!" I wanted so desperately to tell him not to say anything after his usual modest creation. I had a reason to be self-conscious. I had an imperfect head! The voice was booming in my head. I wanted to yell. Nodding silently I just wanted the earth to swallow me up so I could vanish like a thief in flight. In a flash I saw the burning oil lamp in Father's opium den. My imperfect head was a constant reminder that I was raised by Father in a den of criminals, an adopted son, inhaling the injurious opium smoke during the formative months of my life. I grew up to hate the smell of opium.

It was a small—though temporary—consolation that Mother's stick was short and thin. Her favorite instrument of punishment was readily available in the kitchen, where there were always thick and thin, long and short, straight and crooked, pieces of twigs and small branches from our own rubber trees, used for kindling and cooking. Wood-burning stoves, some small (like a shallow pit in the ground), others mammoth, all concrete, (because of large families) the size of a tomb for two, were coomonplace throughout the entire village. Portable charcoal-burning stoves, in the absence of the available firewood, prevailed in towns and cities. We had two that Father used exclusively for cooking and processing opium. Charcoal was abundant but expensive.

I was wrong. Mother was small—smaller than I was—but agile, trailing me like a shadow. A broom with a long handle came charging violently at me under the bed, like a hungry rooster after a worm. I surrendered fast. I could not handle pain like Sister, a born stoic. I came crawling out, crying and screaming for succor. Tears of remorse, however swift and natural, were not enough to mollify Mother. Not even a barrel of ice water could lower her temperature. Switching to a stick she had used earlier, she went after my legs and butt, hammering me all over. By now the whole village heard the commotion. Such cries had never been heard before!

Before Mother could voice the nature of the crime I had allegedly committed and inflict further her deadly wounds on my fragile frame, Eighth Auntie suddenly appeared like a thief in the night. She towered over Mother by quite a few inches. More like Goliath over David. An imposing woman. Stout and square. This was not the first time she had prevented Mother from strangling or killing me. I clung to her for life, sobbing uncontrollably. No one could accuse me of crocodile tears. Mother's arms, like tentacles, were swirling in every direction. My body was still beyond her reach, shielded by the Rock of Gibraltar, Eighth Auntie. Like a bulldozer, she nudged Mother away from me and snatched the instrument of death from her quivering hand. Down the years I could always count on Eighth Auntie to prolong and save my life from harm. From Mother's wrath.

I felt a sense of victory over Mother in the presence of Eighth Auntie. Hail Confucius! Seven times. Confucius—a gentleman philosopher born about six hunded years before Jesus—was my hero, and Mother's friend too. Mother introduced me to him when I was old enough to appreciate and learn what *filial piety* (natural obligations of a son or a daughter to the parents) meant to every child growing up in a traditional Chinese family. Confucius taught us to respect all those in authority, including our parents.

The smell of triumph over Evil (Mother) was intoxicating. Eighth Auntie had come to my rescue, again. For how long?

It was my inquisitiveness about the gramophone (the obstinate British preferred *gramophone,* not *phonograph*) that had gotten me into trouble with Mother this time. Like a young chick, fresh out of a coop, I was more than curious about everything. It wasn't enough to *see* a gramophone in the house. Or to *touch* it. Or to *listen* to the mysterious sounds it emitted. Curiosity almost killed this two-legged cat. Because what I did to the family gramophone was illicit. Insane. Inexcusable. But how come it wasn't Brother who should be after my ass? After all, the gramophone was one of his cherished mundane possessions. Mother was deaf musically. Music was hell and noises to her, she would later declare. Besides the Phillips radio, operated by a battery no smaller than a car's, the RCA gramophone was like a family heirloom. It was. It came from Grandpa. That meant as children you don't touch it or operate it. You could lose your fingers if found guilty of a violation. The possibility of a severe dismemberment if caught red-handed hung in the air like the suffocating black smoke in the kitchen. The few times during a month when Brother played records in the evenings (music appreciation or leisure-time activities were foreign to our family), I became more and more restless. The medley of songs (all in Mandarin) and the mellifluous music of Chinese operas didn't soothe my uneasy nerves. (It didn't matter if you didn't understand a bloody word being sung, like the many western operas in Italian.) Instead it aroused within me an unbearable itch to want to know where these sounds emanated from. I was about to kill the goose that laid the golden eggs. The voices and the music must be hidden inside somewhere. Inside the machine. In the box. I suspected. How did it do it? Too many unanswered bothersome questions.

I couldn't help that I was born a curious child. Blame it on Confucius or Allah or Jehovah! Looking at the gramophone I could see the round head and its sharp needle sitting firmly on a groove of the revolving black disk, going round and round and moving gradually towards the center. Where did the sound come from? It must have come from somewhere deep inside the box through the horn-shaped opening underneath the turntable. Ever so often, when the sound grew weak and the music slowed down, you would wind the machine the way you would start an old jalopy with a crank. For this gramophone the sound was coming through the opening from deep inside the machine. "Don't over-wind it," Brother would caution me. "You had to feel it. You just have to practice it." Brother was always right. You had to feel it with your hand. Yes, I felt the sensation of something tightening up gradually. I was glued to the machine. He did teach me how to change the records. Occasionally a fresh needle. Nothing more. I didn't think Brother had the technical know-how to explain to me where the sound was coming from. But I was, in sooth, overwhelmed with the selfish desire to find it out, my way, no matter how or what!

I thought and thought. I didn't hear any voice. A smart one like Siddhartha Gautama sat by a tree or something and words of enlightenment came to him. I had a quest too, like an unquenchable thirst. Where the hell did the sound come from? It finally drove me to the edge of insanity. In the absence of my Brother one day, I attacked it. Ferociously. Dismantle the gramophone I did, on a table upstairs. You don't have to be an Einstein. Just a screwdriver. Without trepidation. The bliss of yielding to temptation took over, leaving my thinking brain somehow paralyzed, oblivious to fear of any repercussions of my daring. What was I expecting to find inside the box? Miniature human beings? A recording studio, with a live orchestra? An elated silent audience? Mounted on gearwheels and cogwheels ready to perform whenever you wound up the machine? What was I thinking? Something went inexplicably wrong. The greasy metal parts (Brother said to oil the parts often if you expect the gramophone to function efficiently like rice for your stomach) now an eyesore sneering at me, didn't provide me with the one answer I was looking for.

The mystery remained a mystery. Where did the sound come from? Could Brother or anyone in the whole village of farmers and rubber tappers have explained to me scientifically that the sound of the music was buried deep in the groves of the black disk? I could have applied the biblical ask-and-you-will-be-given-what-you-ask-for maxim, but I was a boy of little faith and unschooled in the Socratic method of acquiring knowledge. In my cultural milieu, a child who asked questions was a troublemaker, silenced not encouraged. Ask and you shall be banished!

It didn't help, amidst growing panic and anxiety, that the sound of someone's footsteps, scrambling up the stairs, grew louder. And nearer. And now standing beside me. Almost without breathing, I smelled Brother.

"What are you doing?" Brother stared at me with some disbelief. Eyebrows raised.

"Uh…" My dark face grew pale. Like in the presence of a ghost. Numbed and speechless. But no tears. And the pondering continued.

"It is time for dinner," he said calmly. Didn't loiter. Left without another word.

It was typical of Brother not to question or scold me if he witnessed anything out of the ordinary. Tearing apart his favorite toy, the gramophone, the family heirloom, was definitely out of the ordinary. But you could be sure you would hear it, severely, from Mother. Very soon. Inevitable. Like a heavy downpour after lightning and thunder. I sat down at the dinner table with Brother's children, with a nervous stomach and cold sweat. The guilt, like a speck in your eye. Ah Soh (not her name but a polite customary term used to address a brother's wife) thrilled us with her home-made noodles, this evening special with crabs. Mother was always the last in the family to eat. Children first. Adults later. Another Chinese custom. At times, late in the evening. Soon after dinner I left to play marbles, answering the call of my friends, hoping Brother would intervene quickly without reservation or hesitation and put back together the gramophone. Within minutes, I heard Mother— faintly from a distance—demanding my head on the chopping block. Some immediate accountability. Only Eighth Auntie's quick intervention saved my rear. For now, at least.

It wasn't long before that I had performed a major surgery on the winding alarm clock. Not that it had suffered any discernible ailment. It had served the family faithfully for some time. Rather I did it because it had aroused my curiosity. I wanted to know, like the mysterious inner workings of the RCA gramophone, how it could go on and on ticking away, controlling my every waking moment, commanding me when to go to bed and when I should get up. The family roosters did a good job of marking time, I thought. Their crowing almost synchronized with the hours on the winding machine. And like a surgeon, but without his training and dexterity and the right surgical apparatus, I got inside the body and found a coil of shining spring, like the heart, was responsible for the clock working faithfully day in and day out. Unfortunately, using crude tools meant for bicycle repairs, I manipulated roughly the spring this way, that way, and every which way, causing the coil to distend and the machine to suddenly stop. "Ooh no!" I shrieked! I must have done something bad to the main spring, critical to the life of the clock.

Brother, more than anyone in the house, depended on the alarm clock to wake him up, way before dawn daily, to tap the rubber trees. He demanded nothing less than a public flogging. (The concept of self-esteem or public humiliation was alien to us village folks then.) Would have resorted to a guillotine, if he'd had one. His anger exploded like a firecracker. I pleaded for leniency, promised never to repeat it again. It worked somewhat. I was threatened with abandonment and starvation, given time in a chicken coop. Not bad, come to think of it. It stunk but the enclosure was spacious enough to walk around in without squashing on the chicken poop. I loved chickens. Never had enough of them, growing up. The family slaughtered three or four during a year. Only for special occasions. Like birth. Death. Chinese New Year. Or cooked with potent Chinese ginseng. Herbal roots. For Brother's health and virility.

Another time Mother discovered a number of glittering shells, embedded in beautifully carved lacquered chairs, missing. These chairs spoke of authentic Chinese ancestry and were used on ceremonial occasions. Not just any chairs for any old butts! More of those family heirlooms Grandpa must have carried them with him all the way from southeastern coast of China when they first immigrated to Malaya at the turn of the century. These heirlooms were our only link to China and history. Someone had been so foolish as to destroy the family's historical roots. I was the main suspect. There wasn't any interrogation or trial by the family court. I was found guilty before I was read the rights to a self-defense. "Too much idle time," Mother whispered to Brother. "He is yours. Do what you need to do," she instructed him. Was there a mother-son conspiracy?

Obviously, having a private opium tutor to teach me the fundamentals of Confucius' philosophical ideas since age six hadn't informed or affected my character, they concluded. Did they realize I had no earthly idea what the opium tutor was trying to teach me? I was adept—like a parrot—at repeating and reciting chunks of Chinese characters. And none translated into actions, like good behavior.

Attending a Chinese school at seven might just be the right deterrent, the family decided. Knowledge could be my salvation. In a structured environment, it might protect me from mischief and harm and self-destruction. Soon the world became my beloved teacher. And I, like a lump of amorphous clay, soft and malleable, was ready for the master potter to perform his magic touch. Is it possible to create something out of *nothing*? Assuming I am *nothing*?

TWO

I grew up and spent the formative years of my life in Malaya (now a part of Malaysia, founded in 1963). Surrounded by the Philippines to the east, Indonesia to the west (and southwest), Thailand to the north and Singapore to the south, the Malay Peninsula (or Malaya) is strategically located in the heart of Southeast Asia. No small wonder ancient traders aptly called it "The land where the winds meet." And meet they did. Down the centuries, strong winds had uprooted and swept many Portuguese, Dutch and English to the irresistible, legendary, powerful trading kingdom of Malacca, first established in the late fourteenth century, located in the southeast corner of Malaya.

The last to claim it were the English in 1795. Eventually the tentacles of English intervention and protection permeated the length and breadth of the Malay Peninsula, flying the Union Jack by 1919. Soon thereafter Malaya became a British protectorate,—not colony—and remained in that status until the coming of the Japanese in early 1940s.

Not only was I denied the ability to choose who my parents were (a scion of the fifth wife of a sultan of one of the Malay states would have been most desirable, one of royal pedigree and privileges!), but I was born at the worst of times, on the eve of the Japanese assault on Malaya and Singapore. The Japanese air force was invincible over Malaya. Using bicycles, hordes of Japanese intruders swooped down the Malay Peninsula from Thailand. Unstoppable. Fiercely lusting for power. The British, in their omnipotence, thought the jungle north of Singapore would protect them from the advancing Japanese troops. Instead it became a perfect camouflage for them. The land magnanimously provided the enemy shelter and food. Singapore, once the towering, impregnable colonial center of British operations in the Far East, surrendered unconditionally within two weeks to the Japanese in 1942. For many, especially the Malays, behind closed doors, it was an auspicious time to celebrate the demise of the myth of the white man's dominance and superiority in that part of the world. In fact, many ordinary Malays, those denied superior education because of their birth or without strong ties to the British administration, blamed the British policies for their backwardness and lack of opportunities because the British had brought many Chinese and Indians into Malaya, essentially taking away jobs. The seeds of racial tension—especially between the Malays and my people—had been sown! By the British. And slowly allowed to germinate!

For the moment, our allegiance shifted radically from England to Japan. Down with "God Save the King"! Up with *Hail* to Emperor Hirohito of Japan! Now we kowtowed reverently to the north, for the emperor, since ancient times, was believed to be descended from the Sun Goddess Amaterasu.

Malaya, like an energetic youth, was aggressively seeking a sense of autonomy, individuality, and full independence from England. There was a growing impetus among the Malays, even brewing visibly among the privileged few matriculating at prestigious schools in England, to free themselves from the yoke of the British rule, now that the British impotence was exposed. One wondered how long they had resented the sight and smell of the British, their protection from alien marauders.

My brother was about seventeen. The Japanese Occupation meant snuffing out the fire of hopes, dreams and aspirations of many young people like him, the untimely termination of Chinese education, snatching away the key to their future. For him a fatal blow to his ambitions, like being struck by a sudden, irreversible terminal illness. Brother never fully recovered to pursue his education after the defeat and retreat of the Japanese at the end of World War Two. Not lack of ambition, but dire poverty, had crippled our family. And Brother an innocent victim of a widespread economic collapse the Japanese left behind, like havoc or debris caused by a devastating storm. He rightly blamed the Japanese for his lack of education, which forever doomed him to a life of servitude. He never forgave the Japanese for his sudden descent into despair and meaninglessness.

Brother often said (I was just a baby safe in the warmth of Father's opium den) life under the Japanese was like living precariously on an egg shell, dampened by rampant rumors of rapacious Japanese out to rape, murder and plunder the very sources of our survival: chickens, pigs, fruits, rice, sweet potatoes, tapioca, and garden vegetables. We were able to hide some, like rice in tin cans from ravenous rats. The two-legged bastards! They cursed the Japanese invaders. And lived like babies with meager milk from the breasts for succor. Desperation became an intimate friend.

"*Gin nair Nippon-yan*" (many Japanese sons, in our Hockchiang dialect), Mother would whisper, a warning to all of us to be on the constant lookout for the bastards. Young women, especially, were not safe from the marauding hands of the Japanese soldiers. Many were raped in front of families or taken away and kept for "military purposes." Robust young men could be conscripted for military service or labor, or simply carried off for suspected communist sympathies. Decapitated heads of criminals were on public display! Fear descended mercilessly like the monsoon rain, never knowing what utter annihilation it might bring to those it touched. Many were vulnerable to the onslaught of hopelessness, despair, and near starvation. Living for the moment. Like zombies. Searching for a silver lining in the dark clouds.

Many in Ipoh, the city where I was born, fled to the surrounding towns and villages because the Japanese were bombing and machine-gunning positions supposedly defended by the British forces. Mobility was possible at the inception of the Japanese attacks. During the Occupation, the entire population was registered and every movement controlled, the Japanese way to cut off civilian contacts with the communist insurgents or guerrillas now mushrooming in the jungles.

Being suspected or found with pictures of Generalissimo and Madame Chiang Kai-shek, or the British royal family, or listening to radio news, or associating with people known to have anti-Axis sentiments could lead to torture and death.

"Did you know they beheaded the headmaster of the English school in Kampong Koh?" A town next to our village. The first local Chinese promoted to head an English school, his distinguished tenure ended abruptly. Later it was rumored he and a few other local dignitaries were ordered to dig their own graves. Some were buried alive. The bodies of the headmaster and several other people were never found. A relative bicycled all the way to warn us of the impending doom. "Savage short beasts on the go!" the words spread from mouth to mouth like germs in the air we breathe. It sent chills through our bones. Our weakened and vulnerable bodies shuddered. Who next? What next?

One neighbor reported, on the verge of tears, nervously, "They hung a few men upside down!" We did that to some game animals we slaughtered for food, supplementing our plain rice-vegetable diet. The Japanese did that to our men. And for what? Anger surfaced like spring water sprouting from the ground. But restrained.

Community leaders and those suspected of fraternizing with the British had to flee to the mountain tops or the depths of the ocean, hiding like delicious earthworms from hungry ducks, or face excruciating death from the swords and infamous tortures of the Japanese. In "Operation Clean-up," thousands of Chinese were reported to have been massacred by the Japanese military because they were suspected or accused of anti-Japanese activities after Japan attacked China in 1937.

Another said, eyes rolling side to side like a trapped animal, "They filled his stomach with water until it could stretch no more. Then placed a plank on his inflated belly. Sat on it like a seesaw." Japanese ingenuity.

Villagers breathed heavily in a subdued ambiance. Funereal. Like mourning the death of a beloved family member. Like wells gone dry, tears came hard.

Japanese brutalities committed by the Kempeitai, the secret military police, against innocent men and women—more male than female, prisoners of war, enemies of its imperialism—are well documented and no less heinous and diabolical than those inflicted on thousands of innocent Jews by robotic Germans under the Fuehrer in Nazi Germany. Hundreds of Chinese and Korean women forced into sexual servitude to amuse and relieve the insane Japanese bastards. The records of their atrocities against humanity are miles long on paper.

Chapter Two

Rumors spread like a forest fire.

In Japanese prison camps, prisoners dying of disease and starvation were taunted with abundant Red Cross food and medical supplies (like cruel children teasing stray, starving dogs or crippled beggars with food in my neighborhood).

In Japanese hospitals, countless Allied prisoners were injected with deadly acid and bile.

In a cramped bunker in the Philippines, over one hundred Americans were doused with gasoline and set afire.

During a long march to a prison camp in Thailand, over three thousand prisoners were beaten, starved, and shot to death.

And more rumors. Beyond human description and comprehension. All happened in our neighborhood, so to speak. Where are you Jehovah? Allah? Amaterasu?

By the grace of Allah, Malaya did not become another Auschwitz or Buchenwald even though we industrious and entrepreneurial Chinese were pigeonholed as the Jews of the East. Obviously the Japanese did not share their German friends' anti-Semitic sentiments. We were spared the gas chambers!

Brother also said, a voice strangely devoid of bitterness, "In some strange ways, we were very lucky because we lived in a village. We had our land. A blessing. We grew our own vegetables, like long beans, squash, sweet potatoes and tapioca. We had fruits galore like soursop, pineapple, jackfruit, guava, star fruit, and mango. Sugar Cane. Bananas. Papayas. Coconuts. We lived near the ocean. We had plenty of fish. We dug clams. We raised ducks, chickens and pigs." The one commodity, a staple in the Malayan diet, was rice. And rice was in dire short supply, according to Brother. Imports stopped abruptly. Family income almost evaporated faster than the morning dew in the tropical heat.

Someone in the family, years later, commented, laughingly, "Remember the rice…pet owners used to feed their birds? The raw rice with shells? During the Japanese Occupation when we were faced with a terrible rice shortage, we had to use that pet rice to cultivate seedlings for rice farming. Unfortunately we were not very successful with growing rice. Can you imagine no rice to eat in Chinese homes up and down the land? Of course the poor birds suffered, too."

The Japanese attempt to restore the country's economy to its prewar level was slow. Its attempt to "replace" or "supplant" with everything Japanese—from teaching Nippon-Go (the Japanese language) to inculcating Japanese spirit, manners, and morals—was anything but superficial and tentative. A Japanese bow might take the place of a western handshake but most things Japanese, like a plant, failed to grow on Malayan soil!

The Japanese talk of a Greater Asia under a Japanese military leadership was a false promise. The reality was one of stark insensitivity and extreme harshness to the conquered, failing to win their hearts and souls and support, without which Japanese could not succeed in establishing a new order in my country.

For many, life was a living hell, for at least forty-one long dreary months (February 1942 to August 1945). Like eternity. Until we heard what the Americans did to Japan.

Two atomic bombs, with unprecedented destructive power, were dropped, three days apart, on Hiroshima and Nagasaki. President Harry Truman did not mince words when he warned the Japanese after the first bomb that America would drop more atomic bombs "until we completely destroy Japan's ability to make war." Japan offered surrender the day after the second bomb was dropped. August 10, 1945. About five days later, Japanese people heard the soft but resolute voice of their beloved emperor over the radio, a brave act unheard of in the annals of Japanese history. A real voice from a real emperor, for the first time in their lives.

Japanese troops officially surrendered to Lord Mountbatten in Singapore on August 29. General Douglas MacArthur, the Supreme Allied Commander, had this to say September 2 marking the unconditional surrender of Japan in a twenty-minute ceremony on the American battleship USS Missouri: "It is my earnest hope and indeed the hope of all mankind that from this solemn occasion a better world shall emerge out of the blood and carnage of the past."

Did Emperor Hirohito try to appease the Americans, their conquerors and unwelcome occupiers lording over their land, when on January 1, 1946 (barely six months after the surrender) he issued an imperial decree, to the consternation of his own people, declaring his divinity a "false conception," a fiction? In essence saying to his people, I am just an ordinary man like you, not one descended from the Sun Goddess Amaterasu? Debunking his divine identity? Or did the emperor by his decree aim to usher in a new era of modern government in Japan, "based on democracy, peace and rationalism"?

He also got his wish, an American woman to teach his son English (the present emperor of Japan).

With the war finally over, our family sighed a great sense of relief. Like the first shower after a severe prolonged drought.

But not me. A direct victim of circumstances. Like my brother. But for something entirely different. For something physically painful. And I psychologically scared for life. The family was trying to recuperate from the devastation of war. Our resources depleted. Financially ruined. Forget any access to a medical doctor. Or western medicine.

I was five. It happened a few months after the Japanese exodus from our land. Family members sensed something wasn't right with me. "You are not your normal self," according to their scrutiny. "Something is wrong somewhere," they pronounced eagerly.

Somewhere? I knew where that somewhere was located. Down under. After persistent probing they were able to squeeze the truth out of me, like milk from coconut meat for curry. The cat came out quickly from the bag. I was suffering from *constipation*. A despicable word. *C-o-n-s-t-i-p-a-t-i-o-n*! Why would anybody trumpet this personal tragedy from the rooftops? That was how I felt. Too poor to procure western medicine (blame the Japanese bastards for the family financial woes), the family applied the "soap treatment" without hesitation. Without wavering. The best they knew how. Without consulting me. The victim. Brother judiciously stayed away from this delicate operation. Only the women were in attendance. Stripped of my flimsy short drawers (almost all boys and men wore drawers at home or at work around the house with nothing else over them), belly down on sister-in-law's sturdy lap (she a giant to a small child), I could hear Mother busy shaving away a piece of bath soap to the desire shape, size and length, with the dexterity of a sculptor on a wooden block. All of a sudden, in the stillness of a moment, without warning or lubricating first the bottom end of my alimentary canal, Mother unceremoniously pushed the piece of sharp-pointed soap up my ass, like an aggressive missile into an enemy territory. And the rationale for this rather primitive behavior? To pave and grease the way, my folks asserted, for a smooth, painless discharge! Creating a slippery slope for the shy solid fecal mass to descend unaided. Faster than a baby eager to exit from a womb! Someone no less than a Margaret Mead would be aghast at this quaint procedure among the Hockchiang tribe! I respected my ancestors' resourcefulness but not this one. Sure, it was quick and fast. Initially, a fainting spell. A brief jerk of the body, followed. Shivered, involuntarily. Slight pain lingered, like a thorn prick. Curtailed my misery, the much-anticipated relief. Live or die? I chose to live. Miraculously the soap worked. Next time, it won't be another next time, not after this invasive Chinese torture, I comforted and assured myself. But nobody, in the name of Allah, is ever going to touch me again, I swore. Not my anus. Not anywhere. Next time, suffer the agony silently, avoid any public display of the constipated look, and pray fervently for a miracle!

The soap treatment wasn't optional. Not when the family was destitute and compelled to apply one of the homegrown cures or remedies. I wouldn't be the first patient, albeit a reluctant one, like an innocent sheep led to a slaughterhouse. But I cursed and cursed the Japanese bastards for my humiliation. Suffering. For years I declared myself an untouchable like some of those in India. I blamed the Japanese for the psychological scar that won't disappear. And in my dictionary, constipation remains some indelible bodily pain associated with Japanese unwelcome presence and source of much of human suffering. My suffering!

And not just my delicate anus. But my teeth, too. Later in life, declining and falling fast like trees with dead and rotting diseased roots. With coconut husk (readily available from our own trees, also utilized for scraping dirty pots and pans), a practical toothbrush substitute, I used soot (abundant from the wood-burning stove), to brush my tenuous teeth. A few clung tenaciously to a deteriorating foundation, like a bird's nest on a rickety branch. Dental hygiene wasn't a top priority in the family during or immediately following the Japanese Occupation. It was, without doubt, survival for the fittest. There was a period I had to visit my dentist many times like one spending leisure time with your bosom buddies. I couldn't live without him. His expertise, I desired. Not his closeness. Again I cursed and cursed the Japanese bastards for the dental problems that impacted my health, smiles and pretty face.

The worst infliction occurred after the Japanese exodus. Mother would call me *Nippon-yan* (son of Japan), an epithet she generously bestowed on me whenever she was frustrated with me, herself, Father and the rest of the known world. By the tone of her perturbed voice and her twisted countenance, it wasn't meant to be a compliment. Neither in praise of Emperor Hirohito and his cohorts in crime. By pitching *Nippon-yan* at me innumerable times she was saying to me, *You are just like the Japanese bastards! Evil. Corrupt. Murderous. Diabolical. A rapist. You deserved to go to hell. A disgrace to the family. You short shit-head. You no good.* Damaging invectives more appropriate for the Japanese bastards, now conveniently aimed at a non-combative defenseless child! As a dutiful son, living in complete submission to Mother's control, I deserved my fate. But not to the extent to commit *hara kiri* ("suicide by disembowelment formerly practiced by the Japanese samurai") to end one's life because of disgrace or dishonor to the Ling family. But I suffered because of the Japanese bastards' misdeeds! Psychologically!

The war in the Pacific had concluded with the unconditional surrender of the Japanese but they continued to haunt me. Like ghosts, of the recently departed, visiting their loved ones left behind.

The ensuing peace was short-lived for many of our friends and relatives living in remote kampongs, ten or so miles away from us, suspected of *communist* infestation. During the war and the Japanese Occupation (1942–45), there emerged a group of anti-Japanese communist insurgents, mainly Chinese, in the jungles, ironically aided with arms by the British guerrilla units, together trying to rout the Japanese out of Malaya. What an unlikely alliance vis-à-vis a common enemy! The Chinese communists and the British! Unfortunately after the Japanese surrender, the anti-Japanese communist resistance groups tried to fill the initial vacuum only to be taken over by the British Military Administration. Disappointed they resolved to destroy the economic recovery by ruthlessly murdering British rubber planters and miners, the backbone of the Malayan economy. And any Chinese who dared oppose their agenda. Confronted with the communist insurrection and killing rampage, a State of Emergency was declared by the Malayan government in June 1948 and lasted till 1960.

Translated that meant nearly half a million rural dwellers, including some of our friends and relatives, were herded into new villages, away from the depths of the jungle, walled in by tall fences, under constant surveillance, protecting them from communist depredations, while hoping to cut them off from aiding the communists with food, money and able-bodied men. (Years later we heard that our village Kampong China escaped the resettlement program because we were praised the model citizens! Meaning, we were safely pigeonholed anti-communist and less likely to join any insurrection against the British as they engineered to form a new government in postwar Malaya.) Yes, they all looked alike—the innocent and the guilty (for heaven-sake the anti-Japanese communists were all Chinese!), according to those in the front line of the war. (Years later the civilized world was shocked to hear Americans massacred the innocent ones in Vietnam for the same reason: they all looked alike! because the innocent and the guilty ones were all Vietnamese!) Of course all our relatives denied vehemently any liaison with the communists—granted some communists were once fellow workers or classmates or distant relatives, pleased with the new safe environment, acknowledging a few neighborhood kids had joined the communists because they thought they were fighting against the Japanese. At the same time total victory against the enemies, the government calculated, must go beyond military might. To win the unreserved support of the villagers and their hearts, the government wisely and immediately implemented programs and social services to improve their lives, especially those affected by the resettlement. Friends and relatives sang praises—amidst political turmoil and social unrest—of what the government was actively doing for them. New roads. Health Centers. Midwife clinics. Community halls. New classes. Bridges. Hospitals. Modern methods of agriculture. Even a few small mosques (places of worship for Muslims). Islam is the official state religion in my country.

Tunku Abdul Rahman (a scion of a sultan) became Chief Minister of Malaya's first elected government in 1955. That same year he held talks with the Secretary-General Chin Peng of the Malayan Communist Party, hoping peace settlement would ensure Malay's independence from England in 1957. (Chin Peng's real name is Ong Boon Hua. And his father Ong Sing Piau, a Hockchiang, was once the Chairman of Yuk Ing School, a successor to Hockchiang School started by Grandpa in the village.) The Tunku feared, genuinely, the communist emergency might give the British cause to postpone the independence. The Chief Minister's dream was crushed when the communist leader Chin Peng rejected his peace term offer. "My ideas about communism were determined by that meeting," he said, matter-of-factly. "I became convinced that once a communist, always a communist. They could never coexist with us in an independent Malaya." True to his words, within three years after Malaya achieved its independence from England in August 3, 1957, communism met its demise. The State of Emergency throughout the Malay Peninsula was finally lifted in 1960. Many friends and relatives chose to stay where they were in the new settlements. Few returned to their cultivated lands in the jungle to live and raise their families.

The Federation of Malaya, like an independent ambitious young man, breaking free first from the stranglehold of the British and later a brief occupation by the Japanese, was free to pursue its dreams of happiness and prosperity, peace and harmony for all its peoples—Malays, Chinese, Indians and others.

Happy days are here, again.

THREE

Less than a year after the Japanese defeat and exodus from Malaya, Brother, at the marriageable age of eighteen, engaged for about three years to a girl whose face he had never seen, whose voice he had never heard, was elated about the coming nuptials. For every child, born and raised in a traditional Chinese family, filial piety (thank philosopher K'ung Fu-tse or Confucius who lived and taught our ancestors the rudiments of an orderly society and hierarchy of relationships from the family at the bottom to the government at the top six hundred years or so before the birth of Jesus Christ) meant total submission to higher authorities, your parents; their words and decisions absolute, non-negotiable, indisputable, like a divine mandate from heaven. The parents, in their eternal sagacity, chose the mate for you for eternity. One wondered who actually had the final say in the match making game!

Our ubiquitous village matchmaker, whose mouth, like a fish, never seemed to rest, went about her particular assignment for a big *urn bao* (or read package or envelope of sumptuous gratuity), searching the nook and niche for the ideal match for Brother. She needn't venture far, mostly by foot or carried on a bicycle by her athletic grandson. (For most people in the villages of Southeast Asia, bicycles were then the only means of transportation for humans and goods, light or heavy, big or small. They still are in some parts of Asia. The metal racks installed at the back could haul just about anything—including grandmothers.) We lived in a small intimate village. Everybody knew somebody. Like a huge extended family. Less than five decades ago, our ancestors hailed from the same area in China to settle in this kampong. Everyone knew the matchmaker, in her late sixties, a cherished soul, carrying with her an encyclopedic knowledge of every male and female, beautiful or ugly, born in the village. A catalogue of potentials. Fresh and used—or tarnished!

Once in old China, girls (or parents?) who desired a rich man and a pampered life would readily yield, albeit some contemptuously and grudgingly, to *foot binding* as young as three while the bones were malleable. Tightening strips of binding-cloth tightly wrapped around the growing ductile feet—like clamps—literally crushing and distorting the bones in the process, would produce the much-sought-after the perfect three-inch-length feet. An aphrodisiac in the making! Some contended. She could not *run* far from the snare of a panderer or her husband. Many chauvinistic males heartily agreed. This excruciating painful act of *foot binding* indisputably defined a woman's role in a traditional Chinese society: her utter dependence on her men—husband and sons—for everything. The man's parents preferred a woman with dainty small bound feet, symbol of elegance and good breeding, her erotic walk drew attention to her swaying buttocks, making her vulnerable and desirable. "Show me your feet," the first words a girl would hear from a matchmaker. Big feet guaranteed spinsterhood!

The matchmaker, residing in a small house on our land, had small bound feet herself. Her face increasingly wizened but wiser. Her slow gait did not impede her pawing and scrounging around for the ideal match for a family. More than anything, families trusted her eyesight, her insight, and her intuition. Most valuably her impartial recommendations.

No formal presentations with documents, credentials, references, or testimonials to a potential bride's parents. Causal chitchat. More chitchat. Extended chitchat. Her presence more like a nonchalant friend dropping by for an early morning tea and cookies. Parents raised questions. She answered them, calmly. Matter-of-factly. No embellishments. She spoke, plainly. Everything transparent, expectedly. More like a discreet volley between two sets of anxious parents. She the consummate referee, constantly fanning herself. Tropical heat and chronic skin rash tortured her, Mother said. She carried a light moon-shaped fan, made from one big leaf, wherever her duties led her like a carpenter with his tools. Most times the onus was on her with the persuasive skill of a trial lawyer to advertise the young man to the family. It was always the man's family looking for a match, not vice versa. Trying to sell a female in match making would suspiciously lead people to think she must be a reject, defiled, deflowered, defective, used, like some unwanted worn out tires. Fit for the dump or an old God-forsaken unwanted deep well where neighbors discarded their live or dead animals, the maimed, the crippled and other pests. Stench and fumes of death arising from the hole filled the air around it. A hell hole. The cries of live unwanted kittens or puppies from its depths continued to haunt me, still. One of my nagging fears, as a child, was falling into one, crawling with snakes and other living undesirables. A slice of hell, purgatory! This was the place for the defiled females in our village.

Reject the final proclamations of the matchmaker at your own peril: "He is a good man. He comes from a good family. He has never disappointed his parents. He will take good care of you. He is a hard worker. You can't ask for a better man in this whole village." Her words the gospel truth. Like the final verdict by a judge. Everyone trusted her, implicitly. She was the only one plying her profession in the village, skills honed by decades of experiences. No rival. No competitor. Suffer the fate of bachelorhood or spinsterhood if you dared ignore her magnanimity and wisdom.

The platitude, beggars can't be choosy, applied to both parties. Neither Brother nor his future bride had a good education. (Blame the Japanese bastards.) Neither had any marketable skill or training. (Would you consider raising chickens and pigs, growing garden vegetables and tapping rubber trees marketable skills?) Neither had any plans for the future. (Unless you include sex and procreation as part of the plan.) Neither was born with a silver spoon in his or her mouth. (Unless you think eking out a living from the soil is a silver spoon.) Worse, neither had any voice why they should love each other (strangers in the night) and be bonded like a tenon and a mortise. However, one consolation for Brother and his future bride: many others in the village had married under similar circumstances. Nothing out of the ordinary. Green light flashed.

One consolation for the parents: both sets of parents were winners. The woman's parents gained a son-in-law; the man's parents gained a daughter-in-law. Unlike the Indians living beyond our village, a female would be doomed to a life of despair and servitude from the inception of the marriage if her dowry—her beauty a secondary consideration or a naught—wasn't sumptuous and impressive enough to meet oftentimes outrageous demands of the male's parents.

The parents (they had to be insane!) wanted this union, not them, impatiently. Undeterred consensus led to the engagement, a simple verbal announcement without fanfare, during the first months of the Japanese Occupation. On what grounds? Amidst the social, political and economic upheaval and uncertainties, threats of communist insurgency in the land? Absolutely insane! I thought. What hope for a young couple embarking on a new journey, unable to see the ups and downs along the roads, strewn with social and economic debris, and Japanese soldiers marching contemplatively in and out of our village, like innocent monks looking for food? The parents wanted grandchildren. Aha! The more the merrier! Or was it the more their prestige would climb in the eyes of their fellow countrymen? "What a pity to die alone, without grandchildren to play with," echoed the words of a village sage.

No personal rendezvous was contemplated or allowed from the time of the engagement till the actual nuptials. Blame the presence of the Japanese…or blame the Chinese mores of the day.

At long last there was one final hurdle to overcome before the wedding day. For this, Mother did not consult the pastor of our church, who lived quite a distance from the village. We had become nominal Christians after Grandpa, a devout Christian, returned to mainland China in the late 1930s and never returned to Malaya. Instead, like a pagan consulting an oracle, she sought the divination of an astrologer for a propitious day to hold her only son's wedding without offending heaven and earth, begging for divine blessing. The astrologer—sometimes working as a medium, a supposed intermediary between heaven and earth—did not wheedle the gods, but diligently sought answers from an old, fat, torn book, like a farmer checking his almanac for the time to plant his first crops. The flip of a page or two gave Mother the divine assurance she needed, with no mysterious incantations or elaborate animal sacrifices. Luckily the families did not have to wait long for some gods' approval. It had been spoken many eons ago and recorded for posterity in a book.

The consultation with the astrologer in a Buddhist temple, considered unchristian but imperative, was a family secret.

That accomplished, it was time for earnest preparations, under Father's direction, with military precision. He took charge, planning and executing all the necessary maneuvers to put on a show (a wedding banquet) worthy of the family's name. That meant, in our Chinese tradition, you would be judged severely by friends, neighbors, and relatives by how much you were willing to spend for your First Son's wedding. Be lavish and ostentatious was the right motto to follow. Whatever you did for the First Son or the First Son did to or for you would be the talk of the village for eons to come. Less attention was paid to other children. Most Chinese parents would be guilty of such partiality. Saving and protecting the family's *face* was top priority. Economically, that meant sparing nothing to put out the best wedding feast for your guests.

Truth be told, guests demanded their money's worth without shame, as if their cash gifts could buy a whole restaurant. Be prepared to feed an army of voracious guests. No one ever checked the identities of the guests. Villagers were oblivious to numbers or faces. You could expect a guest's whole family, two to five or more, to be at the wedding feast, like children attending Sunday school punctually for big prizes awarded during Christmas. More guests could be expected now, many having tasted starvation during the recent Japanese Occupation. Weddings and funerals—with plentiful food—were always well attended.

Following another Chinese tradition, especially among the Hockchiang people, Father kept a meticulous accurate record of who gave what and how much to Brother's wedding. Because we were going through lean times, every red package of money was needed to defray the cost of staging a feast. I was soon to learn the record served a useful purpose in the future: primarily so you could reciprocate the same amount or more to weddings at a future date. To kill gossip or not lose *face*, I heard grownups voice this admonition many times while growing up: "Add a little more to the original amount received if you are doing well." Host families would overlook it if you were down in the pits somewhere. Villagers had ears and eyes. Worse, they talked.

I was five, enjoying the fun and commotion as the family and relatives prepared the house for Brother's wedding. But to Mother I was in everyone's way. "Go away. You no helping. Go away. People busy. Go away. Go play." And play I did. I didn't want to disappoint Mother. I trotted away gaily like a wound up toy. Not far from the house, under the watchful eye of Sister, hovering over me like a hawk. Few words. Her wide, round eyes don't blink. I call this period of my life puppy-hood.

Everyone loves a puppy, a darling, cuddly, soft and furry, deliciously enthralling. Everyone wants to touch and hold a puppy. So sweet. So innocent. Tail wagging. Tongue licking. So irresistible! Warm hugs and wet kisses from everyone. You are the center of the universe, like a movie star, they adore and worship you. I enjoyed every minute of my puppy-hood. It ended sooner than I expected.

I don't remember who invented the game, but we played the village version of hide-and-seek. Very often. It required no expensive equipment. No coach. No timekeeper. No field. No spectators to cheer you on. No trophy. Hopscotch or jumping rope if a girl or two were around. Today I played hide-and-seek with my marble friends, one slightly taller and older. I was the youngest of the lot. We used tiny sea and snail shells that were smaller than fingernails. Plentiful, scattered in the backyard vegetable garden, a dumping ground. Color had gradually faded, some bleached because of the sun and blended in with the immediate surrounding. We looked for older rubber trees with huge trunks, like older men with big hanging bellies, and partially exposed roots. Given five tiny shells, some the color of dirt and tree bark, each player, behind a tree, must hide them in the ground, on the tree, under the roots, anywhere within a prescribed area. It was your partner's turn to seek out the hidden shells, so tiny sometimes they escaped detection. You lost the game if you failed to produce the five shells. It was difficult for me to concentrate when so much was going on at home. I wanted to be part of the large crowd at home, a block or two away. I played the game absentmindedly. Using the palm of my right hand, I shielded my eyes from the slight glare of the evening sun as it dived slowly down the western horizon. I lost until Sister escorted me home for dinner. I followed one step behind her, like a rooster picking up rice along an unmarked trail.

A police vehicle in front of our house. We seldom saw a car in the village. Once people would stop, whatever they might be doing outdoors, transfixed by a car hurtling through the village. As rare as an owl in bright daylight. Somebody's out-of-town playboy son, visiting poor parents, showing off his toy, they whispered. The presence of a car aroused great curiosity or suspicion. Seldom jealousy or admiration. And nothing if it was a police car. Two men in uniform were talking to Father. Had they caught someone with opium and traced it to Father, the man in charge of the opium operation in the village? It was no secret that Father had sole monopoly of the opium business in the village. Why were they talking with him? Eighth Uncle was a respected police inspector. We had connections. Partly bought with bribes. Or was Eighth Uncle in trouble himself? Could they be looking for him? He went to work this morning like every other morning. I saw him on his bicycle, happily whistling as he left the house. Did he not report to work? Elope with a new mistress? Did they want to know his whereabouts? Sister and I, with questions in our minds, walked gingerly past the police and Father, straight to the kitchen, wearing masks of indifference.

"Eighth Uncle's friends," someone in the kitchen blurted out. A sense of relief blew through the hot kitchen like a cool breeze. "Don't worry. Nothing serious," Small Sister added, for the moment in charge of cooking. I sniffed a better and more tempting fare because of relatives helping out with the wedding. I ate like parched earth drinking the rainwater. For a while we heard rumors that Eighth Uncle might be transferred to Ipoh. Was he too involved with Father's opium business, compromising his integrity as a police officer? Uncle smoked too, while in uniform. I hated to think Eighth Auntie, my protector, and three cousins might desert the ancestral home to join uncle. The whole family still grieved over the sudden death of the youngest child, Eighth Auntie's favorite daughter, less than a year before. The Japanese Occupation had prevented easy access to a local hospital or western medicine. But Brother's wedding was uppermost in my mind, not some relatives' departure to a big city. Or their inconsolable pain. Or Uncle's rumored promotion.

Though I didn't actively participate in or understand much of what was transpiring all around me (Mother judged me a nuisance and an impediment to everyone), Brother's wedding meant there were effusive joy, happiness, laughter and spontaneous gaiety in the family, again. A momentous rebirth. It was like heaven on earth. A national holiday. Just like a Chinese New Year. Sight. Color. Sound. Smell. Merrymaking. Sufficient to titillate our senses, stirring our hungry souls. The house was spotlessly clean. All the intense scrubbing and mopping were intended to drive out the old evil spirits, awaiting the arrival of a new fortune and good luck, the bride, like an infusion of new blood into a tired family's vein. Everywhere you turned, bright, happy, crimson something greeted and saluted you on windows, doors, or walls in the main parlor. Most attractive and exquisite were ornate scrolls hanging on the walls, gifts from friends and well-wishers, with elegant Chinese calligraphy in brilliant gold or black for the young couple:

"Hundred years good togetherness."

"*Heaven made the match for you.*"

"*Harmony between two families.*"

"*Born soon precious son.*"

"*A match made in heaven.*"

Overtly displayed at the main entrance and other parts of the house, another Chinese tradition, was the Chinese character *luck* turned upside down, confusing to a kid like me, just learning to read and write Chinese. I thought somebody must have committed an inexcusable error. But as I grew older, I would learn to appreciate the profound significance of families proudly pasting the Chinese word luck—written upside-down on square red papers—on a momentous occasion, like a son's wedding. If an error, it was deliberate. In Chinese characters, the words *upside down* and *come* or *arrive* (*dao*) are homonyms. Because the word *luck* was pasted upside down, it had an added sense of urgency or promise fulfilled. Now it meant good *luck* or fortune (the new bride) *has arrived* or *come* to this household. Not just the promise of something good. *It is here. Now!* Truly a time to rejoice and celebrate with the young, happy couple.

No one could rest or sleep peacefully on the eve of Brother's nuptials with the entire household buzzing and bustling like a beehive. The whole house, the front and side yards, the kitchen and its vicinity were brightly lit with kerosene lanterns, hung strategically like a million fireflies. It had to be a propitious day because many considered the most important part of the wedding to be the sumptuous banquet, a twenty-one-course feast (a smidgen compared to the one-hundred-and-eight-course royal banquet in imperial China), prepared, cooked and served entirely outdoors under the spreading rubber trees. The weather had to be as perfect as a bride's fresh makeup.

Some in the village believed that it would rain on your wedding and funeral if it had rained on the day of your birth. I remember once (maybe a couple of times), when a sudden downpour came as I was watching a funeral procession through the village, hearing comments like "It is raining now because it rained on the day of the man's birthday." My family was not immune to such talk but probably brushed it aside as superstition. Because nothing was said openly about rain or no rain on Brother's birthday.

Under a serene, cloudless, evening sky, the chef, who worked for a reputable restaurant in town but lived with his family in the village, had his four heavy, steel-drum, wood-burning stoves delivered and arranged in a semi-circle, with the open furnaces facing away from him, a logical move to reduce the heat while cooking (with one helper constantly feeding the furnaces with wood), in a makeshift, spacious kitchen between the well and the family kitchen. An ideal location, since water for cooking was drawn directly from the well. On two huge woks, at least three feet in diameter, were placed stacks of bamboo steamers with latticed bamboo lids for steaming food or keeping certain dishes warm before serving. The steamer lids were designed with incredible ingenuity and skill to allow small amounts of steam to escape through the lids without droplets of condensed steam to mar the texture and taste of cooked foods. One stove held pots of different sizes for boiling, parboiling and deep-frying. The last stove had a handy wok for the chef to perform his culinary magic, creating a large variety of style and taste of exotic dishes to impress the guests.

The chef came with his own *batterie de cuisine,* an arsenal of authentic culinary tools. I was more than surprised to discover in my first culinary adventure that his assortment of kitchen tools was not much different from the ones now resting contentedly in our family kitchen. Some looked bigger, heavier, sturdier, better made, but seasoned with use.

~

Tools for preparation include the ubiquitous, carbon steel, sharp-edged Chinese cleaver—which some claim is a prerequisite for successful Chinese cooking—in three different weights. A versatile tool for cutting, slicing, chopping, mincing, tenderizing, crushing, and hacking, and its broad blade is used as a scoop to transfer ingredients from the chopping block to the wok, containers or dishes. I have always been fascinated watching any chef (even my own Brother) mince fish, pork, or shrimp using two cleavers simultaneously with deft and astonishing speed. Grasp the handle of the cleaver firmly with the writing hand, hold down the ingredients with the fingertips of the free hand curled, pushing the knuckles against the flat of the blade, begin to cut with the forward down movement (the same front and back movement of a hand saw) the blade slightly tilted at the back, never lifting it any higher than the ingredients.

Yes, the trusty cleaver! I tried to prove to my friends in later years that I am a true Chinese in the dexterity and rapidity of my use of the cleaver. Plenty of o-o-hs! And a-a-hs! They were gasping for breath. Confidence and arrogance bubbling inside me. Followed by the inevitable "Who taught you how to use the cleaver like that?" Intuitively followed by my deliberately cautioning them, "Don't try this at home." Then facetiously adding, "Anyone with a chicken brain can do it!"

After years of trying to master a modicum of the art of Chinese cooking I must confess you spend more than three-quarters of your time preparing ingredients—with the help of a cleaver—and a very short time actually cooking the simple dishes.

We did everything with the cleaver before the appearance of slicers with interchangeable and adjustable blades or ridiculously expensive blenders. No small wonder some culinary connoisseurs call it, because of its versatility, the original Chinese food processor.

A true Chinese chef or a good cook worth his salt would as readily abandon the cleaver as modern Chinese businessmen would trade their simple, efficacious abacus for an electronic calculator.

And the chopping block, as necessary as a singer's accompaniment, usually round and thick, traditionally cut from a tree trunk, is never far from the cleaver. Like a true friend, it will last forever and hangs, like a prized medallion, on a wall next to the stove.

Tools for cooking include the you-can't-live-without all-purpose wok. A pot for boiling water, a separate one for cooking rice and a time-honored carbon steel wok, blackened and shiny from decades of use, for every conceivable style of cooking that had sustained, for thousands of years, over a quarter of the world's population. Quite an extravagant claim, but true. With or without a lid, depending on the style of cooking, use the trusty wok to stir-fry, steam, deep-fry and braise, whipping up a simple meal for a family or a feast of highly sophisticated, intensely flavored dishes fit for the imperial family in ancient China.

Accompanying the wok are three indispensable accessories: a spatula, a ladle and a strainer. Whether in a famous restaurant, a private kitchen, open-air night market or during an outdoor banquet, without straining your ears, you can detect the sharp, distinct clanging of the Chinese spatula from miles away. Designed to fit the curved, sloping sides of the wok, the spatula's shovel-shaped blade (three to five inches wide), with a long handle, is perfect for stirring, tossing, flipping, and separating anything in a stir-fry. I learned that when I was old enough to hold a spatula, working fast and quick like a ping-pong game because it is stir-frying. Yes, the unmistakable clanging of the spatula on the rim of the wok—perhaps to relieve some tension or nervousness (if you have to cook for a few hundred people), or to wait for the food to sizzle or bubbles to rise, but mostly to signal informally that a dish is about done and ready to be scooped out to the serving platters. All in all a busy sound. A happy sound. A sound to announce food is on the way to the table. The waiting is almost over.

Like a twin, the ladle works harmoniously with the spatula. Designed also to fit the curves of the wok, this shallow and wide, cuplike spoon (three to five inches wide) is good for scooping oil or liquid seasonings into the wok. In cooking for a banquet, most seasonings like soy sauce, oyster-flavored sauce, sesame oil, chili oil, rice vinegar, hoisin sauce, chili and garlic sauce (ever wonder why most Chinese dishes are exquisitely flavored?) are in separate bowls sitting on an elevation behind the wok, within easy reach. The ladle is also used to dish out the cooked foods from the wok into splendidly designed serving bowls or platters. Forget measuring cups and spoons. They are for novices and sissies in Chinese cooking. Eyes narrowly focused and brains going at a hundred miles an hour, a chef uses his ladle like a magic wand to measure and spoon out intuitively almost the precise amounts of liquid seasonings required for every single dish he cooks, going back occasionally—after a split-second tasting from a hot ladle—for additional specks from the bowls, if needed for that special touch that finely differentiates one dish from another. Intuition, sensibilities, and years of experiences are the guides that determine the final outcome, not adherence to measuring cups and spoons.

Years later, as a college student new in America, I faced a hungry-looking crowd of American women somewhere in the jungles of Ohio, who demanded relentlessly that I use the ever-present measuring cups and spoons to teach them Chinese cooking. "We need to write down the exact amounts or something," they said, less than a second after I had politely informed them that I grew up in a Chinese kitchen without measuring cups and spoons and had watched my folks cut up things and threw them into a wok with restrained sprinkling of this and that seasoning. It sounded so primitive and devastating to them because they wanted a formal recipe. How many teaspoons or tablespoons of this and that? How many cups of this and that? Sorry, ladies, I don't know of any in my Chinese kitchen. *Did you hear me? I grew up...with no written recipes.* We were lucky if we had rice to eat. A few grains, not cups. At least I endeavored to replicate a few dishes hinging on what I could retrieve from my memories of what I had seen going on in my family kitchen years ago and hundreds of miles away. New and naïve in this wild country, I was initially amused supplying the aspiring women with a list of this and that. But that was not a recipe, they cried. This and that without the measuring cups and spoons were as good as a bicycle without a handle bar to them! I remember wondering why some Americans expect rather obtusely or naively that because you are Chinese you should possess expertise in everything and anything that has to do with the Chinese culture? Speak some Chinese. Do a dance. Sing a song. Write my name in Chinese. Show me kung fu. And mocking, the most detestable sin, height of cultural insensitivity, a Chinese struggling to speak English "You lie fly nice?" with a buck-toothed face for emphasis! You like fried rice? As a teacher, I don't think an average American today knows everything about America because he is an American. Socially? Politically? Culturally? Geographically? Economically? Do most Americans speak eloquently or write American English intelligibly because they were born in America? I think not!

Not all Chinese know and utilize a strainer in their cooking, though it is an essential tool for a chef. I had seen a strainer hanging in our kitchen, begging to be used. The strainer (or skimmer), a wire mesh basket or an oversize wire screen (eight to twelve inches wide) attached to a long wooden handle, is ideal for fishing out cooked foods from hot water or oil, especially in deep-frying. For a poverty-stricken family like mine, deep-frying, which requires abundant oil, was a luxury we could ill afford.

A few chefs might use a set of extra-long wooden chopsticks to keep their hands safe from hot foods, to separate certain ingredients, or to snatch bits for tasting.

~

The renowned chef had his own *batterie de cuisine* all in place (the stage ready for the play). I was eagerly waiting to watch a free performance, right in my own kitchen. And I had the best seat in the house!

The chef and his assistant started early the morning of the momentous event. Guests arrived early, but the banquet would not begin until about one o'clock in the afternoon, following a brief church ceremony in a town nearby and a procession of a few cars with everything to furnish the newlyweds' bedroom. The whole trousseau—mostly financed by the male—on public display, so to speak. The villagers had eyes and noses. They watched. They whispered. They talked. They gossiped. They studied everything like eggs being candled for hatching. Because the procession carried everything—beautifully cross-stitched bed sheets and the hanging over the front of the bed, two large pillows and a bolster with ornate designs on their covers, a cupboard, usually with one tall mirror on one of its doors, full of beautiful clothes and yards and yards of fine cloth from parents, friends and relatives, an adult-size enameled chamber pot, et cetera. Anybody with a sane mind living out in the boondocks would not expect a new bride to use the wooden outhouse, ours pretty rickety, located a few yards away from the residence, especially the first night in an unknown territory. The solution? The chamber pot. (More Chinese ingenuity!) And where might you find the chamber pot in the newlyweds' bedroom? The space between the bed—with its four poles for a mosquito net—and the wall with a thirty-inch wide thick decorative drape, about the width of a bedroom door, hung between the front left corner pole and the wall. Everybody could hear something dripping in the middle of the night! Expected!

And everybody congratulated the matchmaker for another job well executed. Rewarded handsomely by the bridegroom's family with a free meal and a fat red packet of *urn bao,* she was the cunning instrument for a match made in heaven. Even as she sat relaxed and fanning herself at Brother's wedding, she was, like His Holiness the Pope, receiving guests and filtering requests from mothers (not fathers) looking for perfect future daughters-in-law. What better place to advertise the success of her consummate matchmaking skills than at Brother's wedding? For her it was pleasure and business as usual. Her duties were never done!

The loud explosions of red firecrackers announced the arrival of the newly-weds, the bridegroom getting out first, followed by the bride. At this juncture everything was in slow motion, except the muscular young men scrambling up the stairs to the newlyweds' bedroom with all the furnishings (from the groom's house) to add to it color, enticement and seduction. The once Spartan room was transformed instantly into an attractive nest. The firecrackers had two functions: first, to announce the arrival of the procession;

second, to chase away the bad spirits—by firing up more crackers because the louder the better—to make room for the good spirits. (Like emptying the house for some fresh air to come in.) Good luck and good fortune had finally arrived! With the bride.

Added to the hustle and bustle was the delicious aroma from the open air kitchen, the chef mobilizing his men like disciplined soldiers (about ten or so relatives had volunteered their hands and feet) now in earnest and in full steam, gesturing wildly and shouting orders to speed up preparations for the actual cooking. Some preparations had started the night before. The clanking music of the spatula had begun. Transcending everything going on, the sounds, the voices, the colors, the smells, the laughter, the smiles, the greetings, the general commotion, was the joyous sound of a small group of Chinese musicians playing the *Tan P'i Ku* (a small drum sitting on a twenty-four-inch tripod keeping time and when for someone to sing), *Pan* (three wooden pieces with clacking sound for rhythm and emphasis), *Hu Ch'in* (a two-stringed bamboo string instrument with a bowl for singing), *Hsia Lo* (a small brass gong beaten with a wooden stick), and *So Na,* a woodwind instrument shaped like a trumpet. In step with the firecrackers, the *So Na* (used solely for ceremonious occasions, like the regal trumpets announcing the arrival of Her Majesty the Queen) played a solo, the player usually standing up, pointing the instrument at the gathered guests, sounding triumphantly as the bride was gently escorted into the house. Soon followed by a ritual aimed strictly for members of the immediate family. Usually in the main parlor of the house. Father and Mother, uncles and aunties, took turns seated while the newlyweds offered them ceremonial tea, at which time they reciprocated with red-packet gifts of money or gold. At times guests would hunt for the relatives and, when found, drag them to the parlor—like fisherman pulling in a surprise catch. I was one of the spectators jamming the parlor and wondered why a few of our relatives—with tradition in the marrow of their bones—were reluctant to be recipients of the ceremonial tea. Another curious behavior got my attention: the way our relatives tried to pry open the bridegroom's palms and force the gifts on him. And he faked refusal, customarily. Villagers said you don't want to appear greedy for money!

The emergence of the bride from her bedchamber in a less formal dress signaled the beginning of the feast. Anticipation filled the air. Interminable wait for some. Many came just to eat. Big families tried not to sit together. Bad image. Villagers talked. Scattered them like seeds from a flowering balsam plant. Many curious eyes busy surveying the crowd. Still empty benches to be filled. Bottles of orange crush popping. Caps flying. Trays of cold dishes snaking round the twenty-one tables, came finally to you. Over two hundred *paying* guests attacked the first of the twenty-one-course grand feast like our pigs at the troughs. Relax and let the chopsticks do the talking! Soft music soothed the digestion.

Going to a Chinese wedding banquet is liking taking a leisure culinary adventure through one of the four highly recommended cuisines of the world (French, German, Italian and Chinese). The simplicity of the table setting, less elaborate and complicated than a feast for the King of England, would mitigate any anxiety about table etiquette. After years of nothing and starvation in mainland China and the recent Japanese Occupation of Malaya, the Chinese had become a breed of pragmatists. Some basic tools are required to do a job—like eating, as easy as filling a tank with petrol (the obstinate British preferred *petrol*, not *gasoline*), quick and simple and efficient. Follow a sequence: A bowl for rice; a set of chopsticks to pick up meats or vegetables; deposit them on the rice; move the bowl close to the lips; shovel a small portion into the mouth; and with a spoon—Mother always said—wash it down with soup. The process is complete. Bowl. Chopsticks. Soup spoon. Nothing aristocratic. Simple and efficient. For the wedding banquet today foods would be served on a four-by-four-feet table, with a bright tablecloth, room for eight to ten guests on four four-feet long backless benches (imagine sitting on one), sharing it with others for a three-plus-hour banquet? Not to worry. Obesity was a luxury few could afford then. It would be difficult trying at times to anchor the elbows on the table for comfort or to rest. A bowl for soup. A small plate for the main courses. A soup spoon—porcelain, never plastic or metal. A pair of chopsticks—wood, bamboo, lacquer, seldom plastic or ivory. A set of small saucers for sauces and condiments. A glass for orange crush. And a paper napkin—cloth if you want to impress your guests.

Most importantly, underlying every Chinese cuisine, every authentic Chinese should know, is the balance of *yin* and *yang*, two opposing forces in ancient Chinese philosophy. *Yin* the feminine principle, manifesting itself in softer, moister, cooler ingredients. Masculine *yang* is found in hot spicy fried foods, ginger, chilies, and red meats. Achieving a balance of *yin* and *yang* in Chinese cooking is not easy, but essential to attaining and maintaining good health and equilibrium of the body. Consequently, Chinese believe, the imbalance of the *yin* and *yang* in our daily consumption is responsible for many physical ailments and frailties. And the eventual deterioration of health. In practical terms, the clever harmony of *yin* and *yang*, and the dynamic harmony of the five tastes (sweet, sour, salty, bitter and hot, known to the Chinese as far back as the 4th century B.C.), together, under the magical wand of a skillful veteran chef, create a remarkable cuisine of infinite variety in style and taste, satisfying to the senses and the soul and the stomach.

In fact, the *yin-yang* belief and the five tastes are brilliantly manifested in every dish at the banquet because every reputable chef in his years of cooking and presentations must answer three essential questions: Is the dish pleasing to the *eye*? Is the dish pleasing to the *nose*? Is the dish pleasing to the *taste*? The answer has to be an unequivocal *yes* if you are a consummate cook!

To a kid like me, Brother's wedding meant one and one thing only: food galore. Everything looked pleasing to me. Everything smelled pleasing to me. Everything tasted pleasing to me. Everything tasted superior than the plain gruel when many lost their appetite for living under the Japanese Occupation. Just a short while ago. At the moment I had an appetite for something else besides the foods delivered at regular intervals to the table to the accompaniment of Chinese music and singing. I wasn't far from the newly-weds' table. Like everyone else I peered at the bride's every move, body, hands, head and her mouth. Like gazing amusingly at my neighbor's monkey's every funny entertaining move, tied to a post, straining her neck trying to grab the peanuts from my hands. What would this two-legged animal do? I meant the bride, on this festive occasion.

The newlyweds were seated at a table surrounded by faces of close relatives of the groom wearing subtle masks of every kind, studying closely every move of the vivacious creature just added to the clan. If I had the power I would eliminate this part of the Chinese tradition. I mean why put the poor bride, in the first few hours of her new life, through this torturous, grueling ordeal, examined by eight pairs of monstrous unsympathetic eyes. Whether she ate or not, they had the final word. "Unabashed and shameful," if she divulged her liking for the dishes. "Voracious," they would shake their heads. "Selfish and inconsiderate for the first born to come," if she lacked appetite. "How could she!" they would shake their heads, conspiring for a consensus. They were doing it because they too were once under the microscope, examined unscrupulously by different sets of eyes. No less critical and partial. I would plead on her behalf: *Let her alone to enjoy a few morsels peacefully.* She needed the energy and stamina. She had a long way to go before anyone would leave the newlyweds alone. If only I could witness what she was going through on the innermost screen of her mind, sitting nervously next to a man engaged to for the past three years but seeing him for the first time. Brother was young, handsome, virile, congenial and shy. I doubted she had any reason to cry in her heart, not at the table. Private tears, maybe, later in the night.

Guests, relatives, and I feasted our eyes on her. Halfway through the twenty-one-course banquet, the newlyweds left their appointed seats, carrying a bottle of wine, ambling from table to table, offering wine to certain friends and relatives of the groom. Not to appear a drunk or an alcoholic, a guest (usually a male) would gently refuse the honor by putting his palm over the glass (in all my years at Chinese wedding feasts I have seldom seen a guest readily putting forth his glass for the fill), slowly all three were engaged in a kind of tug of war spilling precious drops of expensive wine onto the table, guest's clothes or the dirt below. Not a time for any frivolous guffaw. To laugh or not to laugh when you knew the newly-weds were going through the motions nervously, dictated by traditions, strangers to one another, miles apart emotionally, unable to communicate heart to heart, though in close physical proximity. What a frustration, unable to whisper an endearing word to calm each other's anxiety or boost each other's spirits, not knowing what to say or how to begin a simple dialogue between themselves. Here and there guests stretched their necks—like curious squirrels—to see when the newlyweds would descend on their tables, especially if you were bosom friends of the groom. This brief interlude provided some respite for the chef and his crew, because the attention was diverted from the foods to the newlyweds as they made the obligatory rounds with a bottle of expensive wine. And a busy time for the music makers. I don't remember catching anyone looking or asking for the outhouse. An appropriate time to allow the stomachs to digest the foods for most of the guests. A time for the younger kids to roam freely. some scavenging for bottle caps for games among their friends later elsewhere, some trailing the couple like pet ducks from table to table out of curiosity, some standing attentively around the musicians while they entertained the guests. And I, like a magnet, was drawn to the chef and his clanging spatula.

The older, wiser banquet veterans, anticipating a shift in the style of cooking and the next few dishes, beckoned us wandering little gypsies to return quickly to the tables, because they could tell or predict what dish was coming next. To an untrained eye, or a first timer at a feast, was this based on some kind of hunch of what to expect next? In reality there was nothing random about the order or sequence of dishes served. Remember the different techniques of cooking? stir-fry, deep-fry, steam, braise, stew, and smoke? Remember the five tastes? sweet, salty, sour, bitter and hot? Remember taste, fragrance and color? Achieving a balance is the key to presenting a variety of dishes without boring the guests and their taste buds. The chef might serve cold dishes followed by deep-fried, stir-fried, steamed or braised. The idea is not to repeat the same style of cooking from dish to dish throughout the twenty-one-course feast, but aim at achieving the various tastes and aroma, bringing out the different colors to the foods. The experienced knew what to expect next. We children, like chickens, followed their call.

But amidst the gaiety of the moment, something ominous, like a snake about to rear its head, threatened to mar the occasion. There was nothing anybody could have done, not an astrologer nor a crystal ball, to prevent death from snatching away the life of another newlywed, around noon, not far from our house. Brother's friend was found hanging from a rafter of his house, discovered by his wife returning from shopping. Seemed like yesterday we were at his wedding. Now suddenly gone like the sun disappearing deep into the ocean. News leaked slowly, like steam escaping from a boiling pot, some guests caught its effect, tempted to spread it to others, together in danger of spoiling everything for everyone here celebrating the union of two wonderful young people. Worse, dousing the fire of joy with cold water of death seemed inevitable for a minute. The ill wind blew effortlessly throughout the village, I feared. For now it was a concerted effort to surround the newly-weds with a layer of isolation. But for how long? Then what? Right now my appetite was no less keen.

My perennial favorite dish (I might be young but I had been to a few wedding banquets) consisted of several deep-fried eggs drowned in light, meat-vegetable gravy. Ten eggs or so for each platter, a total of over two hundred eggs for twenty-one tables. For this particular dish, the chef entrusted the helpers to boil and peel the eggs in advance, each with gentleness, the way you would decorate painstakingly a birthday cake, to preserve the smooth rounded surface before gently lowering them into bubbling hot oil. A slam-dunk would cause the sizzling oil to spatter, searing the nearest hands and fingers. And an unlikely spectacle, as they moved and turned the bobbing eggs with a strainer to achieve even browning. Soon a light, brown-yellow crust (without batter of any kind) would encircle the eggs, ready to be scooped out into the waiting platters. By then the chef was pouring a light gravy over them, to be dispatched immediately to the tables. Crispness of the deep-fried eggs is of the essence of this dish.

Other favorites included sweet-sour spareribs (deep-fried bite-size spareribs served with pineapple, bamboo shoots and green pepper), stir-fried squid with assorted vegetables, and the most awaited, delicious, and expensive shark's fin soup, the supreme delight of everyone. Unlike most youngsters whose less sophisticated taste buds limited them to a select few dishes, missing out on many salient features of a culinary adventure, flashing the "I can't eat anymore" grin, heads slightly shaking, the adults savored every morsel of every dish with eager anticipation for the next. Without fail, all the kids would be back at the tables for the final dish, waiting impatiently with spoons ready to plunge into a big bowl of canned fruits, usually grapes, filled to the brim with ice cubes. By now, after gorging all the yin-yang foods in gastronomic abandonment, the young and the veterans sought something cool, soothing, like a shower after tilling the soil in the hot sun. I observed—each time—ice cubes flying, reminding me of fighting fish jumping out of water, and yellowish grapes spilling onto the table because some kids thought that was the only way to get their fair share of the grapes and the icy, sweetened water. Some adults stared in amazement, wordless, giving in to the youthful antics.

For me, the best part of any feast was buckets of leftovers expanding each time the servers brought back the dishes from the tables carefully, dumping in an orderly way what belonged to which unmarked bucket. I had to assume they had been instructed what to do with the leftovers. Divisions according to the methods of cooking—stir-fry, deep-fry, steam, braise? Divisions according to the tastes (salty, sweet, hot, bitter, sour)? Or divisions according to fish, poultry and meats? Overlapping of smells, textures and colors seemed inevitable. The best chop suey in town. A new dish, *sui generis*. With a twenty-one-course banquet, we expected abundant leftovers. When the dust settled, the chef packed his tools for the day. Small pails of leftovers were delivered to close friends and relatives living nearby. I remember heating up earlier leftovers (from relatives and friends) over and over (days before refrigeration in our village)—better and tastier than the original dishes—and wishing for more. I clamored for more leftovers!

With music in the background, friends, relatives, and other guests left quietly, many on bicycles, some walking, not all saying goodbye to or shaking the hands of the newly-weds. Many had been here for the past five to six hours. Time to go home to feed the hungry pigs, a major source of income for many simple villagers. But a few close friends of the groom, mostly young, single men and women, would return later in the evening for a delicious leftover dinner and a memorable evening of intense games and merrymaking with the newlyweds. I don't remember seeing the newlyweds take a shower to refresh themselves, not together of course, before the final ordeal of the day. (Remember we don't have indoor plumbing and the whole village would know if you took a shower.)

With the arrival of dusk and the lighting of several kerosene lanterns (the family owned and operated one lantern, usually providing light first for the kitchen before it traveled to the parlor of the house for the rest of the evening), friends assisted with warming up some of the leftovers for about thirty or so close relatives and friends of the groom for a less formal dinner with the newlyweds, who were casually dressed and appeared at ease with each other and the guests. If Brother had heard of his friend's untimely demise, he didn't show it. Father was busy going through the record book checking listing of each family's name and gift assiduously, a useful guide to reciprocating at future weddings. I was too young to care if the family had incurred any serious debt because of the lavish wedding banquet. I didn't lose any appetite over that, but came to the leftover dinner with, profound gratitude for the abundance of food, guaranteed to please my belly for a few more days. Unlike the earlier crowd, I felt some intimacy with the small group of friends here to enjoy each other's company, humor and merrymaking. With the chef gone, I resurrected my interest in the musicians and their instruments, the only distraction left for the evening.

Having witnessed other weddings and the evening rituals, the newlyweds were not taken by surprise by what was in store for them, essentially games geared to embarrass the young couple and to break the ice between them if it had not already happened earlier in the day. Obviously for a few of the friends present, it was an-eye-for-an-eye evening, meaning you did this to me on my wedding evening, now it was my turn to do this to you. Others were there to learn—like members of a freshman class—what to expect on their wedding evenings. I was there because I had nothing else better to do. The first game that got everyone into a laughing hysteria from the start was the blindfolded groom awkwardly groping for two small oranges (tied to a string) hanging around the bride's neck right above her breasts. Anyone could feign bashfulness, but the crowd would not be satisfied until you had found the oranges. With your hands! Or mouth! A slightly different version of the game had two pieces of dried fruit hanging right on the bride's breasts, the blindfolded groom was to use his mouth, only his mouth, to grope for them and eat them. I never did ask Brother what it was like to perform something this personal, obscene, and embarrassing in front of a hungry crowd demanding blood and action, especially when you realized this was the first time he had seen his bride since the engagement three years before. And this evening they were there to entertain their friends at their own expense, so to speak. Usually the bride needed some nudging and verbal encouragement from the crowd, like pushing her closer to the groom or making her touch the groom in some private places. All in zest, seemed harmless for adults. He might look or feel like a tarantula, neither one could escape from the light-hearted tactile games. They remained taciturn throughout the evening but displayed giggles and nervous laugh, and were cajoled into doing some of the most difficult physical stunts requiring agility and moral laxity. I thought I was watching a silent movie because they were like mindless marionettes on a puppet stage, every act and move choreographed for maximum physical exposure, embarrassment and laughter. At times sexually explicit.

I went to bed around ten or so, laughter and hilarity fading in the distance. Early the following morning, the smell of leftovers from the kitchen wafted through the house, announcing the time to get up, wash, change clothes and join the crowd for the first elaborate meal of the day. Around noon, a little brother of the bride (usually the youngest in the family), according to custom, arrived in a car decked with two sugar-cane plants tied to the top of the vehicle. Today Brother and the bride joined the bride's family and their guests for another banquet. They would return home at the end of the day.

Brother's wedding meant one more mouth to feed in the family.

Brother's wedding meant a brief interlude for me to savor the best of Chinese cuisine, a time of plenty, like manna from heaven.

Brother's wedding meant a new servant in the family, trained to be a good daughter-in-law, graciously taking over the tasks of washing all the family's clothes (using a washboard) and cooking all the daily meals.

Brother's wedding meant an additional pair of hands to work in the farm, raise chickens and pigs, and tap rubber trees, the source of family's income and survival.

Brother's wedding meant additional mouths to feed when the babies arrived, toys for grandparents to play with, and more hands for the farm.

Married less than a year after the Japanese Occupation, with many businesses still in shambles, some gradually recovering from three years of forced inertia, there was no photographic proof or record of Brother's nuptials. "We were too poor to have the wedding pictures taken," Brother would later remind friends and relatives in response to their curiosity.

FOUR

I grew up in a kampong (a word meaning "a small Malay village or cluster of native huts") hidden unobtrusively on the west coast of the Malay Peninsula, not far from the ocean. To reach the coastline, we had to pass through a real Malay kampong, Pasir Panjang, inhabited almost entirely by the Malays, speaking the Malay language (now the National Language of Malaysia). Malays referred to our village as Kampong China because everyone in my village originally hailed from mainland China. I grew up in this Chinese village with everyone speaking the Hockchiang dialect, going to the same schools and worshipping in the same church and many marrying one another within the village. Small but not congested, of fewer than a thousand people in about two hundred or so households, marked by a nameless main road with innumerable nameless tributaries, like the veins of a broad leaf. Narrow, bumpy, dirt roads and well-trodden paths, without pointers or signs, linked the houses to each other and the main road, which led to the village shops, church, school, cemetery, and Kampong Koh, a town with electricity and flourishing businesses that enticed and snatched away the villagers' hard earned money.

Bicycles were the main means of transportation. Either you operated them yourselves or another person would carry you (on the front horizontal bar if you are young and small, and on the back if you are a teenager or someone's grandmother) to your destinations. To a town like Kampong Koh or to relatives in distant villages.

Kampong China, a Chinese village, peppered here and there not with cluster of huts but well-built wooden houses, big and small, with one or two stories, the smallest a one-bedroom house, mostly thatch-roofed, with hardened and leveled dirt floors. Our house was one of a handful that had clay tile roofs. In ancient China, houses of middle class people had thatched roofs, while clay tile roofs topped the homes of upper class families. We had concrete floors and lived in a two-story building, approximately thirty-feet-by-thirty, with an open, fifteen-by-fifteen-feet covered verandah upstairs in front, with left and right benches built into it, and an outside stairway hugging the house leading up to it. Because most houses had dirt floors, it was not uncommon for many villagers, by nightfall, to walk with light wooden clogs (some were decorative and painted with bright colors, the plain ones were less expensive, with front straps at times made from plastic or used bicycle tires) after thoroughly washing their feet before crawling into beds or going upstairs if they lived in a two-story building.

Concrete floors meant the families had wealth, once or now. Two-story buildings belonged only to families who were the first settlers or early pioneers in the village and had, so to speak, made it. I remember that only two of the ten or so families living in two-story buildings had left the ground floor open, with the square support posts exposed (making the houses looked like they were standing on stilts), the whole open space on the ground level utilized for different daytime family activities, crisscrossed wires from post to post for drying clothes away from rain, parking spaces for bicycles, and spaces for storage of farm and other tools. Our ground floor was enclosed, one third on the right with two rooms on one side, the big one for Father and his opium den and the smaller one a sort of storage room for dry goods and bananas from the farm. One third on the left had wires to dry clothes. The middle third was an open space. With Eighth Uncle and Auntie and their three children living with us in this ancestral home, I wondered time and again why the grownups didn't think of adding two or three more rooms on the ground floor. Money was the problem, maybe. Instead, except for Father and his opium den, all of us had our bedrooms upstairs. There were six rooms upstairs, three on either side of the house with the parlor in the middle. Two rooms were occupied by Eighth Uncle and his family and four by our family. My youngest cousin and I had our bed in an open space behind the wall of the parlor next to another stairway, located inside the back of the house, leading from the second flour to the ground flour. Part of the railing of this stairway was hollow, deliberately designed as a hiding place for Father's raw, bulk opium, each piece about the size of a regular brick, usually wrapped in many layers of cellophane paper.

As I entered the parlor from the front stairway few times a day I never failed to see directly in front of me, hanging on the wall (my bed behind it) the black-and-white portraits, which looked hand-painted, of my Grandfather and Grandmother flanking a gigantic mirror in the center. To me they were as dead as a doornail, although there were times I felt they were spying on the family's every move from on high. They meant nothing to me, emotionally. Meant a great deal to the family and many people in this particular kampong, historically.

Below the pictures and the mirror, stood an ornate cabinet with delicate carvings depicting an ancient Chinese motif, one of a few family heirlooms that Grandpa must have painstakingly loaded onto a ship bound for an unknown country called Malaya at the beginning of the twentieth century. Hidden inside it were the family RCA gramophone and a stack of big heavy old records, many still in their jackets. Against one wall of the parlor stood the untouchable, the family's Singer sewing machine. The treadle sewing machine was considered a priceless possession, demanding, in our family, as much reverence as the unseen spirits of our ancestors. Up the wall were frames and frames of family pictures. The other untouchable, sitting halfway up the wall opposite the Singer machine, on the other side of the parlor, was the Philips radio, hooked to a battery the size of a car battery. It looked, to me, like a car battery.

This house, like many other houses in the tropical village, had no ceilings and thin walls without insulation, making privacy almost impossible. Every conceivable human sound (ones that are associated with pleasure, pain or lust)—squeaky beds and furniture—filled my innocent mind with wild imaginings, magnified a million times when kerosene lamps were turned off and silence descended.

Most women did their daily chores in the roofed catwalk between the house and the kitchen. (An ingenious configuration to prevent a kitchen fire from demolishing the living quarters or family valuables.) There, under the roofed walkway and the kitchen and in the upstairs, open verandah—not the parlor—was where my family entertained our friends and relatives.

Many years later a friend remarked to me that he had seen houses similar to ours in Futzing, a town not far from the port of Foochow, in north eastern Fujian province, China. It was no coincidence, I realized, nodding, because that was where Grandpa came from in 1903. Grandpa had built this house, almost a replica of the architecture of houses in his neighborhood in Futzing, China, and bequeathed it to Father and Eighth Uncle. This spacious house looked like he had finally made it in his adopted country, Malaya.

I heard bits and pieces about Grandpa when I was growing up. A fragmented picture of a man, one of the first "colonists," who was instrumental in the establishment of the Hockchiang community, lovingly referred to as *Hockchiang Yong* (officially known as Kampong China on the map). Who could escape the portraits of him and Grandma hanging in our parlor, his dark piercing eyes looking down to watch over us. He might be dead and buried in mainland China, but his presence was real. Children growing up in a traditional Chinese home were told the dead are not really dead, but very much alive, and their spirits could aid or hurt you if you fail to serve their needs. Hence the abundant offerings and sacrifices of fresh, delicious food and golden, paper money to the long departed spirits in private family shrines to the ancestors or at the many cemeteries across the land.

I would not want to have been Grandpa's contemporary, because China in 1903 was a living hell, especially if you were a nobody, a young, able-bodied, struggling peasant like him. At the beginning of the twentieth century, China, urban and rural, was not an alluring place to live, especially if you were one of the downtrodden peasants, like Grandpa, trapped in poverty like a starving dog in a cage. A rapidly growing population, without availability of arable land or a strong economy to support it, added more woes and torment to the masses, and to the already weakened and corrupt imperial court (the last dynasty to rule China). Internal uprisings ravaged the countryside, which was already saddled with heavy taxation because the Ching government needed to pay huge indemnities to foreign governments for the devastations caused by recent Opium Wars and the Boxer Rebellion. Grandpa and other peasants who relied on subsistence farming also suffered natural calamities (typhoons and floods), and famines (droughts and crop failures because of blights). Those young men who had strong will and stamina, as well as some money and connections, were able to escape to distant lands for a second chance in life. One could opt for contract labor or become an indentured servant. Grandpa stayed because he had started a family and had neither connections nor money, only healthy dreams. And a childlike faith in his Methodist God.

Grandpa was going through living hell, when out of the blue came a Moses one day, sent by a government, many miles to the south, Malaya, who came preaching and spreading the good news of a Promised Land for the "poorest of the poor," the creation of an agricultural "colony." Malaya had determined they needed foreigners to grow rice to feed their growing population, hoping that would curtail the expensive importation of rice from other countries in Southeast Asia. Surprisingly, this Moses was no stranger to them, but someone who had learned to speak their dialects when he first came to them as a Methodist missionary years before. He spoke their language. They trusted him. They followed him, as children followed the Pied Piper of Hamelin.

Malaya, under the British colonial government, had experimented with rice growing, employing indigenous Malays first, then Indians and a few other foreigners. (Japanese rice-growers were considered but not invited.) The experiments had all ended in abysmal failure. Not for lack of desire or land or financial incentives. The Chinese already in Malaya, those speaking non-Foochow dialects, many arriving since the 1870s, were drawn to urban areas, to lucrative tin mining locations and ever-expanding profitable businesses in cities. Many, including the government, soon learned the supply of tin was not inexhaustible. The population was increasing rapidly. The British colonial government looked desperately for a way out of the economic dilemma. Diversification was one solution, with abundant arable land waiting for the right kind of people to perform an agricultural miracle. They had experiences in China and knew the Chinese had sterling qualities, indomitable spirit and diligence. Not just any Chinese this time, but the poorest of the poor, with no known relatives residing in Malaya, who might be persuaded to give up the poverty of their present existence for the Promised

Land. And their passage guaranteed free. They knew exactly where to go for help to recruit the potential "colonists." Foreign missionaries working to save souls somewhere in Fujian province. And why not? The Germans and the French, through their missionaries, were aggressively recruiting the poor masses to work in their colonies in Africa and other places around the world. The British would not be the first to try this trick. For they were not just there to baby-sit Malaya—since 1874 when they signed the Pangkor Treaty to protect the Malay states—but to exploit this region for its abundant natural resources. And they knew where to send their Moses to entice and lead the Foochows in Fujian province, China, out of their bondage to poverty to a Promised Land awaiting them in Malaya.

Grandpa heard the good news of salvation and was ready to follow Moses to the Promised Land. About a thousand poor souls, speaking various dialects from the region around Foochow, the port city of Fujian, heard the clarion call but, because of the unpredictability of the shipping schedules and the impossibility of gathering everybody together in one spot and feeding them while awaiting the arrival of a ship, fewer than five hundred, after a few false starts and delays, were able to leave with the Methodist Missionary and his Chinese cohort (a local Hockchiang preacher who had escorted and worked with another Foochow contingent two years earlier) to the Promised Land, the unknown.

It was not smooth sailing for the four hundred and eighty four "colonists" out in the turbulent seas. Five never did reach St. John's Island, Singapore, where the rest were quarantined. During the seventeen days or so of detention on the island, men were forced to work like coolies without pay. Only three hundred and sixty three men, women, and children arrived in Sitiawan, the Promised Land, by sea. Twelve died under quarantine and over a hundred disappeared—probably hoaxed or ensnared by the hustle and bustle of Singapore while waiting for a boat to take them on the last leg of the long journey.

From a small jetty through a jungle path to the mission concession, the Promised Land, the colonists were surprised to hear the promised two thousand five hundred acres for the mission concession had not been surveyed and the lots for them were not ready for settlement. Instead they were divided into groups of over fifty people in seven longhouses for the next six months, testing their faith, resolve, belief, and patience—and whether they did the right thing to follow their Moses and his Hockchiang cohort to this Promised Land.

I wonder how many of the colonists—some Christians, like Grandpa, and some who promised to become Christians—knew that the biblical Moses and his gang from Egypt did not have it easy. But eventually through trials and temptations, according to the Bible, they reached the Promised Land and built a mighty nation because of their faith in their God.

Grandpa and his fellow colonists were now going through their own trials, tribulations, and temptations. The colonial government had chosen this remote piece of land close to the ocean to keep the new arrivals geographically distant from their countrymen (speaking different dialects) who had abandoned their agricultural roots and pursued non-agricultural occupations in tin mines and businesses in urban areas when they first came to this country. The colonial government invited the new colonists for a specific task: grow rice to feed a growing population. Any physical contact with the outside world (the other prosperous Chinese) would undermine the current agricultural endeavor and be detrimental to the colony's future. Segregation from other Chinese—preoccupied with non-agricultural pursuits—was the government's stringent policy. A remote location, in their determination, would achieve their purpose!

Unfortunately growing rice wasn't the first priority for Grandpa and the men with him. Each day, different groups of men had to clear the jungle to build houses for different families. And formal education for their children was also foremost in their minds in a new land. The Foochow School—using the Foochow dialect—was started January of the following year. Within a short time, the three clans of the Foochow immigrants were able to move to their settlements: the Kutian settlement, the Hockchew settlement and the Hockchiang settlement. Each spoke a different dialect from the same region in China. The colonial government promised them a teacher if the people would build their own school buildings. Grandpa and another man built the first Hockchiang School on Grandpa's portion of the Hockchiang settlement. And each clan established its own clan school—using its own dialect—until 1918, when radical political and cultural events in China influenced them to adopt *Baihua* (literally translated *white language*, a new common language for all China, replacing the classical language of the elite and the imperial administration). Thus the birth of Uk Ing Primary School, replacing the Hockchiang School, using *Baihua*, an universal written language for all Chinese-speaking people then.

In time, the Kutian and Hockchiew clans moved away, forming their own dialect communities—the Hockchiew contiguous to us in a town called Kampong Koh, the Kutian less than five miles away, leaving their vacant settlements to the Hockchiang people.

For some unknown reasons, the colonial government did not execute their part of the deal and instead the Methodist concession, with the acres of land from the government, and the Foochow colonists, were now encouraged to plant rubber trees because rubber was becoming a valuable commodity in the surging world markets, fetching enormous profits for people who cultivated the trees. The British, who owned thousands of acres, abandoned coffee experimentation and devoted their vast resources to pursuing rubber traces, using laborers from India on their mammoth plantations. Rice became less important.

Rubber wealth gave Grandpa the opportunity to build his dream house, a tile-roofed, cement-floored, spacious, two-story building for his growing family, like the ones he had longed for and envied in China. Grandpa generously allowed newcomers from China to build their thatch-roofed houses on his land (at least seven houses sit on Grandpa's land). Years later I became curious who these squatters were, and why, during certain Chinese festivals, they would bring gifts of fresh fish, eggs, chickens, and longevity noodles (no cash of any kind) to my family. I never understood why these people would expand their houses without consulting our family or paying rent. They built their first homes on Grandpa's land because of Grandpa's magnanimity, like one beggar sharing his good fortune with other beggars who were new in the land. And also the Hockchiang School he helped build on his land. And what other deeds of kindness, now lost in the past?

My ancestors, the Hockchiang people, were not indigenous to this exotic land. We were natives from the southeast corner of mainland China, from the province of Fujian. Once outsiders, strangers encroaching on a new place, we pursued a vigorous dream and danced to a different tune in a somewhat self-imposed ghetto. It was not a political ghetto. More of a language ghetto. Where people spoke easily and understandably the same language, observed the same traditions (from birth till death), practiced the same customs (from mainland China), made the same Chinese New Year rice cake, raised the children the way you were taught, went to the same Methodist church (there was no competition), and lived a life of simplicity and frugality. We were a homogeneous community.

I am a proud product of this rich Chinese heritage and proud of Grandpa from Futzing, Fujian, China. His grave is in Futzing.

FIVE

At the tender age of six I had a private tutor who exposed me to the rudiments of Chinese classical education, even though we were hundreds of miles away from mainland China where, in bygone days, this would have paved the way for becoming a member of the distinguished literati, a military officer, or a government official in imperial China. This tutor was not a Confucian scholar by any stretch of the imagination, but a squatter on Grandpa's land and a small operator of his own opium den. Rather minuscule compared to Father's elaborate network of opium addicts. A fisherman, when he wasn't dabbling with opium, a coolie with a hoe, if he could stand perpendicular for an extended period of time—usually too demanding for someone who spent a great part of each day horizontally on a wooden opium bed. I had to assume he was preoccupied with opium business during the daylight hours because I don't remember ever going to the house without the use of a kerosene lamp. In the beginning, Mother would lead the way, walking along a path through rows of rubber trees to the humble dwelling on the northern fringe of our land. It wasn't exactly the ideal place to conduct a serious education amidst human voices and busy traffic of people who lived in this house, without separate bedrooms or decent furniture of any kind (typical of many homes of people, subsisting on bare minimum, I had visited in the village). I sat obediently at a wooden table a few feet away from the bed where opium smokers, oblivious to my presence, were engrossed in gradual desecration of their bodies by a foreign chemical, tarnishing the air and my lungs with fumes from the burning opium. Once a week I was exposed to opium and Chinese education, without ever knowing whether inhaling opium smoke sharpened my appetite for Chinese characters (ideograms). For sure, the aroma kept me awake and attentive, waiting at times for my tutor to finish his last smoke.

His cohorts and partners in crime dozed off by the oil lamp in the smoke-filled room.

Unlike western culture, the first book or primer that children were introduced to in old China had to do with the ABC's of Chinese philosophy, unlike the ABC's of the alphabet. *A* for *Apple, B* for *Bat, and C* for *Cat.* The English alphabet I would later learn in an English school had to do with concrete, visible objects. Things one could see or touch. Not the ABC's of Chinese philosophy, dealing with abstract ideas that were as elusive as a slippery eel. Killing two birds with one stone, the idea was to teach the first learners Chinese characters and a basic knowledge of Chinese philosophical ideas at the same time. Called *San Zi Jing* (or Three Characters Classic) each sentence in this slim volume consists of three characters (pronounced like three separate and distinct syllables). The whole book is like a long poem and my tutor would read and I would follow him six words at a time. I learned them by rote. Da da da, Da da da. Da da da, Da da da. There was never an up tone or a down tone. The same flat dull tone. Like some ancient liturgical chant, somber but rhythmic. I must have done it correctly because he didn't ask me to repeat the same words twice or thrice. Or could it be the opium had dulled his senses, making him incapable of distinguishing the right from the wrong tones that his student was anxiously trying to imitate? I was attentive to every sound. I was probably his best parrot. I was able to recite pages of ideograms (words or characters) with ease and absolute delight, after a while catching on to the rhythmic effect of repeating the same words, which became easier and quicker each time when I did it.

My opium-smoking tutor taught me reading and recitation. No brush or ink or paper was necessary, since teaching writing Chinese characters or calligraphy was not his cup of tea. His sole task was to make sure I could read and recite the little booklet. Comprehension, on my part, was not required. Nor an ability to copy the characters. (I didn't know where or how to begin writing a complex looking Chinese characters.) The *San Zi Jing* is really a distillation of the ABC's of Confucius' thinking, written in a way that is appropriate for children to learn and to memorize. A Confucian catechism. Except Confucianism is not a religion. A debatable issue for many people, down the centuries.

I didn't have much choice in my first brush with Chinese education. The opium-smoker tutor did it, I suspect, because it was his way of saying thank you to my deceased Grandpa for allowing him to build a house on our land. On other hand, being raised in a Chinese home, not knowing how to read and write Chinese would be considered un-Chinese and a disgrace to our Chinese culture. Confucius himself believed profoundly—and preached to whoever would listen to him—that the family was the foundation of a decent and harmonious society. Although the *San Zi Jing* was written in the thirteenth century, Confucian ideas of man, family, and society as one big family were planted early in young, fertile minds, preparing them for their eventual roles in the bigger world to come. Like strands of cultural DNA, affecting generations to come, Confucian ideals molded the very fiber of our being, like the air we breathe, from cradle till death.

After a while, recitation was fun. I was never called to perform before visiting relatives or other members of the family. Sadly, the hidden abstruse meanings of the words were never divulged to me by my tutor. Probably too arcane for me to comprehend, even if he did try to speak my language, the language of a six-year old boy. Maybe it wasn't part of his job to reveal the deep secrets of Confucius' thoughts, but simply to enjoy reciting and hearing the sounds of the rhythm of Chinese words. Too erudite perhaps for a young mind to grasp the essence of human nature and the building blocks of a harmonious society. In fact the first six words in the little thin book mean: "The nature of man is originally good." (I grappled with that in college when I was a student of eastern philosophy, years later.) Plant the seeds now, the tutor did, and let them germinate and grow with the passage of time.

I had two things going for me: a primary philosophical education and weekly doses of opium smoke. What happened to a child soaked in the water of Chinese philosophy when he was contemplating most times what his young friends were doing in the neighborhood? For many, the arrival of darkness meant going to bed, for some engaging in secretive nocturnal activities—not a time to engage in philosophy, however cursory, with an opium-smoking tutor. (I often wondered if this innocent beginning had anything to do with my later ardent pursuit of eastern philosophies in college, providing an informed educated perspective, like looking glasses, with which I, inescapably, perceive and interpret events in and surrounding my life.)

Once or twice we were caught in the rain after the lesson. I experienced shivers in the cold wind, the kerosene lamp flickered, slowing down our walk home.

But the evening trips and my introduction to early Chinese education were soon terminated (I had to suppress my gasp of instant approval) when Mother caught the salacious news of a teenage girl in the tutor's house having sex with one of the opium smokers (they said he was so drugged she raped him), fearing I might tempt her with my insatiable curiosity, easy-going demeanor, and emerging seductive charm. "*You*...a willing, loose and easy bait for a slut," Mother said, angrily. Most in the village were unaware of the murky operations in an opium den. Much remained surreptitious to the outside world. Others in our neighborhood were more charitable, less eager to condemn and banish the victim from the village: "The teenage girl's mother is a whore herself, seen lying around with opium smokers for a few cheap smokes. Why blame the little girl for her youthful error?" That was the consensus of a few villagers. Mother didn't think it was merely an error, but the sin of the flesh, the work of the devil, a moral degenerate. Sex outside of legalized procreation, in her estimation, was not to be encouraged and tolerated. Nor practiced for pleasure or carnal knowledge.

What Mother didn't realize or suspect was I had more sex than I could handle at age six. Chinese comic books (one of my friends had volumes of them) and kids unsuccessfully competed for my attention because the world, the whole naked world beyond the doorstep, became the open book, my teacher, with page after page of unabridged and unexpurgated lessons and uninhibited exhibitions by humans and nature, programmed by their creator to go unabashedly after their potential and destinies. I meant sex in all its splendor and glory! The whole wide world became my teacher. Nature was my teacher. Sex was everywhere. The dogs, cats, ducks, chickens, pigs, worms, insects, squirrels, snakes, and Homo sapiens became my teacher. No mentor or tutor or picture book was required. No translation. Life was simple and clear and direct. The world was a splendid stage. And I the audience, my mind, like a huge sponge, absorbing all the images, and natural acts of copulation, most unrehearsed, that informed my thinking and life. Intense mental masturbation. Lurking somewhere in my right brain, I early suspected everything exists for a purpose. There was life everywhere you cared to look, from the depth of the earth to the sky above, nature's creation and work seemed to multiply like untamed weeds out in the farm. Sex!

The best of times was then, days of "puppy-hood," no rules, no pressures, no toil, no worries, no nothing. Free to roam the world of the village. Every day was a happy day. Time to catch dragonflies, as they visited willowy, tall grass and flowers, with a long, skinny pole dipped in a sticky substance made from natural rubber. With other boys I built dikes in ponds, emptying the often muddy water from one section to another, hoping to find "fighting" fish for entertainment and competition. As an energetic, curious boy, I did everything the world had to offer me. Hopscotch. Marbles. Rubber bands. (One version: using the palm of your hand, throw them at five to seven feet distance, you are the winner if your rubber band lands on top of the loser's. Another version: On a wooden or concrete floor, blow your rubber band, you are the winner if your rubber band climbs over the loser's.) Tops. Cat's cradle (a game in which a different design is achieved each time a string is looped over the fingers, passing back and forth between you and your player). Ball game. Pocketknives. Racing with a stick pushing a discarded old bicycle wheel (without tire). On warm nights, filling a glass bottle with fireflies. Only once, I recall, a few of us, boys and girls, played doctor and nurse in my neighbor's house in the absence of the parents. Something to do with pregnancy, delivery, and playing house, like adults. There was some touching, here and there. All done innocently. Details buried in the past. There was nothing to impede my every move in search of thrill, thrill, thrill. And more thrill. In the village.

One of the sights indelibly lodged in my mind was a small group of fun-seeking boys literally torturing two dogs having sex. I was more than a curious spectator. I was a cruel craze-driven participant (more than once), with the others (girls usually shied away from such shameless playful indulgence), hitting the dogs with whatever instruments of torture we could scrounge around us, unfeelingly, in a frenzy, like in a boisterous party, and they (the dogs) meekly, eyes searching for answers, imploring for a modicum of our human kindness. Instant gratification? Copulation in public? No shame? In front of innocent looking boys? What were they thinking?

The bitch whimpered as the dogs desperately tried to break loose from each other. Not easy, locked like two sets of hind legs tied together, at the moment back to back, the stronger male would pull her along with his now twisted swollen penis. *Ouch*! I did not know why the penis was stuck in the vagina. To us kids it was raw sex. Shameless, dirty dogs!

The commotion amidst heightened ecstasy caught adult attention. Since the intercourse took place near a well, the neighbor doused the sore animals with buckets of cold water, a welcome solace for them, mitigating the swelling in the male's gland, easing the way for them to break loose from each other. Each hurried off in a different direction, with no promise of not yielding to the same temptation in the months to come.

I would never know if the two strangers had a good time today. I did. Vicariously. And shamelessly.

The dogs were not the only ones who got me out of life's cocoon and opened my eyes to the world of undiluted pleasures. The squirrels were doing it noisily up and down the trunks of the tall coconut trees, swaying happily with the breeze, a few yards from the house, a front seat in the theater of life. The lucky ones escaped our traps for delicacy. Unlike the dogs, cats, squirrels, ducks and chickens, and certain insects and a few four-legged creatures, the pigs, especially the sows, needed human intervention when it came to sex. There was no need to worry. They spoke loudly and visibly when it was time for male companionship, the sexual kind. Since raising pigs was a vital source of income for my family, we did everything to make the sows happy and satisfied. Help was on the way. A few blocks away.

Two old gentlemen, neither had any substantial formal education, at opposite ends of the village, provided stud service for the whole village. For the pigs, I mean. They would be more than happy to oblige your sow for a fee. I saw the stud often, with huge testicles, walking slowly almost impatiently in front of the owner, down the main road or in the neighborhood, on their way to perform a business function. Not for pleasure. My family and many others in the village depended on our pigs for survival. Therefore paying for a stud was worth the expense. Instead of the sow helping guide the missile, the stud's owner would, most times, nudge the male instrument to shoot in the right direction. Again, I watched, noting that sexual intercourse wasn't a rarity or a novelty. The pigs were doing it. The dogs were doing it. The cats were doing it. The chickens were doing it. The birds were doing it. The insects were doing it. Humans did it, too. So ordinary, I guess, nobody bothered to think about it. Or hide it. Or condemn it. Or be ashamed of it. Such was my early exposure to sex in all its natural beauty!

When a young married woman wore black pants, without anyone indoctrinating me, I grew up knowing that it had something to do with her female reproductive system. Or organs. Morning sickness meant sexual intercourse, obtrusive and loud like the imam summoning the faithful to prayers from the minaret of the mosque. (I grew up in an Islamic country peppered with mosques.) Men, women, and children in the village wore very flimsy clothing in tropical Malaya. At home, many young, married women seldom wore bras except in public places, attending public functions. Breast feeding was a common sight. I grew up wearing very little, not that we were poor, but it was the custom in the village: singlets (a British word for undershirt) and undershorts at home or out working in the farm. Thin but comfortable cotton clothing. I don't remember any female flaunting her breasts or male his mighty erections. Here and there, I heard—once in a while, in public places—young men bragging about their sexual exploits, not with strangers or sluts, but their first nights in bed with virgins. Rumors or cases of sexual deviants were as rare as a poor farmer with a mouthful of gold teeth.

Early on I came to a simple explanation of why so many villagers produced many children. The Methodist Church reigned supreme in the village. Catholicism did not exist in our village. One child was enough to carry on the family name. But many hands were needed to help out in the farm, many eking out a subsistent living from the soil (my family included). There was no electricity. Few homes had radios. Entertainment was non-existent, except movies in another town, if one cared to ride the bicycle in the dark. Few braved the cold and the dark, occasionally. Or the traveling circus in the nearest town, once a year. Few times a year, industrious students burnt their midnight oil for serious state examinations. Most villagers headed to bed early because there was nothing to do after dark. And many, including Brother and his wife and Mother, Eighth Auntie and her daughter had to rise as early as two or three in the morning to tap rubber trees. Yes, sex became the only recreation in the dark, and many multiplied like their pigs.

I became an uncle at the age of six when Ah Soh gave birth to her first child, a baby girl, with the presence of a capable midwife, like the matchmaker, the only one practicing her skill in the village. It started early one day. Ah Soh had to stop doing the family laundry and retreat to her bedroom and prepare herself for the delivery. The family had prepared for this for a week or two and Brother had to bicycle to the midwife's house to inform her of the impending birth. She arrived late in the evening (after dinner), riding her own bicycle, accompanied by her signature black bag. All rooms had thin walls and no ceilings and I could hear everything transpiring in there, many voices, like the Tower of Babel, about this and that, that and this, with Ah Soh's groaning getting louder with each passing hour. I didn't know what to make of it, the shuffling of feet, Brother going up and down the stairs to the kitchen, the midwife's voice of command taking over "Push harder…harder…a little harder…coming…it is coming…good…good…I see something coming…it's a girl." The moaning and groaning were too much for me until I heard someone slapping the baby and her first muted cry. I wonder what Mother was thinking then. A girl would not be able to carry on the family's name. Her first grandchild. If she felt disappointment, we would never know. Nothing was written on her face.

According to tradition, relatives and close friends began to bring gifts, mostly things edible, for the young mother, gifts that would ensure her health and well being: chickens, longevity noodles, cream crackers, eggs, Milo, and Ovaltine (a healthful beverage introduced by the British to our country). And the one-month lying-in was to be strictly observed, at the end of which the young mother and the baby would be joined by close relatives and friends of the family for a big feast (slightly smaller than the wedding banquet). A more ostentatious and festive one if the firstborn was a boy.

Unfortunately Ah Soh's health took a serious turn a week after the birth. I don't remember seeing a doctor visiting the family, but I did witness what Brother had to do to restore her health. Daily, for at least two weeks, Brother had to collect sow's urine (not just any sow but one that had babies number of times) for Ah Soh to drink. Brother would sit quietly and watch patiently for the right sow to urinate. Sometimes she would hesitate or run, sensing Brother coming from behind with a pail to collect the urine. And Brother had no choice but to chase her with pail, trailing her like a shadow. If only she would stand still and make life easy for everyone, Brother must have murmured a hundred times on a day when he had to do it more than once to calm the sow's anxiety and sought her understanding and cooperation. I suspected this was another one of those Chinese traditional cures practiced by our forebears in China. Miraculously, Ah Soh became well after swallowing a large quantity of the pig's urine over a short period of time.

I didn't enjoy it at all, I mean the whole birth event and Brother's wife lying-in business. I suffered a different kind of anxiety and pain now that the woman who had been doing the family's laundry and cooking the family's meals took a month's holiday from her work, leaving the rest of the family seemingly helpless. Mother and Brother took over the kitchen temporarily and I, for the first time, was responsible for doing my own laundry, washing and ironing my own clothes. What started out, I thought, as doing my chore to help the family became, gradually, a permanent undertaking, a first step on the threshold of shouldering adult responsibilities, imperceptibly isolating me from my childhood friends and, later, the rest of the world. Soon Mother, like fate, would decide my every move and destiny.

SIX

When I was seven, the family made, with the formal approval of the Malayan government, a visible documentation of my existence. Mother, Sister, and I had a photograph taken for our citizenship papers. Also a separate picture of myself, black and white, head slightly tilted—a happy, innocent, smiling kid, with no earthly inkling of what was in store for me in the not too distant future.

It started in September, 1945, when the British military administration took over the control of our country after the surrender of the Japanese. Britain's audacious plan, calling for the transfer of sovereignty from the Malay sultans (a sultan is the head of a Muslim state) to the British crown, viewed by many as a devious attempt to re-organize Malaya into one entity, met immediate stiff resistance from the Malays, who smelled colonial power lurking to fill the vacuum created by the exodus of the Japanese. (The Malays and the Chinese had witnessed incredulously how the white men, their once superior protector, kowtowed to the Japanese not too long ago, reduced to impotence by an Asian power.) Incensed by Britain's insensitive plan, the Malays, up and down the peninsula, galvanized successfully to boycott this plan, vehemently rejecting also its conditions of citizenship, which they feared would encourage Chinese dominance. It was no secret to outsiders and insiders that the entrepreneurial Chinese had controlled much of Malaya's trade, industry and business, while the Malays had dominated the political arena. I don't think most Malays are elated and genuinely receptive to any outsider's portrait of them as lazy, easy-going rural folks, contented with their less industrious life style. Racial tension and hostility seemed inevitable and predictable, like the occasional destructive monsoon rains, battering the tiny peninsula. We in the village were less aware of the social and political upheavals permeating urban areas.

The Federation of Malaya, inaugurated February 1, 1948, a plan to appease the Malays, not unlike making animal sacrifices to an angry god, allowed the sultans to remain sovereign in their states with a crown-appointed high commissioner, including specific provisions to protect "the special position of the Malays." While the Malays were granted automatic citizenship, rigid citizenship requirements were drawn up for the Chinese and others. And of the 3.1 million people (out of a population of roughly five million people in 1948) who qualified automatically for citizenship, twelve percent were Chinese. Since our family and many in the village were the original "colonists" from mainland China who had settled in this once remote undeveloped corner of the peninsula at the beginning of the twentieth century, by invitation of the Malayan government, we were counted, I suspect, as part of the twelve percent. A large number of Chinese became citizens by application. Many Chinese, at the time, blamed the Malays for irrationally erecting the unnecessary hurdles they had to overcome in order to become citizens of their adopted country. Mutual distrust and disdain spread like a tropical disease.

Luckily I was outside its sphere of influence.

I had nothing but mixed, gratifying memories of the Malays in my life. As a child, I came face to face with the Malays in my own neighborhood. The same two or three Malay women would bring their rural products to our doorsteps, in tough gunnysacks, not on bicycles but carried on their heads, cushioned by a bundle of cloth, going from house to house, not speaking a word of Chinese, always with a smile. They had walked miles from their kampong, contiguous to us, simple folks, like us, trying to make a living selling fruits, clams and mussels from the ocean (they lived close to it). We had something in common: subsistence economy, making a living off the earth. The neighborhood dogs, by their barking, would always announce their presence. The women's faces told me they feared the harmless barking dogs. There was not a time when any of my family or the neighbors would take advantage of these women by cutting down their prices. Or refusing their offer to sell. I loved their ripe mangoes and other exotic fruits. And whatever they had culled from the ocean and the land.

I wondered often why the Chinese people, my folks included, would purchase many exotic fruits like durians and rambutans, et cetera, from the Malays and not grow them ourselves. Fruits were something for pleasure and enjoyment, not staples. So I was taught. Thus all cultivable land was devoted to cash crops, anything that could be grown and traded for cash. A major source of income for many villagers. Land for a few fruit trees to satisfy the taste buds would be considered a poor investment. Frivolous. Lacking good sense. Some might add rationally these fruit trees didn't come from China, not part of our Chinese heritage. Therefore we should not embrace them.

I came to know the Malay women well, in time learning to utter and exchange a few Malay words by parroting them, zestfully. I had seen Brother engaged in conversational Malay with the Malays in their territory. The Malayan government had once operated Malay classes for some Chinese in the Chinese community, hoping at the time to prepare and motivate those who might want to settle in predominantly Malay villages or towns because of overpopulation or lack of suitable land in the Chinese localities. That would probably explain why a large number of ordinary Chinese could communicate in the Malay language intelligibly with the local Malays. But the government Malay program died a quick death for lack of enthusiasm by the Chinese, who preferred to live, however crowded, poor or deprived, with their own kind.

Mother would be the first to teach and admonish us children on how to treat strangers with kindness and respect. Her version of the Do-unto-others-what-you-would-want-others-to-do-unto-you rule: "Be kind to them. The Malay women. You might be selling something to some people some day." Mother was my moral teacher, always instilling in me to do good to people. Be they total strangers. Or people you know. Including your own parents. Simple lessons with grave ramifications: you cannot escape your actions and their consequences, now and for as long as you breathe. I continue to hear Mother's voice, one of wisdom and caution, in my adult life.

And later, when I had the opportunity to study in an English school, many of my classmates and friends were Malays, mostly from different kampongs, many miles away from the school. Boys were winsome, girls, plain and simple but were irresistibly sweet and charming. And worried at times how they could wear their sarong securely (strips of colorfully printed cloth, wrapped around the waist and worn like skirts down to the ankles), part of their national dress. The Malay girls taught me how to make paper flowers, particularly bright yellow or red roses. The Malays are known for their handiwork and craftsmanship. And our school cafeteria (called tuck-shop because we were under the British then) often served delicious Malay food and snacks along with the Chinese and Indian favorites. I spent not ten days but at least eight years going to school with Malay and Indian kids. And race was never an issue in school.

But there are obvious differences between the Malays and my people. For instance, the native-born Malays or Bumiputras (meaning "sons of the soil") do not have surnames and almost all parents use Arab names for their children. We Chinese all have surnames. The clan or the family name is written first, followed by a person's given name, indicating you are known by your clan or family name first. Our surnames identify who we are.

And the constitution declares all Malays are born Muslims, followers of Islam, allowing religious freedom for the rest of the country's inhabitants. Ironically all non-Malays are free to follow and practice their own religions.

Malay boys are circumcised between the ages of seven and twelve, the elaborate ceremony attended by friends and relatives, a custom unknown in our Chinese culture.

You are expected to remove your shoes when you enter a Malay house because shoes are considered *unclean*. And they want the living room floor clean, a place for their daily prayers. All faithful Muslims pray, always facing Mecca, Islam's holiest city, at least five times a day.

No Malay in his sane mind would have a dog as a pet because dogs are considered *unclean* by Muslims. Dogs roamed freely in our village.

Muslims are barred from eating pork because pigs are considered *unclean* animals. My family's livelihood, like many others in our village, depended heavily on raising pigs. Pigs are our friends. We feed them. We pat them. We rub them. We take good care of them.

Malays usually eat with their fingers. The Chinese with their chopsticks and spoons.

In the absence of a welfare system in our country, Malay and Chinese children are expected to look after their parents.

We all believe that when visiting relatives, it is appropriate to bring food or fruit as gifts.

And while we all possess great craftsmanship, the Malays are renowned for their delicate woodcarvings on home panels, walls, and fishing boats. The Chinese for their ornate carvings on tables and chairs fit for the imperial palace.

And those who love outdoor sports will try to master *sepakt-kraw* (kickball), a popular Malay game played with a round rattan ball. The object is to use your feet to keep the ball in the air or across a net, losing a point each time the ball escapes to the ground.

And children of every race are often entranced by *wayang kulit,* a traditional shadow-puppet show accompanied by a musical ensemble, one of many expressions and contributions of the Malay folk art.

While acknowledging the many differences and similarities in our cultural beliefs and practices between myself in the village and my many Malay classmates in school, the real world out there looked different.

There was always that persistent fear that someone might attack us with their *parangs* (a Malay word for "a heavy knife used by the Malays as a tool and weapon") when some of us kids, sometimes with adults, would ride our bicycles, unusually fast through some sections covered with thick bushes or too close to Malay dwellings for comfort, through the Malay kampong to the ocean when the fishermen would come in from their catch. I wouldn't call them commercial fishermen (some were distant relatives or friends of friends but all from our own village) because they catered mostly to fellow villagers, though some sold their bigger, expensive exotic catch at a huge open market in Kampong Koh. There were at least five or six Chinese families, fluent in Malay language, setting up shops by the ocean, surrounded by Malays, serving primarily the needs of the

Chinese fishermen who worked near the beach after the catch, drying and mending their nets and maintaining some kind of sleeping quarters there away from their homes in the village, few miles away. We had relatives—one family—living among the Malays, speaking and looking like them. I remember wondering, without overtly voicing it, why their skin looked awfully dark for someone who is Chinese, cognizant of the fact they were exposed to the sun day in and day out, with little shade from the few scattered coconut trees, and the unbearable heat radiating from the scorching sand stretching for miles around. "Are you not afraid to live in a place surrounded by Malays?" I raised that question a thousand times in my mind, the few times Mother took Sister and I to visit them by the beach, eyes scanning the surroundings, like a frightened dog. I remember we had difficulties with our bicycles because there was white sand everywhere, inches deep. There were incessant rumors in the air, no doubt, about Malays attacking the Chinese. Not vice versa.

A few times I had gone with Brother, Sister, friends, and neighbors to another part of the Malay kampong where we dug hungrily, after trudging through deep mangrove swamp way out into the ocean because of the low tide, for clams and mussels. At times I feared we might not retreat quick enough with the returning tide. Fear was real for me, someone who didn't know how to swim. And I didn't like the feel of my feet sinking deep into the unfriendly swamp or the howling sorrowful wind. In an alien territory. Easily ambushed by hostile Malays. I shuddered, allowing meandering thoughts of danger to enter my soul. And what if unknowingly I walked into a bottomless pit in the mud. But the worst was praying to heaven and earth nothing would happen to my bicycle or its tires while going to or coming home from the ocean having to pedal miles through a Malay kampong. I never shared this crippling anxiety with anyone because I didn't want anyone to think I was on the verge of lunacy or my behavior, unmanly, or worse, delusional.

There were occasions at home, usually late in the evening, when sounds of distant drumbeats, emanating from the Malay kampong, traveling unimpeded for miles, conjured in my mind imminent dangers on the way like drumbeats in Tarzan movies, announcing the presence of hostile enemies or the possibility of a serious warfare about to erupt, like steam from a rice pot. The Malays were probably celebrating something, less sinister than imagined, some members of the family would say this to assuage my frayed nerves. Still I kept reviewing the Tarzan movies in my head and envisioned the Malays marching to our village with their sharp *parangs*. Fear was as real as the distant drumbeats. Nothing but the passage of time could erase that anxiety. It continued for years till my departure from the village.

Not everything existed in my imagination.

Many Chinese, having suffered more than other ethnic groups from systematic Japanese severity and brutality, had once joined the anti-Japanese resistance movement under the leadership of the Malayan Community Party. The MPC's uncompromising and charismatic leader grew up not far from my village. The Chinese, alongside the British and the Malays, were now vying for political recognition and power, leading a failed revolt to establish a Communist People's Republic of Malaya. Not too long ago, ironically, the British guerrilla units were supplying arms to these anti-Japanese communist fighters in the jungles, now turning the guns against each other for political supremacy and control of post-war Malaya. Over 350,000 British and Malayan troops were engaged in a brutal, bloody guerrilla war. One more reason for the growing racial tension and suspicion between the Chinese and the Malays.

The British are coming! To eradicate the communist insurgents! We were told, as children, to avoid contact with or looking at the faces of the *red-haired devils* (British soldiers) as they marched through the village. I sensed nervousness and uncertainty everywhere, especially after the government declared a State of Emergency in June, 1948, to deal with the communist insurgency. News of communists setting fire early one morning (1950) to a small town some fifteen miles away, destroying seventy-seven shops and a thousand or so homes, did not pacify the nerves of those who had to tap rubber trees in the wee hours of the morning and those who had relatives and friends affected by the blazing fire. Rumors spread like some inferno that some of the victims had ended their ties with the communists, who did it to punish them for failing to continue to support the communist cause. The timing couldn't have been worse because many shops were well stocked for the Chinese New Year, the most important event in the Chinese community. Chinese attempting to destroy their own people? What a shame! Some murmured. Others trembled at the thought of being their next targets. Chinese destroying fellow Chinese?

Now I had some fear of my own people because most, or all, communists (anti-Japanese forces) were Chinese. It wouldn't surprise me if a few of them were my relatives or children or friends of them. While a few relatives some fifteen or so miles away were resettled into new villages (the Malayan government calculated the move would cut off all possible support for the communists, coerced or voluntary), Father felt safe to enroll me at a Chinese elementary school, a walking distance from home (about a mile). Mother issued a stern warning: Don't loiter around. Come straight home from school. Don't look at the *red-haired devils.* Avoid all of them. Mother didn't say they were evil. Mother didn't say they were dangerous. Mother said, "Don't get near the soldiers."

I suspect one reason Mother objected adamantly, years later, to my joining the Boy Scouts was that the uniform somehow reminded her of the soldiers during the war. In her mind, the Boy Scouts didn't serve a practical purpose. The obvious reason, it took me away from working in the farm. Mother had her own pragmatic criteria for judging the usefulness of any activity: Does it help or make money for the family?

One person we were commanded to avoid all physical contact was my Eighth Auntie, someone I would always seek succor when Mother would go after my ass with whatever instrument of torture accessible to her because of the wrongs she thought or suspected I had committed. Auntie would provide a buffer between Mother and me. Tragically, she had contracted Hansen's disease (leprosy) in her right hand, slowly eating away the flesh, immobilizing her fingers, taking away every iota of her dignity as a person, pronounced untouchable even by her loved ones. As in biblical times, a leper was considered unclean, an outcast carrying a contagious disease. Touching her would be hazardous to my health. I cried for days after she was sent far away to an isolated colony for treatment. The one person who could always protect me from Mother's wrath had disappeared from my life. The Malays didn't mean a great to deal to me. The *red-haired devils* didn't mean a great deal to me. But Eighth Auntie. She was everything to me. I learned not to get into trouble with Mother now that I had no one to turn to for succor. For understanding. For protection. I learned to accept the temporary loss and turned my attention to a new pursuit, Chinese schooling.

Eighth Auntie did eventually return home to the family after a successful treatment.

SEVEN

Grandpa had something to do with the Uk Ing Primary School I was attending. When he and three hundred and sixty three other people first arrived at the mission concession in this part of the Malay Peninsula, they organized a day school for their children before members of the four clans (from the same part of China) were dispersed to their respective permanent settlements. About twenty-two students attended this Mission Vernacular School, conducted in Chinese, and they had the first taste of classical Chinese. It was the same slim book, *San Zi Jing* (Three Characters Classic) I was introduced to by my opium-smoking tutor many years later, but I suspect the first group of boys and girls were thrilled to attend a school, even if it was in a simple shed. They were restless for a new experience in a new land (away from the poverty-stricken part of China they came from). For the majority, it was their first formal education in a classroom with a teacher who spoke their dialect, Hockchiang. Totally unexpected. And they diligently learned to memorize and recite every word from the book. Hungry for every morsel of food fed to them. I too remember the first six words from the text (in my Hockchiang dialect): *Ing Chee Chu, Sin Peon Sian.* Translated they mean "The nature of man is originally good." Edible, but definitely not a digestible concept for a child's first classroom learning experience. But the sound of the words was most pleasurable to a simple child.

Within a short period of time, all the students had to discontinue their education because their parents had to move to their respective clan settlements, all within the same village, two or more miles away from the original school building and location. Reports of tracks of wild animals like tigers didn't sit well with the parents, not when their precious sons and daughters had to walk the dangerous distance to school. Eventually Grandpa and another pioneer established Hockchiang School for members of the Hockchiang clan on Grandpa's land. The government, through the Methodist church, would supply the teaching staff, while the local clan community had to come up with their own school building.

By the time I attended the Chinese primary school (about four decades later), the three other clans had moved away from the original village and the Hockchiang people dominated the whole village (with less than a handful of outsiders, like decorations on a cake), re-locating the school, renamed Uk Ing Primary School, to a more central location. Grandpa's first granddaughter's husband was one of the first principals of Uk Ing Primary School (before my time). An old well and a concrete slab of the first school started by Grandpa still exist on our family land. By now Grandpa had returned to mainland China to be with his third daughter. He eventually died and was buried there.

Both Eighth Uncle and Father (Sixth), who shared the ancestral home left to them by Grandpa, did not attain, to my knowledge, any significant level of formal education. Brother's education was severely interrupted and curtailed by the Japanese invasion (schools were shut down, temporarily) and chose not to continue his education, like many other young men and women of the time, after the short Japanese Occupation. The most plausible reasons for not returning to school: times were difficult, savings depleted, money was scarce, confidence plummeted, many young men and women had to help their families survive by working on the land after the economic desolation left by the Japanese. Neither Brother nor my two older sisters had any formal high school education. Sister and I, adopted by the family, had the privilege of attending the Uk Ing Primary School after the Japanese Occupation.

Kindergarten did not exist then. I started with Standard One, the first year in a primary school. In my first day in school, I heard a stranger, my first male teacher, called my name. *Ling Eng Huat,* in Mandarin, the official language of the Chinese people. At home we all spoke the Hockchiang dialect. For the first time I realized I had a name different from the ones I heard daily at home or in my neighborhood with my playmates. Within my family, true in almost all rural Chinese families, no one ever called or addressed me by my formal Chinese name. They always called me by my nicknames: *Ngulan-dea* or *Ardi-yan. Ling Eng Huat* is my real name; the formal name, known to the public, the world beyond the house and the village where I grew up. The school. The government. The police. The hospital. The church. Very few relatives knew my formal name.

In old China, people of means would consult astrologers or numerologists or fortune tellers for a propitious name for a first son or a first grandson because certain words or characters have inherent magical potency. A few parents today persist in this superstitious, quasi-religious practice.

Most Chinese names have three characters written from the top down. In my case, *Ling* is on the top, or the first character, thus underscoring the reputation and gravity of the family name and the family traditions and loyalty. You are known by your family name. From a very young age, you have been instructed that your whole life is to preserve and uphold that family name. Philosopher Confucius taught that the family is the backbone and foundation of an ordered and harmonious society. If you are a Chinese, you zealously guard your family name and protect it with your life. Defaming or tarnishing it, therefore, could result in one being ostracized, or worse, eventually banished from the family, excised like some cancerous tumor and fed it to a world of hostile hungry wolves. *Eng Huat,* my given name, means "forever or eternally prosperous." A long way to go, I figure. A charming name, not a guarantee of eternal prosperity waiting to be dumped in my lap. I didn't expect the road to be paved with gold or strewn with easy pickings and valuables. Nevertheless, a goal worth striving for, if not monetarily, at least spiritually.

All males in the Ling's clan (specifically all uncles' sons) would have the middle character *Eng (or Ing),* according to some old families and traditions. The character *Eng* had been chosen long time ago by the Ling's family for that particular generation of males. My generation. The next generation could pick *Wong* or *Ah* or *Chong.* Or whatever the respected elders had chosen, preserving an extensive genealogical chart of names. There were no known criteria for the choice of Chinese characters. I know of a family who had chosen the middle names for the next eighteen generations down the road. (Deviations from the norm do happen.) All my male cousins' given names in my generation begin with *Ing. Ing Tai. Ing Huat. Ing Wong. Ing Sing, Ing Nan.* Et Cetera. Another one of the family traditions. (The really poor were too preoccupied with survival, not playing this name game for posterity.)

I had to get used to someone calling me by my Chinese name (in Mandarin) in school. Or in Sunday School (in Hockchiang). At first I had to listen carefully in class to make sure the teacher had called my name. Because at home and with neighborhood friends, no one would dream of calling me by my real name. Not in my village. Or any other village. Only in school was I known by my real name.

I don't remember if the teacher ever used the Hockchiang dialect to facilitate our transition from home to school, for many, the first time hearing everything in a new language, Mandarin. I suspect he did or he had to because I had never heard Mandarin spoken anywhere in the village, though a few older kids and grownups had attended Chinese schools before me. They instinctually reverted to the Hockchiang dialect when conversing with their parents, neighbors, friends and relatives, away from schools. I started watching Chinese movies from Hong Kong (all in Mandarin) in my early teens in a movie theater in Kampong Koh.

The Hockchiang dialect is just one of many dialects spoken in different parts of mainland China. An unassuming fisherman married a woman who spoke Hockkian dialect and lived with their two boys few yards away from our house. She spoke Hockkian only and seemed able to communicate with the Hockchiang people without any problem. Her children grew up speaking Hockchiang and had no difficulty understanding their Hockkian mother. To my knowledge she was the only human being in our village speaking a different dialect. Grandpa came to the village with his Hockchiang people and three other groups speaking three different dialects. Within a radius of less than ten miles or so from my village, there are people who speak at least five or more different Chinese dialects.

Many dialects but one language. Because miraculously all the dialects share the same written characters. We may not understand each other orally in the markets or streets or train stations or planes, but we can read and understand the same information, no matter what dialects we speak at home. That is the one enlightening aspect of the Chinese language unknown to the outsiders and non-Chinese around the world. How does more than a quarter of the world's population communicate with one another speaking unaccountable number of dialects within the same borders in old and contemporary China? They read and write utilizing the same written characters.

The Chinese language or Mandarin that I studied as a kid in Malaya is now referred to by communist China as the *Putonghua* (literally translated Common Speech), in reality the Northern dialect spoken by more than 70 percent of the Chinese-speaking people in China today. More than that, it has become one of the world's major languages (used by more than a quarter of the world's population), one of the official working languages at the United Nations and other international bodies. The Chinese communist government continues aggressively to encourage its adoption and usage by Chinese-speaking people in every niche and nook of mainland China for at least two reasons: 1. To transcend all regional and local dialectal diversity and differences (using one Common Speech to unite all peoples); 2. To facilitate, encourage and enhance cultural, political and economic growth as an emerging economic dragon in the world. Every road leads seemingly to China, today, and for good reasons: many on this shrinking global village are suffering an incurable itch to procure a piece of that vast economic pie, laden with gold, at whatever costs! Speaking Mandarin might get you near the entrance, at least to catch a jealous glimpse or smell of the pie!

I grew up speaking the Hockchiang dialect, not Mandarin. I grew up in a home without any reading materials or picture books for children or challenging toys to stimulate one's curiosity or tickle one's imagination. Not raised by people who loudly advocated or clamored for the desirability of education. I did hear biblical stories and color religious pictures and recite verses from the Bible in Sunday school (in Hockchiang dialect), a short walking distance from the house. My world was the farm and the village. Simple and uncomplicated. Isolated. A simple dot on a map. Mother's perennial and unabashed philosophy: a farmer's life is good enough for anyone. Going to a regular school wasn't my or any family's top priority during the topsy-turvy years following the Japanese Occupation. Neither something encouraged nor discouraged but just something for a kid to do. Fortunately it was compulsory education, mandated by the government. There was less than a handful educated people in the whole village, working for the schools. Not many role models to emulate or follow during the formative years of my life. Sadly the only role models were the farmers pursuing subsistence living out of the soil. Singers from Hong Kong who gave live performances at a nearby theater were the only people who caught my fancy. The closest I could get to them were autographed photos. What role models? They were females. And movie stars from Hong Kong. They were total strangers fading in and out of my awareness. The farmers were real to me. We were all farmers with no steady income, an uncertain future, and totally dependent on nature's magnanimity for our survival. And Mother's gospel: *If they can do it,* so *can you.*

Her message failed to gain a willing adherent. I rejected it from the start.

For now I tried to be a student. One particular detail was etched in my memory about my life as a student in the school. It had nothing to do with formal education. We were cautioned, one day, not to drink any water from the well, sandwiched between the kitchen and the principal's residence, that was used by the principal's family and the school. The principal's wife, also a teacher, was very sick and remained unnoticed and closeted in the house, adjacent to the school building. Something to do with the well water, we suspected after we witnessed, from a distance, white-robed people spending an enormous amount of time around the well, examining and studying the well water. I remember the presence of a microscope, like the one I used in a science lab later in my high school. The students were never told the true nature of her illness. We knew not to ask.

In class, students were introduced to the Chinese characters and repeated them loudly and in unison, following the teacher word by word. I could hear many animated voices and echoes from other classrooms doing similar repetition drills. In the absence of electricity or ceiling fans or air-conditioning, the school's screenless windows and doors were left open for ventilation. Like most primary school children, I was totally engrossed in learning, indifferent to the outside interferences. We were hungry for knowledge and new experiences and nothing could deter us from giving a hundred percent of our attention to the teacher and the task at hand. I was a product of a strict Chinese upbringing and Confucianism, which instilled in me unbridled respect for my elders and those in authority. My teachers included.

I soon learned that every Chinese character or word has one and only one sound. It didn't matter how simple or complex a character looks. It has only one sound. Each character owns that sound. To learn Chinese correctly and effectively, we as children learned the sound of each character by heart. Memorize. Memorize. And memorize. With English, a word could have more than one syllable, and therefore more than one sound. Count the sounds in a word like "antiestablishmentarianism". Ten sounds for one word. Or a simpler one like "governmental". Slightly less, four sounds. Also in learning a new English word, a learner can guess at the pronunciation of a word by deliberately dissecting and grouping the letters to form certain sounds for a simple or a multi-syllabic word. Unlike English, with an alphabet of twenty-six letters, the Chinese language that I learned has no alphabet. Every Chinese character comprises a number of strokes. The combination of these strokes appear artistic but do not produce any sound—unlike the grouping of letters in an English word—making it difficult to pronounce a new Chinese character. You could dissect and group the brush strokes of a simple or complex Chinese character, but they do not assist in the pronunciation of a word, any word. Therefore good acute hearing is needed to listen to every word uttered by the teacher. Listen. Repeat. And most importantly, commit the clear and distinctive sound of each Chinese character to memory. Be a good mimic!

How does a teacher know if the students are hearing and repeating the same sounds, accurately? I compare him to a choir master. A trained and sensitive choir director could easily detect a wrong pitch in a cacophony of voices during practices. He desires to achieve certain harmony, not discord, if all the voices know their assigned parts—soprano, alto, tenor and bass. Every Chinese character, like a bird, has its own sound. We are like parrots when it comes to learning the correct pronunciation of Chinese words. Only years later (in fact I studied Chinese in college realizing I had only two years of Chinese schooling as a village kid and the urgency of speaking Chinese in the twenty-first-century world economy) I also learned that not only does each Chinese word have its own sound, but each word also belongs to one of four unique tones. I simplify the four tones as straight, up, curl, and down in one's voice. Some say Chinese is a tonal language. Some words could have the same sound and the same tone. Or the same sound but a different tone. The sound and tone of a word and its context decide the actual written character and its precise meaning. Again, there is no easy way out of learning Chinese characters but to memorize and memorize and memorize.

From the beginning, I thought learning to write a Chinese word was much easier than learning the different sounds and tones of words we had to commit to memory. Of course to the uninitiated or non-Chinese, it is a daunting task and a dilemma trying to learn to write or simply copy a Chinese character. Writing was the next order of business and I could not wait to use the brush, ink-stick, ink-block, and writing paper. Called the four treasures, according to some traditional Chinese. Unlike learning the correct pronunciation of each word, writing is a routine, meaning one learns to master the fundamental steps (all brush strokes of a character follow a specific sequence) in the writing of a word, which are applicable to all words, however simple or complex they are.

First step first. And that meant we students were given writing exercise books with printed Chinese words in squares—exactly nine little squares within one-inch-plus squares—to achieve proportion and balance. Chinese writing, or calligraphy for some, is an art form requiring years of mastering the brush techniques. All Chinese characters can be reduced to simple strokes. And, according to eminent Chinese calligraphers, there are seventeen strokes in practice today. All grouped under eight types of basic strokes: the horizontal stroke, the vertical stroke, the point, the lift stroke (left to up right), the downward slant stroke (right to down left), the sweep stroke (left to right), the hook, and the curve stroke. Each brush stroke of a character on paper is numbered starting with Chinese numerical one. Like a picture coloring book with numbers. But with a huge difference. In writing a Chinese character, following the number sequence is not optional but must be adhered to faithfully and consistently. Without deviation or personal preference of any kind.

Whereas there is more than one way to write the letters of the English alphabet, capital or lower case, there is one and only one correct way to write a Chinese character. *"Follow the sequence of numbers,"* the teacher said, to write the characters correctly, not magically.

Now came the messy part of the whole process: preparing the black ink using water, ink-stick, and the ink-block, following a tradition going back hundreds of years in our Chinese culture. The idea is to not get the ink on your hands, body, and school uniform, especially the white shirt and shoes. With a few drops of water on a two-by-three-inch ink-block, grind the ink-stick slowly to produce sufficient amount of black ink with the right consistency for the immediate task of writing. Holding and taming the brush, for us kids trained to eat with the chopsticks, was as easy as combing our hair. (The use of brush, according to historians, dates back to as early as 4000 B.C.) Refined skill and dexterity with the delicate brush would take time to accomplish—years, for some.

After the teacher had explained and demonstrated—in some cases holding and guiding the students' nervous and wobbly hands—we held the brushes upright, perpendicular to the paper. The middle and ring fingers and the hand control the movement of the brush strokes. The thumb presses gently on the brush against the index finger to steady the brush. The exact locations of the numbers in the brush strokes indicate the movement and direction of the brush, usually from top to bottom and from left to right. For each character, there is a specific sequence of strokes. Dip the brush in the fresh black ink (too much ink would drip) and turn the bristle around in it to achieve even soaking in the ink before applying it to the first brush stroke. The brush pressure depends on which directions the strokes are moving and tapering.

Remember, the teacher reminded us daily: 1. Clean the brush after use and let it dry before trying to squeeze the swollen bristle back into its cap; 2. Never leave a wet ink-stick on the ink-block because it could get stuck to it; 3. Wash the ink-block after use each time to maintain its smooth surface. After weeks and months of dauntless practice and practice (and now many years later) I could write any Chinese character with careful precision like I would letting my fingers run triumphantly the keyboard (on an old typewriter or a piano) with confidence, ease and a sense of personal accomplishment. I often wonder if it is my fingers or the brain or both that are doing the Chinese writing because when it comes to a keyboard of a typewriter, it is without doubt my fingers that are doing the writing. The letters, it seems, are magically built into my fingers after years of practice. The same is true now when I write Chinese characters. It comes naturally through my fingers, from the first stroke to the final one, without conscious effort.

Along with reading and writing, my early Chinese education included reciting multiplication tables from one to twelve in front of the class, which took some courage and lots of self-confidence. If you didn't volunteer on your own, the teacher would insist you stand in front of the class and do your recitation. He called randomly, but your name would not escape his glance. I volunteered, ambitiously, many times, for different things. Pleasing my teachers wasn't that much different from trying to please Mother at home. Mother was a difficult one.

One day she went into a frenzy when I failed to walk home on time. The chance of being kidnapped for ransom was nil. Our family was nobody and our earthy possessions were meager. Mother saw it simply as willful disobedience and downright subversive defiance of her authority and specific orders not to loiter around with strangers. She forgave me once when—hoping for some charity, like candies, dried fruits, or cookies—I visited relatives (Mother's sister was married to a rich merchant) whose prosperous grocery shop visible from the school campus. The gifts more than compensated for the physical punishment I gladly endured from Mother. This time it was my curiosity, not hunger, that did me in. On this sunny day, there was a noodle man, halfway between home and the school, practicing the unique art of making *mee sian*, a kind of wheat noodle originally from Foochow, Fujian province, China. I had seen him a few times on my way home from school, but today I could restrain myself no longer and had to satisfy my curiosity. I stood there—the only audience—and watched the man threading fifteen to twenty strands of 6-inch noodles to a sturdy bamboo stick and then pulling and stretching them, like elastic, till they were about fifteen feet long, and letting them dry in the hot sun for less than an hour. As a kid, I had seen him performing some kind of magic, stretching these noodles without ever breaking any of them. Not magic on this day when I was curiously watching his every move. Fifteen feet? Like pulling and stretching the colorful rubber bands my friends and I played with at home. Many in the village celebrated their birthdays by eating *mee sian* (symbolizing longevity because they are long) and one or two hard-boiled eggs (symbolizing life). The rich could add Chinese Red Wine (many villagers made it themselves, with rice as the main ingredient) to the dish. Women were generously fed this *mee sian* with Red Wine especially during the thirty-day, lying-in, recuperative period after birth.

Today the *mee sian* got me into trouble with Mother. I had deliberately stretched my leisure time walking home. Obviously a behavior not to be condoned or encouraged.

"How come you didn't come home straight from school?" She screamed at me. Luckily I was spared the stick in her hand. I remained unrepentant because I was a good student only trying to avail myself of every opportunity to learn something new each day. All she did was look at me, mystified and speechless, sensing early a child with a mind of his own. "He wants to learn," it dawned on her. "When and where will it end? I adopted him for something else." She must have been searching her heart and soul for a revelation. I enjoyed learning and going to school. Something admirable, I thought. But to Mother, less and less time tending the farm and chores around the house.

Once I learned the simple sequential brush strokes for Chinese characters, writing my Chinese name (Ling Eng Huat) was easy, not from left to right but from the top down. Three characters. In a row. In three imaginary, perfect squares. I did not pursue calligraphy, a highly stylistic art form of Chinese writing, because of a lack of artistic inclinations and aspirations. But after two short years of Chinese education, Father and his chauffeur decided I should attend an English school in Kampong Koh, a town contiguous to our village.

In existence and in practice at the time, some parents adopted "double education" for their offspring. Children could attend Chinese school in the morning and a different school for English education in the afternoon. Sometimes in the same building. And vice versa. The prerogative belonged to the parents. I could have the ultimate benefit of studying Chinese and English at the same time. I was too young to know anything except to follow mutely the desires of the elders. Father's decision was to send me to an English school, exclusively. (I wish I had both). Because most of my friends, and some relatives, were educated exclusively in Chinese schools. Ironically it didn't really matter much then because we all spoke our Hockchiang dialect, here and there and everywhere, transcending our educational differences.

Many of the young people in our village continued to attend the Chinese schools for a cultural reason. For many uneducated Chinese parents, it was the right thing to do. The patriotic thing. Chinese should be educated in Chinese, no matter what, they reasoned. It didn't matter that most jobs in the country required proficiency and fluency in English and Malay, not Chinese. Especially government jobs. It was no secret that the British had lost their preeminence after the Japanese took over Southeast Asia, including my country, however briefly. Many disdained the British after that. Father never did divulge his reason for sending me to an English speaking school. Inexplicable move, to me. I acquiesced to Father's order, like all dutiful Chinese sons and daughters, and attended the English school, not knowing then it would be a major turning point in my life, gradually and devastatingly abandoning my Chinese culture and losing the ability to speak fluently the Hockchiang dialect that had informed and nurtured me since I was adopted by a Hockchiang family.

EIGHT

One warm early Saturday morning, there was a commotion, according to Mother, breaking out in the church building a few blocks behind our house. A lorry with an Indian driver had delivered many marked bags of goods, donated by some far away foreigners, for the poor families in Kampong China still recuperating from the Japanese Occupation. A large crowd of noisy women and children had congregated and were ferociously grapping or fighting over something like pirates dividing up some ill-gotten loot.

Many of us in the kampong were reduced to indigence during the Japanese Occupation and were grateful recipients of many generically labeled cans and bags of foods to supplement our meager resources. Rumors had it that some ate banana skins and potato leaves to ward off starvation when the Japanese were in control. Not wanting to appear ungrateful, many concocted new ways of using unfamiliar cornmeal and other foods that were alien to our Chinese culture. All Chinese cooking is done on top of the stove—stir-fry, braise, steam, boil, deep-fry. Oven cooking is non-Chinese and non-existent in most Chinese kitchens, even today.

And now the clothing. Fascinating, I thought. First the surplus food from abroad. Clothing wasn't a big deal in the tropics like Malaya. Most men were half-naked most of the time at home or out in the farms. Almost all women in the village wore simple, traditional Chinese clothes, sewn with their own hands. Few could afford sewing machines, treated like precious gold and diamonds.

While clothing is universal, American clothes were something else. People marveled. They giggled. They seized on something to speculate. We were grateful recipients of bags of second-hand clothing from America. The only American I had met as a kid was a nurse running a small clinic operated by the Methodist Church in Kampong Koh, who visited our village Sunday school, usually with her guests (presumably other Americans), every so often. Their arrival (preceded by a gentle honking and the sound of a purring vehicle) meant kids abandoning everything we were doing at Sunday school and crowding around the car like adoring fans beseeching their favorite movie star for an autograph. A touch or handshake was like a visit with a member of a royal family. They were different—usually taller, bigger and all white. Like rare animals in a zoo somewhere. A different breed from us. And of course they spoke a strange language. The nurse would mumble a few Hockchiang words in her greetings. Like a child uttering the first words. Touching and adorable!

On this Saturday, Eighth Auntie and her daughter, Mother, Ah Soh, Sister, and I couldn't resist the urge to join the crowd to see who could grab and snatch and run away with the most from a huge assortment of used clothing worn by strangers we had never met. Whose smell and presence, we felt. What bodies could have worn these clothes?

Some people simply chuckled. Some shook their heads.

"I could cut this one up for my girls," a joyful mother said, stretching an unusually big dress (like a small, shriveled tent) on a wooden bench. Most Chinese women that I knew, including those in my immediate family, were rather short and petite. Much of the clothing, male and female, was rather large by our Chinese standards. Double or triple the size suited to our frames. Giants, by my estimation. Because I was small and short, I could hide or get lost in some of the clothes.

Many dresses, blouses and skirts, I could only imagine, must have once adorned the bodies of Amazon women somewhere. Some American women, we were told. Most men's clothing was meant for baboons, not us in the village. Worn by big people with big necks, long arms, plump bodies, long legs and bulky waists. One size here didn't fit all. The American size could accommodate quite a few youngsters in our village. Women's voices, like a chorus, sounded blissfully their brilliant, creative thoughts. Cut here. Cut there. Fold here. Fold there. Shorten here. Shorten there. Join here. Join there. Plait here. Plait there. Women in the crowd spilled out their intentions with the abundant materials strewn all over the floor, excited by so many possibilities. Most of the clothing— in colors and texture new to our village—had to be reduced to sizes to fit the Chinese physical realities or transformed for their children.

Handouts or hand-me-downs, it didn't matter when you were poor. We were grateful and happy recipients of the unbounded goodwill of people halfway around the globe.

On my way home, alone in my elation of some new shirts and trousers to wear to school, I was interrupted by a relative, who was out in front of his house washing and polishing his bicycle. Next to the well. He and his brother and two sisters and mother lived a block away from our house.

"*Ardi-yan*," he called my name, waving his washrag in the air to get my attention. "What's going on in the church?"

"Nothing." I shook my head in response, not wanting really to engage in any serious conversation about what had just taken place in the church.

Not too long before, he had quietly beckoned me to his house, but I had six ducklings to feed, leading them with a *changkul* (a square blade attached to a long wooden handle commonly used by farmers for loosening or turning over the soil) to areas where I might find worms in the ground. On barren land between our two houses. The same worms sought by kids in my neighborhood as bait for fish. After a while I could sense worms by studying the surface of the dirt, one slightly damp and suitable for cultivation. You could see visible tiny pores in the dirt, like warts on a skin, for the worms to breathe. I had to be careful not to bury the ducklings under chunks of dirt while they expertly went after crawling worms, some digging their beaks into the soft crumbling dirt, dragging out their victims. Some pulling a worm and stretching its fragile body, like kids in a game of tug-of-war. One beak gnawing at another, playfully.

This was one of my seasonal chores, helping to raise the family ducklings. Nature is benevolent and generous, I learned at a young age. Abundant worms to loosen the earth and fertilize the land. A bountiful feast for the hungry ones.

But the dirty dirt can be fatal to your health, I soon learned. In attempting to break up the dirt to expose the worms, my fingers had voluntary come into contact with the soil that had been infected by animal and human feces, invisible to the naked eyes. As children we were always playing out in the dirt, assuming it was clean and disease free. All yards in our village, except the school playground, had dirt, not grass. (For some people in the village, outhouse was any place to defecate in a hurry or the first convenient spot nearest from the house. You had provided a ready meal for hungry animals, especially the neighborhood pigs.) There were times I would simply wipe my hands and not wash them at all before eating something, allowing round worms from the infected dirt to enter my mouth. Some had grown a few inches by the time they emerged from my body with the feces. Partly from nutritional deficiencies. Partly from contact with contaminated soil.

Raising ducklings can be hazardous to your health.

Today I had no excuse. I was ambling home, like a happy dog, without a care in the world.

"Come here. I have something I want you to see," he continued, casually. He was looking, his head slightly cocking to one side, at his bicycle, shiny and glimmering in the morning sun, like a thief at a stolen jewelry. This, his pride and joy. His one worldly possession.

"You have a beautiful bicycle," I joined him in his admiration of his bicycle, not wanting to appear disinterested in his magnificent job.

I saw a half-naked bearded man crouching by the stairway to the house. That was his uncle. But the family didn't want to commit him to a mental institution. Because he was a deaf-mute, with uncouth behavior and an unkempt appearance (his penis was often hanging out), many villagers thought he should be locked up somewhere or receive some kind of treatment. He lived way out in the boondocks in a small hut (closer to the Malay kampong), but would visit his sister when he ran out of supplies.

"My uncle is waiting for my mother," he said, feeling the need to explain his presence.

"I think I saw your mother and sisters at the church," I said, watching him communicating this information to his uncle using some universal hand gestures.

His house was a little strange, I always thought, sitting about four feet above the ground. After climbing five or six steps, he led me into this huge unfinished room on the left. In one corner a bird was chirping away merrily in a small cage. Many boards on the floor were in place but some ends had curled up slightly, making the surface uneven. I didn't feel safe at some spots for fear of causing the boards, a few warped, to move and injuring myself by falling into a hole. *Why's a sawhorse sitting in the middle of the room?* I asked myself.

Maybe he wanted someone to help him to nail down some of these boards. Or help steady them while he nail them down. But neither nails nor hammers were present.

"Do you know how I got this bird?" he said, breaking the silence after eons.

"Did you buy it?" I asked, exposing my ignorance as to the nature of the bird in the cage. He is too young to keep birds for company or hobby, I thought. Older people do for pleasure in some wealthier Chinese communities, I had heard.

"I was out cutting some sugarcane the other day and there was this bird just sitting there in the bush. So I got myself this small bird cage. You like it?"

"I like fighting fish, not birds really," I blurted out. I wasn't afraid to express my true feelings. He had seen my friend (Ah Dea) and me looking for fighting fish in the ponds not far from his house. I had a few in a clear soda bottle at home to prove it. I told him Brother and I had set up traps for squirrels, especially the ones going up and down the coconut trees. Bad for the coconuts, Brother would say. But quite a delicacy for the stomach. Not much to consume after chopping off the heads (first death by submerging the trap in a bucket of water) and removing the skins and other parts. "Have you tried squirrel meat?" I asked, not knowing what he would say.

I didn't mean to change the focus of our conversation.

I could see he changed his mind, withdrew his hand slowly from the cage and closed it. He realized I wasn't the least interested in talking further about the bird or holding it in my palm.

I saw an empty stare, like his spirit had suddenly left him. His face drained of blood.

For a minute he seemed gasping for words. Maybe I didn't say the right thing. I should have pretended to like his bird. By then I heard some trifling voices outside fading into the kitchen, located at the back of the house. The family had returned.

Before I could say anything more he had firmly pushed me down on a bench, pulled down my short loose pants and from behind tried to introduce his swollen bird up my alimentary canal. I told him if he continued I might faint and I didn't like the pain. Then a strange feeling of suffocation. He tried but the plug was too big for the socket. There was no pleasure in this. He was tall and lanky, in his late teens. He had attempted to sodomize me but stopped as quickly as he had started because of my protest. My physical body refused admission. My small body was trembling. He got the wrong person. I wasn't about to shout because I didn't want anyone to know about it. Shame would be unbearable. He turned away from me and finished his job, shooting into the air.

I had a flashback…someone in the family had introduced the soap treatment because I was constipated. It was a medical necessity then, not for pleasure. This time the pain was unwelcome, someone trying to inflict it on me for pleasure. The body rejected it like an amoeba a foreign particle.

He didn't say anything. Probably treating it like a child's play. Some kids were doing it in the village—the heterosexual kind, in the bushes, half imitating the dogs and cats and chickens and ducks and pigs around them. Sex was part of growing up. Nothing to talk about. Nothing to be ashamed of. No big deal. Only once we played doctors and babies in Ah Dea's house, with one or two girls, I remember. Some touching. Nothing else. All in innocence, without guilt or sense of wrongful action. No teenage pregnancy, not in my immediate neighborhood.

I left his house shivering, without a whimper, because I was frightened to death wondering what would happen if Mother found out I was somehow involved in an indecent act. It didn't matter that I was the victim. I imagined being quarantined for the rest of my life. I couldn't bear the gossip in the whole kampong. So I kept silent. But nothing in the world could erase it from my memory.

My emotional problem was less visible and critical than the family's preparations for Small Sister's wedding, which was less elaborate than Brother's wedding, even from my vantage point. At the same time, Mother was concerned that I should visit the mission clinic soon because a teacher in my new English school had complained that I had not paid attention in class, that my head, like a radar, was turning this way and that way while she was talking to the students. In my defense I had told her I had some hearing problem and had often turned my head to listen better. Mother must have thought she had magically solved my ear problem by sticking some cotton into my left ear every time she saw some smelly stuff slowly dripping down my ear lobe. I had never seen a doctor for this because we were poor. Blame the Japanese! The best hope was a visit to the clinic started by American missionaries, originally for people who first populated this area on mission land.

I had deliberately kept some problems from Mother because I didn't think I would be safe from her if she knew about them. A female teacher had brought a basket of eggs to school one day and one of my legs had gone astray and kicked it accidentally, breaking a dozen or so eggs. I was so frightened I had cried in front of the teacher and promised to replace the broken ones. Only Sister knew about this. I had visited the chicken coop, hoping for the hens to cooperate and be fruitful. My prayer was answered. I stole the eggs without Mother's knowledge.

During recess one day, a few boys and I were playing in a construction site for a new row of classrooms next to our building. I don't remember seeing any KEEP OUT signs posted anywhere. It had rained heavily for a few days and many holes in the ground were covered with water. I must have been after something, because I was on the edge of one of those holes and the next thing I knew I was screeching for help. I had fallen into one, a few feet deep. Because I was of small stature, everything seemed like a bottomless pit. I had a genuine fear of deep holes, especially ones filled with water. A thousand bogeymen waiting for my flesh and soul! A deep-rooted incomprehensible fear of the unknown lurking everywhere! At home I had this fear, when drawing water with a bucket from the well, that the weight of the water in the bucket might mysteriously pull me into the deep well (at least fifteen or twenty feet deep). At school I got off easy. Just a warning from the headmaster to be careful: Look out for the KEEP OUT signs!

I told no one but Sister about this incident. I had to share my burden with someone. Sister had become my confidante.

As long as Mother was kept in the dark, I reasoned, I would be spared the rod. The only person I could trust with my secrets was Sister. But for how long? I had betrayed her at least once.

Father usually carried a lot of cash because of his opium business. He dabbled unsuccessfully in the fishing business. And with a few friends, he had formed a gambling syndicate, playing numbers (using the winning numbers of the national horse races). Many in the village possessed a copy of a dream book that conveniently converted your dreams into numbers. There were numbers for every conceivable dream. Some got lucky, not rich, buying these numbers. Family members helped write these numbers and kept carbon copies of every transaction. I don't remember how long the gambling syndicate lasted, but Sister, Mother, and I helped count the money and wrapped it in bundles according to the denominations of our Malayan currency. Father had a habit of leaving bundles of cash in the pockets of his shirt or pants, which he left hanging by the wall in his opium den. He could be asleep or serving his clients. Once Sister had cleverly, she thought, removed a bill or two from each bundle, thinking Father was asleep and would be oblivious to her crime. When Mother heard of the theft, she didn't think it was an outside job. She couldn't imagine any loyal opium customers, who spent at times hours in Father's opium den, would resort to stealing to support their habits. Only two culprits in the house could be responsible for the missing cash: Sister and I were the main suspects. And since Sister was two years older than I, Mother went to her first. Mother suspected she was the guilty one because of some inconsistency in what she said. All the bloody flogging with a cane in the world, Mother soon realized, and even death would not elicit any confession from her. She remained stoic, no matter what. Not me. I couldn't take any pain, no matter how or where on my body. I told Mother immediately after the first strike descended on my sensitive butt that Sister had shared her loot with me. That she had planned this all herself. That I was just a recipient of her generosity.

I learned a bitter lesson, too late. Maybe two. Not only I had betrayed my Sister, who had kept all the secrets I had told her. Because from this day on, Mother would always know who to go to when things went wrong in the house. I could be trusted, in her eyes, to tell the truth and nothing but the truth, at all times, with just a small dose of pain!

The truth? I did it to save my own hide. Not because I was an honest child. In many ways I was a sensitive child with sensitive skin. It had very little to do with morality. Everything to do with delicate sensitivity to pain, the type meted out to unrepentant criminals. Self-preservation was uppermost in my mind. This included hiding dark secrets from adults, especially Mother.

Hectic preparations for Small Sister's wedding took precedence over my personal misfortunes. I became invisible for a while because every ounce of energy and drop of sweat was exploited, expeditiously, for her aggrandizement, her marriage to a farmer, sometime fisherman, in a distant village. An arranged marriage. Like marrying a ghost. She had been plodding for months on her trousseau. The most cherished and conspicuous were expensive yards of cloth given by close relatives and jewelry by my parents, and the new clothes specially designed for the wedding feast and evening party at the bridegroom's residence the first day, and also one for the second day when she returned home for another feast, attended by friends and relatives. Rich aunts and uncles might also bestow gold to adorn her fingers or something around her neck. The gifts hinged largely on the nature of her relationship with close relatives. Small Sister wasn't chosen for anything, she didn't receive any rewards from them. She was the inconspicuous mild one in the family.

While some Indian women were judged or valued (in some cases punished) according to the size of the dowry they could offer the men they married, Small Sister's husband's cash gift to my parents would be the talk of the village for some time. Some parents bragged about the amount, others tried, in vain, to camouflage it. Indirectly, his wealth or lack of it would be on public display because my parents would use a portion of it to purchase a cupboard and a vanity (rumor mongers looked for size and quality and other conspicuous features), which would be carried in a procession to the man's house on the wedding day.

Small Sister spent many hours doing cross-stitch on pillow and bolster cases—personal items on public display on the bed on the wedding day—sewing clothes for daily wear, never betraying at any time she was in a hurry to abandon the household for a greener pasture elsewhere.

She had as yet to pass the toughest test before flying off the cuckoo's nest. Any potential bride would consider this wedding eve's ritual archaic, preposterous and unnecessary, involving her sobbing (more than simply shedding a few tears or weeping) with different relatives throughout the evening. This was no ordinary sobbing. The veterans, older relatives like aunts, had mastered the words, and when sung, sounded like a long recitation with sobbing the musical accompaniment. I had heard the same tune and song many times before in other households. Many voices. Seldom in unison. More like three- or multi-part rounds I had heard and participated in youth meetings at church. A mixture of joy and sadness. The nature of the sobbing didn't seem much different from the one at a funeral. The words were different, predictably encouraging the bride-to-be to be obedient to her husband and a dutiful daughter-in-law in a new household.

A bad daughter don't cry, the villagers said. But a few crocodile tears were expected. The bad one couldn't wait to start a new life somewhere beyond the constraints of the old household. She couldn't tolerate any longer the present and was impatient for the unknown. She wanted out, like a dog in a trap.

A good daughter would sob, her tears worth a thousand words, the villagers said, because she was loyal, virtuous and wouldn't conceive of leaving the beloved parents. It was too painful to leave the safety and comfort of the nest, her home since cradle.

A good daughter would sob, her tears genuine as the morning dew, the villagers said, because she wouldn't be seeing her beloved home, relatives and parents for an indefinite period of time. Especially if you married someone beyond the village. Transportation wasn't readily available. The thought of that alienation seemed unbearable.

A good daughter would sob, her tears remembered for eternity, the villagers said, because she was afraid of the unknown, especially the future husband she would be meeting face-to-face the first time. Who is this man I would be spending the rest of my life with? What manner of person is he? What about the in-laws? Nothing had prepared her for this new life. Like moving into an alien territory, living with total strangers. The anticipation of the unknown seemed unendurable.

I don't remember how hard or how earnestly Small Sister sobbed with our female relatives (strictly a camaraderie among the females, males excluded), young and old, with regular intervals away from her bedroom to engage in small talks with friends and relatives. For others, a respite from the intensity of the moment. Everybody returned, like clockwork, to the bedroom and the sobbing resumed.

Once again Small Sister was being a dutiful daughter and kept the Hockchiang tradition alive. And her good reputation intact.

Only relatives and close friends, living within a short distance, turned up for the wedding day. Fine wedding garments for the bride and bridegroom were rented. Fresh bouquet, for the bride, with sprightly delicate little pink flowers, smelling like sweet-smelling perfume, seemed to enliven everyone in the house. Most relatives and friends waited and attended the wedding banquet the second day at our house. Small Sister didn't sleep well. The flawlessly executed fresh make-up, the next day, covered partially her sadness and anxiety, giving color and vivacity to her skin. The joviality had the effect of lessening the gravity of the occasion, which was going to be a personal loss for my parents. She would soon be leaving the nest.

Chinese had been saying for centuries that females are not important. Dispensable. Families who practiced female infanticide were exonerated, in ancient and modern mainland China. A female belongs, from day one, to somebody. To another family, somewhere. Only the males will stay on the land, bear proudly and continue the family name. Obviously, for our family it meant two fewer hands to till the land and tap the rubber trees and raise the pigs and one less mouth to feed. For me, it meant more pressure from Mother to work harder and play less. And to be treated more like an adult than a child of eight, going on nine.

It seemed like every external event triggered a turning point in my life. At times I thought of myself more as an unwilling victim than an instrument of positive change during the formative years of growing up in the village.

When the cars arrived around noon, the crying started again. The hidden pressure was on. Last chance for Small Sister to prove to the world she wasn't ready and not about to desert the old habitat, that it was our parents who had conspired with a matchmaker to find her a husband. She was being obedient to their will. Only a bad daughter with diminishing morals would scrounge around for her man. While relatives helped loaded the cupboard, vanity and her personal effects into different cars, the matchmaker carrying the bright red chamber pot, I saw Small Sister, dressed in all white, accentuated by shimmering gold necklaces, bracelets and rings, looking radiant and calm, being led and pulled slowly into a waiting vehicle. Someone bellowing: "Time to go. Time… to… go." A bad daughter would walk unaided to the car, the villagers said. She would run, if she could. A good daughter, the villagers said, must show some reluctance to leave her parents and, in some instances, had to be dragged out of the house into a car, gingerly because of the wedding dress and the fresh make-up. The voice continued: "Time… to… go…time…to…go." The engines were humming. The drivers getting impatient. I witnessed Small Sister, tears in her eyes (someone in the crowd cautioning don't let tears mar your makeup), pouring out in mine, holding tightly to her bouquet of flowers, being dragged by Father into a waiting vehicle, leaving little room for bystanders to gossip. She was, in public view, a good daughter. The procession soon departed, at least an hour's ride to the bridegroom's house. Mother still weeping. A few wiping off their tears. Guests soon dispersed. Few stayed for lunch.

I felt a sudden emptiness but I knew I would be seeing her the next morning at her new house. Big Sister came home with her husband and son; Eighth Uncle came home with his mistress and an entourage of city folks. I didn't feel I had lost a sister. There was no time for sadness.

Later in the evening the chef arrived and preparations for the wedding feast soon began. I knew it wasn't as big and elaborate as Brother's wedding, but the same chef was in command and I knew I was in for a heavenly treat. Within the next two happy years, two of

Eighth Uncle's three children would be married, one male and other female, their spouses all living within less than two miles from our ancestral home. All from the same village. Oldest cousin, with very little education, had a steady job working for a construction company, marrying a woman without any education or a job. Cousin sister, without education or a job, married a good-looking farmer with a decent house and some inherited wealth. He was the only son of a widow. I said happy years because (growing up poor with watery rice gruel three meals a day, making me vomit a few times a week, with homegrown vegetables, salted fish and fresh fish from the ocean and not much of anything else) wedding feasts meant abundant tasty foods for a delightful change for a starving child. It didn't matter to me who got married, in or out. Where? or to whom? Or who passed away? These celebrations, sad or happy, meant nothing to me personally but opportunities to gorge myself. A time of plenty! A time to have something decent to eat! I prayed for marriage. I prayed for death. Ludicrous? Absurd? Sad? Yes, but true.

Mother insisted I go to bed on time, despite the incessant noise all around me because of guests, relatives, and the growing excitement in the kitchen, which had been completely taken over by the chef and his helpers. Father entertained his friends in his opium den—part business, part pleasure—and the scent of freshly burnt opium wafted to noses experienced in discerning its smell. Eighth Uncle, a police officer home for Small Sister's wedding, could not resist Father's offer of free opium. The dimly lit room was filled with smoke. Some coughing. Their voices almost inaudible to passers-by.

A big day for you, a relative said to me. I slept soundly.

The next day, I was up early. Mother made me take a cold shower. No time to boil some water. I had a fresh hair cut a week before. Big Sister gently daubed my hair with Yardley brilliantine (Father's favorite British hair product) on my hair before she combed it. She was in charge of making sure I dressed properly, in a short-sleeved white shirt, a dark blue short pants, white socks and a pair of well-polished black shoes. I waited nervously, like being summoned to the headmaster's office, for a car to arrive. Few paid attention to my part in this wedding tradition because they were busy with getting ready for the wedding feast early in the afternoon.

Relatives tied two sugarcane plants, at least the length of the car, one on either side of the top of the car, symbolizing happiness, I was told. I was the lone passenger in the car and didn't mutter a word to the driver on the way to my new brother-in-law's house. The driver tried some small talk but I was too preoccupied to respond to a total stranger. This was the second time I had ridden in a car. A year before, Father and his chauffeur had taken us children in a compact British car to visit Ipoh, where Eighth Uncle and his mistress lived. For me then it was like going to China, roads winding and meandering, causing dizziness and vomiting. I remember seeing my blood brother, a teenager then, living with Eighth Uncle and his family. In an amusement park, I saw a female singing in a large room with people dancing. I enjoyed the merry-go-round, but not for long because of my dizziness. I was thinking about that trip to Ipoh and feared the dizziness might return. It didn't because the distance was shorter and the road mostly straight without the abominable curves like the ones on the way to Ipoh. As we neared the house, I saw monkeys swinging on treetops, chattering away, incoherent to a non-monkey. And I could smell unmistakably we were not too far from an ocean. Also the sight of tall mangroves at a distance buttressed my intuition.

"Are you hungry?" my brother-in-law asked me politely as he led me inside the house. Nothing fancy but a clean two-story building, I noticed immediately. I wished for nothing but to lie down because I did feel some dizziness from the ride. My sister in her new cheerful dress soon appeared and introduced me first to the rest of her new family, her husband's brother and her mother-in-law. I nodded my head in acknowledgement, remaining silent at all times—a sign of good breeding. I told Small Sister I had to lie down somewhere because I wasn't feeling well. She led me to her room, away from the prying eyes so I could rest. "Is he fine?" someone asked my sister. Voices subsided. I closed my eyes, wishing the dizziness to quickly vanish, so I could appear like a normal child, meeting strangers and participating in the day's activities.

I recovered shortly and joined Small Sister and the crowd. Some relatives were warming up leftovers for lunch, which I graciously declined because Sister and her husband and I would soon be returning home for a wedding feast. The penetrating odor from the mixed leftovers was irresistible. The few I tasted seemed better than the feast itself.

"Come back again," I heard a chorus of voices as they waved to us while the car—with Small Sister, her husband and I, in the front seat—pulled away from the yard. I had never understood the meaning of my presence. Was it to escort them back to the house? Or something heavier than that? For sure it was another one of our inscrutable Chinese practices, dating back to ancient China.

Many of our relatives saw Small Sister's husband for the first time. A tall handsome young man with bushy eyebrows and a set of unbelievably white teeth, always wearing a broad smile when he talked. Nothing today could be worse than what he had gone through the day before. In fact there was not much of anything expected of him or the new couple except to return home to enjoy another fancy feast with friends and relatives of my family. It was a quiet affair with no Chinese music to celebrate the occasion.

I suspected the young couple had many ups and downs during their first year of togetherness. I prayed for divine intervention or a miracle for two complete strangers to live together for the first time, in search of a perfect harmony and love and understanding. Small Sister came home to visit many times alone and I always saw her crying in the presence of Mother. Her eyes always swollen and red. She might as well be an alien in the house because she moved around like a deaf-mute. Mother would not be the best person to offer advice if Small Sister experienced any marital discord and distress because Father had deserted her for other younger women years ago. Mother had shriveled up emotionally and sexually for years, which might have been one reason why she watched my every move like a hawk as I grew older and bolder. Father was beyond her reach, but I was forever in her presence. Mother and Small Sister seemed to whisper all the time. As a kid I wasn't allowed to hear the family secret. There must be trouble in paradise, in her marriage, I concluded. Why would she be crying every time she came home to visit the family? Tears of joy? Elation? I doubted.

NINE

The title "breadwinner" did not exist nor apply to our family because in reality the whole family toiled ceaselessly to keep our bodies and souls intact. Mother was the silent band leader who watchfully orchestrated our every move, making sure both Sister and I were singing, playing or marching to her tune, our slightest deviation evoking not only her suspicion but a stern call to obedience, duty and obligation. Though her physique was small, her presence spoke louder than words. She was incapable of using a tyrant's voice; most times Mother didn't seem to say much of anything but once you encountered her murmur or persistent, face-to-face presence, it meant resolute, unwavering action from us, neither resignation nor an opportunity for a protest or an argument. Her words were like a divine mandate. Clear and unequivocal. *Get busy with your hands! That is the reason for adopting you!* Her silence spoke eloquently. That this was her goal for me and my life became glaringly clear as I was dumped with more and more adult responsibilities by the time I reached ten.

In the beginning, my own inquisitiveness got the best of me and I was anxious and ready for action, wanting to learn and indulge in just about anything as part of growing up to be a man, I reasoned. I didn't think much of anything but responding wholeheartedly to excitement and opportunities around me. It required neither prompting nor coaxing. The truth: there was not much of anything going on in the village or home, except the maternal calls for endless daily chores in the farm and around the house. There was no blueprint for my existence known to me. Nor a prescribed path to puberty. I was, I thought, listening to my own inner voice, happy as a lark, nevertheless marching to a mixed tune. My own, temporarily suppressed, seemed less urgent than Mother's loud trumpet. Her commands, my duty. This made Mother supremely happy because what I was doing was fulfilling her dream. I was adopted *for my hands only.* And as I grew older, everything I did wasn't a game or a delight or a journey of discovery anymore. It dawned gradually, as assuredly as the rising sun in the east, that I was raised, praised and valued *for my hands only!*

That meant working many hours in the heat of the day in the farm—daylight hours after school and full-time on weekends. The only enemy was the rain or my silent protest.

That meant preparing and cooking, in the open air with a hole dug in the ground and barrel resting on solid concrete blocks, almost daily, barrels and barrels (in huge at least four-feet-tall metal drums) of slop for the gluttonous pigs; commercial feed, like copra, was available but too expensive and thrown in sparingly, mixed with the cheap home-made concoction.

That meant working side by side with Mother initially doing the rubber trees and later, as we grew older, by ourselves.

That meant assisting Father in his opium business. (Going to jail was always a possibility, a constant danger, if caught engaging in this known illegal activity.)

That meant I had no life of my own. Like in a communist state, where the individuals do not count or matter.

That meant I mustn't play with the neighborhood kids: because leisure (absent in my vocabulary while growing up) was a luxury my family could not afford or encourage.

That meant education was neither very important nor Mother's top priority because, as Mother would put it, "There are many people in our village who never did go to school and are doing just fine, working hard to feed many mouths and raising a decent family."

That meant I felt trapped, like an innocent but hungry squirrel wandering into a tantalizing cage on the trunk of a coconut tree, against my better judgment, realizing, even at the tender age of ten, that there had to be something better than this life of poverty and toil and unhappiness. Subsistence living. Cycle of poverty. I wanted something better! Beyond my hellish home and suffocating village!

I was allowed private thoughts and private ambitions. I wasn't allowed to express my personal desires openly and freely. Like all children in a traditional Chinese home, we were taught to obey our parents, follow their orders and pretend to live happily ever after. But something was churning deep inside my being. Like a small but a visible ripple at the bottom of a deep well. The inception of something, like the first weeks of a human conception. Inarticulate but there.

Where was Father in all this? In my life growing up? After all, he was the one, I was told, who adopted me from a city somewhere. Father's role in my life was like the occasional visits of our relatives. Now and then. Like two parallel lines that never seemed to meet or touch. Neither a constant nor a dependable factor in my life. But Father never failed me when I needed cash because he always carried cash in his pockets. Because of the nature of his opium business. He never once asked me why I needed the money. He was a man of few words, one who could be trusted with the deepest secrets of your life. I cannot retrieve from memory any words of wisdom, encouragement, or advice from Father. There was never a serious father-son conversation or a moment spent to know and appreciate each other. Father was always on the periphery of my life, like the clothes I wore, two distinct entities without bonding or mutuality. Sadly, I never knew what interested him in life or his early ambitions or his upbringing. He remained a total stranger to me, an enigma, while living under the same roof for a short period of time.

Maybe, just maybe, his non-assertive and non-aggressive personality did not help advance his career in his various business pursuits. He seemed incapable of advancing his ideas, ideals or personal thoughts. Eventually a victim of his own ineptitude and circumstances.

The opium business was Father's main preoccupation and he could count on the rest of the family to be there when he needed some assistance.

Before Brother was married, he and Mother helped Father with his opium business. Now that Brother had a growing family of his own, Sister and I were initiated into Father's opium enterprise, replacing Brother's and Mother's four hands, learning from A to Z how to prepare, make, package, and sell opium to the public in the small village.

I was the most qualified to work in this opium business because I grew up as a baby with Father in his opium den especially during his hours of business. The spiraling opium fumes from countless exhalations, I imagine now, were enough to put me to sleep or subdue any urge to cry or demand attention. Or make an addict of me after many critical hours of unprotected exposure to the opium as a baby, lying inches away from Father's opium-smoking clients. An unwilling partner in crime. I didn't hear any complaint from Father or his clients about my presence on the bed with them. And why should they? After all, most times their minds had gone up with the smoke into an illusory world, rendering them blissful and content, temporarily oblivious to their immediate surroundings.

There was nothing secret about Father's preparation of his raw opium for use and sale later to the public. It was done openly, right in the family kitchen, usually late in the afternoon because Sister and I were in school earlier in the day. We grew up seeing and smelling the whole operation many times and were called on to help with our hands in the different stages of the process. Father, Mother, and Brother had trained us every step of the way, not unlike cooking a pot of rice or making egg noodles the Chinese way, from scratch the first few times. Making opium was easy if you had abundant patience and time, even if you questioned the value of the drug.

Father got his raw opium, usually wrapped the size of a regular brick, from dealers who traded with the producers in Thailand (formerly Siam). Chinese had known opium smoking since the seventeenth century. But blamed the British in China for importing opium from India, corrupting and exploiting the Chinese in the process, and allowing it to flow generously to the south, eventually to Malaya, the country of my birth. Or wherever there was a Chinese immigrant community. I was never impressed with the value of the "black gold" that Father was dabbling with. In fact, most times I thought it was one of his personal hobbies, not something the family depended on for our livelihood. It was Father's selfish business experimentation, with more downs than ups in the months I was an active and willing participant in the operation. Earlier in his business pursuits, Father had been to Thailand many times, I was told, and it was rumored that my biological mother was a Siamese. Mother had called me *sima-yan* (son of Siam) in moments of anger and frustration with me. Thailand had licensed opium dens until 1959, when such privileges were revoked. I had never heard from Father or anyone that licenses were issued in Malaya. Bribery, large and small, was the key to safety and protection for Father and other people who operated opium dens, in the absence of our government's approval of an evil drug or a deleterious practice.

I never heard Father questioned or doubts raised about the quality of the raw opium he had procured. As a child every heavy package, before cooking, looked and smelled the same to me. The final product after the cooking process, I assume, could indicate the quality of the raw materials.

The paraphernalia for making opium included, in our case, two portable charcoal stoves (the cost of charcoal was too inhibitive for daily family cooking), two large size pots (with round bottoms), a bamboo fan, and a sturdy cotton sieve. The initial stage involved softening and dissolving the raw opium by boiling and boiling in at least two gallons of clean water. I had to watch carefully because too much heat from the charcoal could cause the opium to rise inside the pot and cause an overflow. The sin would not be dereliction of duty but profit lost to the fire. Punishable by scolding. And usually a prolonged almost unbearable fixed stare. Not from Father. But Mother. The bamboo fan could regulate the heat or the boiling solution. No switch to turn on or off or a button to push, but I could always add or remove a few glowing pieces of charcoal, depending on the intensity of the heat required, to expedite the cooking process. A long wooden spatula was used to stir the bubbling solution to keep it from from sticking to the bottom of the pot or overflowing.

No explanation was given—because I didn't ask—but the extended boiling time was critical in trying to extract the essence of opium from the original, thick, glutinous, black, raw opium, like the secret flavor from boiled soup bones or shrimp shells. After an hour or so (like an eternity) some of the water evaporated and we used a cotton sieve to strain the solution into a second pot. The filtered solution looked like dark black coffee with its distinct smell. Its aroma killed my every desire to feel its taste. I then added additional clean water to the residue in the first pot, and continued the process of boiling. Father was always there when it was time to strain the solution. Up to that point he would be smoking in his opium den, alone

(I don't think Father wanted his clients to know we were preparing opium in the house), while Sister and I were cooking the opium. I don't remember seeing Father home unless he needed a new batch of prepared opium. We boiled and strained at least three times. I don't remember what Father did with the residue. The final process was long and boring but critical and required careful vigilance and the patience of a saint.

Part of the reason we all remained silent during the entire time was to maintain some semblance of secrecy in our operation. More than that, our ears were trained to function like radio antennas, sensitively attuned and responsive to the slightest provocation by an approaching car or lorry. Who else—since father was the only one in the entire village at this time who owned a British vehicle—but the police would have the legitimate reason to prowl suspiciously in the village for potential law breakers or answer to rumors of criminal activities. One or twice our hearts would sink and our bodies would shake with fear, like a swift current snaking through the body, when a car would abruptly stop in front of the coffee shop—just across the road a few yards from our house. In reality it was someone seeking directions to a relative's house, usually hidden in the woods somewhere. The sound of an approaching car was sometimes a signal to dismantle the whole operation and run for safety into the fields of tall banana trees and thick tapioca plants, behind our kitchen. It was a consolation to know there was an option other than readily submitting to the handcuffs. We were never caught red-handed cooking opium, its distinct aroma wafting through dry air identifiable only by trained noses or a connoisseur of opium. Bribery, however large, did not calm our nerves completely.

Everything about cooking the opium was done in silence, without music or interruption in the background, and Sister or I constantly fanned or tamed the charcoal. Opium cooking was done before evening meals for a reason. I suspected the strong odor of opium, intermingling with the delicate smell of cooked garden vegetables or fish or cooked rice, would be chaotic to the taste bud. The family had been involved with bootlegging once, miraculously unmolested by the local police despite the strong smell of rice wine saturating the air. A coffee-cum-grocery store could be seen from our house and it wouldn't surprise me if a few shoppers had raised some questions, in their heads, about the smell. Rice wine and opium. But since they were not opium-smokers, it didn't matter much to them. They simply treated it as another one of the indistinguishable smells emanating from the animal farms or the surrounding areas.

After hours of boiling and evaporation, Father, using a slender wooden spatula, always tested, during the final stage of the cooking process, for the distinctive aroma of the optimal consistency of the product (definitely not a burnt smell). From watery to syrupy to sticky, the final product that emerged at the bottom of the pot was a black, gluey substance, like a thick paste, known as *chandoo* or prepared opium, with a silky, shiny surface. Priceless black gold! It was cooled, then stored in bottles for safekeeping.

Sister and I helped Father make the opium a few times and we were never caught or raided by the police. I suspect the police had a reason to stay away from this model Chinese community. Maybe there were more pressing matters in towns around us. Maybe we were out of focus because of our distance from the police station. Maybe Father and others in the business had fattened the pockets of those in leadership positions in the police force.

Surprisingly, our house was raided once, one late night when I was about twelve. Father had a special railing built for the second staircase inside the house. Instead of the balusters sitting on a fifteen-foot long two-by-four, Father had a carpenter build a hollow bottom support for the balusters. With two or three screws the side panel could be removed to expose the hollow cavity for hiding. That was Father's ingenuity. And strategy to fool law enforcement officers. At least fifteen feet long (the length of the railing) and six inches tall and six inches deep, big and spacious enough to hide raw or finished opium. And family treasures. This night there was a commotion going on inside the house. And enough nervous anxiety to explode and expose our criminal activity inside the house. I heard grave low men's voices, belonging to strangers not acquaintances or neighbors or relatives. Not in our Hockchiang dialect. Everything didn't make sense since I was rudely awakened from my sleep. The bed I shared with my cousin was next to the railing. I wasn't sure if there was any opium hidden in it tonight. I remember trembling, teeth chattering uncontrollably, seeing two police officers standing inches away from the railing questioning grownups in the family. A few times touching and leaning on the wooden railing. How could he not smell something? Especially if there was raw opium at the crime scene. Despite layers of cellophane wrap, the raw opinion exuded a distinct odor. This was before the days of the sniffing dogs. Maybe they were not trained to sniff drugs like modern dogs. We escaped police detection and felt invincible and victorious this time. The nervousness vanished when I awoke the next morning. But it bothered me: Whatever happened to the bribery and police protection?

Preparing the opium was the first step. There was a time we moved the cooking operation with the portable charcoal stoves to a building adjacent to our kitchen, not exactly a perfect hiding place to commit a crime. It had dirt floor, unlike the clean concrete floor in our kitchen, and smelled like a perfect hideaway for some of the unwanted nocturnal animals. One consolation: Brother hung unripe and ripened bananas, from our own farm, in this shed. An irresistible temptation to someone, like me, who loved bananas, anywhere, anytime. There was no ventilation except the door into the shed. On a hot day, the stench from the animals' dung was stifling.

Cooking the opium was only half the game. The next step was packaging it for sale.

Sister and I had to cut dried, soft bamboo leaves with scissors to package the opium for sale. We learned to handle the leaves to avoid the undersides, some of which were covered with fine hairs, a source of severe itching. With a pattern, we cut the leaves according to size. On our square wooden dinning table, with an adjustable homemade weighing machine, I would dole out, from a bottle, a large drop of prepared opium and placed it onto a cut leaf, weigh it for the right portion and Sister would then fold it into shape and warm it over a flame to solidify it. One package at a time. My fingers came too close to the flame a few times, not to my comfort. We were never told why, but later Father used cellophane instead of the bamboo leaves to package the prepared opium. I was glad of the change because cellophane was cleaner and easier to manage. Away from the flames and minor scorching. We made hundreds of these small packages for sale to the public. Father took most of them but left a few for local consumption. Father would be gone for days or weeks and returned when he needed fresh supply of prepared opium. The whole process would be repeated when the supply was exhausted.

Usually users of opium in the village would send sons or daughters to our house to purchase packages of prepared opium. A few were relatives and most were plain farmers in the village who depended on opium to keep them going from day to day. Sister and I did pocket some money from the sale without reporting everything to Mother or Father. I did it because I needed some pocket money since we were not paid for our time and effort.

Eating opium was not a common Chinese practice although employed in some parts of the world to cure dysentery, diarrhea and rheumatism, et cetera. It would be much easier to consume opium straight without the requisite tools. However to smoke opium, addicts or users must own the necessary paraphernalia or visit the nearest opium den. I knew of only two such venues in our village, one operated by Father in the house and the other by my opium-smoker tutor. I don't see many customers coming to Father's opium den at home, which was more like a place to entertain his opium friends or relatives. Father operated another one in a house in Kampong Koh, where he had his mistress. That opium den in Kampong Koh was busy day in and day out. Right in the middle of the town. And I knew intimately of three or four other operations within a block of houses. I would visit Father at his opium den when I needed some cash. Or to carry news of family matters to him, usually after school hours. My English school was not far from Father's opium den.

Every opium den looked and smelled the same. Never hidden away in the boondocks or beyond the arms of the police in a subterranean maze but arrogantly on display in private homes or in spacious rooms attached to a house or a shop. In the middle of a civilized world. Usually without windows. Dimly lit, except for the oil lamp in the middle of the bed for processing the opium for smoking. The bed, covered with a cool mat, was no more than a raised wooden platform, slightly bigger than a normal Chinese bed, with the smokers facing the door. The host lay on his side on one side (it didn't matter which side of the bed), the guest or client on the opposite side. They seemed ambidextrous. They rested their heads on wooden pillows. In between them was a small tray with an oil lamp, protected by a thick glass with the concentrated heat rising and coming out through a hole on the top. The glass top, which intensified the heat from the flame for processing the opium, looked thicker than normal. And lying next to the tray was the pipe, the most indispensable utensil for smoking. I had sat transfixed watching Father prepare the opium—without ever deviating from a set ritual—for his clients many times in his den. Strangely I was never tired of watching them perform the ritual, not knowing or questioning the reasons for their habit.

Yes, the pipe. It looked like a long bamboo stem (slightly thicker than a broom's handle), about two feet long, with a stone bowl screwed on to its side four inches or so from its end. Father used a metal dipper or thin wire to pick up a mass of thick opium and roast and twist it gently over the flame a few times, less than a minute at the most, then skillfully work it into the orifice (size of a pin's head) of the stone bowl after it was first warmed over the flame. Father then turned the mouth piece to the client, who in turn steadied the stone bowl over the oil lamp, you could hear the opium frizzle instantly, and the smoker readily inhaled strongly three or four times, thoroughly massaging the walls of his lungs, then exhaled the smoke through his nose and mouth. He would then sip some Chinese tea. The body collapsed into a bundle of satisfaction. I was sure I had watched a pantomime show. Except a slight cough now and then. Or the creaking of the wooden bed. Or the sound of tea dripping from a teapot. Without windows or ventilation (the operation had to remain hidden or under cover for fear of the police), the opium smoke and smell would stay in the room for a long time. Second-hand smoke, still an unknown factor at the time, saturated the air. The old clients would move to another bed for a rest or leave the den immediately after their turns. The whole process would be repeated again. And again. I never asked Father how much he charged his clients for his laborious work. Or did it come with the purchase of the prepared opium? Not a sensible way to earn a living. Neither a viable scheme to get rich. Essentially he was working for the police, with very little left in his own pockets.

I, in one strange way, personally benefited from Father's opium business. Granted, he would console and enrich me with some cash every now and then. The family never counted on Father's precarious business enterprises for financial security. We knew all along he did it for his own personal gratification. There was nothing for the family to boast about in Father's business acumen or the profitability of his business. But Father's opium business bestowed on me an unprecedented opportunity to meet and mingle with, every July of every year (for a few years in my early teens), a troupe of Chinese opera performers, who would descend by the ocean in Pasir Panjang to perform during the birthday of a god, whom many fishermen in our village looked up to for protection from evil or harm out in the unknown, at times perilous sea. A few men who came with Grandpa from China to settle in the village were fishermen and some of their descendants had continued the family tradition. A few, tragically, had lost their lives out in the turbulent sea. The superstitious few believed some evil spirits were offended, angry or displeased with sacrilegious human conduct, snatching away the lives of their loved ones. Like some kind of punishment for deviant behavior by wayward believers. Each year the fishermen of the village would put on a Chinese opera to celebrate their god's birthday, a way to worship and appease him. Elaborate, irenic offerings of foods—mostly fruits and meats—were carefully arranged on the altar. Bundles of spirit money and incense were also burned in the god's honor.

Growing up, I was warned never to walk near or go inside a temple, big or small, humble or majestic, erected to the gods because, according to Mother, "they are evil and they might hurt you, because of your carelessness, by taking away your life." So I grew up fearing the temples and also tiny places of worship erected by Indians in nearby villages. Sacred, but dangerous to non-believers, Mother always said. I grew up believing the spirits from the underworld are alive and everywhere. Few were benign. Most were capricious, irascible, and easily offended by humans. The only safe place, harmless place, was the church. Every other place of worship was considered bad and evil, according to Mother.

One of Mother's brothers, a strong and tall farmer in his early forties, who seemed like a giant of a man to me, died mysteriously in an outhouse, behind a coffee shop in the village. It was the devil who did it, Mother said. Many others, no relations to our family, in the village concurred. The family's godson, about my age, playful and energetic, always wearing a serene smile, mysteriously died after a brief illness. It was the devil who did it, Mother said. Many religious fanatics in the village also concurred. The chief suspect in both cases was not any known physical causes or terminal diseases but some unknown vengeful evil spirits, according to neighbors and friends and relatives. At age ten, I didn't know anything better and had no reason to question my elders. People, some Christians, many non-believers, talked ignorantly and they believed in their own voice, that some evil spirits had taken away the innocent souls of my uncle and godson. They died the same year, a few months apart. Mother was inconsolable about her brother's sudden demise. She had her doubts and questions but she was positively sure it was the maleficent doings of the devils. In that superstitious milieu I lived and breathed, in fear of the wandering dissatisfied spirits, avoiding all the dark and unusual places, anything that looked out of the ordinary, be it a tree or a stone or a mount or whatever; "Respect your surroundings at all times," Mother continued to sound the alarm. Always on the look out for the unseen and the invisible forces around you. Worse, it could be the spirits of deceased family members, surfacing to get the living, for being mistreated when they were alive, or willfully neglected before and after they departed to the world beyond.

Much of what I knew about gods and religious beliefs or superstitions came from Mother and others in the village. Religious training or education did not exist nor were the village folks, including my own family, inquisitive enough to venture into the world of books, to gain some slim perspective or cursory knowledge of the religions and religious practices, prevalent among our relatives and neighbors. The village Christian pastor held the key to our religious safety and survival and protection from the evil ones.

Burning incense or offering foods or paper money to a god or a deity in a temple, big or small, was never a part of any organized religious activity like the church I grew up in. In fact worshippers in temples did not belong to any organized religion, with memberships and regular dues or tithes. Common folks visited their local temples and gods, many were humans once, when they needed succor or solace or escape from life's tormenting vicissitudes. But not every Sunday or at an appointed time, adhering to a schedule. Appearance at temples or attendance was random, most times optional. They could offer incense and prayers in any temple anywhere in the country in their travels. They could be the only souls inside a temple seeking divine guidance or spiritual intimacy with their god, embodied in a miniature carved model or one painted on paper, with names of the gods written in fine bold calligraphy. People who entered such places, including myself, would never doubt the mysterious presence of someone or something. Like a light breeze touching your skin. You felt it, the divine presence. For me it was something, amorphous, not someone.

Every year, by the ocean in Pasir Panjang, in front of a small temple to their merciful god, protector of the seas, the village fishermen, their pals, and benefactors erected a huge edifice, like a house with tall ceilings, the whole front removed exposing the centre, the main stage, with empty spaces all around, for a few days of Chinese operatic performances, a respite from the doldrums of village life, for those who professed to be heathens and worshippers of idols. Many Christians whom I knew stealthily bicycled to the shore to enjoy a few hours of free performances.

This huge building, sitting on round posts five to six feet above ground, a few feet away from the sea water on a sandy beach, was solidly built for operatic performances and as temporary living quarters for everybody connected with the troupe, children, and the stage hands. More than fifty people claimed it as their temporary domicile. And there was room for Father to ply his trade, performing his ritual in a makeshift opium den for some members of the troupe.

I had the best seat in the house, so to speak, roaming freely the back stage, intrigued by the multi-colored costumes and meeting the real people and faces behind the elaborate facial make-ups, like camouflage, employed in all Chinese operas, to indicate their different roles in a story unfolding on the stage. For this particular week, these people, I felt, consecrated their time and their bodies to a holy cause—speak no evil, do no evil, in praise of the protector of the seas, while entertaining us simple village folks, once a year. We sat on wooden benches, cooled by the ocean freeze, fed by vendors proud of their delicious offerings of foods, desserts and exotic snacks, made and sold only on such occasions. There was only one severe impediment to my enjoying all the variety of foods and that was my fear of the flimsy outhouse on stilts with the ocean water below, ever so gently lapping the stilts, catching your discharge. You watched the ocean beneath you as you squatted on two precarious planks. The outhouse stood like a jetty built out into the ocean. The less I ate the less the possibility of having to walk the rickety plank, seeming to sway with the ocean waves, from the beach to the outhouse thirty or more feet out into the sea. Dark brown or black human discharge was deposited along the shoreline. That didn't help the appetite for exotic snacks. But food, while a major attraction, was less interesting than watching the opera itself.

As the always-appreciative audience faced the stage, we were constantly watched by, and in the presence of, the protector of the seas, in a small temple behind us. At least once a year, I was in the presence of a deity acknowledged and worshipped by the fishermen in my village, and participated innocently in ceremonies seeking divine blessing, favor, and protection in the years to come. Most importantly, safety and divine protection for all fishermen who depended on the seas for their simple livelihood. Growing up, we often bicycled to this place, waiting for the fishermen to bring in their catch, however meager, and engaged in quiet bargaining for the fruits of their toil.

I followed Father to the annual religious festival and to the stage where I had the unique privilege to learn a thing or two about Chinese opera first hand from performers and stage hands, as well as those sharing the opium bed with Father. Aspiring actors were either born into an acting family, learning and perpetuating the art form from father to son, or they could apprentice themselves to professional actors, usually from a young age. One peculiar practice or tradition had persisted: a person was trained to play a specific role or part, for his or her entire professional life. From the beginning, one picked (based on natural talent or proclivity or mentoring) a role from four main categories to learn: male, female, painted face or comedian. Male roles were either military or civil. All male actors were trained to play the different male roles. (But backstage from year to year I saw how one female actor with elaborate facial makeup and brightly colored costume would transform herself into a tough-looking military general. She wasn't tall but had the physique and voice to match the demanding role. I recognized her because of her gold teeth. I had not seen her in female roles.) Each role within the male category had its distinct costume, voice, and mannerisms on stage. Having watched a few Chinese operas on stage, I could spot or identify instantly any role in a Chinese opera by keen observation of its costume, voice, and mannerisms. For example, emperors and members of the imperial families wore yellow; men of virtue or high rank wore red; low-ranking officials wore blue; et cetera. A scholar or a mandarin official displayed refined manners and a general polished disposition. Old man used a soft but firm voice, a young man a high-pitched shrill. Every male role had its distinct costume, facial makeup, shoes, voice, walk, and mannerisms.

Mannerisms included movements and gestures involving the eye, hand, body and leg movements. Only a trained eye could grasp the full range of symbolic representations by subtle, intricate and stylized use of eyes, facial expressions, fingers, fists, hands, and sleeves. Yes, sleeves, long strips of white silk added to the sleeves of the original costumes to create movements like waves. When a woman held up one sleeve over her face, it meant she was embarrassed or bashful about something. And if she shook her head slightly while holding up one sleeve over her face, it implied doubt or disbelief. If she flicked a sleeve, it indicated anger or disgust. There were myriad ways a woman could use a sleeve to indicate she was going through a doorway, was exposed to cold in winter or heat in summer, or was returning home from a trip somewhere. But all I could think of was how easy it was for women to wipe their mouths with the long sleeves at dinner tables!

What I was truly after in every performance, usually based on mythology or history, was the highly stylized fighting scenes of warriors in bright-colored costumes—small flags strapped to their backs, hats gaily adored with pheasant feathers, high-soled boots—wielding swords and spears, ducking and twisting their bodies in spectacular somersaults all over the stage. There were moments I sat nervously on edge, or stood on the bench, fearing the flying swords and spears might cut someone badly, as gongs and cymbals worked themselves into a frenzy, like music in an old movie with Tarzan engaged in a fierce battle with his enemies in the jungle.

Without the orchestra of seven or eight players, usually seated at the left-hand corner of the stage (a view from the audience), there wouldn't be Chinese opera. For example, *Tan P'i Ku*, a small drum, is the most important instrument for keeping time, indicating entry and exit movements and when for a performer to start singing. Percussion instruments, which included drums, gongs, and cymbals, provided musical accompaniment for military and non-military scenes and stirring moments. And string instruments provided musical accompaniment for singing.

None of us could understand any of the words, spoken or sung, because they were all in a different dialect, Hockkien, even though it used the same written Chinese characters as my dialect, Hockchiang. Most times few in the audience understood the dialogues or monologues on stage because all performances were executed in Hockkien, granted all of us hailed originally from the same province in mainland China. I went because of Father's opium business with the troupe. I went because it was one free entertainment. I went knowing Christians in the village condemned everything at the religious festival as heathen and the work of the devil. Few knew Father catered to the needs of a few opium smokers on stage each year during the festival. I went because I felt privileged to go backstage to rub shoulders with the performers.

As I grew older, I could see Father's continued involvement with opium had a sorry impact on the family and his own eventual health. He would usually spend some time at home going after Mother for money when he didn't fare well in his business. Rather quietly, most times, without getting anyone suspicious of his presence. By now Mother was practically a widow because Father was raising another family with a mistress in another town. He didn't come home to spend time with the family, but more and more to harass Mother, squeezing every ounce of hard-earned money from her, the way I squeezed water from my clothes before hanging them up to dry.

It seemed it was his right to beg, but she had none to spare. That meant more hardships for Sister and me, who had to work longer hours on the farm, helping Brother and his wife with endless daily chores, procuring raw materials from near and far to feed the pigs.

The ingredients for the pigs' mush, cooked at least three times a week in a huge oil drum over an open fire, came from banana plants, cassava roots, and sweet potato leaves (some as long as ten to fifteen). They all came from our own farm, grown year round because we lived in the tropics. Sister and I spent long, boring hours gathering and chopping bundles and bundles of sweet potato leaves. Once banana plants had their fruits, they served no useful purpose but would eventually rot away. Many—like the Malays, Indians, and other Chinese ethnic groups—used banana leaves to wrap exotic foods and cook in them, adding a special scent to the foods when opened the first time. Some—like the Malays and Indians—used them like plates for meals.. Well fertilized, some banana plants could grow as tall as ten feet or higher and measure more than a foot in diameter. One banana plant (belonging to the rhizome family) could produce clusters of plants around its roots after a period of time. We tried not to hurt the young ones when cutting down the old ones. The robust, clumsy, big ones were as heavy as some rubber tree trunks and we (usually boys and men) would carry the whole plants home on our shoulders. They too had to be chopped up like the sweet potato leaves and cooked in a huge oil drum.

At an early age, Sister and I were trained to master the heavy-duty cleavers, each pursuing a different speed, the goal to chop up, without cutting off your fingers, all the leaves and the banana tree-like plants. Harvesting cassava, one species grown solely for animal consumption, involved uprooting them first with a *changkul* (something like a hoe), breaking up the clusters, brushing away all the clinging dirt with bare hands, then hauling them home in gunny sacks to be grated by hand. Hundreds of these roots, big and small, long and short, had to be grated. The grater was the size of a sturdy washboard. When we had time we would grind cassava roots, employing a special machine, using our legs to keep the machine running (like a treadle), to make our own starch for cooking and clothes. After processing, the lumpy residue would be used to feed the pigs. Like cooking Chinese foods, it was all in the tedious preparations. Hours spent harvesting. Hours spent preparing them for cooking. Imagine stirring the thick mixture of banana plants, sweet potato leaves, and cassava roots in an oil drum that sat on huge cement blocks and towered over me. In the open air. There was always a person there to keep the fire going (in the hot afternoon sun) and to stir the mixture for even cooking. Feeding the noisy, hungry pigs daily was the job of Brother and his wife, sloshing in mud and dirt to the chorus of blissful noises from satisfied pigs.

Preparing the soil and high ridges for growing sweet potatoes and cassava meant paying some women laborers in the village for the hard work with the *changkul.* I tried every which way to avoid exposing myself to the heat of the oppressive sun. A big hat did not reduce the level of sweat and discomfort. If only I could just work during evening hours of each day. Because Brother and his wife were uneducated and Sister and I were children, our lives depended on the land for survival. Mother ultimately gave us orders to do the work, knowing Brother was behind in everything that went on in the farm. There was no escape from the farm and the pigs.

Because of the middlemen, we didn't get much for the pigs. It was quite a sight to watch how pigs were caged and sent off to a slaughterhouse. One man would try to pull the tail of a pig, the other holding and directing the opening of a rattan-woven cage in front of a pig, gradually releasing the tail and pushing the reluctant one into the cage. There was absolutely no room for any of the pigs to move or stretch once inside these cages. After they were weighed, they were stacked on top of each other, driven away in a lorry, some squealing all the way to the slaughterhouse somewhere. I think Brother got most of the money from the sale of pigs.

Mother, like a taskmaster, wasn't about to let me stray from farm work after returning from school each day, unless there was some divine intervention, like a sudden rainstorm. Mother was under pressure to produce more to make some money. More so if Father didn't do well in his opium business. It was no consolation to be reminded (a million times) that Mother, as a young girl, helped her father raise a family of four or five boys and a girl or two. Her mother died young, and being the eldest, she was like a surrogate mother to all her siblings. All her life she knew nothing but work and work to survive. "You can't blame her for that? She had a hard life," so I was told. Yes, I saw all her brothers, my uncles, living within a radius of less than two miles, raising families of their own, but their lives undistinguished and confined to the walls of the kampong, for lack of vision, drive, education and opportunities. I disdained them for their lack of success in life. I don't want any part of Mother's admirable and much talked about sacrifices in raising her siblings. I don't think she deserved an award of some kind. Neither was it a blessing to be told (not a few times) that "Mother adopted me and promised Brother that someday I would be his helper." Even at age ten, I was beginning to question what else was in store for me as Brother's helper on the farm. My skin color and my look (Mother labeled me a *sima-yan* for some obvious reasons!) didn't exactly help me acclimatize to a village life, having been adopted from an urban milieu. I looked and felt like an outsider. I suspected something was going on but I didn't know who or what was the cause of my growing misery. I felt deprived, neglected, and hindered from growing and advancing socially and intellectually. And I sensed something better beyond the horizon, from the core of my being, not a calculated response to any external propaganda or influence. The church in no way advanced my personal cause. Later my high school teachers were taciturn, as though following an interdict ordered by a judge, about exposing us to the world of possibilities, excitement and opportunities out there.

I felt trapped in a doldrum of mindless activity, valued for my hands only. Worse, I didn't know who to share this personal predicament with. I never believed in prayers, like some of the teenagers in the village. I cared openly for this earthly life, not some nebulous heaven somewhere in outer space. I wasn't seeking temporary respite. Now I saw Father's indulgence in opium contributed partly to my agony of defeat. He was my only hope for an escape from servitude but doomed because of his inescapable bondage to opium addiction and his lackluster opium business

Opium, in my mind, wrought deleterious effects on Father. Years later, I witnessed his wrecked body on his deathbed, a pathetic, shrunken body ravaged by opium, not illness or old age. All skin and bones and tearful sunken eyes and not much of anything else. "In his death bed, he cried out for opium, begging me sorrowfully," Mother said, unsympathetically, realizing that at this stage feeding Father more opium would only prolong his agony and suffering. I wasn't there in his last moments but knew death was knocking on the door. He died in his late fifties.

TEN

The birth of a first grandson, Brother's third child, was an occasion to celebrate with controlled fanfare and a small extravagant feast for close relatives and friends of the family. Females are dispensable, like some undesirable pests, but a male grandchild is a good omen. He will carry on the family name. Like the arrival of a much sought after heir to the throne! I did not sense the same exuberance and unbridled jubilation with the birth of the first two grandchildren. They were females. I might be small but I wasn't blind or deaf. They were tolerated with as much disinterestedness and warmth as you would for a stray. This male grandchild was special in the eyes of generations of your ancestors, worth more than all the pigs and rubber trees in the farm. The celebration provided a brief moment for the family to forget and transcend life's inexorable poverty. Ultimately it meant a further drain on the family's limited resources. When so many people around you were eking out a living from the good earth, no one spoke about surviving on the verge of poverty. Or an additional mouth to feed, in our expanding family. You suffered quietly.

The word poverty was never in our vocabulary. We Chinese—at least my Hockchiang people—were not inclined to advertise our private sorrows, disappointments and life's vicissitudes. We rightly deserved being mocked and pigeonholed as "inscrutable" or "secretive" by non-Chinese around us.

But I knew we were poor because I was eating thin porridge three meals a day. Seven to ten times more water than the rice in a cooking pot, stretching quantity and thinning nutrition to feed the hungry mouths. And a growing family. My throat became unduly sensitive to the mushy texture of the gruel and, like an emetic, caused me to throw up time and again. Vegetables from our own garden and salted fish mercifully, at times, added some color and taste to the bland porridge. Or the porridge was simply cooked with a few yellow or purple sweet potatoes, making it palatable to swallow in the absence of salted fish or vegetables. Friends' tables always seemed irresistible and had more variety if not abundance or ostentatious display of class or money. Mother or Brother occasionally spent money on some fresh vegetables and pork from the town market. Especially after sales of pigs or rubber or during the few Chinese festivals. Especially during the Chinese New year. At least once a year I had plenty to fill my belly. Such times were few but greatly cherished and greeted with happiness, like our tree squirrels dancing with joy on finding the first nuts.

I knew we were poor because our lives depended on the well being of our pigs and the productivity of our rubber trees. And on the mercy and prices of the markets beyond our village and control. And on the over-used, fragile, calloused hands commanded to do all the dirty work. And acknowledging stolidly that nothing was about to change in the foreseeable future. We would continue to cling precariously to the wheel of poverty.

I knew we were poor because I often yearned for relatives to visit us because they would bring some goodies and fruits and cookies for us children. Thank God for this Chinese custom: you never visit your relatives empty-handed. The sight of an approaching relative meant some manna from heaven. And children would be the first to abandon everything and rush to the guest with open arms and carry the gifts to the house. Unless the guest insisted, it was impolite to attack the gifts, however desperate you were, in the presence of the guest. And if you were one of the family's favorite relatives, Brother's wife would be out in the backyard chasing a chicken to spice up a simple noodle soup for our guest. At least on such occasions there would always be a few crumbs left under the table for us to savor. But such visits were infrequent, like storms on a bright, serene, cloudless day.

I knew we were poor because I was praying hard for someone to die (it didn't matter who) because there would be abundant food on the tables for those involved with the funeral. Perhaps carrying the banners in the funeral procession. Or ushering the mourners along the way or at the gravesite. Or pretending to be a relative of the deceased. Your attendance guaranteed you a free meal, usually at a local restaurant. You could be certain that most family members of the deceased would be oblivious to your identity or your presence at the funeral. When you were hungry you felt no shame or guilt for taking advantage of any situation, even tears and sorrow over the loss of a loved one.

I knew we were poor because Mother made Sister and me tap the rubber trees until some stopped producing latex. Or literally dried up. A normal human being knew that the trees, after many indiscriminate tappings (like removing thin layers of flesh from a body), needed rest and time to regenerate, allowing new bark to grow and mature. But driven by survival instinct under abnormal circumstances, we had blindly forced the trees to produce and produce, finally exhausting most of them, the older ones especially.

As children we spent long carefree hours, interrupted only by hunger, and played many innocent games under the lush green canopy of the rubber trees around our house. We searched the ground with our keen eyes, like chickens after plumb worms, and picked the shiny dark-brown nuts of the trees, unintentionally thwarting nature's way of insuring its posterity. We competed to see who had the most in our tin cans. And some of us used them as marbles. Left on the ground, undisturbed by children or the squirrels or the forever-voracious wandering pigs, with their stout noses ceaselessly grubbing for whatever seemed edible, the abundant nuts—like seeds—would give birth to young seedlings, dotting the weedless leaf-covered landscape.

Our family inherited a few acres of land with rubber trees from Grandpa. Four decades later I grew up seeing rubber trees in every nook and niche of the village. Many owners of rubber trees, including Grandpa, became rich, especially in the years between 1911 and 1929. Not only were rubber-tired vehicles used to transport troops and supplies during World War I, but the automobile industry developed phenomenally in the United States of America, which imported more than half of the world's supply of natural rubber.

In 1839, Charles Goodyear, an American from Connecticut discovered the process known as vulcanization, which enhanced the strength and elasticity of the natural rubber. Germany first experimented with synthetic rubber during World War I when their supplies of natural rubber were cut off by the Allied blockade. German and American scientists separately continued to research for a more viable synthetic product, but it was Germany that came up with two types of synthetic rubber at the onset of World War II (1939).

In 1942, Japan marched into the rubber producing lands in the Far East (including my country Malaya), cutting off nine-tenths of the supply of natural rubber to the United States. Overnight the government of the United States developed a huge synthetic rubber industry to meet the challenges of World War II. We blamed the Germans for creating the synthetic monster that killed the world's interest in natural rubber, thus impacting my family directly, which depended on natural rubber for survival. First we blamed the Japanese for the economic devastation, then the Germans deserved our full hatred and disdain. Unpredictable international demand and prices for natural rubber had created hell for me personally because I had to work harder and harder tapping rubber trees just to stay alive. The Germans created a new hell for us all!

The ubiquitous rubber trees (*Hevea brasiliensis)* that grew in our front yard and back yard, and everywhere in between in the village and beyond, came originally from the Amazon valley in South America via experimentation in the Royal Botanical Gardens of England, Ceylon and Singapore. Malaya, because of its geographic location, had the requisite rainfall and temperature to grow these Amazon trees, known for their excellent quality latex. Columbus was said to be the first European to have seen native Indians in South America play with a heavy black ball made of rubber.

At age seven, I quickly learned that the rubber trees, along with our beloved pampered pigs, would be our salvation, a viable source of income for the entire family. Soon—on weekends and school holidays—Sister and I followed Mother at the first of dawn from tree to tree, cleaning the cups for collecting the latex while watching and learning the skill of tapping rubber. It was our initiation into a new occupation, not a pastime. It was fun initially because we had something new to learn and do, not realizing then Mother depended solely on rubber for some meager income to carry out her duties as head of the family. Father was living on a different planet, totally unaware of our daily toils and struggles. I was impatient for Mother or Brother to let me tap the trees. It looked easy to a novice.

By age eleven, during weekends and holidays, I was up at two or three in the morning. After having a cup of hot Ovaltine with biscuits, I dressed warmly and followed brother on a bicycle to his holding, about ten miles away. Located beyond the boundary of our village, the three-acre holding was bounded on one side by a stream at least twenty feet wide, and in some places just as deep, with clear water and little fish, and on another side by rubber trees and thick bushes. On Brother's land, you could see, unhindered, clear rows and rows of rubber trees, making you feel exposed, surrounded by thick bushes all around you.

I never liked the feeling of goose bumps or chills and shivers through my freezing body pedaling behind Brother because of the early morning cold air or my nervous reactions to something I thought I saw in the dark, unfriendly eyes in motion, either coming at me, or trailing behind me or fading behind the trees or into the woods. And riding a bicycle across a twenty-feet long and five-feet wide, rickety, wooden bridge without railing terrified me because I knew the water was deep and I was not a swimmer. My fear of heights was worse and crippling. After the bridge, we cut a path diagonally through a rubber plantation that covered thousands of acres and had been owned and operated by the British since the turn of the twentieth century, when rubber was first introduced into British-controlled Malaya. There we encountered well-trained Indian tappers the British had brought over from India. By the time we arrived at Brother's holding each morning, I was a nervous wreck, having gone through many paralyzing emotions. I chose not tell Brother of my mental or emotional state.

You had to start early if you had only two hands (Brother's) to tap hundreds of trees before dawn—slightly over three hundred trees in his holding. The real reason for the pre-dawn start, however, was that the flow of latex was greatest in the early hours of the morning before the sun rose. A little heat would cause the latex to harden, strangling its natural flow and reducing the yield from the trees.

My job was to follow Brother from tree to tree, cleaning the cups or replacing a broken one or one too small for its purpose, placing each cup firmly on its snug-fitting holder, a wire strapped around the trunk. It sat right beneath a metal tap, which directed the flow of latex into the cup. Brother never once said he appreciated my company. Despite news of rubber tappers in some localities being attacked by tigers and other predators, we continued to brave the cold and the wild surroundings to tap rubber trees because our livelihood depended on them.

We took a break after tapping all the trees, at times lending a helping hand to others closer to home who were still working the rubber trees. Some villagers tapped from one holding to another, in different locations, allowing younger members of the families to collect the latex. Division of labor and practiced efficiency allowed the veterans to engage in the difficult task of tapping.

As the sun slowly rose, peeking through the dense bushes, looking bright and cheerful, we always had something hot to drink and we loved to dunk biscuits in it. Brother loved candies and there were wrappers on the ground to prove it. He would pick up an old wrapper, covered with dew, hold it up skyward to show me the design, stretch the corners and place it on his bare arm and slap it hard to produce something like a tattoo. He did this many times, as though trying to prove something to me. I tried it. It worked every time. We shared a smile with each attempt. I don't remember anything momentous or critical said between us. Brother's wife was a storyteller, not Brother. Though whistling came naturally to him, he was stingy with his talent. Sometimes we tried to catch the little fish in the stream. They looked like fighting fish and were difficult to catch without the right gear.

After our break, we would check to see if the latex had stopped dripping, signaling the right time to start collecting it. We each carried a two-gallon pail, collecting the latex painstakingly from each tree, emptying the pail into a larger container when it became heavy. (When we returned the next morning, we first removed the thin strip of dried rubber on the bark from the previous tapping—wound into a ball and later sold as inferior grade rubber—before commencing to tap again.) The left hand carried the pail, leaving the right hand to pick up each cup, pouring its content into the pail, then letting the left hand hold the cup sideways, wiping the cup of every drop of latex with the right index finger. Once in a while I lost my grip—if the cup was wet and slippery or too large to handle—and the cup slipped disastrously into the pail, causing it to splash all over, especially into my face and eyes, not to mention my clothes, already smelly and sticky with sweat. I tried to be careful each time to avoid wasting our precious latex. With two pails and our slow—almost leisurely—movement from cup to cup, it usually took us a half an hour or more to accomplish the task.

I always had a sense of having done something successfully while riding home on my bicycle, the warm air caressing my face and neck. I knew the same process would be repeated hundred more times in the days to come. I wanted nothing more than a chance to hold that sharp gouge and prove to everyone I could do the job—tapping.

A few times we lost some precious latex after all the hard work because of a sudden, unexpected downpour. Although we tried not to venture out in a drizzle to tap rubber. the family—from day to day—had no way to know impending weather conditions, even in our own back yard. Once in a while we listened to Chinese music on the radio (hooked to a battery the size of a car battery), not to any weather report...if there was such a thing then. We knew the seasonal trends, certainly, and were able to sensing some changes in climatic conditions. *The wind is coming our way*, someone might announce. *The stars have disappeared tonight*, could be another observation. *I smell something in the air* (signaling a change in weather), would be a voice to heed. *Do you see the dark clouds over there?* I could see Brother's wife up on her feet hurriedly gathering all the clothes from the clotheslines strung across the front of the house. Dark clouds meant rain to all of us. We knew rain was good for our crops and vegetables, but it could be disastrous during the critical morning hours, if you depended on rubber trees for subsistence.

A few yards from the house, we had built a shed to house two machines used to turn the rubber into sheets for sale. There Mother and Brother's wife usually took over the next step in processing the latex. They added some clean water to the latex, passed the mixture through a sieve, then poured it into a twenty-by-sixty-inch wooden tank. About six inches high. More latex meant more tanks. Then they added a tablespoon or so of a coagulant with water into the tank. (A few villagers, especially women, had committed suicide swallowing the highly toxic liquid sodium silicofluoride, which burned the flesh as it traveled down the throat, I heard.) I always watched with amazement as we gently stirred the thickening latex with a spatula, before we placed wooden slats at every foot across the tank, with each compartment measuring twelve-by-twenty inches.

After we cleaned up at the shed, we returned to the house. There were other chores to be done. Working on pigs' food was the next top priority. Within an hour or two, Sister and I would return to the shed to find the white milky latex had turned into white, doughy mass (coagulum) floating in the liquid in the tank. We would lift each piece (twelve-by-twenty inches, about two inches thick) and lay it on a slanted platform. The solution of organic matter and minerals dripped onto my legs, hands, and other parts of my body. It burned your eyes if you were not careful. Then, using a two-foot-long, the thickness of a broomstick, as a roller, we pressed the rubber down with all the weight and strength we could muster, crisscrossing once or twice, to flatten it to the thickness required by the rollers of the machine. The soft, doughy coagulum was malleable. While Sister turned the wheel to start the rollers going, I held the thick mass and fed it through them to further flatten it evenly, squeeze out every drop of solution in it, and achieve the desired thickness and shape, thin enough so we could dry them in the open air instead of heating them inside a smokehouse. After the next machine cut a design on each sheet, we transferred the sheets from the shed to the house and hung them up like clothes to be dried in the hot tropical sun. After a few days, the sheets turned from white to light brown and became firm and elastic raw rubber.

As we did with the pigs, our family sold the rubber to middlemen. One was a tall woman who always wore a smile on her face and gold earrings. She spoke a different dialect and was not one of us. She often carried news, both good and bad, about people who did business with her. We enjoyed some of her tall tales. The other was a tall man, about the same age as the woman, who was one of us in the village. A man of few words. We would sell the rubber to the one who offered us the best price.

After the war, the price of rubber rose and fell like the ocean waves. I knew it had an effect on Brother, now a father to a growing family. I knew it had an effect on Mother because she had obligations beyond the immediate family, like births, weddings and funerals. I knew Sister and I were finally allowed to tap because more hands were needed to boost the family's meager income. We cursed the Germans for the world's decreased demand for natural rubber.

Brother explained, in his own way, how to avoid cutting too deep into the wood of the tree because that would eventually end its economic life. Know the bark of the tree and how to take good care of it, he insisted. That is the source of our livelihood, I gradually understood after spending time with Brother. He made sure I knew my tapping could aid and prolong or shorten the economic life of each tree.

Covering the bark of a rubber tree is a layer called the cork. Then comes the hard outer layer of the bark, which has few latex vessels. Next to it is the soft layer of the bark, which contains the most latex vessels. Pay undivided attention to this layer because this is where the rubber is coming from. Between the inner wood and the soft bark is a critical layer called the cambium, thin as a sheet of paper, which the knife must avoid bruising it because it is the seat of growth with new cells for the wood and the bark.

When a tree is five years old, it is ready for tapping. The first time I tapped a tree, after many months of trailing Mother later Brother from tree to tree, from one location to another, and learning everything they could teach me about tapping, I approached the bark with a great deal of uncertainty and nervousness for fear of tapping too close into the cambium. Tapping involved skillfully removing a shaving of bark with a sharp gouge, following a pattern that had been set for me—the first cut made by Brother or Mother, about four feet from the ground. Depending on the tree's diameter, the length of the shaving was anywhere from one-half to one-quarter of its circumference. Subsequent tapping followed same track until a rectangular panel had been shaved to within a few inches from the ground. That could take weeks and months. While waiting for a completed panel to regenerate with new bark and latex vessels, we continued tapping by starting a new panel above the old one or on the opposite side of the tree.

To preserve or extend the economic life of a tree, every move with the sharp gouge had to be just right, which required endless practice and uncommon dexterity. If the tapping was too shallow, reaching only the hard layer of the bark, the yield would be less substantial. I often tapped too deep into the wood, shaving unevenly beyond the cambium, thus preventing the bark from regeneration. If tapping is done correctly, a panel will regenerate itself in a short time, extending the economic life of the tree.

I grew up to regret falling in love with the rubber trees, eager to master a new skill. That love turned after a few years into intense hatred because I realized my slave labor—with the farm, the pigs, and the rubber trees—did little to ameliorate either my own sense of hopelessness or the family's pathetic subsistence living. Where did all the money go? I could see, without prying too deeply into family finances, that we didn't get much money from the sporadic sales of pigs and rubber. Market prices fluctuated unpredictably, seemed more down than up. I never witnessed an outburst of a we-are-all-so-lucky praise to the Almighty or an excuse for a family celebration because of the generosity of the world markets. As a family, we were not going anywhere, only staying afloat, navigating the course skillfully to avoid starvation.

Most students in my mission school anticipated spending their holidays doing fun things, or doing nothing, or visiting interesting places and people. (We attended school from January to December, divided into four terms, with four holidays, the longest about five weeks in December, at the close of the academic year.) I dreaded having to spend those days—supposedly of leisure, relaxation and recuperation from books—in intensive labor, like the slaves under Pharaoh's taskmasters, in stories I heard in my Sunday school class. Mother would be at my bedroom door, sitting on the floor like a monk, next to a flickering kerosene lamp with its rising, light black smoke, every morning at two thirty or so without fail, quietly calling my name as not to disturb the rest of the household. She deserved an award for patience and perseverance. Many mornings her exhortations fell on deaf ears, like water on slippery surface. Malingering did not work with Mother. She was uneducated but I couldn't fool her. Sister took less coaxing and would be down in the kitchen drinking something hot and waiting for me, the sluggard, to join her. Mother's insistent pestering could go on for minutes before I gave in to her annoying voice. I also hated the smell of kerosene a few inches from my sensitive nose. Sometimes I prayed earnestly for forty days and forty nights of rain. That would be the only way to find some calm in my soul and respite from drudgery, doing the same trees year in and year out. I had finished basic training with Brother. Sister and I were to work together on our own with hundreds of trees in two separate holdings close to the house.

Mother's actions caused me a great deal of embarrassment. The trees needed some rest too, so most owners would alternate between different acres of trees, tapping some and leaving others to regenerate or rest. We tapped the same trees twelve months of the year. It was no wonder that, in time, we had to leave alone a tree here and there because the latex simply stopped flowing. With each passing month, more trees were added to this list. I felt sorry for the trees, their economic life over, and for Mother because she had only the rubber trees, her income dwindling with their slowly ebbing yield. No matter what, the morning ritual continued.

Sister didn't seem to mind getting up early in the morning because of the pocket money she received from the sale of rubber. From Mother, of course. By age eleven, I viewed the pigs, the farm, and the rubber trees as obstacles to my dreams and aspirations. Something wasn't right, I thought. Most decent human beings in the village readily lived with the status quo. Some cultivated their own farms or worked for others who owned farms. Some raised pigs and chickens and ducks. There were a few fishermen, their number declining each year because the younger ones detested the dangers of the seas. Fewer than six shops, one of which provided limited grocery items, operated in the village. Most people still bicycled to Kampong Koh to purchase their everyday needs they could not produce on their individual farms. Fewer than a dozen, mostly educated in Chinese, had ventured to cities seeking economic betterment. Fewer than a dozen in the village of under a thousand people had guaranteed, income-producing, eight-to-five jobs. Most of them in the teaching profession. The rest depended on heaven and earth and sturdy bodies to stay alive. All the neighbors are like us, they reasoned, complacently.

There is a saying in my village that if you compare yourself with other people, you might as well die. To me it didn't make much sense because how could you not use someone as a yardstick to measure your own progress (success is an alien concept), unless you grew up like a monkey, chained to a pole, taunted by cruel children, your existence subjected to the whims of the master. I was a different kind of monkey and refused to dance for stale peanuts. I felt chained to the backward village life and suffocating family traditions. There had to be something better than my life at the moment. I was yearning for something beyond the village. I didn't know what that something better would or might be but resentment simmered inside me, like yeast in a dough, against the adults in the family. They were responsible for my backwardness, blinding me to the outside world. They created the walls, responsible for the hurdles and stumbling blocks along life's bumpy road. Their lack of education and enlightenment only made things worse for everyone. They had absolute power and control over me—without a visible muzzle. Maybe they had a hidden blueprint for my future. Good or bad, I didn't care. I buried the growing, debilitating feeling deep within myself because I had no one to turn to. It didn't take much resolution or scheming on my part to camouflage the turmoil within, preoccupied as I was with the daily drudgery.

School was my friend and salvation at that time. Mother and Brother were not impressed with my scholastic achievements, but I loved my school and my teachers. At age eleven I knew that it wouldn't hurt to kiss a teacher's ass at the right moment. I had developed an affinity for a soft-spoken, slightly hunched teacher, partly because his ailing father depended on Father for opium. I suspected the gluey opium had something to do with our bonding, but it was not a topic for discussion between a teacher and his student. We were close, but without undue familiarity between us. After he graduated from a bicycle to a small car, I often volunteered to carry his personal stuff from the car to the classroom or vice versa. I reveled in the role of a teacher's pet, which I had created for myself in order to get ahead in my class.

Unbeknown to my teacher, I had watched him copy test questions on the blackboard from one of his notebooks. Inquisitiveness, not greed, goaded me into committing an offense deserving of caning in the headmaster's office. News would spread from the inner sanctum like leaves scattered by an ill wind. Public disgrace, for sure. But I ignored risk, stupidity, and culpability. I peeked into the teacher's notebook and secretly copied the questions a few times during stealthy detours between the classroom and his vehicle. I wasn't about to sell or share the information with anyone. Selfishness, I decided, could save my skin. I had studied diligently and most of the stolen questions didn't motivate me to study any harder. Those questions were expected based on past experiences with the teacher and the nature of certain texts and the nature of most of the tests. Most test questions involved regurgitation of facts. Memorization, we were taught from day one, was the key to success. The word *comprehension* was rarely spoken in class. So we grew up swallowing chunks of material, some palatable, most insipid, so we could ace the tests. And receive, in the presence of adoring and envious classmates, the crown of success. It was customary for teachers to post names (I had not heard of registration numbers in school) and results on the front classroom wall for everyone to see. Especially your ranking in class at the end of a school year.

There was one student, from another town, I really wanted to befriend and help, even though he didn't speak my dialect and usually keeping his distance. None of our teachers said anything about his deteriorating health, but the other students and I saw that he was losing weight rapidly, his firm face was changing from robust to pale yellow, his posture of arrogance was replaced by pathetic cowering. We wondered why he continued to come to school. The clothes were the same. But his body was shrinking. I never understood the animosity between us. I wanted to touch him. To find something in common. It seemed we were moving further apart, in opposite directions, his illness making him more aloof and unapproachable. Each day he became more fragile and had difficulty breathing, like someone experiencing a severe asthma attack. Whatever his ailment, I knew it was something irreversible, knew death was on its way. So young and brave. Not a word was spoken among us, but many students were counting the hours and days. One day he simply disappeared. Soon someone took over the empty seat. Teachers' lips remained sealed. We were not told of his death nor given time to grieve his passing. We knew he had passed away. You got a distinct feeling this was none of anyone's business. Classroom life went on as usual. Nothing eased my profound sense of loss at his quiet passing.

Earlier in the week, we had witnessed, from our classroom in the second floor, across a low bamboo fence, the beginning of the funeral procession for a parent of one of our teachers. Funerals exuded a recognizable, sweet smell from some flowers. A familiarity distinguishable, say, from the smell of a bridal bouquet. And the band and the dirge sounded mournfully familiar. People close to the deceased wore black and others, according to century-old Chinese traditions, were expected to wear clothing without red or other bright cheerful colors. As if to say, let's be slightly subdued, not overly jubilant, on this funeral occasion. We somberly watched the scene from our classroom, without a word from any of the students.

Ironically, knowing the questions ahead of time—through devious means—didn't change the way I studied for tests. I was in the top five in my class for a few years. Yet not a reward or a word of praise or an encouragement from either Mother or Brother. I concluded early I was valued for my hands only, my brawn, not my brains. The two older sisters didn't attend schools. Brother himself refused to complete his education after the Japanese Occupation. Education didn't mean much to the adults in the family. Worse, I could count with my fingers the few from our village who were working as teachers. They were discarded as my role models. Most people, according to Mother, were doing well without ever going to school. They were often held up as role models. I didn't get her approval or encouragement to do well in school, because she couldn't see beyond the walls of the village culture and traditions. She clung to the wheel of life she knew. I wanted no part of it, saw pervasive poverty as only temporary for me.

The school was preparing me for something. One day in early February, 1952, we got news of the death of our beloved King George VI from coronary thrombosis after treatment for lung cancer. Rumors of his deteriorating health had lingered on the periphery of our lives for some time. Pictures of the royal family, especially young Princess Elizabeth and Princess Margaret, had been plastered in almost every classroom since their father unexpectedly ascended the throne. Their uncle, King Edward VIII, abdicated the throne for the sake of an American divorcee in 1936.

My instinctive reactions to some of the pictures seemed normal for my age and level of curiosity. Why is she, especially Princess Elizabeth, doing this or that? Is she, as heir to the throne, trying to show her subjects in the British Empire around the globe that she is an all-rounded person? capable of handling all manners of human activities that her subjects are going through everyday in their lives? She looked pretty and feminine, not like someone I would readily entrust with the burdens of the British Empire at the time. The black-and-white pictures, most ten-by-twelve inches, adorned the walls and were pretty to look at. A constant reminder that we lived under a British monarch thousands of miles away in a fairy land. I knew absolutely nothing about the role of a monarch.

I loved the tune to *God Save The King* and my eyes became misty the few times a year we assembled before the school assembly hall and sang the song in perfect unison. Most of us learned of the life of the royal family from magazines in our school library, or newsreels in our local theater, or in newsreels our government propaganda machine sent directly to our village when the government felt the imperative to say something urgent or important to its citizens (a practice started after the government declared a state of emergency in June 1948 because of a communist insurgency).

There were no visible tears but a brief moment of shock when news of the royal demise was announced to the whole school. We will not be singing "*God Save The King*," some joked. For most of us he was too far away to mean anything personal to us. Weeks later I learned that King George VI never recovered from a lung operation. Princess Elizabeth and her husband were on their way to Australia, taking her ailing father's place for a scheduled visit, when she was told of the news of his death.

Before Princess Elizabeth's coronation, slightly more than a year later, the school sold a variety of souvenirs to the students. With limited pocket money at my disposal, I chose the most important item, in my opinion, a miniature gold crown pin with sparkling stones on it, symbolizing the very essence of her coronation and the monarchy. Many of the other souvenirs seemed trite, frivolous, shallow, and hollow to me. The Union Jack was too common and ubiquitous. I wore the little crown (not on my big head!), with pride around the time of her coronation on June 2, 1953.

We heard that The Coronation Joint Executive Committee, Sir Winston Churchill and his cabinet, and her advisors expressed concern that allowing television lights and cameras into the Westminster Abbey for the coronation—something never done before—could impose an intolerable emotional strain on the Queen after a grueling day. According to the story, she objected courageously to their objections, expressing her desire for all her royal subjects to participate and watch her coronation on television. She reminded Prime Minister Churchill that it was she, not his cabinet, that was being crowned. She was determined that nothing must stand between her coronation and her subjects' right to participate in the glorious event.

When it was made public earlier in the year that the coronation of the Queen would be televised, sales of television sets went through the roof, especially in England. Her advisors consulted the British meteorologists (as the Chinese would consult Buddhist priests to determine an auspicious day for a momentous event) and decided that June 2 was the most consistently sunny day in England. Needless to say, there was a heavy downpour on the day of the coronation.

I was home eating dinner (the school was closed because of a national holiday to mark the event) when, around noon in England, the coronation of Her Majesty, Queen Elizabeth II, took place in Westminster Abbey on Tuesday, the second day of June, 1953. For the first time ever, aristocrats and ordinary people in England and around the world—an estimated twenty million television viewers—were able to watch a coronation in their own homes.

I read many years later that the carpet in the Westminster Abbey had been laid with the pile running the wrong way, which caused some inconvenience for the Queen's robes, almost stopping her from going forward. She was heard to have said to the Archbishop of Canterbury, the man who was to crow her Queen, "Get me started!"

The holy oil that had been used in her father's coronation was destroyed during one of the disastrous WW II bombing raids over many parts of England. The company that made it had gone out of business. Luckily for the royal family—it was reported—an elderly relative of the company's owner had kept a few ounces of the oil.

I saw the majestic event in a newsreel at the local theater. Television was still in the distant future for me.

That same year, I had a serious encounter not far from my house with one of Her Majesty's English subjects in my country. A *red-hair devil*, he had been sent to my country by a major rubber company in Britain to manage a huge rubber plantation (one of many British-owned estates dotting the Malayan landscape), the one Brother and I had to cut through to reach Brother's small holding. I was twelve and with each chronological year it seemed more responsibilities were saddled on my shoulders. Finding firewood was one of these manly responsibilities. I went one day, rather excitedly, with a group of people—teenagers and young women—with our bicycles to gather some dead wood on the British-owned rubber plantation. Wood was the primary source of fuel for cooking in our village. No wood, no cooking, no food—it was that simple. Here and there, between orderly rows of young rubber trees, lay piles of fallen old trees. Maybe left to rot away. I had no idea what the *red-hair devil* would do with all the dead wood. Or what the company in England, which sent him here, would do with all the fallen trees.

I did know—because our family also owned rubber trees—that old trees had to be periodically replaced by new ones for the estates to stay alive and viable, supporting hundreds of Indians recruited directly from the Indian continent. Why not let poverty-stricken village people like us have some of this wood, I remember saying to myself. I was speechless when I first came upon the abundant fuel lying everywhere, the way Ali Baba might have reacted when he beheld the treasures inside the cave. What a waste, I thought. Old wood from rubber trees was not good for anything except firewood. Rubber sheets could be dried in smokehouses or in the open air. Though the plantation smokehouses needed endless quantity of wood to keep the fires going, they had more than they could ever use.

When we arrived at a spot in the plantation, chosen unanimously by the group, we left our bicycles near the trees by the side of the road and rushed to our destinations with our *parangs*. We knew we had to work fast to avoid being caught by the *red-hair devil*. In the quiet of the evening, all I could see were leaves dancing in the wind. I felt my heart beating faster and faster. The chopping of branches with sharp *parangs* could be heard miles away. Could there be eyes and ears—Indian sleuths trained by their British masters—lurking in the woods? I had been lucky a few times but not that day. Out of nowhere, a jeep seemed to come right at me, screeching to an abrupt stop next to my bicycle, spurting dirt from its spinning tires, and stirring up clouds of dust into the air around the vehicle, like smoke from a thousand Chinese firecrackers. I knew there and then my days were numbered. I was within reach of the long arms of the *read-hair devil*. My companions parked further away were able to escape apprehension and the wrath of the *red-hair devil*. I was caught, hands suddenly damp and shaking, sobbing hysterically, realizing something terrible was about to happen to me. Four of us, two boys and two young women, didn't escape.

The Indian workers loaded our bicycles to another vehicle, and pulled us up by our hands to the back of the jeep driven by the *red-hair devil*. They spoke a different tongue, with their heads turning slightly this way and that way as if to emphasize the gravity of each spoken word. I had always been intrigued by female Indian dancers in my school moving their heads rhythmically to music while vigorously tapping their bare feet on the stage. I used my hands a lot when I talked. The Indians used their heads. Thinly clad, I shivered because of the evening air as the sun disappeared behind the tall trees. He drove us first to his well-attended and elegantly manicured residence, then to the police station for questioning. News of our capture had spread and Brother and my parents were at the station to greet us. The electric lights were on. I trembled because of the evening breeze, with guilt and shame written over my face. I wasn't properly dressed for the occasion, half-naked because it was hot earlier in the day. People don't normally dress up to steal firewood.

The charge was trespassing. And there was a small fine. On the day in court before a Malay magistrate, uncontrollably shaking all over like a dog slipping into a ditch of cold dirty water, I was instructed by a well respected young lawyer, a relative, to say, "I am young and I didn't know what I did was wrong. I was just following some older kids in my neighborhood. I am deeply sorry for my mistake," and thereafter remain silent. The truth was we were stealing wood that didn't belong to us because our families depended on us for firewood. Young and innocent, I learned quickly to listen to my lawyer carefully and do whatever he insisted I must do to save my skin. I learned to lie, to wear a mask of contrived penitence. It didn't matter that I had a mind of my own and knew what I did was wrong before I went to the rubber plantation, contradicting what my relative wanted me to say to the magistrate. Thankfully, the torture lasted only a few minutes, but the hostile feelings I harbored against the *red-hair devil,* England, and the entire British Empire lasted till I finished high school.

ELEVEN

At first, the whole household must have staggered at the size of Big Cousin's quivering, swollen penis. His hands gently held its now limp shaft like the wounded head of a once proud snake while Eighth Auntie (his mother) generously applied Tiger Balm ointment to it. The active ingredients of the ointment were menthol and camphor. The aromatic analgesic instantly produced a warm, soothing sensation, a temporary distraction from stinging pain. An unprecedented event, in the family. A predicament confounding the adults. One consolation was that no one in the village had died from a similar attack—usually in a less critical part of the human anatomy. Almost every family had a small bottle of Tiger Balm in the house. The Chinese concoction, a well established brand with a running tiger on its cap, was used by some as a first aid measure, by others as a panacea for all minor ailments—from coughs to colds—in the absence of a medical doctor.

Hearing the sudden, sharp, disturbing cries of pain upstairs late in the evening, you would have thought my twenty-one-year-old cousin—tall, athletic, muscular, and soon to marry—had been attacked by a man with a sharp *parang* or by the violent ghost of a dissatisfied, deceased member of the family. There was an attack, certainly, by one of the most feared monsters in our midst. I too was once a victim of this attacker's painful but non-lethal bite. My bite was on my leg. Cousin's was on the most sensitive private part of his anatomy. His penis. A little suspicious, in view of his impending nuptials. This attacker, hidden during the day, loved damp places and crevices and could run very fast because of its many legs. Despite its Latin name, *centipeda*, this carnivorous invertebrate actually has about fifteen pairs of legs, with each pair slightly longer than the one before it. Anatomically, it has a head and a segmented body, with a pair of legs sticking out of each segment. I grew up hating and fearing its dark red head with two long antennae constantly in motion, searching for something. Some adore its existence, and are convinced it is nature's way of taking care of some unwanted insects and spiders. It was anybody's guess how one crawled onto cousin's penis this evening. With the gentle patter of rain on the tiled roof, and most of the household sedated by the calm, I suspected one hungry centipede, out looking for its prey in the dark, lost its grip crossing the exposed rafter and fell on unsuspecting Cousin while he relaxed on the wooden floor, probably listening to some Chinese music from the family radio.

The centipede bite caused severe pain and swelling, bringing an adult a thousand times bigger than this small predator to his knees. Everyone wore a helpless look amidst the cry for help. A local application of ice would have been great, but where would one find ice late in the evening? I don't remember if there was any kind of analgesic in the house, but Tiger Balm was always handy. A doctor's care was beyond reach. In a case like this you remained stoic, bit your teeth (in local parlance) and suffered silently. Cousin's moaning soon faded into silence and he succumbed to painless sleep.

While cousin's penis attack became a public affair, I was secretly nursing a private pain, which could have been damaging my reproductive apparatus. We had two mango trees beneath tall coconut trees in the land adjacent to our house. One was at least thirty feet tall. The other, mowed down by a strong wind, continued to grow and bear fruit lying down, with its roots still buried firmly in the ground. Sister was fearless in just about anything, like climbing a tall tree. I was small and timid, so Sister would climb a fruit tree, pluck the fruits and throw them down to me. I grew up—for no known reasons—afraid of climbing anything tall or faling into anything deep, like an imaginary bottomless pit out in the blue ocean. This time, in the absence of Sister, I decided to go after the mangoes myself, way up in the air, with the help of a twenty-feet bamboo pole, its diameter an inch and a half at the base, tapering slightly to its tip, with a strong metal hook tied to it. This particular pole had a nail hammered into its base, with at least two inches exposed at an angle. Sometimes a pail full of water would break loose from a rope and fall to the bottom of the family well. Or the rope escape from our wet hands. The bamboo pole was the only tool we were taught to use in any salvage operation. First you lower the pole to the bottom of the well—we could see everything at the bottom—and with a little maneuver catch the handle with the nail, and pull up the pail. I used the same pole and went after the tantalizing, ripened, light golden-brown, juicy mangoes way up the tree, half hidden among the leafy branches. Just feeling the touch and the succulent taste drove me into action. Because I feared heights, the pole was the best alternative. I made the grave mistake of trying to steady the long pole between my legs and using my hands to move it up and down as I pulled the clusters of mangoes with the hook. At one point, the nail on the pole between my legs caught my testicles. I released it immediately, leaving it hanging among the branches by its hook. I sank, breathless, to the ground in excruciating pain. I thought I was going to pass out and lose consciousness. Tears came swiftly, followed by a dry cough and dizziness. For a second I thought I was going to die. But soon I forced myself to touch my scrotum. There was very little blood, so I concluded the nail hadn't torn deep into the testicles and that my injury wasn't serious enough for me to make a public announcement about it to anyone in the house. It was one of those things too personal to share with anyone. Some profound embarrassment and shame attached to it. You died with it. After a while, I gathered my senses and the mangoes on the ground, left the bamboo hanging from the tree, and tried to walk normally to the house. I remained taciturn the rest of the day, as if traumatized by a ghost. At age twelve with, a robust, heavy body, the minor wound, to my great relief, did not cause any infection but healed quickly. Memory of it remained indelible.

And my cousin got married. The ancestral home was getting too crowded. The centipede episode was soon forgotten. And his penis seemed to work just fine because his wife soon had morning fever and her gait became a little awkward. It wasn't a product of my young active imagination. I heard things. I saw things. He was still a virile man.

And the bamboo pole remained a trusted family ally for months and years to come. Days later Sister and I were out and about with the bamboo pole, balancing on my shoulder, not far from our house looking for dead limbs for fuel. Sister carried the *parang* to cut the limbs into suitable lengths for the wood-burning stoves. The two of us worked together because there were numerous times when the energy and muscles and weight of two or more were needed, since we were too light and petite to sever or pull down the dead limbs alone. Sometimes the metal hook at the tip of the pole would break loose because of a stubborn limb or the weight of our two bodies. *I think this one is still very green*, Sister might say to me, failing to break it loose after a few tries. Or *this one is not worth our energy*, I might volunteer my opinion. Once in a while I found myself swinging with the pole—with Sister's nudging—hanging from a stubborn limb. I don't remember the family ever entertained the thought of deliberately demolishing a rubber tree, however decrepit, for the sake of firewood. Only once did the family make a unanimous decision to cut down all the old rubber trees—because of drastically diminished yield of rubber—on the three acres of land where the ancestral home stood. And where the family now lived. For now Sister and I were kept busy scavenging for fuel to keep the kitchen going. Illegally pilfering wood from the British-owned rubber plantation was a risky business, no longer attractive. Once bitten twice shy? I couldn't face the same magistrate in court twice. We went about our undertaking unrelentingly, knowing our daily survival depended on it. No scrimping on fuel for cooking. No ifs or buts. Most rubber trees were healthy. Dead limbs were as scarce as Christians praying for divine solace in a Buddhist temple. But we never returned home empty handed. Even if it meant poisoning a tree or two. We had to intensify our efforts because of the impending Chinese New Year, the Year of the Snake. For almost every family, the kitchen became the centre of activities. And the wood-burning stoves were kept more busy than usual toward the end and the beginning of Chinese New Year.

Our parents' generation was more at ease with the Chinese calendar and used it to mark, remember, and celebrate certain events happening in the family and the larger community. But I always knew the Chinese New Year was coming because Mother would insist we pay an annual visit to our family seamstress, just as the family each year paid respect to the departed at the graveyard, a walking distance from our house. Our seamstress was also the mother of a teenage friend of mine from church. A single mother, she managed to raise two boys and a girl. The eldest son and daughter were married and lived in Singapore, a city island many miles south of our village. She was a tall, dark woman who had to talk down to me and sat on a chair while taking my measurements, her black hair, with a few visible grey strands, neatly bundled on the back. She always wore traditional Chinese clothing. The snug fit made her look bamboo tall. She and her youngest son, my friend, also tapped rubber trees, on land—right behind our house—that belonged to another Ling's family and shared the profits with the owner. (The Methodist Religious Education Center, built in 1937, sat on this three-acre property. I attended Sunday school here.) She was meticulous about the measurements and holding the measuring tape around my thin waist might say something gently without being offensive like "we need a little bit loose here because you are still growing," jotting down the specifics in a note book. She did everything including procuring the requisite amount of cloth from a clothing store in town. For the Year of the Snake, I was showered with two short-sleeved white shirts and two pairs of dark-blue short pants—school uniforms for for our junior high school. (In high school we wore everything white.) Like something instinctual and ingrained, we *will wear* new clothes on New Year's Day. The same clothing I wore to all public places: school, church, theatre, and town. The traditional Chinese thinking or superstition about donning new clothes on New Year's Day is that if you can't afford new clothes on the first day of the year, it is bad news for the whole family for the rest of the year. I grew up adhering to this belief unwaveringly, even though I disliked intensely the smell and feel of all new clothes, any time of the year. A new hair cut, a must (not a suggestion), would go well with the new clothes. A visit to the barber was as necessary as washing your dirty feet before going to bed.

Preparations. Preparations. Preparations. The whole village was up to something to usher in a new year. There was something going on in every house, like getting ready for the judgment day.

It is more than putting the final touches to a Christian pageant at church or a Shakespeare play at school. It is more like pulling out all the thorns that have poisoned the flesh, thus weakening the body, this past year, and preparing the body for a rebirth or regeneration, a new beginning. This coming new year has to be better than the last one. It is on everybody's agenda. Rich or poor. A dream worthy of consideration and striving, which remains elusive like a slippery eel for some unlucky folks.

The whole family was involved with a thorough house cleaning—front to back, top to bottom, side to side—as if preparing for a wedding or a visit from Gabriel, the divine representative. Spruce it up, fix, scrub, wash, wipe, and paint. An auspicious time to do minor repairs to the house and replace worn-out or decrepit household items from the kitchen to the bedrooms. I was the self-appointed sweeper, obsessed with the orderliness and the external appearance of the house ever since I could hold the broom (many inches taller than my stunted height) in my hands. Cleaning the house spick-and-span took on a whole new significance and urgency because the house had to be emptied of all the evil and the bad luck of the past year to make room for good luck, happiness and prosperity of the new year. And sweeping out (not in) is the correct modus operandi, leaving not an iota of dirt for the past to cling to, literally opening the doors and windows to recuperative fresh air for the whole household. But this same motion (sweeping out) would be considered ill-advised and against Chinese traditions on New Year's Day because you would then be sweeping out and away everything that is considered wholesome, lucky, good, and prosperous for the household. Call it superstition, but not a soul would want to tempt fate by sweeping out any dirt on New Year's Day. But if you suffer the itch to sweep, sweep it in and leave it in a corner somewhere to be removed a few days later.

Some Chinese don't sweep in or out on New Year's Day, at all.

As I grew older I never once felt that the house was neat, stylish, or appealing to my growing circle of teenage friends from the church (most of my school friends didn't come from my village), so I avoided almost all social contacts and activities in my house. I was genuinely ashamed of my disheveled-looking house with farm tools and bicycles everywhere, a stone rice grounder to the right and a huge grater for coconut and cassava to the left of the front door, with clotheslines running every which direction from the two front posts holding the verandah. A partial, disharmonious view of the front of the house. Add to this the 6-feet-by-10-feet roofed bath house (the outhouse was located a short distance away) with a cement tub—built cleverly with half exposed to the outside—using water drawn from a well two feet away for the daily cold bath, the same well serving the kitchen about twenty feet away in the opposite direction. Many villagers built a seven-feet-high enclosure around their wells, drawing cold water pail by pail from the well for bathing. In our family, anything that had to do with water, from laundry to bathing—children in their underwear in the hot sun—was done on a concrete slab around the well, allowing the waste water to run freely into a long mud puddle stretching for yards into the farm, a haven for pigs to wallow in, a few ducks now and then. Not a breeding ground for mosquitoes, surprisingly, because the puddle was never the same. A delight to our two- and four-legged friends, but a terrible eyesore.

A ten-feet-tall chicken-wire fence encircled the front portion and yard of the house, keeping the chickens, ducks, pigs, and any four-legged strays from encroaching on the house. Another terrible eyesore, to me.

Occasionally a relative or two might show up and for a short duration. Most people in the village and those immediately around our house were saddled with the responsibilities of raising children, pigs, chickens, and rubber trees and farming the land to feed the animals and themselves. Thus most villagers were not in the habit of visiting one another except for weddings and funerals and occasionally seeking advice or help with small family issues. Maybe the reason why the appearance of the house was never an issue or cause for embarrassment. You could also say everyone was in the same boat. The poor looked poor to the poor. The Christian youth fellowship—anywhere between fifty and hundred boys and girls—would hold an occasional prayer meeting after dark in my house (every member would host such a meeting at least once a year), lighted by kerosene lanterns and a bright full moon. I was never present when the women of the church met for their prayer meeting in the house. To accommodate such a big gathering, we had it out in front of the house, borrowing benches from neighbors. That saved my face (ego and pride) because they could not see much of anything in the dark except each other, their bicycles, and the hot snacks we served at the close of the meeting. I had attended a few such meetings. I went for the occasional great hot snacks—most families put out their best, traditional Chinese favorites—not the hymns, fellowship or the Bible study. Maybe seeing a friend or two. I didn't care what the house smelled or looked like.

There was only one bright, cheery spot in this whole tarnished scene, which remained boringly the same year in and year out. Luxuriating in the hot tropical sun, a hibiscus shrub grew wildly next to the bathhouse. Known to the locals as *Bunga Raya,* a Malay word meaning *Queen of Tropical Flowers,* its profusion of bright red flowers greeted us each morning, only to wilt in the late afternoon, like some of us feeling drained after a few hours in the hot sun. But new buds continued to bloom each morning, brilliant and cheerful, like the rising sun. I don't think Mother allowed this one indulgence because the *Bunga Raya* is our national flower. That wouldn't mean anything to her. Granted the luscious soft petals were used by some people to polish shoes or make wine or dye. Mother allowed it to grow because it wasn't in anyone's way or a drain on our limited resources. I fell in love with the hibiscus because it looked like a huge permanent flower arrangement sitting there, idly reminding us poor, struggling country folks that there was more to life than the daily endless toil to survive. Something fragile but soothing to look at. I had no doubts the pigs were beautiful to other pigs. So were the chickens and the ducks to other chickens and ducks. But they didn't touch my soul like the sweet-smelling hibiscus flowers. I knew I was born different from the others in the family, something the Creator must have secretly planted deep inside me, because I saw beauty, charm and elegance in the natural world, plants and animals, and the world around me. I found time, however limited, to savor the simple things of life all around me.

On the way home about eight or nine in the morning, feeling exhausted after helping Brother with the rubber trees on weekends and during the school holidays, I would slow down my bicycle as I approached one particular house, intrigued by the sight of what seemed like clusters and clusters of stunning, purple blooms hanging lazily over a wooden fence. Similar ornamental garden plants, with a variety of colors, had adorned the yards of the nouveau riches in certain neighborhoods, outside the village. I learned you could propagate the bougainvillea—named after Louis Antoine de Bougainvillea, a French sea captain—by stem cuttings,which gave me hope. And it required very little attention, perfect for someone like me because the daily chores from morn till dusk left me starving for leisure time. The clusters that I had seen from afar were actually layers of colorful bracts, surrounding almost inconspicuous, white-yellow flowers. Like the hibiscus, the bougainvillea bloomed all year round. Like the rubber trees, the bougainvillea—called *Bunga Kertas,* meaning *paper flower,* by the locals—was also a native of South America. I was given a few cuttings and planted them anxiously—without consulting anyone in the family—right by the chicken-wire fence in front of the house. In time, I should be able to assist it climb and trail on the fence, imitating what others had done with their yards. Except the front yard of our house was covered with concrete, not dirt. About five feet of dirt stood between the concrete and the fence. This was my first modest beautification venture. But it became an immediate problem for Mother. Not that we needed space and land for planting crops. Mother considered any activity that had no economic value to be wasteful and nonproductive. And growing flowers for aesthetic reasons met her vehement disapproval. To her, it was a frivolous engagement for the well to do, who had both the money and the time for what Mother considered non-essential pursuits, definitely not for the poor like us, who should be growing garden vegetables for humans and crops for the pigs. The only blooms that went undetected or unappreciated by Mother were those of garden vegetables, like the gold-yellow blooms hanging from the vines of certain squash and the variety of tropical fruit trees that decorated the land around the family home. The many blooms of the tropical fruit trees almost went unnoticed because most of them were on tall trees, but their sweet smell permeated the air.

When Mother first saw the bougainvillea plant, she went at it like a cat after a mouse. Her hands, not her mouth, sprang into action. She pulled the stems from the ground unapologetically and threw them over the fence, thus ending prematurely my leisure time occupation and—more damaging—stunting my growth aesthetically. I watched with sadness the demise of my newfound joy, my bougainvillea, but try as she would, Mother failed to nip completely my innate propensity to surround my private world with things that were intrinsically part of who I really was.

The hibiscus somehow escaped Mother's plan of annihilation. The vibrant reds of the hibiscus blended well with the reds we were pasting on doors, windows and walls to usher in the New Year. One legend has it that *Nian* (meaning year) was a feared monster that terrorized many villages, but over time the villagers learned that *Nian* was afraid of anything red, loud noises and bright lights. So, many Chinese families, down time immemorial, decorated their doors and windows with bright red papers, with couplets on themes such as prosperity, happiness, wealth, and longevity written on them with fine calligraphy. And the loud firecrackers young people set off on New Year's Eve (around midnight) in my village were to welcome the Chinese New Year. The firecrackers were never meant to entertain by lighting up the midnight sky on New Year's Eve, but to drive away the evil spirits that might have infested the old year. And wearing anything red was believed to ward off evil spirits. Red candles, red flowers, and red firecrackers were not uncommon in many homes. I remember seeing a red banner or a red piece of cloth hanging from the central beam of a new house, the main purpose to protect the new dwelling from evil spirits.

And as children, we each would receive an *urn bao* (Red Packet) from the grown-ups, especially married couples and our parents, on New Year's Day, making us hopeful and rich at least the first day of a new year. One year Father gave me a gold ring. I saw it once and it mysteriously vanished into thin air. I suspected Mother sold it at some point to fund Father's opium business. And his incurable drug addiction. For sure every child in a family—however poor—would receive some money in an *urn bao,* auguring well for the rest of the year. Because money meant prosperity and good luck. Sensible adults would not dream of carrying over old debts into a new year. A new year means a new year, a new beginning, a fresh start, uncluttered with the debris and burdens of the past, allowing room for growth, expansion, happiness, prosperity and good luck.

The Chinese New Year is therefore the most important, the oldest, holiday in the Chinese calendar. In mainland China, the land of my ancestors, where it all started centuries ago, it actually signals the end of winter and the coming of spring, and is still popularly celebrated as the Spring Festival, culminating fifteen days later in the Festival of the Lanterns. Since it is a movable holiday, the exact date on the Gregorian calendar (I grew up calling it the western calendar) varies from year to year between January 21 and February 19, but always on the second new moon following the winter solstice. Every home had a western calendar with the traditional lunar calendar in Chinese usually in small print, above it a smiling face of a winsome Hong Kong movie actress. The Chinese New Year or the Lunar New Year officially marks the first day of the first month of the Chinese lunar calendar. Because it is the coming of spring in mainland China, the Chinese New Year has always been a time for a fresh start in life, a new beginning, and also a time to reunite with and honor the family, both the living and the dead. A time to drive out the evil spirits and bad luck of the past and seek gods' blessings for a prosperous new year. The customary Chinese New Year's greeting, *Kong See Fat Choy*, means literally "Wish you become prosperous," something I didn't hear much when I was growing up. An unrealistic dream or goal—like reaching for the moon—for many in my village. It would not surprise me if parents saved all year so they could be lavish at least once a year, the most important time of the year, buying new clothes, food, materials for decorations, gifts and good luck items. Indeed *Happy New Year*, a modest aspiration for many, was a more common greetings on New Year's Day in my village.

Since I grew up in a poor family, the Chinese New Year meant one thing and one thing only: the one time in a year when I wouldn't be starving for food. I wouldn't be wondering why some of my friends always had more variety of food on their dinner tables. I wouldn't be looking for a wedding or a funeral so I could gorge myself. Chinese New Year meant, however destitute your family, *you must begin the new year with plenty to eat.* Rich in symbolism? Yes. I had implicit trust that my family would have plenty for us to eat at the beginning of every year. An annual ritual many practiced in the village was the making of steamed buns. Our whole family was involved with making dozens of steamed sweet buns and *Nian Gao* (meaning Year Cake) a week before the New Year. Family members took turns grinding the pre-soaked glutinous rice. One person turned the grindstone with a T-shaped wooden handle bar in a clock-wise motion, and another person fed soaked, glutinous rice into a hole in it with a ladle. Sister-in-law took charge of the whole operation. There were plenty of eager hands to do the grinding, and eventually to roll a small piece of rice dough in our palms, to produce the desired shape before crowding the bamboo steamers with buns. This team activity usually took place after the evening meal because it would take all the available space in the kitchen. Everyone in the family took turns keeping the wood-burning stove fully fed at all times, watching vigilantly for the rising steam popping out from the steamers. There always had to be sufficient boiling water in the wok to create the steam, and sufficient firewood to keep the boiling water going. The family members were always there to gobble up the first few batches of the steamed buns, like chickens awaiting the feed, the first taste since the year before. Most Chinese enjoy food hot. You could say, from the wok to the mouth. Sister and I were dispatched with a few, the best looking ones, to our neighbors. Soon only Brother and his wife were left in the kitchen to finish the task of making more sweet buns and *Nian Gao.* We would enjoy the taste of sweet buns for the next few days and everyone would eat a piece or two of *Nian Gao*—a symbol of family unity—on New Year's Day.

It was not uncommon for most families to store away the *Nian Gao* for weeks and months until they became moldy (years before electricity and refrigeration came to our village). We learned to remove any mold with a wet cloth, slice it into small pieces, dip them in an egg batter and fry them in some oil. Every year I looked forward to eating the old, moldy *Nian Gao,* which seemed to taste better than when it was fresh. The coconut oil and the egg batter did something magical to the old *Nian Gao*. Simply delicious! I clamored for more, long after the New Year.

The kitchen became the center of activity for every family during the festive season. I watched a peculiar ritual practiced religiously by pagans in our midst. Something about *Tsao-Chun*, otherwise known as the *Kitchen God*, one of the most revered of the ancient Chinese gods. Legend has it that this once mortal man abandoned his wife for a younger woman, who left him penurious and starving. When he came to his senses, recognizing the widow who fed him was his first wife, he incinerated himself by jumping into the oven and became immortalized as the *Kitchen God*, an honor bestowed on him by the gods. (Many in the Chinese pantheon were once mortals, not unlike some of the saints my Catholic friends pray to.) *Tsao-Chun's* presence—a statue, a picture, or simply the Chinese characters for *Kitchen God* written on a red paper—was seldom obtrusive in some of the kitchens, but resurrected and taken seriously by the households, because he was scheduled to return to heaven on the twenty-fourth day of the twelfth month (of the Chinese lunar calendar) to report to the Jade Emperor—the almighty god—the good and the bad about the individual family he had the pleasure of residing with and watching over for the whole year. A family could do a thing or two to sweeten his tongue by offering *Tsao-Chuan* sweet rice dishes, fruits and cakes, and smearing his lips with honey, ensuring he would say something sweet—or nothing at all—about the family. They burnt his image, along with paper chariots, as he returned to heaven. The simple ceremony ended with firecrackers. To signify his return to earth on New Year's Eve, the family would put up a new statue or picture of *Tsao-Chuan*, at the same time honoring him with ample offerings. Christians didn't do this.

And because we were Methodists, greeting the spirits of our ancestors or the gods, or making offerings of food to our ancestors on the family altar on New Year's Eve (we had portraits of our grandparents on either side of a huge mirror in our family parlor but no family altar), was foreign to our beliefs and New Year rituals. Such practices would have been incongruous with our Christian teachings. But one ritual that had become a local tradition was the slaughter of pigs on New Year's Eve. For a small village, this was a big event and it happened not far from our house, in front of the coffee shop, lighted by kerosene lanterns. Where and when the pigs were slaughtered was of no interest to anyone but I could hear and feel the commotion as people crowded around the butcher's table, their bicycles parked a few feet away, and everyone seemed to be pointing to the same piece of meat. Every year there was never enough meat to go around. Due to fewer pigs or smaller pigs or a growing population? Demand far exceeded the supply. Everyone agreed. The mood was lighthearted and there was abundant cash. The same two or three entrepreneurs had been doing this for some time, only during the Chinese New Year, and it seemed the whole village was there to buy whatever was offered on the cutting board—pig's feet, pig's blood, pig's intestines, pig's head, pig's ears, pig's tongue, et cetera. Every part of the pig was good for something, magically transformed into some Chinese delicacies. There were no prescribed dishes for the special meal of the year. Basically we cooked and ate what we could afford. Our delicate palates ruled by our pockets, not traditions My favorites had to do with different fried noodles—egg noodles, bean noodles, rice noodles—with shrimp or pork or chicken, sweet and sour pork or fish, beef noodle soup, boiled whole chicken, and stir-fried vegetables. And fried, hard-boiled eggs in light meat-vegetable gravy. The affluent could indulge in oysters, believed to bring good fortune. And the traditionalists, for their last meal of the year, might insist on ten cups of wine with ten bowls of vegetables and ten bowls of meat as part of New Year's Eve celebration because ten is the perfect number Yet the most popular dish had nothing to do with pigs, but rather with fish.

And why fish? Because the word fish, *yu* in Chinese, has the same pronunciation (or sound) as the Chinese character (word) for *abundance*. It is necessary to grasp the significance of homonyms and rhymes of certain Chinese characters and their symbolism in the celebration of the Chinese New Year. Chinese characters for foods, decorations, and gifts that sound like or rhyme with words for happiness, prosperity, good luck or good fortune, good health and wealth are believed to bring good luck to the family for the new year. Grown-up children returned in droves to their roots and families because New Year means unity and wholeness. With the dead and the living. And so much the better if the family could serve the fish or the chicken or the pig whole, underscoring the importance of wholeness in our lives and relationships. Some families went to the extent of eating part of the whole fish on New Year's Eve and the other half on New Year's Day, spilling over the abundance from one year to the next. Take a simple fruit like the orange, ubiquitous in every Chinese celebration because the Chinese character for orange has the same sound for the word *gold*. And the same is true for words like tangerine, kumquat, raw fish, and lettuce. The affluent Chinese decorated their homes with peonies, orchids, pineapple flowers, chrysanthemums, daffodils, and plum blossoms because they were said to bring good luck.

There were a few dos and don'ts for the celebration of the Chinese New Year that were instilled in us as children. Some of us grew up to view them as superstitions and abandon some of the old rituals. Some families, for example, gathered on New Year's Eve to share Chinese folktales about happiness, prosperity and good fortune in the hope of attracting good luck to the family. Some children stayed up late on New Year's Eve because that would add more years to their parents' lives. Some families would dress and behave well because they believed the gods and the spirits of their departed loved ones would visit them on New Year's Eve. And the loud firecrackers were encouraged around midnight to drive out the evil and bad spirits of the old year. And on New Year's Day, only appropriate words should be used. Take the word *four, ssu* in Chinese, which is pronounced the same as the word *death* in Chinese. All of us tried to refrain from uttering the word *four* and any obscene or negative words on New Year's Day, focusing on the positive and words like hope, happiness, and prosperity for a new beginning or a fresh start for everyone in the coming year.

Every year I watched the family cautiously avoided cutting or slicing anything with knives or scissors on New Year's Day because that would mean cutting off the family fortune. So my family did all the cutting and chopping on New Year's Eve and did light cooking on New Year's Day—making simple soup or warming up the dishes cooked the day earlier. And Mother reminded us, without fail, to wash our hair on New Year's Eve because doing it on New Year's Day would be washing away our good luck. And what a tremendous pressure on children not to cry or say a bad word or fight, or the parents to refrain from punishing the kids on New Year's Day! You considered yourself a lucky man if you heard or saw a red-colored bird on New Year's Day. And the very superstitious might consult the Chinese Almanac on when to leave the house and which directions to go on New Year's Day.

Those of us who were Christians and those not preoccupied with further preparations for the New Year would put on our elegant new clothes and attended a New Year thanksgiving service at our church the first thing in the morning on New Year's Day. A time to thank God for our good fortunes and good health the past year and seeking God's blessings on our families and dreams for the New Year. I often wondered why there were so many happy faces in the church that morning. The answer wasn't hard to find: *many Chinese honestly believe that what you do on New Year's Day sets the tone for the rest of the year.* Live well. Dress well. Eat well. Speak well to and of others. Think well. Behave well. Do well. What I do today, according to tradition, will determine what will happen to me the rest of the year. A truly sobering thought!

And everybody in the neighborhood would serve the same things to their guests and visitors: red or black watermelon seeds, shelled peanuts, and orange crush soda. Again the affluent might serve an eight-sided tray—eight is considered a good-luck number—of lucky snacks like watermelon seeds, plums (individually wrapped), lotus root, candied ginger (individually wrapped), pineapple chunks, and other preserved fruits. And oranges too.

The Chinese New Year celebration would be incomplete without some kind of noisy parades in towns and cities featuring the Dragon Dance as the main attraction. I had to bicycle, like many others, to Kampong Koh to witness the Dragon Dance. The dragon, a symbol of the coming spring in mainland China, could be a hundred to a hundred and fifty feet long, carried by fifty or more young dancers who had been trained to make the animal come alive by twisting and twirling its flexible body, accompanied by loud drum beats and cymbals,. The person maneuvering the huge dragon head had the most challenging tasks of making its ears twitch, its eyes move and its tongue roll in and out, while at the same time moving the head up and down, side to side, and forward at all times. The dragon seemed to be chasing after a big yellow ball representing the sun. The rest of the dancers held firmly the lengthy body covered with fish scales, trying to keep in step with the main dancer who controlled the dragon's head and the noisy drums and cymbals. Some people were tempted to throw firecrackers at the procession as the dragon glided through the street, driving out the bad luck.

Only one custom I had trouble understanding and giving my full support. Add one year to your age on "Everybody's Birthday," on the seventh day of the Chinese lunar calendar, prompting some to ask "Is this your Chinese birthday?" or "Is this your real birthday?" Imagine, if taken seriously, every Chinese and a faithful adherent or believer would be consuming lettuce and raw fish—highly recommended—on "Everybody's Birthday" on this planet, on the seventh day of the lunar calendar.

Without doubt the Chinese New Year is swathed in rituals, traditions, and beliefs. And rich in symbolism. Growing up poor, I would be well fed. But the majority of the Chinese—in mainland China and in every corner of the world—continues to celebrate it not because it is centuries old but because we are Chinese, and this is one momentous link to our glorious past and history. All the way to mainland China, the country of my ancestors. And it categorically infuses us, like the Passover in the Jewish faith or the Ramadan in the Muslim culture, with a sense of who we are as a people, deeply rooted in a rich culture, unsurpassed in the world.

TWELVE

Not too long after the Chinese New Year, Eighth Auntie announced—after heart-wrenching deliberations and financial scrutiny—that she would build her own house on her own property, not far from the ancestral home Grandpa had built when he came to Malaya from mainland China at the turn of the twentieth century. Grandpa had bequeathed the ancestral home to Father and Eighth Uncle when he returned to China in the thirties to be with his youngest daughter. He died and was buried in China. He left us a sturdy enviable two-story house, with ample spaces for two families. By now Brother and Ah Soh had four children—two girls and two boys—and first cousin and his wife had a baby boy. There were thirteen people living in this humble abode. Father and his mistress and their unruly brood lived in a town nearby. Eighth Uncle and his mistress lived in a city thirty or so miles away. Eighth Auntie had her own kitchen—added some time later—at the back of the house. Ours was connected to the main building, a part of the original ancestral home. All the bedrooms of the two families were upstairs. Truthfully, we could have pulled our heads and resources together—if we wanted or were confronted with a dire need for more rooms—and added three or four rooms downstairs easily. I don't remember anyone in the families suggesting that or any other ideas on how to accommodate two growing families.

I don't blame the gods or what we did or didn't do right during the recent Chinese New year for the growing tension fermenting beneath the normality of everyday living between the two families. It was obvious that the chief culprit was my cousin's wife whose presence seemed like a stinging thorn in everyone's flesh. She was a bundle of unhappiness that oozed out through every pore of her body, contaminating everything she touched. Tension started soon after eldest cousin married her. She came from a small, intimate family and had a tough time adjusting to her new mother-in-law and to my family, objecting silently to her husband spending time and money on Brother's children. She had no way of knowing that my cousin had become a part of our family during the many months when Eighth Auntie was away at a leprosy hospital. Our family at the time treated him like one of us and we fed him in the absence of his mother. Brother was slightly older than Cousin but they got along well, like brothers. Cousin would often bring home candies after work for Brother's children and one time he surprised Brother's eldest boy with a huge inflatable animal. A tiger. His wife was after his ass for weeks because of that. She went insane over the doll. Worse, her relationship with Eighth Auntie was strained from the start—one possible ramification of an arranged marriage. Eighth Auntie was caught somewhere in the middle of a growing tug-of-war, with everyone else walking gingerly on eggshells. Just waiting for something or someone to explode, shattering the tenuous family relationships.

This was reason enough for Eighth Auntie to want to move away from the ancestral home, before allowing anything worse to descend on and plague us all. She did not ask for any compensation from Mother. Neither was my family willing to offer any kind of financial assistance. The two families were like two angry dogs snarling at each other. In our case, rather quietly. When they finally emptied all their rooms and moved to their new house, I was devastated beyond consolation, the one who missed her the most because Eighth Auntie, tall and square and big, always shielded me from Mother's rage whenever she was around or heard my loud screaming for help. And there were quite a few times her intervention saved my sensitive hide and face. She would rush to my side and I had learned to count on her for protection and empathy whenever Mother was on a destructive rampage. I cried for days, missing her tender assuring voice and presence, like the passing of a dear friend. I could visit her but only stealthily, like a thief in the night, at my own peril. Not much was spoken around me before or after Eighth Auntie and her family evacuated from the house we had shared for years.

With or without Eighth Auntie, I was spending less and less time with my childhood friends. I was too busy with my hands, shouldering more adult responsibilities, squeezing every drop of latex from the rubber trees twelve months a year, ceaselessly finding, preparing, and cooking barrels of slop for the pigs, and spending every waking moments outside school hours on the farm. At the callow age of thirteen, my skin was dark, my palms and fingers were calloused, social life was discouraged and kept to a minimum, and I was grudgingly on the way to becoming a full-fledged farmer, a nobody. It wasn't a case of being inveigled into performing tasks against my will. It was part and parcel of growing up in the village with the family who adopted me. Like everyone else, I went along with the rhythm and the flow and became inured with what life and circumstances had to offer me. Mother wrote the script and I was a reluctant player.

But I was soon listening attentively to my inner voice and marching to a different tune, like allowing a seed to germinate and grow naturally without human interference of any kind. To nurture it, I had to protect it from Mother. I searched and utilized every avenue for personal betterment and intellectual growth.

Childhood friends and the world beyond were always within reach. At a very young age I discovered the mind, especially my mind, had no limitations on what was possible. I could travel anywhere, anytime, and Mother had absolutely no control over my intellectual travels and pursuits. School became my savior. Mother had stopped me from planting flowers but she could not stop me from doing many other things that were essential to my intellectual growth. And I was bent on pursuing my own dream. The world and its artifacts became my ardent teachers.

There were the Philips radio and the RCA gramophone and stacks of black records without fingerprints or scratches, fresh in their pristine jackets, that the family had inherited from someone. Maybe from Grandpa or one of his children who had left the nest seeking fortune elsewhere. Brother might have purchased a few contemporary songs, but he wasn't in the habit of following the top tunes of the year. Sadly, no teacher in school ever taught me or any other student how to use the radio (at home) and the newspapers and magazines (at school) to access information from near and far and around the world, especially those of us living out in the boondocks, feeling deprived and out of step with the modern world. Ironically, how could you feel deprived if you had limited exposure to the vast world of opportunities, knowledge, and technological advances out there? But leisure time—whether listening to a radio program or records—was a luxury we could ill afford. By early evening hours, most of us, young and old, usually sought refuge in silence and solitude, our fatigued bodies pining for quiet repose. We were oblivious to the sound of music and radio. And the outside world.

But I refused to be a dodo!

A church friend introduced me to a bible correspondence school, which I decided would increase my status as a serious Christian youth. It was the inception of a spiritual journey that resulted, visibly, in a slew of certificates next to the display of American movie stars on the wall in my bedroom. The chapters and verses and questions and answers did little to activate or fuel my spirituality, but opened my eyes to the good and the bad, the wisdom and folly of ordinary human beings, some choosing hell, others heavenly paradise in the world to come. I had problems with believing in a heaven somewhere beyond the blue sky at a very young age because of my worldly orientation and a pronounced philosophical bent in my thinking. Blame it, partially, on Confucianism and Buddhism, two "isms" that had nothing to do with religion, though our traditional lives in the village were steeped in their moral and ethical teachings. Neither ism had room for a divine being or intervention or presence in its teaching. *Why speculate or think about the heavens when you can't even handle this life on earth*, Confucius was reported to have uttered to one of his followers. Even if Confucius hadn't actually mumbled these words, I would preach that gospel myself. Why bother about believing in something beyond the blue skies and human comprehension, when many of us mortals are screwing up so atrociously this life, here and now. Maybe, just maybe, communism has something insightful to say about the effects of religion on the masses. Do-unto-others was good enough for me. It would guarantee me a place in heaven, if there is one.

Then I went on a different journey, while in high school.

My art and English teacher, also the school's Boy Scouts leader, took us all in imaginary flight to a faraway country called the United

States of America. You didn't have to be there physically, but could experience vicariously the multifarious aspects of American life, he would say. Always accompanied by a broad grin on his smooth, youthful face. And the inexpensive ticket there was the *Reader's Digest* magazine. Long before I took this journey to America with my English teacher, I had met white people from the far west who looked, smelled, talked, and behaved differently from the people I was accustomed to, whose main preoccupation was subsistence living and survival, living from day to day in a vicious cycle of poverty. The missionaries, those who catered to our souls, bodies and minds—health care workers, doctors, preachers, and teachers—maintained a certain distance from us, treating us like lepers. Foreigners. They were not, in my experience, coming down to us on our level and speaking to us in our language. In truth, none that I had met spoke our language. Part of their callous indifference, I suspected, was rooted for decades in the notion that the local culture with its diverse manifestations, religious beliefs, customs and gods were the work of the devil, to be demolished, replaced by the superior God of the white man and the superior culture of the western world. Ours were unworthy of attention, study, imitation, admiration or perpetuation. Total eradication instead of trying to build on the given cultural base, their superficial attempts proved not only ineffective but detrimental to many early missionary endeavors. Why did many early converts take rice more seriously than the black book—the Bible? Maybe the white men had never fully understood, for lack of skills, interest, or training, the local cultural manifestations. Truth be told, formed by unblemished observations, many missionaries lived a life of luxury in western-style homes, with gardeners, cooks, maids, chauffeurs—beyond their means in their own countries—away from the ignorant, unsophisticated, uncultured people they were sent to serve. And worse, what could they—representing the most developed nation in the world—learn from us, the ignorant, unsophisticated, uncultured people of the Far East? Forgetting that we simple Chinese folks in the villages and small towns in Malaya represented a centuries-old civilization that was once the envy of the world. All roads once led to China—not Europe or the Americas—the economic and cultural giant, protected by the Great Wall, the country of my ancestors. Sadly, many of my countrymen were captivated by the power and wealth of the white men and therefore kowtowed to their whims and fancies and put them on pedestals, as Chinese heathens did with their idols and ancestors. And worshipped them. I was no less guilty of this idolatry, forgetting that the white men were messengers and servants sent by God. Humble servants from a major denomination in America? They were not, by any measure.

However, missionaries from non-denominational groups were more effective in their missions because many chose to live among the people they served, often times speaking the local dialects, and were attuned to the local cultures and diverse religious beliefs and alien practices. The missionaries in my life did little to advance our causes.

But as a student in a mission school, a Methodist school, I was eager to take an unforgettable trip with my English teacher to America, for a very different kind of encounter and experiences, hoping to add color to my life and inspiration to my intellectual development. At least exposure to some innovative knowledge and thinking. I was hungry for challenges, ready for a foreign diet to whet my intellectual appetite. "I want you to know Reader's Digest will open your eyes to the wonders and excitement of a whole new world," my English teacher said to us a thousand and one times. He was proud to show his students, on a rare outing to his home, his collections of the American magazine and Reader's Digest Condensed Books. "Only the best articles from the best magazines in the whole of the United States are reprinted in this magazine," he preached ardently, often reading to us the titles of the articles in each issue—like chapters and verses from the holy book. "And best of all, it is arranged for your convenience. About thirty main articles in every monthly issue, one for each day of the month. You read it at your leisure," he added. Out of curiosity, I checked the list of articles—printed on the front cover—in every issue and he wasn't lying. "Each article," as he would persistently point out to us at every opportunity, "is a piece of superb writing." His convictions and a slight smile spoke loudly to all his adoring students of English. And article after article was on current issues, pertinent not only to the immediate audience, the Americans, but to those beyond the American soil. At times he would pick out randomly different sentences from different articles to demonstrate what a good sentence should look and sound like, whether it had ten or forty words in it. "And if you care to learn," he challenged all of us, "the magazine teaches you anything and everything from A to Z." Needless to say, I was hooked. I read and continue to peruse the magazine voraciously like a devout Muslim his Koran, or our Chinese petty gambler his dream book for numbers.

What a strange irony that I was attending a mission school, founded by American Methodist missionaries a few years after they helped lure—with tantalizing bait of a Promised Land—Grandpa and his countrymen to come settle in a virgin land they had negotiated with the Malayan government. The school followed a British curriculum—from sciences to the gospels and geography and American history, et cetera—and now my esteemed Chinese teacher assigned to teach us American English. And not English English. Because our most feared but respected headmaster was a pragmatic, lanky, and tall American missionary, all the movies shown in our school were American movies—mostly those depicting the wild west, the western frontier, and wars with the American Indians. Drastically alien to our culture and thinking and understanding of legends and history. Nevertheless a rudimentary introduction to American culture and history. He initiated vocational classes in metal and wood. The aggressive headmaster built a huge pond—serving also as a holding tank for rainwater from the soccer field and the surrounding area, et cetera—for abundant, healthy lotus plants with their broad leaves and charming flowers. And he added a small projection room, about fifteen feet above ground, outside the back wall of the school assembly hall, necessitating cutting a hole in the wall, and trained a few senior students to operate a single movie projector, allowing students time to stretch or pee between reels. Who could blame a thirteen year old boy from spending his meager savings on American comic books and pasting passport-size, colored pictures of American movie stars—Alan Ladd, Roy Rogers, Gene Autry, Doris Day, Esther Williams, Gary cooper, Grace Kelly, Montgomery Clift, Victor Mature, Randolph Scott, Maureen O'Sullivan, Elizabeth Taylor, Tyrone Power, et cetera—on my bedroom wall, daily staring at winsome faces of total strangers with their turquoise and sparkling blue eyes looking down at me? Meaningless images, but they brightened the walls and enlivened my draconian village life. I cared little for the candies but cherished the pictures that came with them, giving away the duplicates. Few of my friends had taste for strangers. We Chinese had our own movie stars from Hong Kong, on Chinese calendars, decorating the living rooms of most Chinese homes. I too had autographed pictures of female singers from Hong Kong who performed every so often in our local theater. But not a single picture of an English actor or actress—or a British movie—anywhere. And to think that Malaya and all the inhabitants of this peninsula were under direct British protectorate and control for five decades or so before Independence from Britain in 1957.

Using the British curriculum meant that any student anywhere in the British Empire (outside the United Kingdom) stretching across the globe—in places like India, Hong Kong, Malaya, Singapore, New Zealand and Australia—would be studying from the same text books. And the major exit examinations for Form III (the end of junior high school) and Form V (the end of high school) came from Cambridge University, England. You felt you belonged to a special breed of students around the world, all working indefatigably to achieve the highest standard of education possible. Fortunately or unfortunately, that meant we studied and memorized our materials diligently, from cover to cover, and knew almost every relevant question and answer by heart. It wasn't uncommon for some of us to memorize chunks and chunks of paragraphs instead of striving for comprehension and knowledge. Teachers adhered stringently to the curriculum and, on test days, students regurgitated whatever they had sponged from the texts and teachers. Serious students were expected to burn the midnight oil during the major exit examinations because we knew our lives and future depended on scoring high on these tests. In some cases you had no choice but to repeat the same form (grade) if you failed some critical tests. Sister didn't do well in some of the tests and she had to attend a different school from mine—a second chance for an education—for students who were behind in the regular classrooms or older than the age limits. Textbooks were our friends because we spent an enormous amount of time with them, more than with our friends, God, Bible, or the family pigs and chickens.

Most books in my house were textbooks, something I especially looked forward to own the beginning of each school year (January) because it meant I had successfully completed another year of studies and been promoted to a higher form. It was a moment of personal achievement and pride to be able to go to the school bookroom, next to the principal's office and the school main office, with the precious family savings to purchase new textbooks (I never forgot the smell, that invigorating scent, of new printed pages as I flipped through them the first time), pencils, ruler, easer, exercise books, composition books, and any specialty items for the coming school year. Second hand books were hard to come by because most families saved them for the younger ones. From sibling to sibling, not from a relative or a friend to another. You walked away from the bookroom with your head held high, rather arrogantly. You were on the way up to a different level but also to a different block of classrooms surrounded by a whole different colony of students.

We spent the first six years in a primary school (Standard One to Six), and the next three in a secondary school (Form One to Three) and the final two years (Form IV and V) in a high school. By the time we reached Form IV and V, we were classified or separated according to our interests and academic achievements: sciences and mathematics in one class, humanities (history, geography, et cetera) in another class. Those who performed well in Form V exit tests (prepared and administered by the University of Cambridge, England) were encouraged to apply to teachers' training colleges in England. Not a single teacher during my last two years in high school ever hinted or spoke encouragingly or knowledgeably about the world and the opportunities out there for those who could not further their education beyond Form V, for whatever reasons. My teachers, I concluded, were well versed in pedagogy and strict interpretation of the curriculum, but not the welfare of the students in their charge. Their primary task was to instruct, not to advise kids on their future. "It's too much trouble for us teachers to get involved with the students and their ambitions. And their lives. And their families. Just too much hassle and paperwork. The best thing is to stay out of it. And don't get involved." I heard this from a missionary teacher years later. Those who had the brains and the money could proceed to Form VI (an additional two years) in a boarding school—another Methodist institution—in Ipoh, the capital of the state of Perak, thirty or so miles away from home, the next step to university education. There was the usual waiting list of eager social climbers and overachievers with wealth, brains and connections. One would think the reputable boarding school would offer and advertise some scholarships to down-trodden students like me, motivating us to combat and transcend poverty and continued deprivation. That was not to be. Nothing on my own, could alter my fate, however hard I tried.

When I was in Form III, I had an incurable aspiration to attend the boarding school in Ipoh because I knew that close to a hundred percent of the students from that Methodist institution would be matriculating in institutions of higher learning somewhere, here or abroad. And that inevitably meant universities somewhere in the British Empire because British degrees were deemed to be of higher value and standards than their American counterparts. And there were cases of graduates from American universities doing additional post-graduate studies in British educational institutions—a requisite detour, before returning home, like procuring a stamp of approval and acceptance first by the British—before they could contemplate applying for jobs in our own country. It was no coincidence that certain elite Malays studied in and graduated from elite British institutions of learning in England. And those Malays, the poor ones or those from rural areas, educated in Malay schools would be denied prestigious government jobs. The poor Malays and I had one thing in common: restricted or no access to higher education. Especially in British universities.

I tortured myself by fantasizing about the exclusive, boys' military-like academies advertised in the glossy pages of the *National Geographic* magazines in the school library. Knowing these were elite boarding schools for children from elite American families, I was satisfied to accept my status quo, one born, like some of my Indian friends in school, into the lowest socio-economic class in Malaya. I knew where I wanted to go in life but finding a benefactor seemed beyond my reach. It required a great deal of diplomacy and skill, desirable but urgent social skills at which I was a total novice.

Incredibly, I wasn't shy about begging for assistance. If only, like beggars, you knew where to find the food. Begging was the game. Too cocky and aggressive for a thirteen-year-old, ambitious lad because of a burning desire to attend the boarding school in Ipoh. There was a Chinese Methodist preacher from Ipoh, round and fat, wearing thick glasses, who came to preach in our village a few times. Driving a well-polished, glistening, black car. A friend of our pastor. A prominent man in the Methodist Church, both locally and in the nation. He spoke some English and I befriended him for a selfish reason, hoping someday to approach him for some financial aid. A potential benefactor, I thought. Acting on presumptions and boundless optimism, I did write him a few letters sharing with him my village upbringing. That I was born in Ipoh but adopted by village folks. That life wasn't easy for me from the start. That I was beginning to feel trapped, at thirteen, in an unending cycle of poverty, the family solely dependent on pigs and farm and rubber for subsistence. That I had been adopted for my hands only, not for my brains. That my folks didn't appreciate my academic achievements, because none of their own children had finished high school. That education would be my road to salvation, a ticket out of meaninglessness and poverty. That I desperately needed his understanding and generosity so I could attend the boarding school in Ipoh because that would put me on the road to a promising future. And that I—a simple country boy—had no way of rustling up the necessary funds to achieve my goal. I appointed him my savior. And audaciously demanded—by the tone of my voice, a benevolent response.

How presumptuous on my part to plead my case before a complete stranger, expecting naively that a servant of God would perform a miracle because I proclaimed myself a needy, neglected, deserving child. I didn't consult anyone for guidance in writing the letters and didn't think to be less aggressive in the way I approached a man of his stature for money to fulfill a selfish dream. Weeks and months elapsed without a word from him. Not a word of solace. Maybe he thought his investment in a village kid would be like a leap in the dark, that I was an unworthy or risky protégé. I blamed myself for probably saying the wrong thing at the wrong time to the wrong person for the wrong reason. That disappointment did not deter me from writing a few letters to one particular cousin in Singapore, from whom I received words of praise and encouragement but no promise of financial support. At the time I didn't believe prayers would do me any good. The glaring absence of humble prayers and my shallow religious faith in my missives to the pastor were probably part of my downfall. I kept my dream alive but to what avail? No matter what, I continued to look to Ipoh for my salvation, like the devout Muslims to Mecca.

The one man who could or might have done something for me was my history teacher and choir director in high school. He married a relative of mine, but I could not exploit that connection to expose certain family secrets for my individual selfish pursuits and gains. Such betrayal would be considered a violation of a social taboo. What goes on in a family stays in a family. I could never strip before him that disguise of adolescent charm, smiles, happiness and innocence. I played the piano for his choir. I spent hours in the school print shop under his supervision, learning and working with a few other students, from setting the type (manually putting the metallic alphabets together to form words and sentences, et cetera) to printing and putting together the finished products, like letterheads, address cards and even the school's annual student magazine. I bicycled frequently to his residence because he had jugs of fresh squeezed lemon juice drink in his refrigerator, which I was envious of because my family could not afford one. Always a refreshing, soothing drink in the heat of the day. Feels like a cool shower on a hot afternoon. I would use his telephone to call long distance, most times without his knowledge. He never suspected I was living a life of pain and suffering, hovering precariously between despair and hope, denied and deprived of every opportunity to grow up as a normal child, fighting against Mother at every turn because I refused to dance to her tune, essentially defying her every move to transform me into her image of who I should be—just another uneducated, poverty-stricken villager, eking out a living from the soil. I kept my dream from him, though he was probably the one—like

Moses in the Bible (that was also his Christian name)—who could lead me out of the land of bondage!

I approached only one man and I felt at ease divulging the family secrets to him, but he seemed not to hear my cry for help. I did not persist in banging on his door.

This was a temporary setback known only to myself. Life as a student went on, with renewed interest and determination to take advantage of every opportunity for learning.

Geography and history, biblical studies and English literature took me around the world, allowing me to visit and study places beyond my physical and intellectual limitations. I was introduced to and fell in love with *Treasure Island, Quo Vadis, Gulliver's Treavels, Great Expectations, Macbeth, The Merchant of Venice, Oliver Twist, The Pilgrim's Progress, The Prisoner of Zenda, She Stoops to Conquer, Silas Marner, A Tale of Two Cities, David Copperfield, A Christmas Carol*, et cetera. I read, memorized, and recited poems by renowned English poets. I read extensively all major works by English authors. I would bicycle all the way to Simpang Ampat, a town at least five miles away from home, to visit an Indian store because that was the only place I could search for and acquire story books published cheaply in India. (India and my country had the same British masters.) I soon developed an insatiable appetite for storybooks by English authors. Ironically, none of my American missionary teachers introduced us to American authors for private pleasure or leisure reading. In fact, the two—a male and a female, recent college graduates—were mute about the land they came from. A student discovered a copy of *The Decameron* in our school library and it became an instant hit and the most borrowed book for months. Something, the rumor spread quickly, about sex within the pages: good sex, bad sex, illicit sex, dangerous sex, liberal sex. The book became hush-hush among some students. I had enough sex in my life growing up on a farm with pigs, dogs, cats, chickens, and ducks, so the sex in any book held very little intrigue for me.

I did not limit myself to books to broaden my horizons.

At least once a year, for a few memorable years, I followed Father and his opium business to the Chinese opera performances by the beach in Pasir Panjang, a fishing village, and joined the fishermen in their celebration of their god's birthday. Devout Christians would chastise me for intermingling with the heathens in their place of worship or being a willing participant in a pagan festival. I went for the operas while Father conducted his opium business on stage, literally behind the scenes. Many of the village philistines truly missed a cultural experience.

Periodically our whole village would gather at dusk on the Chinese school ground to watch cartoons, newsreels, and short documentary films. This was the work of our government information (propaganda?) service to educate its citizenry, especially those in rural areas, on the major issues—economic, cultural, political—confronting the country as a whole and how the government was dealing with them or how new policies on these issues might affect all citizens. Like some kind of warning, though highly informative and educational. It was common for one of our local village leaders to address us in our Hockchiang dialect during a brief interval on critical issues affecting us, especially the health and general welfare of the villagers. Less than a handful of homes in the village could afford newspapers and few listened to radio news, and this was our government's smart way of carefully disseminating vital information and keeping in touch with the people. Most came for free entertainment, but were grateful for our government's continued endeavors to bring urgent information to where we lived. For me, it was another avenue of free education.

With the state of national emergency still on, the government used the evening—and many similar evenings—to keep in touch with the people, spread their message of hope and betterment for the people, and trumpet the many programs now miraculously available to us to better our lives, however remote we were from the central government.

What seemed most unfortunate growing up Chinese in a village, physically a short distance away from the British, American missionaries, Indians and Malays (true, the white people—*red-hair devils* in our local parlance—would appear, in their full regalia, like some out-of-this-world window dressing, in our school's annual sports event drawing hundreds of parents and local citizens, the top athletes considered an honor to shake their hands, their presence adding some significance to the sporting events, like some exotic sauce on a bland dish), was the simple fact there was not a single attempt by anyone, in the churches or the schools or any civic organizations, to foster a better knowledge, awareness and understanding among us of our sameness and differences, socially, culturally, economically and politically, and our common goals and aspirations. There was never a conversation about our religious beliefs and differences—Confucianism, Christianity, Buddhism, Islam, and Hinduism. We knew almost nothing about how the others were celebrating their major holidays. Mother was my voluntary religious instructor, instilling in me fear of and antagonism against Islam, Hinduism and Buddhism. For years I would not walk near a Hindu or a Buddhist place of worship for fear of malevolent spirits.

We had Malay, Chinese, Indian, and Christian schools we could attend. There were western, Chinese, Indian, and Malay movies in different theaters in different localities. We harbored fear and misconceptions about the religious beliefs and cultural practices of people other than our own. The Malays were the indigenous people of the land and many young Malays were forbidden by their adults, from hearsay, to socialize with non-Muslims, especially the Christians. Many distrusted the Christian mission schools and their purposes. The only thing that seemed to unite us was the singing of "God Save the Queen." Or exchanging Christmas cards when the majority didn't even belong to any church. Or celebrating the New Year according to the Gregorian calendar—when the Chinese, the Indians and the Malays had their own new year celebrations according to their respective calendars. At least most tried to wear a mask of congeniality.

THIRTEEN

Our family's fortune, however measly but life-sustaining, went up and down like a bouncing ball with the fluctuations of market prices beyond our control. Especially, in the case of natural rubber, subject to supply and demand in the international markets. Blame that on the Germans! Our natural rubber fetched high prices during WW I and in the 1920s, with the mushrooming automobile industry driving everyone dizzy for ownership of the new toys in the United States. Inundated with profits from rubber, many locals went wild and crazy and borrowed heavily to invest in more land and rubber trees—ignoring the exorbitant interest rates charged by Indian money lenders—in anticipation of a booming demand for natural rubber. Those economic decisions dictated by myopic visions, lacking diversification, proved disastrous in later years because of unbridled, unanticipated competition from synthetic rubber. Our livelihood depended solely on rubber and pigs. And there were rubber trees and pigs everywhere in the village because most families were in the same boat, tossed and blown about listlessly by the storms and wild winds of international events. For example, the Depression in the United States of America in the 1930s, WW II in the 1940s, and the short-lived Japanese supremacy in Southeast Asia drastically changed the economic landscape of my country. For many, life-long savings evaporated into thin air, worsened by lack of education and opportunities and a national depression that affected the village poor like a deadly malaria.

We lived in and through hell in the 1950s because of a lackluster demand for our rubber while we were still recovering morally and economically from Japanese exploitation of our human and natural resources. Grandpa must have planted the rubber trees in the 1920s or 30s. Mother and Brother decided it was time, since the rubber latex in most trees had literally dried up (imagine squeezing a drop of juice from a shrunken, dehydrated orange), to cut down all the trees in the three-acre land in front of the ancestral home and replace them with new, high-latex-yielding rubber trees. The fact that a female stops producing milk doesn't mean she is dying or dead. The same with the rubber trees on our land. Making that decision was easy, but severing the robust roots around the bases of vibrant trees, felling the 40-60-feet tall trees (some with luxuriant canopies), sawing the trunks (ten to twenty feet or more in diameter), chopping up the unruly branches, and finally uprooting the stumps and burning them, all done manually, took many exhausting hours and months, sweat, tears, and numerous bruises, before the land was somewhat ready for a new planting. Many friends and neighbors, with little persuasion, helped themselves to the wood for their kitchens. With the trees gone, there was no place to hide from the burning sun.

At thirteen I wasn't sure whether hauling the heavy tree trunks—cut into varying lengths—on my bare shoulder improved my physique or stunted my growth. (I knew nothing at the time about the importance of nutrition and genetics and how they would inextricably impact my physical growth and development.) Chinese ingeniously used human shoulders to move heavy trunks from one location to another. Sister and I had used our shoulders instead of bicycles to carry home bundles of firewood. Women on farms and children in villages carried tons of water in tin containers suspended from a flexible pole balanced on their shoulders, like students in training in a martial arts temple. Enough physical workout and endurance to last a lifetime. Most importantly, I witnessed, throughout the ordeal, altruism at work, with friends and neighbors, relatives and families dirtying their bodies and hands, aiding each other to move one step ahead in our continued struggle to better our lives.

From our house I could now see the stretch of fertile, sun-baked, barren land marked by four dwellings, one used as a shop rented to a family friend, next to it, on the opposite side of the village main road, a simple thatched-roof house of our beloved village matchmaker, the one furthest from our house belonging to my opium-smoker tutor, and the one nearest to us belonging to relatives on Grandpa's side of the family.

Rubber trees thrived in hot, moist climate and well-drained soil. A long blind drain, at least four feet wide and five feet deep was laboriously dug along one side of the land, the furthest away from the main road, for purposes of preventing erosion of the top soil and collecting generous rain fall. The more the humus, the better the soil, a common knowledge among veteran farmers. And a final warning from the government experts—not to be viewed lightly: any wood left rotting in the field could become a potential source or carrier of diseases hazardous to the young rubber trees, in the months and years to come. In one word: no soil should be left unturned. We planted about three hundred trees in each acre, in rows about thirty feet apart. A tree will mature and be ready for tapping in seven to ten years and will continue to produce latex for at least the next twenty-five to thirty years. And if they get, like children, the right amount of attention and nurturing, they will grow up healthy and productive. They will certainly not disappoint us.

Since this was our family's first taste of replanting the land, Brother spearheaded the audacious decision to venture into tobacco growing on the same land while waiting for the trees to mature. After all we would not be the first ones to engage in this profit-making, labor-intensive enterprise in the village. Fueled by a titanic desire to improve the lot of the family and goaded on by the lucrative potential of a tobacco crop, the family was armed and ready to engage in a new economic adventure, recognizing our lack of expertise, not commitment, in this new bold endeavor. Like the rubber trees, tobacco too loved the hot, moist climate and well-drained soil. No additional preparation was necessary since the soil had been tilled for growing just about anything besides the rubber trees. The original tobacco plant had traveled all the way from Mexico in the sixteenth century to Spain, Europe, England, USA, Asia and now Southeast Asia. The minute seeds were first sown in nursery beds, well watered, and later shaded to protect the seedlings from the tropical sun. There was ample land between rows and rows of young rubber trees for us to transplant the seedlings into rows and rows of ridges three to four feet apart, with liberal utilization of the foul-smelling night soil, fresh from the outhouse—one of my first lessons in husbandry growing up poor in a farm and in a traditional Chinese culture—helping to replenish the soil with nutrients beneficial to both the growing trees and the tobacco. That odor wasn't strong enough to drive away pests and worms—out in force in the bright daylight—that feasted unashamedly on tender, savory tobacco leaves. Since we chose not to use expensive insecticide, we used our fingers and feet to do the task of simply squeezing and grinding the nasty trouble-makers to death and stamping them into the soil, temporarily coloring and moisturizing the thirsty dirt.

And like the stealthy unscrupulous hawks after our chickens, we were constantly nipping young suckers (shoots) sprouting out between the leaves and the stems or topping the flowering buds, thus channeling the food and energy to developing ten to fifteen leaves—the most valuable and desirable part of a tobacco plant. I could handle easily the tall plants, many taller than my height, but not the scorching heat of the sun, feeling the burn on my naked arms, like putting your hands close to the wood-burning stove in the kitchen. In the absence of a sophisticated irrigation system, all of us—Brother, Sister, Ah Soh and I—with watering cans hanging from a pole on our shoulders, watered each plant carefully three or four times a week except on days when we had abundant rainfall, which we collected in two huge square deep holes on the land. There was never a need or talk to bring water from the outside to meet our needs in the field, blessed as we were with plentiful rainwater. The blind drain was always filled with rainwater, a few feet deep, now alive with happy little fish and a thousand tadpoles, a possible resource should the water ever dry up completely in the holes. Unfortunately, mosquitoes were everywhere, but we got used to their presence and annoying music. Their demise imminent and swift if they landed on our sweaty faces or unprotected arms, their blood splashed like red, shimmering tattoos on our skin.

Despite a modicum of success growing rice to feed the family, with little to trade, whether in water or on dry land, in years gone by (Grandpa and his cohorts were brought to this country originally to grow rice for the Malayan government, perturbed by rising importation of rice to feed a growing population and the disinterestedness of the locals despite numerous government offers of land and other incentives to engage in increased production of the cash crop—a staple consumed by all the Malays, Chinese and the Indians), Brother opted cautiously this time for tobacco, partly because rice was cheaper to buy than to grow. Partly because others were doing it successfully in the village—with plenty of cash to taunt and impress landless neighbors and distant relatives. Partly because there was an unending, universal demand for tobacco, once attributed with healing powers, now processed for smoking, chewing or in powder for snuff. A viable pursuit, the family nodded. Something rewarding economically for the family while waiting for the rubber trees to mature. It was like saying to the soil: you could not be left partially fallow. What a waste! Or to the rubber trees: you need company, so we will surround you with hundreds of tobacco plants. And the more the merrier, until you are fully grown, independent, and ready to prove your worth.

Tobacco, imperceptibly at first, had taken over my life, with every waking minute devoted to the farm, like a faithful wife catering unsparingly to the whims of her husband. I soon felt like one of those intricately-woven, pear-shaped bird nests dangling from a small tree, swaying in a light breeze—a marvelous creation, but lonely and isolated amidst a forest pulsating with life and vigor and the perennial music of its diverse inhabitants. Friday nights provided some welcome respite, however momentary, away from Mother, Brother, rubber trees, pigs, farm, and now the tobacco plants—all in all the crux of indescribable boredom and bitter drudgery—to be with my favorite people. One teenager with a covey of other teenagers. A time to breathe afresh and partake of youthful innocence like a normal human being. One Friday night I attended a Methodist Youth Fellowship (MYF) fun night—less than a ten-minute bicycle ride away—of camaraderie, singing, games, and snacks, but the tobacco trailing me like a twin, its invisible residue permeated my skin, hair, breath and even my clean clothes. No amount of soap could scrub it away. I was tainted, a slave.

Kong Ing and Hook Bing (not their real names), two of my closest friends in a budding relationship, were always there to amuse me with their antics and silliness, unaware of the horrendous life I was going through, which I had camouflaged from all outsiders. At thirteen, on the way to fourteen, making friends was easy for me because of my sweetness, charm and easy-going personality. But Mother wasn't about to let building friendship, especially with the opposite sex—it didn't matter if it was in the church and on holy ground or in the presence of the Almighty—affect my marriage and unswerving devotion to the farm, the only entity that had meant anything to her since her own deprived childhood. The public masks I wore, different ones for different occasions like a seasoned chameleon, remained impenetrable because I continued to fear that a careless revelation about my family and myself might undermine or destroy my public image, one of steely will and determination, cheerfulness, confidence, someone well-adjusted, full of ambitions and going somewhere in life. I was wholly responsible for half-truths and some false fleeting images. And what I feared most was the lingering suspicion I wasn't going anywhere in life because Mother's myopic and parochial attitudes and philosophy, the family's inescapable poverty. My failed attempt to seek outside pecuniary aid to further my education in a better school seemed to have grounded me in the village for life. Or at least for the moment. Nonetheless resulting in a paralysis of some sort

The boys and I had a few things in common. Females, the obvious distraction. Or attraction. Even though they attended a Chinese school and I an English school—an ocean apart in our intellectual pursuits—we all spoke the same Hockchiang dialect, they cleverly avoiding my English, and I slyly their Mandarin. Only Kong Ing and I were related—his grandfather and my grandmother, both deceased, were brother and sister. All of us were active in the Methodist church (the center of our social life, especially for the young people in the village), Sunday school, bible study, MYF, weekly youth prayer meeting, and had the same piano teacher—the first female pastor of our church (who years later became the first female superintendent of the Methodist Church in Malaya). I could never join them and others in ping pong or badminton at the church because Mother decided that tending to the well-being of tobacco plants and killing the insidious worms were more important than friends and frivolous recreational activities. Pressed, Mother might defend herself by saying "Do ping pong and badminton make cash for the family?" Mother became this way because life wasn't kind to her, and forced into the role of a surrogate mother to her many brothers and sisters after the sudden death of her mother. Both my friends knew practically nothing, my deliberate choice, about Mother, or the oppressive goings-on in my family.

Most people in my village lived and died with dark hidden secrets. Their mouths sealed forever. A few daring young men, uneducated fools I called them, boasted about their virility and sexual exploits or, was it, their fumbling sexual experimentations. I was one of those who mindlessly helped spread their rumors, sinfully indulging in some sexual fantasy, albeit vicariously. A few unfortunate suicides, something about failed love. Others pronounced them the work of the devil. Most people in the village practiced silence, preferring to mind their own businesses. Unless of course you were the nosy but eminent village match-maker whose preoccupation was to gather—by hook or by crook—every iota of information, good and bad, about every marriageable young man and woman, whose destiny and future bliss depended on every word that proceeded from her mouth, few from her brains. Her words a redemption for the socially challenged, awkward in appearance, speech and gait, doomed otherwise to a life of single-hood! Nobody questioned her gift and propensity for embellishing facts to sell used, spoiled or contaminated goods—the few morally decadent and unworthy of a second chance in life. Or marital bliss. Yes, she rescued a few unwanted strays. Or pests. Yes, she, like a criminal lawyer, wielded enormous power. Few challenged the tradition of arranged marriage in our village. Most followed meekly, like sheep, the dictates of their parents, like mandates from heaven. And many found compatibility—at least the few moments in bed—and lasting satisfaction with complete strangers at the inception of their union.

At my age the immediate problem was not the matchmaker, but how not to betray my true feelings and self and family to my two friends. And sometime during the fun evening at the Christian youth fellowship, Hook Bing asked me if I would like to spend the evening with him after the meeting, something about his birthday. Something about going with him to his house. I was elated beyond words.

"You sure it's okay with your parents?" I said grinning, innocent as a puppy. I was eternally grateful to Hook Bing for even asking, an excuse to be away from home. I liked surprises. Should I or shouldn't I hug him for the invitation? He interrupted my thinking in progress.

"My mother decided we won't be tapping rubber trees tomorrow," he said casually. "That's why I would like you to come over tonight if you have nothing to do."

Rubber trees? Why, Mother would never understand why the trees, like me, needed some time to rest, relax and recuperate. Just ask the Indian rubber tappers at the British-owned rubber estates, nearby. They strictly followed the schedule of their British bosses to tap one section of rubber trees and let it rest for two weeks, minimally, while moving on to hundreds of other sections. A stringent rotation was scientifically healthy for the trees in the long run. And a practice not unlike the desired rest one needs after giving blood, for charity or personal gain. "Your trees are lucky to have a mother like yours," I mumbled into the air, envious that my friend had such an understanding mother.

"Did you say something?" my friend said looking puzzled. "Did I hear you correctly something about—"

"You did." I had a chronic habit of cutting people off in mid sentence, sometimes before they could complete the main subject or the critical verb, considered rude by my teachers in school, who cared to remind me not infrequently of my manners. "Try not to be so rude," they admonished me. "Mother makes my Sister and me tap and tap twelve months a year. Only a heavy downpour could save us from this. We are exhausted and the trees, believe me, are exhausted too," I continued, careful not to spill too much of the family secrets. If Hook Bing could hear or read between the lines, so to speak, that meant we were utterly poor to be slaughtering the trees twelve months a year. An inexcusable crime against the trees, committed only by people who desperately needed cash for something. It was survival, plain and simple for my family. One secret out of the bag was too many I thought. Maybe he didn't hear it as a secret as the gaggle of teenagers was getting louder with everyone having to impart their last words to their friends before leaving for the night. So it seemed.

My friends and I were the last ones to leave the premises, making sure the hall was in the same condition as we entered it earlier in the evening. "See you tomorrow at piano lessons," someone shouted at me while balancing on his bicycle seat.

"Where is your bicycle?" Hook Bing asked, leaving me wondering if he had heard what I had said about Mother or postponed it for later.

"Over there." I pointed to the spot where I had parked my bicycle. "I will follow you." No one was in a hurry to go home and everything was in a slow motion like some of our pigs in our farm on a lazy hot afternoon. I had never seen so many dawdlers in my life. And why not? There was nowhere else to go but to bed. Staying up late to entertain a friend or a relative was out of the ordinary unless of course you were an overachiever, alone burning the midnight oil preparing for an important examination. (Looking back, one cannot help but think that rubber trees and kerosene lamps were an indisputable deterrent to juvenile delinquency in the village. You went down too when the sun went down the horizon—many preparing to get up at two or three in the morning to attack the rubber trees, and others to take care of the many chores around the farms during the daylight hours.)

By nine or ten in the evening, the sun had gone to bed and the air was relatively cool, gently massaging my face and arms and chest (anything that was exposed) as we rode leisurely side by side—barely running into any human traffic in the late evening—on our merry way towards my friend's house. Less than half a mile up the road, further away in the opposite direction from my house, like going to school, we turned left for a third of a mile, then right for another half of a mile, his house silhouetted against the trees in a moon-lit night sitting motionless at the end of the road. The building loomed larger as we neared the doorstep. "I don't see any light in your house. Your parents must have gone to bed," I said softly as we parked our bicycles on one side of the house. The dynamo that generated the bicycle light worked with the rotation of the back bicycle wheel, automatically turning it off once the bicycle came to a complete stop. I was sure there was a roof above where we parked the bicycles even though we were blinded by total darkness. At home we left all our bicycles, seven or eight of them, unlocked, under the veranda. Only in a crime-free village. "They like to go to bed early," he said, gently pushing the front door open, locking it behind us, then, with a flashlight, tiptoeing to his bedroom, the first room on the right, like one blind man leading another blind man to a destination. With a match he lighted the one kerosene lamp with a clean chimney on his study table. I could see immediately one textbook left open, others neatly stacked around it, another lamp hanging on one wall, and, with a bright lamp bringing everything into clear focus. I followed him like an obedient child to the kitchen, without a word between us. His kitchen, like some better village homes, was in a separate building, joined by a covered walkway to the house in front. Smoke, despite well-connected chimneys, from wood-burning stoves and possible fire were responsible for this rather pragmatic design. While I could faintly hear birds and animals singing or chattering away in the distance, silence reigned supreme in this household. Using some weird sign language, more of a pantomime, he had me sit on a bench near a big square dining room table and he began the ritual of making two cups of hot Ovaltine—a British beverage. (No sane person in any home would build a fire for the sake of two cups of boiling water. Many Chinese homes had one or two sturdy flasks filled with boiling water at all times, sufficient to meet all needs, especially convenient for the sick or young mothers, having to make bottle milk using condensed milk for babies in additional to breast milk.) "Do you want anything in it?" my friend said, breaking the silence. He knew where everything was in the kitchen. "I would like some condensed milk if you have some," I said. Again most of us grew up using condensed milk and not sugar in our hot beverage. A bad habit we copied from the British. I knew my request wouldn't be an imposition on him. I was fed with condensed milk when I was first adopted as a baby. Most of us grew up with it, a product essentially made up of sugar and milk. He went to the pantry and returned with a glass jar half full of condensed milk. Without doubt, the Ovaltine always tasted lovely, hot or cold, with the milk.

Then came the bonus or surprise for the evening. Hook Bing went over to the stove and removed the lid from a bamboo steamer, still in a wok, and picked a few pieces of something golden-brown his mother had made earlier in the day and brought them to the table. "I can eat hundreds of this stuff," he said. "Try a few."

A few? Thousands! I had to suppress my gasp of sudden excitement and instantly aroused interest, meaning never expose my true state of mind when offered something so irresistibly palatable by a host. Always pretend you are not hungry, according to the social etiquette Mother had taught me since I mastered the dexterity to handle the ubiquitous chopsticks. Mother belonged to the old school and I had to believe this affected behavior was part of the Chinese culture and traditions. Let the host do all the talking. Let the host pile it on your bowl. Even though your heart was aching or dying for a morsel of the treat. "I am not very hungry after all the snacks at the church," I said lying through my teeth. Mother would be proud of my performance. But not for long. *Yield Not To Temptation*? Ignore the warning of a hymn we sang often in church. I threw the social etiquette out the window and started with one piece. And slowly, without any trace of voracity. Like aged Chinese rice wine, it tasted better each time. And the hot Ovaltine washed it down smoothly, as Mother would say.

"More over there," he pointed to the steamer. The snack was made from a few simple ingredients readily available in most Chinese kitchens: Chinese sweet potatoes, ground peanuts, and some brown sugar. A bamboo steamer, some water and a good steady fire.

Shortly after, we returned to his room and to bed. He made sure I was comfortable sleeping without the lamp on. He slept on the outside, and I automatically on the inside, our feet facing the wall, not the door. (Many Chinese, a little primitive and superstitious to educated urban folks, believe you carry the dead with their feet first through the door. And sleeping with your feet facing the door invites death! Or means death! Don't tempt fate!) We were on the way to dreamland, at least I was when Hook Bing decided to resume our conversation, the one we started at the youth meeting.

"I told you earlier at the church mother and I won't be getting up early to tap rubber. And you said to me something about tapping twelve months a year," he said both turning our heads sideways about the same time so we would be facing each other, intentionally so as to reduce our voices to a loud whisper without disturbing his little brother and his parents somewhere now visiting a faraway paradise in dreamland. "That doesn't make sense to me."

I said, "My sister and I tap the trees during weekends and all the school holidays. She spends additional hours with the trees on weekdays because she wants more pocket money to spend. I don't. She goes to a different school. Her classes start later in the morning." I knew I wasn't telling the whole story, with a hot debate boiling inside me. Should I tell him everything…why, I think, Mother makes us kids work to death like slaves not only tapping rubber trees, but working in the farm day in day out, raising pigs, and now caring for tobacco plants? Because both Sister and I are adopted kids, I wanted to shout from the rooftop. "What doesn't make sense to you?" I asked, suppressing all the thoughts rushing through my mind like a bicycle losing its brakes down a hill. I caught myself hesitating again, reluctant to share my private thoughts.

"I thought your folks are doing well. I mean your father must be making tons of money selling opium," he said.

"I hate to disappoint you," I said and I thought what a perfect time to clear a rumor or two about my father's opium business. "My father dabbled in everything. He tried to put some money into the fishing business over at Pangkor Island. We didn't hear a thing about it. And the opium business? I think he spends too much for police protection."

"I thought you have an uncle who is a police officer."

"That is my Eighth Uncle, but he lives and works in Ipoh. Too bad he is not working here in town to protect Father."

"So how is your father's opium business?"

"By the way," I said, as something just popped into my mind, "Father and a group of friends also tried their hands at gambling. Have you seen people looking at dream books and hoping to find the winning numbers?" A dream book consisted of numerous pictures, from trees to birds to rivers to mountains, et cetera. Each picture had a number or numbers attached to it. In other words, all your dreams could be translated into numbers. The family helped sell some small amounts. And if you were lucky that numbers from your dreams you bought could well be the winning ticket. "He and his friends lost some money on gambling. Again Father never uttered a word about his share of the loss in gambling."

"I have never met your father but I've heard a lot about his opium business in the village. I've a relative in Kampong Koh who is also involved with the business. But I heard he is a small dealer, compared to your father."

I could no longer hold back the dam from breaking. I was about to let a big cat out of the bag early in the morning while in bed with a friend. "Father is not a smart business person. He thinks he is a big guy and has a chauffeur driving him around in that little British car. He has a mistress and a few offspring in Kampong Koh. People said he had no business having kids at his age. Now when he comes home we can expect trouble. He is constantly after my mother for money. And you know what that means?" I was about to let out a bigger cat out of the bag. "Since our daily survival depends solely on rubber and pigs, my mother has no choice but to force us to work harder and harder every day. Of course my father increasingly threatens to sell the family land he inherited from Grandpa." Selling off the family land and the ancestral home was not an option. The family would lose face in the eyes of everyone in the village. The most humiliation any family could bear.

"With the price of rubber so low in the market," my friend said, "my parents are looking for something else to do. We too depend very much on our farm, pigs and rubber trees to keep us going."

"You have to be in my shoes to really understand what is going on in my family. You see me once or twice in church during the week and I always put on my smiles." I added. My eyelids were getting heavy. Worse, I felt I had betrayed my family.

We had had quite a night and soon we were dozing off going on our separate journeys. I was never a sound sleeper since being forced to get up three or four in the morning to tap rubber trees. And I don't usually sleep well in a new bed with another person, though I did share a bed for a while, for lack of space, with my second cousin, now living with his father and his mistress in Ipoh.

It didn't seem long when I started hearing a distant dog barking. A stray or a wild animal on the prowl? Maybe? Must be a big prowler because a few more joined in the barking. Some kind of ripple effect was in the works when it struck me the sound was getting louder near my friend's house, with more dogs joining in the chorus. Soon I saw a light across the rafters (most village homes don't have ceilings), then I heard someone talking in the house. The rafters got brighter as she approached the front door. "Hook Bing," she said, "I think there is someone coming to our house." It was the voice of my friend's mother. By the time we got dressed and joined her, the neighbor's dogs were drawn into the early morning vocal exercises. Everyone singing the same tune. Definitely not a sprightly one, most awakened from their slumber.

I said solemnly, "That is my mother out there looking for me." Sounded like someone caught stealing red-handed with my head slightly bowed. And found guilty!

"You are not in trouble, are you?" my friend's mother said and sauntered to meet my mother.

"What time is it?" I asked no one in particular. Numbed and befuddled that she could find the house in the dark.

"About four," my friend finally broke his silence. He stood there speechless.

This was Saturday morning. It was time for my sister and I to get up to tap rubber trees. Mother must have had the nose of a dog to track me all the way to this house. I might have said something about going to see Hook Bing during the week or some time in the recent past. Mother had a rubber tapper's kerosene lamp strapped to her forehead and rode her little bicycle. It was quite a distance between the two houses and I doubt Mother had ever been to my friend's house. If she did it must have been in her previous life. But she did it. "See you later at piano lessons," I told my friend and left quietly. Ephemeral but grateful for the fun. As I rode away I heard Mother said, "Children don't understand things nowadays."

The two mothers didn't usually talk to one another. They had nothing in common except worshipping the same God in the same church. Mother was way older than her and I could not conceive the two doing something together. Two very different people from two different planets.

Nothing she did was fortuitous. I was adopted for my hands and my hands only. But I was deeply hurt and humiliated in public before my friends by Mother's intransigence, because she believed everything she did was right, in her eyes and in her scheme of things. I should have known better because this was not the first time Mother had gone after my hide because I chose to disappear for a night away from home for the sake of regaining some peace and quiet and sanity of mind. Not too long ago I attended a youth meeting and opted to spend the night with Kong Ing, next door to the church, and Mother raised hell then. I was with a relative, not a stranger. She woke everyone up in the wee hours of the morning because the houses were closer together and the dogs couldn't stop hollering. She screamed and yelled and said I had become an intractable child. And said something awful like "I should have known better than to let you join the youth fellowship" or something.

"Doing God's work?" I moaned in protest. "Or at least to be near people who are doing God's work in His vineyard? What's wrong with Mother?" I was grateful for the diversion and jollity with my friend.

She forgot I was young, energetic and gregarious. I wanted to grow up like a normal teenager. Her mission seemed to be to erect every possible barrier around me, denying me the freedom to be the real me and the experiences vital to my social and mental development. Like allowing a plant to grow in its natural environment, planting it in the best of soil and location. But I found the home environment suffocating and not conducive to my procuring a good education and personal growth.

Mother's ideas and my ideas, her thinking and my thinking, her plans and my plans would never dovetail, one seemed too big for the other, with too many rough edges, more like one person veering off from the main well-trodden path venturing into an unknown territory. Not unlike what Grandpa and the families faced when they first arrived at this virgin part of Malaya, from the moment the ship landed, literally cutting a path through a thick forest to their destination with well-sharpened *parangs*. With each passing year, I didn't find Mother satisfactory, failing to talk to me about what I truly wanted for my life and future or give me unstinting support as a parent so I could be a successful student. But she seemed satisfied with the mediocre, with her deplorably, in my judgment, fossilized approach to life, present and future. She couldn't see beyond the four walls of the village or her own life, that there were other things one could aspire to doing. We had relatives, not in the village anymore, children of uncles and aunties who flourished conspicuously in their legal, medical, law enforcement, and teaching professions. And they, steeped in Confucian teachings and ethics and Chinese culture, never failed to shower their parents with money, care and deep affection. I refused to believe Mother was blind to what was going on in the Ling clan. We heard stories about our relatives and their successes. Especially about their grown-up children. You could never stop Chinese parents from talking about the brilliance and achievements of their offspring, with seldom a word about their own accomplishments. Because their children's success is their success. Their future their future. Mother took Sister and me to visit some of their homes, though infrequently. She was partially blinded, I was sure, by the vicissitudes in her own life.

Mother had led a life of poverty for too long. All she knew was pigs and rubber trees. Father's infidelity must have ruined her life for years. She looked small, withdrawn and wizened. Most times she was expressionless, sitting at the top of the back stairway looking out the window. Her tears, many and bitter. Her smiles, few. Her joy, barely visible. She suffered in quiet despondency. If only there was someone who could help mitigate her burdens. She was never a deeply religious person. God and prayers didn't mean a thing to her. More likely she would go to a temple seeking divine solace if she was down in a deep hole. I had witnessed innumerable times Mother listening tearfully to Small Sister's problems, seldom seeing her coming home without rivers of tears, eyes red and swollen because of too much crying and groaning, because of her husband's addiction to gambling, threatening to drain the family's resources. But Mother was never good at telling others about the troubles and frustrations that almost drowned and killed her every step of her life. For years she was the surrogate mother to her siblings, the same no-nonsense uncompromising stance and toughness she continued to project in her life till this day. And she was the head of the family for all practical purposes because Father had left her and the family and the village for various business pursuits and mistresses.

One of Mother's biggest problems at the moment was trying to coerce me into following in Brother's footsteps, someone I tried hard to admire but not to emulate. His shoes were not my size. I didn't belong in this family or the village.

FOURTEEN

One steamy hot afternoon I received an urgent message to go by the matchmaker's house, conveniently located on the edge of our land by the main road. Someone came running across the field to deliver the message verbally. One of her grandsons. Big and fat and tall as a giant. His boobs waggled as he ran. "Now what?" I shrugged my shoulders. A worm wriggled on my left palm, about to die mercilessly. Sister and I were busy with the tobacco plants, working hard spying on the worms' activities. The house was a short distance from where I was.

"Go," Sister said, "I'll be here."

I loved my sister, a tough nut to beat. We came originally from two different families. She a little older than I. We never indulged in self-pity or exchanged thoughts on our common misery or misfortunes that had plagued us. I wished she would study harder in school. At least she knew how to enjoy life, worked hard tapping rubber trees without complaint, and spent her pocket money her way. She loved Chinese movies. I usually tagged along—she would carry me on the back of the bicycle, and did most of the crying and sobbing, less of laughing or cheering because there was nothing humorous or funny in the ones we saw. I cried when the Emperor ordered his taskmasters to whip, discipline and bury those who refused to work, for reasons of health or conscience or obstinacy, right at the site of the famous Great Wall of China. Just a movie! I consoled myself. (The truth? With overpopulation, China had many young men to spare!) I cried when the misunderstood, jilted lover plunged herself into a surging river, gurgling for breath, drowned, and was swiftly washed away. I cried when a pretty woman was transformed into a snake by the magic of a displeased monk, who condemned her evil incarnate, then buried her under a pagoda, She was rescued and released by her son decades later, in a sequel to the first movie. I thought we had enough tragedies in our own lives growing up in the sticks without having to witness more tragedies in black and white on the big screen. But Sister embraced and loved them all like iced water on a hot day.

I did try to replicate something I saw in many of the Chinese movies: the electric wall lights. Something to brighten up my room. Without electricity? It wasn't that difficult a project. All I did was to hang my kerosene lamp on the wall and scrimped on a one-foot by two-foot piece of white paper, folded it into a half circle around the lamp and used thumb tacks to hold it in place. It looked, to me, a slightly modified copy of the ones portrayed in the movies. I was pleased with my own creative impulse. I felt like I was in a movie, basking in my own creation.

Anyhow, as I approached the front door of the matchmaker's house, I smelled something terribly odiferous coming out, in the absence of any breeze, from inside the house. Something that could only be found in abundance and free in a chicken coop. The old lady must be raising some chickens to supplement her income because of a slump in her matchmaking business. Maybe there was a snake inside the house after the chickens. I hated snakes and I would be the first one to run away from one, dead or alive. What I saw next was far worst than my suspicions, depending on how you look at it. With a bowl on her left hand, using something like a Chinese spoon, Mother was dishing out this chicken shit like a paste onto the match-maker's back and gently smearing it—like icing on a birthday cake—from side to side, up and down, some dripping down the sides of her body. Using my right fingers to block my nose, I felt something eerily unpleasant springing up my throat. I had vomited at the sight and smell of baby shit. And shit from other animals, two- or four-legged. It didn't matter. Mother instructed me to go home, scoop up a few cups of fresh chicken shit from our coops, and bring it to her in a pail because our friend needed fresh applications at least twice a day, for a few days. I had heard that she had had a rash for a while, which was exacerbated by the prolonged tropical heat, now that her thatch-roofed house was exposed naked to the scorching sun, without the tall rubber trees that once flanked it and provided a huge canopy over it. It was no secret that her condition worsened about the time we felled the trees in her vicinity. She could blame us for her ailment. But we also knew she suffered chronic itch, and western medicine didn't seem to ameliorate her physical condition. In fact nothing did. Hopefully, this old-fashioned Chinese cure—the power of chicken shit—might do the trick.

Our garden vegetables, vines (Chinese squash and melon), sweet potatoes, cassava, et cetera, all grew fast and robust after we fed them chicken shit. Another lesson in husbandry for someone growing up dirt poor. Everything could be used for something, including chicken entrails, feathers, blood, and shit. Coagulated chicken blood fried with Chinese chives was one of my favorite dishes. Not having any medical or scientific knowledge, I suspected the chicken shit contained certain chemical ingredients that needed further scrutiny and experimentation to determine their efficacy. Seemed like a soothing moisturizer for the poor lady, at the moment. The offensive odor, in my teenage thinking, could kill just about anything, including the hardiest and most stubborn germs and bacteria.

I wasn't exactly thrilled with the mission because I anticipated I would have involuntarily emptied my stomach before the task was over, without having to snake my index finger down the throat or swallow a drop of sugarless emetic. I did station some Tiger Balm ointment in my nostrils to filter the foul smell, and a block of Chinese sugar to fool my throat with something sweet before I entered the coop to do my job. Mother was pleased that I had secured more than the amount she requested. I suspected that stale mud, especially from our pig wallow, might have done the same job for the old lady!

By the time I returned to the field, Sister had covered quite a few rows of tobacco. A few suckers still appeared here and there. And they had to be removed. The worms continued to pose a challenge, a perennial problem as long as we had tobacco plants out there. Today we were students again as Brother attempted to show us how to harvest the mature leaves. "When the leaves, especially the big ones, at the bottom start to change color," Brother pointed to them and plucked a few to show Sister and me, "it is time to harvest them." And when Brother held the ripened leaves next to the others still growing, I could see the difference in color. The mature ones had a lighter shade of green. Some could have a few spots of yellow. Interestingly not all the leaves mature at the same time. The leaves aged or matured usually from the bottom up. The gradual change of color was a clue to prime the leaves singly. And you could do it with ease standing, squatting or bending over to pluck each one carefully without bruising it. Sister had to go home early because she said she felt like vomiting or something. I didn't say anything to her about the chicken shit. I doubted I had become infected with something and unknowingly passed it on to her. With fewer hands, we had to hurry to harvest all the mature leaves. And more ripened with the day. The timing was perfect. The sun speeded up the maturing process.

Sister and I were out of school for the next three weeks or so, which meant more hours helping Brother in the field. At the end of each day, we had piles and piles of leaves under the veranda ready to be wired—Mother, Ah Soh, and my oldest niece all volunteered their hands for the wiring—and hung up to dry anywhere and everywhere, by the sides of the house, kitchen, under the veranda, and in the sheds. When dried properly, the leaves turned golden or dark brown, ready to be cured by the tobacco companies.

Brother was exhilarated by the success of his first venture into tobacco growing and was seriously contemplating a second planting before the year was over. I prayed for rain—forty days and forty nights—to escape from the insufferable heat everywhere, the worst radiating from the sun-drenched soil and setting your body on fire from the bottom up.

After a day or two, Sister wasn't doing well and Brother got some Chinese herbal medicine from Kampong Koh. Mother asked me to help her prepare something using the herbs for Sister to drink. We went upstairs to Mother's bedroom. She set a bowl on her bed. She slid out one drawer, then another one and placed them quickly on her bed and asked me to catch the crawling insects inside the drawers. With speed and determination, Mother pulled off the legs so they wouldn't run away. I followed her every move. We managed to catch a handful, now severely crippled but their antennas still active like searchlights. How could we tell these cockroaches—looked like cockroaches to me—that they had to die so Sister could live?

Into the kitchen we went and Mother dumped the insects unceremoniously into a small pot, adding the herbs and a cup or two of water, and boiling it for about twenty minutes. It took more time to set up a fire than to boil the concoction. Soon it emitted a mild odor. I wasn't there to see Sister drink it. But one thing I did know—Chinese people were not in the habit of adding sugar to their bitter medicine. Sadly, I had not seen, growing up, any Chinese medicine in the form of a pill. Everything had to do with some cooking and swallowing the nasty stuff. You did it in one gulp with your eyes closed. The aftertaste seemed to linger forever. Immediate rinsing might help. And you bundled yourself up tightly in a thick blanket, because the more you sweat the better it was for you, releasing the poison from your body. Mother would place her fingers on your forehead and pronounce the magic words: "The fever is gone."

Chinese medicine, mainly of herbs and animal parts, has been in use for thousands of years in the country of my ancestors. Wherever they went, Chinese immigrants carried their medicinal secrets with them. I grew up with Chinese medicine and never had reason to question its universal use and efficacy. I did, however, grow up hating its taste, never drinking it without some protestation and tears.

The only affliction I had that wouldn't go away for a long time was the occasional canker sore. Because I had too much *fire* in my system, the Chinese would say, symptomatic of acute imbalance in the consumption of foods. What foods! Eating might as well be drinking—three meals of watery porridge a day with salted fish and garden vegetables was our daily fare. But the *fire* part I knew to be true because I was forever thirsty and would buy blocks of ice to make cold drinks. I complained constantly about the heat and the sun. It was the heat building up within, supposedly because of all the foods I ate, not the heat from without, that was the cause of my canker sore. And there was only one way to douse that fire and that was to drink and eat things that were considered to have, according to the Chinese Yin-Yang philosophy, *cooling* effects on my body. Mother made plenty of barley water for me to drink whenever I complained of pain in my mouth. Eating Yang foods would be like adding more wood to the fire. And eating Yin foods would have the opposite effect. One must always strive, according to Yin-

Yang philosophy, for a proper balance of Yin and Yang foods to avoid sickness, disease, and suffering. Acupuncture is one accepted way that many traditional Chinese correct this imbalance. The best guide to follow is to eat what nature provides abundantly according to each season of the year. Nature is still the best teacher in matters of growing and eating the right foods for health and longevity.

But food was only one part of the formula for growing up healthy. The other was work. Physical labor, without doubt, kept me lean and strong. But work—tapping rubber trees, preparing slop for pigs, tending the farm, and now caring for the tobacco plants—was gradually affecting my mind and concentration. Because by the end of each day, fatigued by work, this drudge didn't have any appetite for books, but only wanted rest and sleep. At fourteen I was also the uncle to Brother's brood of five growing children, two girls and three boys. The oldest, about eight, was a girl. She and her sister were now attending the same Chinese elementary school I first attended about fourteen years previously. Mother helped Ah Soh raise the kids. I cradled a baby to sleep once or twice. Sister and I spent very little time babysitting the children because our hands were needed for work at all times so our family would have decent meals each day, decent clothes for everyone, a decent roof over our heads, and a decent chance for some of us to get a decent education.

Suddenly a decent chance became accessible for me to excel in something no one had ever done in the whole village since its inception. We built the first parsonage for the first full-time preacher of our Chinese Methodist church, an outstanding achievement, considering that most parishioners were farmers, with a few fishermen, businessmen, and government workers (including teachers) added to the throng. The Chinese Methodist church became the focal point for many of the Hockchiang people, my hard-working people.

And when I heard that the female preacher was giving piano lessons to the youth of the church, my interest in the church and its activities jumped up quite a few notches! My faith in God may be a little shallow and shaky, but my faith in my hardened fingers to play the piano was unshakable from the start.

In school I was simply thrilled to touch one or two of the white keys. For no reason except curiosity about where the sound was coming from. And how! I didn't forget what I had done to Brother's gramophone machine years ago. For almost the same reason. "Beware, the headmaster is on the loose." Students would remind each other to behave, because if caught violating any school rules, the punishment could be severe. One of them was "Don't touch the piano without permission" on a stiff card sitting on top of the piano in the school hall,. You could hear the public reprimand and caning miles away. Everyone feared his presence. Something about his height—a tall American giant, like a tall tree among the bushes. Something about his no-nonsense speech and puffing, leaving students wondering if he was genuinely angry or simply impatient with us. Anyway, at the time I knew of two fat students in our elementary school, children of a filthy rich medical doctor in town, who were chauffeured to school in a British Jaguar every day and traveled to Ipoh for private piano lessons every weekend.

Finally, I could remove that sting of jealousy and concentrate on my own opportunity to learn the piano—also from a private teacher—without having to travel to Ipoh. Few in the village ever ventured beyond the village, except to contiguous towns for government business, school, theater, and shopping for any necessities not grown or produced on our own farms.

And here in my own church, in my own village, for thirty minutes every Saturday morning, for the first time in my life, I had the opportunity to learn how to play the piano for an almost insignificant monthly fee. The same amount could have gotten me a few sticks of ice-cream from the ice-cream man selling from the back of his bicycle. But I was in for a real surprise during my first official piano lesson—my music teacher did not know how to play the piano. That couldn't be! But I heard it from her own mouth! I remembered seeing her teach the congregation new hymns before the church services many times on Sunday mornings. She used four fingers—two on the right hand and two on the left—to play just the melody (without all the fancy chords and harmony) for everyone to sing. It worked. She was playing the same four notes, octaves apart, with the stretched fingers. In fact she was very good at it. Patiently she first taught them the words—many in the congregation had very little education, and then she taught them to sing a phrase or a portion at a time. There were at least two or three hundred people in the pews, men and boys on one side of the aisle, women and girls on the other side. A strategy that worked incredibly well for her. Nobody ever introduced an unknown hymn during a regular church service.

Within a short time we had a teacher—another Ling, not related to me, whose father was one of Father's longtime opium partners—leading in the singing. Not in Mandarin, which the kids learned in school, but in Hockchiang, the dialect used and spoken by every soul in the congregation and the whole village. Thereafter a choir of the young and the old was formed, performing in front of an uneducated audience every Sunday up on the dais. There had never ben a choir before. A new exciting experience for anyone who could crow like a chicken.

And there were many other innovations to the church services and programs. The new pastor visited just about every member's home in the village with her bicycle (later she had a car), a daunting task that would intimidate anyone, especially one who was new to the village. None of the roads in the village had markers or signs and there was no printed directory of the addresses of the local inhabitants. But she braved the unknown, always with a smile and a trove of kind words. She was an effective communicator, aggressively sowing the seeds of the good news wherever she went. The church became alive and a powerful force in the community because of her dedication. It grew by leaps and bounds. Without doubt, she was a true servant of God! Under her spiritual leadership, she trained and groomed many young men who later became some of the most outstanding leaders of the Chinese Methodist church in Malaysia and Singapore. I knew her—Reverend Lim Swee Beng—as my first and only piano teacher.

She might not have played the piano like a true pianist, but she could show us where our fingers should be on the keyboard and how to keep the proper timing. She was never able to physically demonstrate on the keyboard how it should be executed or what the music or the piece should sound like. But she did not hesitate to tell you—shaking her head and gently tapping your knuckles—when you were not doing it right or according to the book. The fifty-six-page *William Smallwood's Pianoforte Tutor* opened the gate to a musical wonderland for me. It was my introduction to the world of piano playing and heavenly music that was to add a whole new dimension to my life. *Pianoforte* seemed to me at first an old-fashioned word, a classical word. But I felt calmly assured I would be learning the rudiments from the book, like from an old but experienced teacher. I was the only bold and promising one out of her ten students who moved gleefully from lesson to lesson, page to page, beyond her and my wildest expectations. I was always ahead of others because I was endowed with the gift of sight-reading. It was like picking up a storybook and reading it with ease without the bumps and potholes along the way because I had mastered the basic vocabulary. I had been waiting for this for too long and nothing could bar me from coming to church, however sacred the piano, to practice and practice and play new lessons way ahead with confidence—two, three or four pieces at a time—leaving all the others behind. "A natural talent," my music teacher said, "and try to use it to glorify God." What a felicitous remark, I thought—the part about my talent. The part about glorifying God would have to wait. I had to work harder to deserve her adulation and trust in me. I was her pride and joy!

My reputation was soon to spread far and wide, from the little community to the school. I was lionized and became the darling of admirers, here and there. But Mother wasn't the least bit pleased or touched by what I had accomplished with the piano. She probably thought my hands could have been used for a better or a more utilitarian purpose, like tapping rubber trees, raising the pigs, tending the farm and taking care of the tobacco plants. "He makes too much noise," she was rumored to have said when told of her son's astounding display of talent on the piano keyboard, "and for what purpose?" She was, I considered, an unrepentant philistine. She had my flowers pulled out of the soil and threw them over the fence, once, but not the piano.

Every Saturday, starting as early as eight in the morning, without fail, rain or shine, each student must come prepared for a new lesson for a thirty-minute session with the piano teacher, using the only piano in the whole village, the one up on the dais, near the pulpit and the altar. I believed we were on sacred ground. And in the presence of God at all times. A busy day for her. And during the week, depending on the schedule, you could have more than thirty minutes for practice without competition. I was one of two or three of her students who attended English schools and with me she would use pidgin English when spoken words were absolutely necessary during the session. With the others, who attended Chinese schools, she used a mix of Mandarin and the Hockchiang dialect. The lesson began with the routine playing of a scale. The *scale in contrary motion* was my favorite type of scale where you started with the thumbs on the same note—usually in the middle of the wide keyboard—and running the notes up (right hand) or down (left hand) for the next two octaves in the opposite direction then returning at the same speed back to the original note where you started—like two cars heading to an intersection from two opposite directions without a collision. *Scale in contrary motion* was like a warm-up exercise followed by a quick review of the lesson she had taught us the previous week. Quick if you had done your work, but slow if she perceived you had not done your homework, but had instead wasted your time socializing or goofing around rather than practicing your music. After I had had a few lessons, we leapfrogged over the perfunctory routine and followed the trail of my musical journey to wherever it might lead, working on piano compositions other than the ones prescribed in *William Smallwood's Pianoforte Tutor*.

I soon realized I did not learn—partly because of my teacher's musical limitations—the difficult technical dexterity and virtuosity required to play the advanced compositions that caught my fancy. Truth be told, we never had a metronome, which was a critical instrument for learning the correct and exact tempo of a piece of music according to the precise ticking of the machine. Failure to master this rudimentary aspect of piano music had serious consequences for my musical development and my later execution of unfamiliar works by classical composers. (I cared little for contemporary, avant-garde composers.) I failed to make the fine distinctions between say *Vivace* (an Italian word for brisk and animated) and *Animato* (with spirit) or *Risoluto* (firmly, decided) and *Vigoroso* (with strength and firmness) or *Pompos* (with dignity and grandeur) and *Brillante* (in a brilliant, showy style). Most times, in all honesty, I played everything in *Fortissimo* (very loud), oblivious to a call for say *Crescendo* (increasing the sound gradually) or *Dimineundo* (diminishing the sound gradually) or *Cantabile* (in a graceful and singing style), persisting in playing embarrassingly like someone delivering a dull monotonous speech without any variations in tone or pitch or emphasis. But I was determined to master and play even the most difficult pieces for my own edification and gratification, and later, in my adult life, to entertain students, friends and strangers, wherever I saw a piano somewhere in a corner, lonely and unappreciated, in homes and in public places. I graduated from the *Tutor*, way ahead of the rest in the pack, and started to work on hymns, which required a different style or technique of playing. I knew she was preparing me to glorify God with my musical talent, which, as far as she was concerned, came directly from the Almighty Genius, who created me in the first place. Use your talent to glorify God, she persisted. It sounded like a royal command performance.

Gone were the days when I could pound "Swiss Gallop" in *Allegro* (quick, cheerfully) on the keyword, or "Bay of Dublin" in *Tempo di Vase* (waltz tempo), or "St. Patrick's Guild March" in *Tempo di Marcia* (march tempo), or "New Killarney Polka" in *Tempo di Polka* (polka tempo). Because with the hymns and other edifying compositions sung by the choir, all to the glory of God, I had a solemn tempo to deal with and only three, my young mind told me, were acceptable to God: *Andante Cantabile* (rather slow, in a graceful and singing style), *Andante Tranquillo* (rather slow, in a serene manner), and *Andante Moderato* (rather slow, moderately quick). And most in *Pomposo* (with dignity and grandeur). To glorify God. I grew up believing, wrongly or rightly, that God would not tolerate frivolity or triviality while in His presence on the dais, singing, preaching or playing an instrument. (How would anyone know if He remained silent on the issue?) And now I was playing in the Chinese church where I took piano lessons for six months, in the school choir (chosen over someone, my classmate, who was a great piano player with formal training afforded by parents who were teachers), in the English-speaking church, where my headmaster, an American missionary, briefly pastured. And I was a paid piano teacher to a few students who attended the same school. And when invited, I played for weddings and funerals. My piano teacher was delighted but expressed concern that I was "adding too many notes to the music!" I took it as a compliment: insanity or creativity? She made sure I continued to glorify God with my music and my life.

While I excelled musically and became a darling of many people around me, trying hard to slow down the inflation of my tender ego, my friends in the church, especially the young men, joined forces with the pastor to tackle a much more complex problem with a member of our congregation, who happened to live a few yards away from my house. (A handful of these Christian young men shouldered leadership positions in the Chinese Methodist Church in our nation in the years to come, under Rev. Lim's spiritual leadership and tutelage.) I would say the new task facing the young men and the pastor demanded deep personal faith in themselves, God, and the power of Jesus Christ and His words and His promises that with God nothing is impossible. Yes, faith can move mountains. Yes, faith can perform miracles. Yes, faith can make you whole. And nothing can stand in the way of his Son Jesus Christ if you truly believe in Him, His life, His Death, and His Resurrection.

They studied the Bible, its every word imbued with divine power. I was there. They prayed, their confessions, their pleas, and their cries spiraling up—like smoke from burning incense—into the heavens. I was there. They were prepared and ready armed with indefatigable faith and God's invincible power to fight a war against Satan. I was there.

But I wasn't there when, with their pastor, their brave commander, they marched into the home of my neighbor because a young woman was possessed by demons. Because I knew I didn't have their kind of dedication, commitment, and faith in their God, Jesus Christ, the Bible and the efficacy of their ardent prayers.

When the family called for help, the Christian soldiers came ready to do battle. The young woman's face and mouth contorted, her piercing, agitated eyes rolling and searching the room, her body pulsating uncontrollably. The soldiers had to restrain her from hitting someone. And with each fervent prayer and vociferous chorus of supplications seeking God's power to come to their aid to subjugate the demons, the woman became more violent with a cacophony of rasping voices—deep and low—like you had never in your life heard before. And she spat ferociously at everyone. As prayers became more intense, the soldiers had to restrain her, like an untamed animal violently tearing through a cage to escape. It was a spiritual and a physical tug-of-war, but it was God's presence and power that would decide the outcome of the ordeal. The neighbors had gathered, watching from outside the house, wondering nervously who was going to be the victor in the highly emotionally charged battle. And I was there. A witness.

After some very tense moments, whispers had replaced the loud commotion, and peace had descended upon the household like a soft rain. They had declared victory for the moment and God was in control. Armed with God's words and divine power, these soldiers, with their dauntless commander, won many other battles as we all marched triumphantly to win more people for God's kingdom here on earth. Today the church has grown from its humble beginnings to be one of the most powerful Chinese Methodist churches in Malaysia because of the vision, faith, and determination of one indestructible woman warrior—armed with the powerful word of God—to win humbly the souls of many for God's kingdom. And she was my piano teacher.

FIFTEEN

The year was 1956, the year of the Monkey according to the Chinese zodiac. I liked monkeys and they could be instrumental in my success or failure this whole year. I was actually born a Snake, according to the Chinese zodiac. And Snake people are supposed to be elegant, accommodating, intuitive, attractive, compassionate, philosophical, decisive, well-bred, cerebral, lucky, and amusing. And Monkey people are passionate, acutely intelligent, independent, achievers, enthusiastic, fascinating and witty. I don't think I would have problems getting along with the Monkeys of the world! But I had never seen these two creatures, a monkey and a snake, in *National Geographic* magazines or in real life somewhere in a public or a private zoo, playing together. I very much doubt a wise snake could tolerate the stupid antics of a frivolous monkey! Should I worry? Should I try to curry some favors from a monkey? I should resolve to treat my neighbor's monkey a little kinder from this day onward. I had cruelly teased her with peanuts before. I should worry.

I was in Form III. I was fifteen. Short for my age but cute. And I wasn't worried about being short—granted a few friends, relatives and acquaintances were cyclopean in size in my social landscape—but about my life and my future because this year would be a pivotal turning point in my life, according to my government. A good government can do a lot of things for you, so I heard many villagers say to my Brother when he was trying to get assistance in obtaining high-yield rubber seedlings and tobacco plants for our land. In my mind I had to do what I needed to do—don't monkey around was one terrific idea—to pass the Form III exit examinations before I could be allowed to enter Form IV and Form V, the final two years of my high school education. And some guys somewhere in England, nesting high up in some ivory towers with their late afternoon tea and scones, would be judging us and our abilities. They would be writing the questions based on materials everyone in the British Empire was supposed to have studied and memorized. Once you had successfully completed the Form III exit examinations, you could branch off to either science or humanities classes for the final two years of your high school education. And kiss your girlfriend's or boyfriend's ass goodbye temporarily. But if you failed because your were asinine or lazy, or you thought you had some connections to Buckingham Palace or some big shots in the British Parliament, you had no choice but to repeat Form III again. (Automatic promotions maybe happened in your parents' or in-laws' companies, but not in the world of education. *You Fail You Repeat* was the motto every student or parent dreaded but upheld.) You realized quickly that you were graded according to your abilities to sponge the texts and reproduce them on test days, like some cows regurgitating their cud. And kiss your British connections and accent goodbye! And if you were overage at the time, you were not allowed to repeat this in the same school but were sent to another school.

There was nothing shameful or humiliating about all this in our school culture. You learned to accept it and move on, hoping to learn some kind of lessons from your failures. Parents didn't go around beating their chests with ashes on their heads, feeling guilty because their children had decided to fuck up their own lives. They don't go around pointing fingers at teachers saying something self-righteously like "How dare you fail my kids?" Or, "My kids failed because you didn't teach them anything the whole year." Most parents didn't say anything. There was plenty of work to do out in the farms. And those children who failed didn't go around vandalizing school buildings or join gangs burglarizing their towns or villages or debauch by drinking or smoking or terrorizing their neighborhoods. I should know because I was there. Because Sister now attended that so-called other school for students who didn't do well in a regular school and who were overage. That also meant higher school fees.

Everyone paid the same school fees in my school, to be collected by your homeroom teacher at the beginning of each month without any silly excuses (from January till December, our school year) and bought your own textbooks and other supplies. No textbooks, no school for you, that simple. You studied the same subjects with the same students in the same classroom each day, while the teachers of different subjects would go from one classroom to another throughout the school day. Students in each classroom would select a *classroom monitor* whose primarily job was to assist the teacher in maintaining peace and quiet conducive to serious pursuit of knowledge, and other duties, and also, at the beginning of each period, to announce "Please stand," followed by "Good morning teacher." About a dozen senior students had the honor of being chosen "School Prefects" with their distinctive badges, their presence radar to detect or to deter any mischievous or malevolent behaviors in the campus. Peaceful co-existence within the four walls of the classroom was the modus operandi, but each student was free to choose and cling to different cliques before school and during our lunches. It was difficult to decide who you wanted to spend your free time with because of your varied loyalties to different activities in school. Chinese students dominated the student body, with a generous sprinkling of Malays and Indians.

For example, the whole school was divided equally into four major sports teams with rigorous practices being held almost daily throughout the weeks prior to the annual sports festival, by representatives from each team for each specific event—chosen by your teammates because of your athletic prowess and physical agility. A film-star body or model-like, sexy looks didn't matter in the evaluations and selections. Then there were all the different clubs to further your interests, develop your potential, or hone your skills: choir, drama, science, photography, table tennis, geography, et cetera. I was chosen captain of a table-tennis team…or something.

I was active in Drama Club, where I learned for the first time in my teenage life what the word *hiccup* really meant. That stage directions in a script were to be acted out, and not a part of the spoken words by an actor. My English teacher kept saying "Hiccup, Eng Huat?" "Hiccup, Eng Huat?" and I kept repeating the word *hiccup* innocently (or ignorantly) after him. Fellow student actors and my beloved English teacher from America broke out laughing hysterically on stage, shaking their heads in disbelief because of what I was doing. A clown or a joker or a court jester, I was definitely not. My innocence questioned, feeling defenseless. My face registering different shades of colors and expressions. The impasse came to an abrupt end mercifully when the teacher asked simply "Eng Huat? Do you know how to *do* the hiccup?" *Do* the hiccup? No sooner he could finish the sentence I heard a slight cough—like a signal—then a voluntary response from someone on stage *doing* the hiccup. With a sudden realization—like Moses unexpectedly enervated by a divine voice from the burning bush—of my ignorance of the meaning of the word, I felt embarrassed beyond words. Without further ado, I *did* the hiccup according to the stage direction and we resumed the rehearsal, William Shakespeare's *The Merchant of Venice*. I didn't know I had wowed the crowd with my ignorance!

I was active in the English-speaking Methodist Youth Fellowship, where I was readily seduced by square-dancing—first time touching intimately a female body—taught by two young American missionary teachers. Years later I learned that they had been very green, ignorant of the Chinese and Malay and Indian cultures of the people they had been dispatched to serve by the American Methodist missionary board in New York. "We were literally thrown into a lion's den without much preparation," one said, "and I am willing to say we knew nothing, yes nothing, about your culture and your people in Malaya. And I was young, just out of college and really scared of my job, first time teaching in a foreign land. It wasn't that we were not interested in your culture, but we didn't know what to do most times in your country. I am sorry you felt like we were avoiding you. Nothing like that"

One day in the science lab, while I was doing an experiment using the Bunsen burner, test tubes and some chemicals, my science teacher—an Indian imported from India, who was rumored to have an oversized and overactive male reproductive organ—called out of the blue to me "Eng Huat? Can you spell for us the word *wrap*?"

I don't remember if the question had any bearing on our experiment. No one seemed to pay any attention to what he said because of the experiment, and I blurted out, instantaneously with confidence, *r-a-p-e*. The chatting and industry suddenly stopped at all stations—they did hear my voice or something else, after all—with the exception of the hissing sound and gaseous smell from the thirty or so Bunsen burners. Most of the students started giggling, the girls with the palms of their hands slowly rising up over their mouths.

And the teacher patiently repeated, "Try again, Eng Huat? Spell the word *wrap* for the class?" By now all eyes were on me like arrows drawn at the bull's-eye.

This time I made sure everyone heard each letter enunciated slowly and accurately: *r-a-p-e.* Now what? The laughter grew. I had created a mayhem.

For fear the sudden rowdiness might impact the delicate nature of the experiment with chemicals and burning test-tubes poised precariously on some tables, my science teacher called the class to order immediately after "Well…well! Thank you Eng Huat….Class I need your attention!" Not a sound was heard after that. His words like a muzzle. He didn't make any comment about the minor chaos. From the corner of my eyes I saw him shaking his head this way that way flashing a broad grin on his face, dark and smooth, marked by a well-manicured mustache, a sign, I always thought as a boy, of sexual prowess.

None next to me in the lab volunteered anything except a silent chorus gushing at me, "Look up the word *rape* in the dictionary!" as we marched quietly back to our regular classroom. They said *rape*, not *wrap*. What happened! Nothing registered in my brains. A few continued to giggle. I left things as they were lacking the diligence or urgency to pursue a dictionary. Things got progressively worse at lunch—I quickly discovered—because of the notoriety the faux pas in the science lab had caused me. "He? *Rape*?" I was self-consciously reading the lips of many students, presuming some pointing their index fingers at me. Lip reading wasn't my forte. Putting words into strangers' mouths supported my growing suspicion that I had become the laughingstock of a school-wide conspiracy of sorts. I became an instant object of curiosity? Or derision? But why? Nonchalant at first but slowly drawn into it like being sucked in by a whirlpool.

Like the word *hiccup,* the word *rape* didn't mean anything to me. Nobody ever used the word in the village. My teenage friends never uttered it in our daily exchanges. I was an innocent child living in the cloister of a monastery, sheltered from the sins of the world!

When I finally had time to look it up in the dictionary at home after dinner, it was too late. Sex!...What an ignoramus! I meant the meaning of the word *rape*, not sex! Shit! I said it three times. Slamming the shit dictionary violently against the shit wooden wall right below the shit movie stars! Lucky it was Friday. It should all vanish into thin air like water on your face by Monday, massaging my slightly bruised ego. God Save The Queen! I said, one time only. I felt better already, letting go of my pent-up anger. The inner upheaval dissipated quickly, as I was in a hurry to attend the MYF meeting at church.

But one important experiment had a huge impact on my thinking for years to come. And that had something to do with the study of an amoeba under a microscope. "You are looking at a microscopic one-celled animal and I want you to watch it carefully." I listened with rapt attention to my biology teacher's running commentary, as students peered at the specimen through thick lenses, adjusting them up and down for clarity. "See how it engulfs and imbibes what it needs and rejects or throws out what it doesn't need." Most students responded with "I can't believe it! That little thing is doing it!" If we are as smart as an amoeba, I often said to myself, we should not take in anything and everything that are injurious to our bodies! Physically! And morally! But only that which is beneficial to our survival. The amoeba lesson haunts me still, for good.

SIXTEEN

Unknown to me, Father had come home one afternoon when Sister and I were in school and stirred up a hornet's nest. Like so many other times, Father had come home thinking he could bully Mother into waiting on him hand and foot and giving him what he always wanted: money, and more money. There never was a cornucopia of easy cash anywhere. Sister and I had been pushed to the limits of what we could do with our hands, sacrificing our lives so Father could pursue his many failed business adventures. A mistress and a brood to feed. Mother had one and only one source of income: rubber trees. Our existence could best be described as penurious, the family's best kept secret from our friends and relatives. She could sell the family property, if that would solve anything. Grandpa, who worked hard for the land and left it to us, would probably turn over, resurrect, and protest from his grave, somewhere in southeastern China. Brother's limited income from the pigs, rubber, and tobacco was needed to feed the whole family, including his five growing children. Mother did her share, bringing home groceries every so often without Brother's knowledge or urging. It mattered that Brother, not Father (gone) or Mother (aging), had become the sole breadwinner of the family. Sister and I understood what we had to do to support Brother's role as the unofficial head of the family. The trees were growing old, less generous with their milky latex, but we continued to butcher them, squeezing every drop from their veins every morning, fetching less and less for our labor because of the world hunger for more synthetic rubber. Blame the German Bastards! Cheaper than natural rubber. And when Mother stood her ground and refused to comply with Father's outrageous demands, he resorted to using a kitchen cleaver (according to the account later by Ah Soh, one of the few witnesses to the whole episode), and chased Mother, who was small but agile, all over the house, she screaming for her life. Brother intercepted, angrily. "She is getting old," he shouted. "She is not a bank. She doesn't print money." Father left, dejected and empty-handed. A man of few words, Brother had spoken ruefully to Father for the first time. Brother was devastated by Father's flagrant attack on Mother, and by his own disrespectful, unfortunate, volcanic outburst against Father…something like that, according to Ah Soh. Something unbecoming from a dutiful son.

The house was very quiet when we came home from school. You would have thought someone had just passed away. But the children were playing as if nothing had happened. Sister and her girl friend chose to spend the evening at the theatre. Brother and Ah Soh were feeding the pigs according to routine. Their loud grunting cannot be ignored. After a dinner of steamed rice, egg soup ,and some garden vegetables, I saw Mother sitting motionless at the top of the back stairway, deep in thought, her look distant. I told her I was going to a youth meeting in church. I knew I was less of my usual exuberant and effusive self when I bicycled to church because of what I had heard from Ah Soh about what Father did to Mother earlier in the day. My subdued countenance said everything to my friends. They were curious, but respected the *Do Not Disturb* sign on my anemic face. I wasn't about to put on a façade of gaiety, considering the ominous conditions at home. My future was at stake. My friends tried to draw me out of my shell, but I remained shut tight like a frightened clam and chose to be a spectator and not an active participant in the evening's bible study. I saw words dancing on the page, unable to focus on God's holy words. I was busy with my own thoughts. I had heard for days that Father and the mistress might be migrating south to Singapore to try something different with a hand from Seventh Uncle and Seventh Auntie, who had no children of their own. Seventh Uncle was doing well in gambling and prostitution, so I heard, and owned a few acres of farmland on the island's northeast, less populated side. Brother had worked with Seventh Uncle years before up in Cameron Highlands doing some farming, like growing tomatoes and tea. "Singapore is an island of opportunities," people proclaimed, "a paradise and the Promised Land." A few kids from my village had pursued professional careers there. Almost all of Father's oldest brother's children were making a mark for themselves in the island city. I was torn between the bible study and Singapore. Between Mother and Father. Between two loyalties. More, between the devil and the deep sea. I knew it was a dead end road with Mother. And I had had enough of the rubber trees, the pigs, the farm, and the tobacco plants. Sick of the whole fucking village, feeling trapped by Mother's long arms, as menacing and suffocating as octopus tentacles' grip on an innocent victim. And I refused to get married, bear her many grandchildren and perpetuate a life of poverty because that had been her plan for me ever since I was adopted. *For my hands only*. I would be her maverick adopted son. And I would not give her the satisfaction, not for a second. With Father there was a possibility to embark on a promising new journey to the Promised Land, and begin life anew with new possibilities and opportunities. With money from gambling and prostitution and no children, Seventh Uncle might be persuaded to look kindly on me and invest some of his pocket change from prostitutes on a deserving relative. He could expect to collect years of dividends if he were willing to invest in my education and future, a practice not uncommon in the Chinese culture. Helping or taking care of one's own—like the Ling's clan—was a praiseworthy, humanitarian deed, practiced and approved by our ancestors. In a few months I would be taking my Form III exit examinations, a turning point in my life, and I could follow Father to Singapore, the Promised Land. I was there at the bible study and I wasn't there. I had traveled to the Promised Land and back a few times during the reading and expounding of the scriptures. My dream of making it big in Singapore was about to take over my entire being. I allowed myself to be carried away like by a sudden blast of good wind from the heavens. God and Jesus and the Bible would have to wait, tonight and the foreseeable future.

I told my friends not to worry about me when I left the bible study with a heavy heart. Cutting through the chilly air on a slow ride home, I felt invigorated with tears down my face, like raindrops from the sky, just thinking wistfully what life could be like with Father in Singapore. "So near yet so far," I said to myself, "it's within reach." I desperately wanted to have a better chance in life than the hellhole I was in. There was no future for me in the village if I didn't do something quick and soon. With or without God's help and approval. There was no glue or cord that could not be destroyed by my will power. I wasn't an indentured servant. Nothing was immutable. I wanted my life to count! It had to mean something!

I descended quickly to earth when I saw something unfamiliar going on as I neared the house, reminiscent of a scene in a black-and-white movie where people gathered with burning torches looking for a dangerous fugitive or a stranger in their midst. Yes, neighbors and relatives with kerosene lanterns and lamps, I soon learned, with Mother and Ah Soh wailing uncontrollably—reserved for the dead—in the background, were anxiously looking for a known fugitive, Brother, who had disappeared earlier in the evening, threatening to kill himself. Either by hanging from a rubber tree or by drinking something corrosive, resulting in a slow painful death. People around us might never know the truth, but I refused to believe it had come to this tragic end because Brother, a young man looking each day older than his age, had to raise a family of five and the rest of us without the benefits of a good education and a career because of what the Japanese bastards did to him and all of us during the Japanese Occupation. And added to this, as if punished for some wrongs in his life, past or present, was Father's unrelenting harassment of Mother for money when she had none to give. I hurried and joined in the search and we fanned out in small groups, scouring the thick bushes dotted with rubber trees not far from the house. I don't think the neighbors' dogs knew what we were doing, but they led the way, tails firm and wagging playfully. They found Brother not far from the house sitting on some thick sweet potato vines, spread out like a thick carpet for rows and rows, his hands over his face, quiet as a statue. His whole life seemed unhinged by insuperable burden and grief. I wouldn't want to wear or walk in his shoes. In my mind I still had a chance ahead of me to escape from the predicament that had so engulfed Brother that death would seem the only feasible alternative.

A poor Chinese family like ours wasn't in the business of analyzing and solving problems. Or the luxury of having someone professional come to our succor. Saving face or preserving a family's name was uppermost in everyone's—if you were a Chinese—mind. Don't air the dirty laundry for your neighbors to see. Air it somewhere, like in China or Singapore—far away, among strangers. There was this simplistic notion that bad things would just vanish from sight, or dissolve in the mist of your mind, the less you dwelled on them. Burning a few joss sticks and muttering a few incantations to your gods might not be a bad idea if you were a non-Christian. Saying a few words to your God might not be a bad idea if you were an authentic Christian, which most in my family were not. In one word, we were left with no one to turn to but each other. I grew up with a taboo against probing each other too deeply. I grew up helping to build a bulwark of secrecy around our family.

In Brother's mind, the Japanese bastards were the culprits responsible for his life's predicament because the Japanese Occupation abruptly ended his education. And he blamed the German bastards for introducing synthetic rubber into the world market, crippling the very economic foundation of our village. Yes, I saw the writing on the wall: get away from the village before it would consume me too in the fire of destitution and meaninglessness.

Not a word ever was said about the suicide incident. Brother miraculously regained his composure. Peace returned, not prosperity. We trudged on as a family.

SEVENTEEN

I did turn to my friends to get away from the family turmoil. What perfect timing, I thought, when our Christian youth fellowship organized a picnic for the annual get-together at a beach, some fifteen or twenty miles away. The instructions were simple: bring yourself, your swimming trunks for boys, modest one-piece swimming suits for girls, large towels and money for food. Of course the ubiquitous Chinese Bible, representing God's omnipresence. For food we usually had cold bottled drinks, our favorite onion-sardines sandwiches freshly made on the spot, and packaged snacks. A noisy covey of about thirty teenage boys and girls gathered one early Saturday morning at the church. "Watch out for the traffic," one of the youth advisors cautioned us, "be sure you stay together."

Our transportation was our bicycles and we rode quietly, with ringing of bicycle bells here and there, every now and then, like music in the air, like on our way to Kampong Koh. Less than a quarter mile before we reached the town, we veered off the main road to the left and meandered through a coconut plantation, known for its toddy production, a few Indians going up or coming down the coconut trees, until we reached a major highway. A mile or so along this highway to Lumut (a town by the ocean) we saw the luxurious bungalow of the British overseer of a mammoth rubber plantation (I was there briefly, once), with gorgeous flowers and bushes lining the half-moon driveway. Two Indians with scythes were cutting the grass of a huge yard—the size of a soccer field—extending from a lush ivy-covered porch to the highway. A glimpse of what wealth could do for your ego and status! About a mile further along this highway, we took another short cut on a dirt road, which led to a pristine, sandy beach, lined with lanky coconut palms, some bent like old people, with leaves blowing graciously in the wind. A post-card picture of paradise, a portrait of one of God's many creations.

No sooner had we parked our bicycles, than some, who couldn't wait to disrobe to expose their swimming trunks or suits, rushed to the water like soccer players after the goal. You could tell these were the Olympian swimmers eager for a competition. They soon disappeared, their heads bobbing up and down like the corks on fishing lines. Others leisurely surveyed the beach, enjoying the sun and the light breeze, letting the warm water touch their naked feet. The waves were calm, lapping the shore and the huge rocks jutting out of the water like miniature mountains.

There was a white house on the beach, empty at the moment, where we could wash or shower or relieve ourselves. The famous Outward Bound School stood not far away from the beach where we had our picnic. The school, I had heard, was for the rich and the famous who could afford the money and time for a period of very rigorous physical and survival training. I don't think it had anything to do with the military. I had the feeling the filthy rich sent their kids here for discipline or simply to get rid of them for a short period of time so the adults could pursue their sinful pleasures. From a distance, they seemed to be dressed like soldiers in a boot camp, the loud orders to do this and that carried through the air. Not exactly a playground for the rich. But good for your resume to colleges or high-powered corporations.

With all the physical training and stamina I had mustered through thick and thin at home on the farm, I might be a good candidate for the school. Unfortunately, that was not to be because I was a nobody and poor. What I needed at the moment was someone to teach me how to swim. That might be less of an issue—everyone could at least paddle like a dog—but divulging and getting rid of my paralyzing, entrenched hydrophobia might require more than an empathetic friend or a veteran lifeguard. Falling into a bottomless pit covered with muddy water, after days of heavy downpour, thinking it was a shallow hole, one of many in a construction site for a new school building a few years ago, had made me extremely nervous, even just stepping into a shallow puddle of dirty water. I was sure I had fallen into a family well once when I was little even though you could see clear to the bottom. A few fishermen from my village had disappeared out in the open seas because—some said—

the gods were angry and out to get you by first drowning you. I was taught to believe in spirits and there were, in my mind, evil spirits everywhere, like stinging, sleazy jellyfish in the deep-blue waters. If there were any other deeply buried causes of my hydrophobia, only a professional could unearth them. This was one of many personal secrets anchored deeply in my soul, hidden from my friends. Unlike the squirrels, I feared I might never be able to uncover a few of the buried secrets. For now I was happy as a child, using an inflated, well-patched, inner tube to float around and mingle casually with the more experienced swimmers, whose bodies slithered effortlessly like snakes in the water.

"Hey, Eng Huat, let's go for a walk along the beach," a friend called, large drops of water on his body glistening in the hot sun. I envied the muscles on his arms and legs, defined and firm, Adonis in the making. He ran for his camera and I joined him and another friend for a stroll along the beach, with small foamy waves caressing our ankles.

"I am sorry you were a little upset at the bible study the other night," Kong Ing said. "So what is going on?" Hook Bing echoed the same concern. I wasn't about to spill the beans about Brother's failed suicide attempt or my clandestine plan to vanish from the village.

"I was a little worried about my coming Form III examinations," I lied to them, with a thick veneer covering my insincerity, hoping to detour our conversation to something lighthearted and less personal. The opportunity presented itself like some divine providence right before our eyes. I directed our attention immediately to two beauties on a rock, who were unaware of our looming presence. "Hey girls?" I shouted, as if through a horn, startling them. "Do you want to join us for a walk?" I asked. By now we were waving at them to get their attention.

"What are you girls up to?" I said, my friends watching with some curiosity. The girls had slid into the water, a few inches covering the base of the rock, as I inched closer to them, especially to Ching Lang, the notorious one.

"Do you see these barnacles all over the place?" Ching Lang spoke out, pointing to a wall of these crustaceans clinging tenaciously to the rock. Both Ching Lang and Su Ming knew my two friends because they all attended the same Chinese high school and spoke very little English. Ching Lang, in fact, lived a stone's throw away from my house. Her younger brother, preparing to embark on a ship for Taiwan for university education, was working with the older brother running a grocery-cum-coffee shop directly opposite my house on the opposite sides of the main country road. Ching Lang was well endowed for her age and guys would kill for a chance to trace her curves with their fingers. She had an on-and-off relationship with one of the older boys in our youth group. A lady, you might say, with a reputation. The boy couldn't spread the graphic details of his amorous adventures fast enough. I was the first to volunteer to examine the barnacles closely, the protrusion of her chest area distracting my main focus. "I think some of these are actually small oysters," I said, trying with my bare fingers to break one or two pieces loose from the rock wall. In my mind I saw myself pressing on her bare bosom, the way Ah Soh used deliberate pressure from all angles kneading her dough. I heard a distinct click from the camera. The moment of my intimate encounter with the barnacles, with me eyeing her bosom, was frozen in time. The trance ended as quickly as it started. My friend the photographer didn't say a word and he wound his film forward ready for another shoot. "The tide is coming in," Su Ming said, leaving the water for the dry sand. We all followed her over an unmarked trail. The shadows had shortened considerably as the sun had climbed almost directly over our heads. It was time to assemble at the long tables on one side of the white house for our lunch.

Another dietary secret we stole from our British masters was eating sardines sandwiches, with bread, sardines and plain cucumber. Ours a modified Chinese version. Still the favorite for a picnic. Simple and quick, the few essential ingredients easy to assemble. Cold bottled drinks and small packaged snacks like candies and crispy rice completed the menu for lunch. After grace we devoured the food, some easily gulping down stacks of plain white bread. After lunch we had a short inspirational talk, partly because we were discouraged from swimming with a full stomach. By now, a few were in a slight stupor. Spiritual nourishment came with the picnic. Most of my friends don't sunbathe because we had enough exposure to the sun working out in the farms. I avoided the sun like a mouse in the presence of a cat. Instead we relaxed, visiting one another under shady trees and coconut palms. Someone played the harmonica, unobtrusively, and others joined in the hum. I dozed off briefly, having been up since three in the morning tapping rubber trees with Sister.

A few kids returned to the warm water for a last swim. Most, including myself, went combing the beach for seashells, large and small, always hoping for a rare find to add to our individual collections and memories to last a thousand years. Mangroves with huge prop roots forming dense masses grew profusely near the coastline in Pasir Panjang, the fishing village near our house. Thankfully absent along the stretch of wide sandy beach where we had our picnic today. Soon we would be packing up and going home for the day. A quick shower helped remove every salty contaminant from head to toe, like stripping off all your dirty clothes, so we could return home feeling fresh and energized.

We dawdled all the way home, having spent some precious time with friends, sharing the simple joys of life, like bicycling together, swimming together, laughing together, eating together, praying together, and combing the beach together. I continued to grapple with the existence of God, the Bible, and the efficacy of prayers. Because the philosophical bent in my thinking and outlook I was unable to have the kind of faith—like the one some of my friends had—that moves the mountains or heals the sick. Worse, my own poverty-stricken life in this village was an unequivocal testimony that God, if there is one, had long abandoned me to fend for myself.

My immediate concern was survival and how best to prepare myself for the coming examinations in November. Eat well (three meals of porridge and garden vegetables?), sleep well (irregular sleep patterns because of having to get up at two or three in some mornings to tap rubber tress?), and study well (constant nagging about preparing the pigs' slop and tending the farm?). Easy for our teachers to say that from their ivory towers. What about the real burden on my bare shoulders to work hard just to survive from day to day in my family? I was fifteen and where was God in all this?

About a week after the picnic, I came home one late afternoon with the photograph of Ching Lang and me that Kong Ing had taken of us while I was examining the barnacles on the rock wall. The three oldest of Brother's children, Sister, Brother, and I were enjoying the special dinner Ah Soh had prepared for the family. Special because it was very time consuming for Ah Soh, having to take care of the family's meals, laundry (granted I had been doing mine since I was seven or eight), children, pigs, and limited farm work. She might do this once a month if she had time to make it. For me it was a break from the three meals of porridge daily. Mother, whatever the nature of a meal, was always the last to eat. Except the Chinese New Year's Eve family dinner. All, including the ghosts of the deceased, were expected to eat together then, symbolizing family unity and wholeness. So, with the cheap craps we bought directly from the fishermen down at Pasir Panjang and homemade egg noodles, Ah Soh had cooked a wok-full of crap-noodle soup, enough for an army. The trick was always to add more water. For more mouths. And while everyone was eating, I passed the photograph around the table. "Who is that?" the children asked. "Ching Lang," I said, "the one not far from our house. The family with the monkey." No one seemed to care very much about the photograph. Just a photograph, I said to myself. They ate and left and I helped to clean the table.

Until Mother came to the kitchen for something. It wasn't Ah Soh's cooking but the photograph on the table that aroused her intense interest and curiosity. She held it close to her eyes because she wasn't seeing well. She examined it this way and that way without a word. But something in my guts and her face, suddenly growing tense, told me I was in for some shit trouble with Mother. Suddenly, as if possessed by a demon, with the photograph in her hand she rushed out of the house and zoomed straight to Ching Lang's house. I was the only one in the family who saw the whole thing unraveling, unstoppable, before my eyes. I had no idea what Mother was going to do with the picture. But something was going to happen. I went upstairs to the back window by the back stairway and I could see the roof of Ching Lang's house, straining my ears like an insect's antennae to see if I could hear something of Mother's angry outburst against Ching Lang or Ching Lang's family.

Days later in church Ching Lang told me the whole story. That Mother had called her every obnoxious word that existed or was possible in Hockchiang dialect, that she had no business morally corrupting every young man in the village, that she should establish a whore house so she could sell her body cheaply, and that she was sick of her reputation. Of course Ching Lang's mother listened indignantly to Mother's long tirade against her daughter and decided wisely to let Mother blew off all her steam. Mother had to leave because her enemy refused to budge an inch and fight her.

But she came home with enough fury to kill a tiger. I could hear her coming up the front stairway and shouting for me from the verandah. She thought I was in my room, but actually I was at the back window spying on her. As I stepped into the verandah words came flying out uncontrollably from her mouth. Like a bad vomit. "Bad woman. Evil. Sell her sarong. Sell her body. Gamble. Prostitute. You son of a Japanese bastard. You no good. You and your whore…." Her words, like a dam suddenly broken, hit me unexpectedly. Like arrows piercing my heart. "You whore…," she kept going. Mother was also hitting hard on my chest with her two hands. She tried to pin me down hammer and tongs. Tore and pulled the white singlet off from my body. I was crying and screaming because I thought I was fighting someone possessed with demons, many ferocious demons, trying to kill me. Eighth Auntie wasn't around anymore to save me from her wrath. And every minute Mother became more violent, not her usual quiet mild-mannered self anymore, and pulled my flimsy shorts down threatening to castrate me, trying to grab hold of my penis and testicles. I was naked as the day I came to this world. I had nothing on except shame and humiliation. I was struggling with all my strength for life. "You pig stud. You fuck prostitute." For a second I thought I saw the cleaver the family used in the kitchen to chop up everything. Mother's herculean strength could only have come from the demons. I was small but she was smaller than I. All of a sudden I could see and hear in a flashback the pitiful squealing of a young boar, sandwiched belly up with testicles facing Brother's face on a gunny sack between his strong legs, his partner holding down its front and hind legs , and Brother, with a straight razor in his right hand and his left holding one testicle at a time, made a quick two-inch-incision, the testicle popping out, cutting it off and throwing it into a waiting pail. After both the testicles were removed, inhumanely I said, with the boar worn out by all the squealing for help, Brother then smeared a mixture of soot from our own kitchen wood-burning stove and coconut oil, made it from our own coconut trees, into the empty, bloody wounds, releasing the boar before he started on the next one. I was little. I was there and felt the pain with each cut into the testicles. Curiosity turned into fear and disgust. All the young boars had this waiting for them because castration would help them concentrate on growing up strong, healthy, and fat, ready for the chopping block. I saw myself squealing for help as Mother sharpened the straight razor up and down on the strap ready to make the first incision, my hands and legs tied to a wooden bench, making any kind of escape impossible.

"Mother I won't do it. I won't do it," I cried and pleaded for mercy, pushing her away from me. And all because of a picture? Mother finally sat down, exhausted physically and emotionally. I withdrew to a corner with my shorts, feeling a horrible sense of impotence because of Mother's mocking castration, and sat staring blankly at the evening sky. Nobody came to my rescue. Children must have been cowering in a corner somewhere downstairs, hearing Mother's condemnation and my desperate screams for help.

And all because of a picture? What I had done, in Mother's eyes, was going against a tradition that the Hockchiang people had carried all the way from mainland China. Sister came from one family. I was adopted from a different family. And we were supposed to marry each other one day in Mother's scheme of things. And according to a Chinese custom. To me that was incest! An act morally offensive to me. And here I was, smart in school, a darling of many people because of my piano playing, handsome and attractive, and now, in her eyes, flaunting my penis for the females out there? A stud? A whore? Our relationship had become less and less of a mortar and a pestle, deteriorating faster than a ripened mango falling from its tree. I was adopted for my hands only, my duty in Confucian ethics to obey her implicitly, and support her whims and fancies. A dutiful son I was not and I refused to fit into her mold. She saw it coming. I was determined to follow my own conscience, and stand up for my rights. The right to be myself. The more reason I must break loose from Mother's grip and follow Father to Singapore, to the Promised Land.

EIGHTEEN

Less that a month away from the November examinations, I complained to Mother of the sudden swelling on the tip of the index finger on my right hand. No, Mother, I wasn't bitten by any kind of poisonous insects. Yes, Mother, I remember the centipede that stung Big Cousin's penis. No, Mother, I didn't accidentally sit on it. No, Mother, it didn't happen two weeks ago. No, Mother, I wasn't ignoring it when the pain first started. No, Mother, there weren't any symptoms to warn me. No, Mother, I didn't go near a thorny bush of any kind anywhere. No, Mother, I didn't see any splinter of wood anywhere. Yes, Mother, I asked Sister to examine my finger in the bright sunlight. Worse than the interrogation at the police station when I was caught stealing firewood from the British-owned rubber plantation. Yes, Mother, the pain is unbearable. Worst at night, the throbbing pain has kept me awake all hours of the night.

A blessing in disguise of sorts, because I was excused from tapping rubber, temporarily. But a curse, really, because the pain was making it almost impossible for me to concentrate on my studies for the coming examinations. And what about my typing, my piano playing? After three or four days I could feel the skin at the tip tightening, something fermenting and growing inside, now appearing a size larger than my thumb. And pressing it against a cold hard surface seemed oddly to provide some relief from the excruciating pain. We had a conundrum at hand. Mother approached our *quack doctor,* the village matchmaker (she was known for wearing a few hats) for advice about this stupendous development. The *snake disease* had stricken my innocent index finger, she concluded brilliantly without having examined the patient. Maybe it did begin to look like the head of a snake, but I was the unwary prey.

Mother sprang into action and in less than a day she produced a packet of herbal stuff from the Chinese medicine shop in Kampong

Koh. She managed to scrounge around for a small pot about six inches in diameter and filled it with water and the magical herbs. Instead of the wood-burning stove, she used the charcoal stove we used for preparing opium for Father. And for a pragmatic reason as I would soon discover. You could control the heat in a way with charcoal but not with the unruly flames from the burning wood-stove. Mother made me sit on a small stool in front of the twelve-inch-tall charcoal stove and the boiling pot. With the steam shooting into the air, Mother told me to put the snake where it should be, right into the rising steam an inch or two from the surface of the stormy water. "It is unbearably painful," I groaned. Her eyes unblinking, Mother said, "You die or snake die. Steam kill snake." You might as well be boiling the finger with the herbs, like a crab leg in Ah Soh's crab-noodle soup. And not for a minute or two, but to sit there holding my snake steady over the steam till the snake died! I felt the pain gradually creeping up the arm to my right shoulder as if the snake was looking for an escape. Mother announced "We will do it at least one more time tomorrow before the snake is completely dead." Dead? Another day? Gee! "You die or snake die." Tomorrow came and went. And the stubborn snake refused to die because it looked worse and bigger than before the herbal treatment. Looked like the snake was getting pregnant. The skin on the tip was stretched so thin it might break any minute.

"Why didn't you come to see us earlier?," the Chinese nurse at the mission clinic in Kampong Koh—located on the edge of our English school's soccer field—looked at me as if it was my fault. I didn't want to embarrass Mother by telling the nurse it was a case of a snake gone wild and crazy! And uncontrollable! Long live the snake! "This is getting bad," she continued, towering over me like an Amazon. Not that I was sitting down on a chair and she was standing up. She reminded me of my Eighth Auntie, tall, square and stout. Like the Rock of Gibraltar. She was wearing a different hat today, the nurse hat, because she was also the village midwife who had delivered Brother's five children. But the village was unkind to her, condemning her for wearing a very different kind of hat once. Though a spinster, she had a boy and a girl. Many spinsters in our Chinese culture had adopted children. But they said she was a different kind of spinster. And she suffered quietly—her house between my village and the town—years of gossip, pain and shame because people in the village and the town pigeonholed her a *whore*. She didn't adopt the boy, they taunted her mercilessly, maybe the girl. They knew of only one Virgin Mary in the world. And she was no Virgin Mary in their cruel estimation. She might as well be wearing the letter *W* (for *whore*) on her sleeves. The boy grew up a tall handsome giant (no one could deny she had a part in the conception of this kid!) and later became a doctor. The daughter was vivacious, with dimples on her cheeks, a star pupil, and her charm and sweetness could easily have won her a beauty title. Anywhere. "You sit tight because we have to do something with this finger," she said, preparing for a minor surgical procedure.

She literally had to cut off a portion of the tip of my finger to save it. Mother was sitting patiently outside in the small waiting room. I always hated the arrogant diminutive receptionist, a single mother (something about her husband being killed by the Japanese soldiers) raising two girls and a boy, living next door to the house where Father and his mistress lived, ordering the patients around because most don't speak a bloody word of the English language. Excuse her for doing her job, my friends calmed me. "Make sure you give him these pills to help him with the pain," the nurse told Mother. She handed Mother a few more things to help clean and dress the wound at least once a day. I always thought her life as a midwife was the easiest in the world. She was generously compensated by ignorant villagers, including my family, thinking she had done them a big favor by the saving the lives of these women by the successful deliveries she had miraculously performed when in fact it was the ladies, lying helplessly in beds, doing all the hard work. "Push a little harder," the nurse would coax a mother, at first her voice in *Pianissimo* (very soft. in music). She could move to *Con spirito* (with quickness and spirit), then to *Prestissimo* (as quick as possible). And finally with the baby's head coming into view, "We are there!" in *Vivace* (brisk and animated).

The mission clinic was built in the early 1900s to replace a hospital that was never built to serve the needs of the early pioneers who came with a Methodist missionary from the Fujian Province of mainland China to settle in this area. Grandpa was one of them. It continued to serve the descendants of those people and others who were too poor to see a private doctor. Of course major cases were referred to a local hospital.

"Thank you for saving my life," I said to the nurse, as she gently patted my shoulder. "I don't want to see you again," she said with a grin on her face. Mother and I did some grocery shopping since we were in town. A surprise dinner treat for the entire family.

With the bulky bandage on my index finger, my first concern was if I could still hold a pen firmly to write my answers. The snake died an unnatural death in the hands of a skillful nurse, destroying it with a surgical knife. Neither Mother nor I wished to talk about the failure of the herbal medicine to do its job. The finger got better each day, allowing me the peace of mind to study and prepare for the examinations. The rubber trees had to wait a little longer. Like everything else in life, the tests came and went. I was confident the results would propel me to the final two years of my high school education.

The December holidays meant a long fifty-plus days of hiatus from school. On the one hand I dreaded having to get up every morning at two or three for the next fifty-plus days to tap rubber trees. Without fail, Mother would be sitting by my bedroom door with the rubber-tapper's lamp sitting beside her and trying to wake me up, usually mumbling something without ever calling my name. Sister and Brother would be in the kitchen having something hot to drink before venturing out into the morning cold air. The family also owned a few acres of rubber trees about five miles away from the house. Sister and I would be working on this patch of rubber trees. Mother usually worked on the trees within walking distance of the house. We were still waiting for the rubber trees to grow on the three-acre tract where the house sat. Brother continued to grow tobacco on the same land.

On the other hand, Christmas was also the best time of the year for me. The church always had a Christmas tree and the youth helped to decorate it. The choir prepared their specials. The young and the old volunteered to put on a Christmas pageant, one year with live goats, and the congregation, usually reverent and quiet, broke out into a sudden burst of laughter because one of the goats decided to take off, jumping over the dais and right into the pews where the congregation sat. An elusive one to catch. I loved to recite, as my contribution to the program, a few verses from the Bible. And for years I had won top prizes of big towels, toothpaste and toothbrushes, and school supplies for the best overall Sunday school attendance. But the best part of every Christmas in my memory was the caroling we did on every twenty-fourth of December, literally walking from house to house delivering the good tidings of Jesus' birth to every member of the church. We had some members of church choir join the members of the youth fellowship—a total of thirty to forty people—and walked and sang from dusk till dawn. Having done this for years, certain members of our congregation were scheduled at certain hours during the caroling to feed us with hot drinks and warm foods. Maybe this was the best part of the evening or morning because people always put out the best of snacks and desserts and everything for us to enjoy, a part of giving and sharing in the joyous Christmas celebrations.

And also during the long holidays, Brother could use my help to work on some improvements around the house. It seemed like we had to constantly enlarge the chicken coops to accommodate a growing colony of chickens. The pigs seldom used the sties because they preferred the mud and the dirt and the open space out there. We used the sties for the sows to give birth to their young or to keep the young in till we felt they could handle the real world out there. And there was always work on the farm: to grow, to harvest, and to replant crops for the pigs. And everyone helped with growing garden vegetables on a patch right behind our kitchen. Besides the rubber trees and the tobacco plants, I was married to the farm.

I helped Brother dig the holes for the four posts of the new chicken coop. We didn't use any concrete for the posts because the coop was never intended to be a permanent residence for our birds. The land might be used for something else in the near future. Next we attempted the roof. In the process one of the rafters got dislodged and fell to the ground. "You are going to ruin the whole thing if you are not careful," Brother finally broke his silence. I had been waiting for an opportunity to vent my feelings and he broke the ice for me.

"Use your hands in the right way," he added, waiting for some kind of response from me.

"My hands, huh?" I said. I had been thinking for a while about what I wanted to say to Brother, at the right place and at the right time. I didn't want to miss this opportunity to do so. And I hated to spoil this beautiful afternoon. And our so-called brotherly relationship. After a long pause, "Tell me what is wrong with my hands? Sister and I have been doing our share of the work, but it seems someone is never satisfied with our efforts. Shall I tell you why you tried to kill yourself?" He stopped working and stood there speechless. "The reason is obvious to me. It wasn't my fault you didn't want to finish your education because of what the Japanese did to everyone in this village. It wasn't my fault you got married young and have five children now to feed. It wasn't my fault that you couldn't go anywhere in life because you don't have the education and the skills they are looking for out there. And Father isn't of much help to anyone of us. You know what? I *am* your problem." I repeated slowly, "I *am* your problem." I didn't want to keep him in suspense. He had no idea what was coming to him. But I knew where the monologue was going and I didn't care about the consequences of what I was about to tell him, to his face. "I was told by someone that when Mother adopted me, she promised you something. That if you would help to raise me, *my hands* would be yours forever. So you went to Mother every time you were upset with yourself or with me because you realized you had no control over my hands and my life, that I was going somewhere in life with my brains and talents And you pushed and continue to push Mother to the limits. And this is why Mother tried so hard to keep me working and working on the farm. And all Mother cared about was my hands. I suspected long ago I was adopted *for my hands only*. I didn't impress her or you with my education, my popularity, my determination to be somebody someday. In fact you never uttered a word of praise or encouragement to me. Never. You felt you were at the end of the rope. So you wanted to kill yourself." And the final blow to his ego or self-image, if he had any. "*And just because you are a beggar, it doesn't mean I have to follow in your footsteps*." And with that I knew I had driven a huge wedge, an unbridgeable chasm, between us.

NINETEEN

Soon after my painful and combustible discourse with Brother, I said goodbye to the village that had bestowed on me more sorrows than joys during the formative years of my life, and willingly lodged myself in an alien world dominated by Hockchiew speaking people, next-door neighbors in mainland China. Hockchiew and Hockchiang, like so many other Chinese dialects, share the same written characters but differ in their pronunciations. I moved to Kampong Koh, a town next door, and lived with Father and his mistress, and the mistress' mother, and a sad looking bunch of children, ranging from age one to six. The oldest boy, doted on by his grandmother, was rumored to be the son of a communist who had been killed during the insurgency against the Malayan government.

Malaya went through a tense time following the defeat and exodus of the Japanese in 1945. Having failed to come to power in the country with the immediate return of the British Military Administration to fill the political void, the anti-Japanese Communist resistance groups soon engaged in a campaign to retard and paralyze the economic recovery, targeting the rubber and mining industries, which were indispensable and critical to the country's survival and recovery, and those who opposed the communist cause. Thereafter the Malayan government declared a State of Emergency—1948 to 1960—to deal with the insurgency. A house divided, they understood, would ensure chaos, anarchy, and racial outbursts.

Two or three of the children, oftentimes dirty and scrawny looking, were found loitering in the back alleys every other day, like homeless wild cats in the neighborhood, bringing deep shame to Father. I became the Big Brother, by association, but was unschooled in how to discipline the children. We had a young teenage relative from my village living with us as a maid. Her main duty was to look after the children. The brood of six (there was one timid female) was difficult to manage. Because the house was crammed between other dwellings, like sardines between two pieces of white bread, in a row of wooden houses—a tinderbox baking in the tropical sun, ready to explode at any moment—I found myself gasping for fresh air and pining for space, which the village I disdained and had just left had in abundance. I missed the bucolic ambience of country living. To fend off claustrophobia and get out of the house, I volunteered to help with the children. Accompanied by the maid pushing a black baby pram, I led the children—Like the Pied Piper of Hamelin—to a nearby playground, which was in a huge lot right in front of the local theater, Sister's favorite place to watch Hong-Kong-made Chinese movies. Occasionally I borrowed a cart with four kerosene tins from a neighbor (a rich relative, whose daughter, a teacher, would later cause a scandal in town by dumping her long-time, live-in, educated boyfriend for an unknown poor boy from my village) to fetch fresh water from one of two famous wells in town, in front of the Chinese Parsonage, wells dug by the Christian mission for the pioneers in early 1900s. Symbolically living water to quench their thirsty souls! The well was located opposite my school. The school, a few hundred yards from the house, soon became my playground and haven.

For the first time in my life I had the freedom to roam the universe freely, to pursue my dreams full-time, free from the snare of the pigs, rubber trees and the farm, and the people who frowned on—and tried to snuff out—my individualism and aspirations, which had become a threat to the fabric of their beliefs and traditions. I was drawn into a friendship that was to sustain me throughout the last two years of high school. He and I had many things in common. Education topped our priorities. Both tempted and attempted to exploit the maid to satisfy our hedonistic urges; once I chased her inside the house, upstairs and downstairs, she shrieking at the top of her lungs, while the kids watched in amazement, trying to scare her into some kind of submission. To no avail. My newfound friend, in the meantime, unfortunately fell into a trap set by a girl from his home town. Days and nights he was on the move, like an agitated predator, stealthily watching her every move from the moment she stepped down the school bus till she stepped up the bus to go home. Once or twice I became his seeing eyes surveying the surroundings like a Sherlock Holmes for a criminal. And my target, his silent but deadly competitor. "She is going after him because he has money, and you are a student, a poor student, without a career and money in your pockets," I consoled him the best way I knew how. He and a teacher, not exactly a spring chicken, were competing for her love. My friend was irresistibly seductive, sentimental, humorous, charming, eloquent, well mannered, sensitive, passionate but poor. The teacher wasn't exactly a Romeo, with pimples like monkey scratches on his face. He was, students said, manipulative, rigid, this-worldly, impetuous, ostentatious, ruthless, and unfeeling, but he had money. In this case the plumage of a peacock, my friend the young stud, was of no consequence. And the poor girl was indubitably seduced by the jingles in the teacher's pockets. Looks were for the dogs, in her judgment! Many nights in my house I felt his grief and frustrations and saw his tears pouring out like the monsoon rain. Unlike my friend, I was sensual but cautious in looking for a voluptuous body. I flirted with one to convince classmates I wasn't impotent, sexually.

An older female, tall and elegant, foreign and exotic, did encroach on my life and thinking, with her song *Que Sera, Sera*. I fell in love with Doris Day, but part of her song gave me indigestion. One of my classmates lived four doors down where I lived and he would play for me on his radio console any record I would request and I had him play Doris Day's newest hit over and over. One verse got my philosophical machine working overtime. "Que sera, sera/Whatever will be, will be/The future's not ours to see/Que sera, sera/What will be, will be." And if I genuinely believe in *Whatever will be, will be,* I would not, as a dutiful son, decry nor reject adamantly Mother's earnest endeavor to raise me as another mediocre, introverted, dependent, insecure, old-fashioned, rigid and poverty-stricken farmer! *Que sera, sera* is not for me! Sorry lady, I grew up to believe I am the master of my fate, and the captain of my soul. And not fate or chance! And I had to kiss Doris Day good-bye! Gladly!

If Shakespeare's insight that "All the world's a stage" is true, then *my performance* is at stake. I would demand nothing but the best script. Who but I would be the most qualified to write that script!

Moving to live with Father was the beginning of a new chapter in my life.

Father operated an opium den in the family residence and another one in another part of town. A walking distance away. It wasn't unusual to see grown men and a woman or two coming in and out of the house through the back door. The only presence was the aroma or the hissing sound of burnt opium inside the house. It wasn't exactly the time or place for active verbal volley between Father and his clients. Most times the sound, emanating from the dark room, was inaudible even to a sensitive ear. The mistress spent a great deal of her waking moments in bed, helping Father entertain his loyal opium customers. To her, I assumed, it was work with her hands, lying sideways facing a client. I suspected she slept with one or two of them. Because the children don't bear the image of Father, more like children from assorted families.

Opium continued to be illegal and the penalty if caught with this stealthy operation was severe.

The mistress' mother was a distorted replica of Mother: impatient, energetic, critical, manipulative, power-hungry, petty, vindictive, authoritarian, stubborn, resistant to change, loutish, vain, uncompromising, quarrelsome, hotheaded, old-fashioned, devious, loud-mouthed, judgmental, irritable, demanding, vengeful, phlegmatic, unfeeling, predatory, selfish, ruthless, tactless, capricious, unscrupulous, opportunistic, long-winded, short-sighted, defensive, and gullible. In one word, a thorn in my flesh!

And she hated me because I used too much electricity (it was kerosene lamp back in the village) to study late into the nights, prompting my friend (at times spending a night with me) and me to cover our study lamps with the thickest blanket we could find on earth. She was a common laborer, continuing to work in her old age, but she—not Father—was definitely in charge of the house when she was home. She cooked most of the evening meals and did most of the family laundry. She tolerated my presence and most times communicated with her fierce eyes and stern countenance. Words were never necessary between us!

Life with Father was heaven on earth.

EPILOGUE

For reasons never explained to me, Father postponed the departure to Singapore, allowing me the luxury of finishing high school with flying colors. Thereafter, we packed and moved the whole family (without the grandmother) to Singapore to the Promised Land. My dreams intact. The village a history, I thought, and remains indelibly imprinted in my memory as clear and vivid as the tropical blue sky. Every moment, like each individual frame in a reel, is a momentous highlight of my life.

Time will heal, but not erase, the bittersweet memories of the formative years of my life in a poverty-stricken and God-forsaken village. I returned to the village once to see Father on his deathbed and later to attend his funeral when I was a college student in Singapore.

I have not returned to the village since, as if to say, let the dead bury the dead.

I got a scholarship to study at an interdenominational college in Singapore. And eventually moved to the United States of America with more scholarships. I continue to entertain my dinner guests with the anecdotes of my pathetic upbringing. And as an English teacher, I realized profoundly I have my own inimitable unique story to tell my students (and the world), less to entertain but to instruct, inspire and instill in them that they too can become the person I am today, despite all the seemingly insurmountable hurdles that once stood in my way, growing up adopted, neglected, deprived in a God-forsaken poverty-stricken secluded village, somewhere in a remote corner in a country called Malaya.

And my victory is no less significant and memorable than Caesar's over Pharnaces: *Veni, Vidi, Vici.* I came, I saw, I conquered!